A DARKNESS
DESCENDING

CHRISTOBEL KENT'S previous books include
*The Dead Season, A Fine and Private Place, A
Time of Mourning, A Party in San Niccolo, Late
Season* and *A Florentine Revenge*. She lives near
Cambridge with her husband and five children.

D1136511

Also by Christobel Kent

The Sandro Cellini Novels
A Time of Mourning
A Fine and Private Place
The Dead Season
The Killing Room

Christobel
Kent

A DARKNESS
DESCENDING

Corvus
An imprint of Atlantic Books Ltd
Ormond House
26–27 Boswell Street
London
WC1N 3JZ

www.corvus-books.co.uk

CORVUS

Published in trade paperback in Great Britain in 2013
by Corvus, an imprint of Atlantic Books Ltd.

This paperback edition published in Great Britain in 2014 by Corvus,
an imprint of Atlantic Books Ltd.

Copyright © Christobel Kent 2013

The moral right of Christobel Kent to be identified as the author
of this work has been asserted by her in accordance with the
Copyright, Designs and Patents Act of 1988.

All rights reserved. No part of this publication may be reproduced, stored in
a retrieval system, or transmitted in any form or by any means, electronic,
mechanical, photocopying, recording, or otherwise, without the prior
permission of both the copyright owner and the above publisher of this book.
This novel is entirely a work of fiction. The names, characters and incidents
portrayed in it are the work of the author's imagination. Any resemblance to
actual persons, living or dead, events or localities, is entirely coincidental.

10 9 8 7 6 5 4 3 2 1

A CIP catalogue record for this book is available from the British Library.

Paperback ISBN: 978 0 85789 328 4
E-book ISBN: 978 0 85789 327 7

Waltham Forest Libraries	
904 000 00407781	
Askews & Holts	08-Aug-2014
CRI	£8.99
4381130	H

For Rowan

Acknowledgements

I would like to acknowledge the great debt I owe Angus MacKinnon, without whose clever, careful eye and impeccable instincts Sandro Cellini would never have become the man he is.

Prologue

SHE HAD TO LEAN right down into the cot to set him down. It was a movement she had almost perfected over these first six weeks of his life: it might as well have been a decade, because now it seemed to her that the time before him had receded, impossibly out of reach.

The movement had to be slow and steady, then the arm had to be eased out from under that surprising weight that was his warm, damp head. The soft light glowed from the shelf above the cot: she straightened, set her hands on the rail and looked down. One small, plump arm in the white terry-cloth sleeve was raised and folded against his body like that of a little praying mantis; his cheek was just flushed from the feed, his mouth slightly open. His rosebud mouth with its milk blister: he was perfect. Born perfect, in spite of it all.

Next door she heard Niccolò shift in his chair, heard the rustle of the newspaper, and held her breath. She heard him cross his legs. She didn't need to see, to know. They had been one soul, one unit, since they were nineteen years old. She knew what he was thinking. She didn't move: she was waiting to be sure that the child was asleep, he knew that. She felt as though she would like to stay in here for ever, buried in the warm half-dark, postponing the moment.

It was not quiet: the Piazza Santo Spirito was almost never quiet, and September was a busy month. She could hear the restaurant sounds, the clink and clatter, the hum of conversation in different languages, a waitress bellowing into the kitchen. The midwife had reassured her, He'll be used to it. They learn in the womb: these sounds are life to him, they're his world, like your heartbeat. Some babies had Mozart played to them; her child would have the singing drunks of the Piazza Santo Spirito.

It was early still. The raucous sounds of the later evening had yet to begin. She liked to put him down by seven, although her mother-in-law found fault with her schedule, as with almost everything else. With the fact that they lived on the Piazza Santo Spirito, where drugs were dealt on the corner and there was always one alcoholic rough sleeper or another fighting, reeling under the statue or parked in a heap of rags and carrier bags against the fountain. The fact that they had never married, that they wouldn't have the child baptized. Niccolò's mother even found fault with her age. *You make yourself ridiculous. Babies should come at nineteen, twenty.* Her mother-in-law's own age when she had had Niccolò, her only child, her treasure, which meant that she was a young grandmother. She could go on for years yet.

'You put him down at seven, you can't complain when he wakes you at three.'

She didn't complain, though. If she had a complaint, she would not bring it to her mother-in-law. She stood on, still looking down: from next door a tiny exhalation of breath that meant, what are you doing in there still? Not that he would ever voice it. Niccolò did not seek confrontation, he took an age to rise to provocation, which was just as well, given the path he had chosen. Stern, just, certain: his face lifted before her, questioning, and lowered again to resume his examination of the newspaper. As if in confirmation, there was the sound of a page turning, carefully.

It came to her that the child didn't need her, not really: milk came in bottles too, after all. She was not strictly necessary, not with the steady presence of Niccolò, his certainty, his resolution. His goodness.

In the kitchen the pots stood ready. She had made a sauce with aubergine and tomato. She need only turn and step back out of the warm, hushed gloom and light the flame, lay the table. Sit, push the food around the plate while Niccolò averted his eyes. She hadn't eaten, it seemed, in months, but Niccolò said nothing.

Leaning down, gently, slowly, she pulled the white blanket over her son, to the chin. Up she came again, out of the cot, out of the child's orbit, his sweet breath, his innocent, milky flesh, set her hands back on the rail to keep them still.

And it began: she was powerless to stop it. She tried to delay it, as if she might fool her own body; she stood very still, breathed as slow as she could. It's in your head, she told herself, it's your head that got you into this. Don't do it, don't look. Outside the night was cooling, the blessing of September after August, but a sweat broke on her upper lip. Don't do it to yourself. She reached up to the shelf where the nightlight sat, felt along it with her hand, stopped, lifted it. Looked. No.

The sweat bathed her, from her brow to the backs of her knees. She felt the most sudden terrible urge to run to the window so quickly she wouldn't be able to think and the momentum would propel her through, through the shutters, across the too-low sill and down three floors, twenty metres, she would fall, shocking in her house slippers and nightwear, between the restaurant tables. And there would be a silence. The silence was what she wanted: she wanted it all to stop.

Moving the hand along further, she reached for the baby monitor. She pressed the switch and its blinking green light came on. She turned for the door.

Niccolò's face raised to hers, taking in the flush on her cheeks, the sweat on her neck, the dress sticking to her too-thin body, to the hips that had once been rounded, the breast that had been full. She felt a hundred years old under his gaze, a shrunken thing.

You make yourself ridiculous, at your age.

He could see the tremor in her hand as she pushed the door behind her because she saw it reflected in his face, but he said nothing.

'He's down,' she said.

Chapter One

S HE CAME IN PAST the journalist, a big man taking notes, handsome if you liked that kind of thing. Giuli didn't. She'd seen him before; he smelled of cigarettes and good aftershave.

The meeting room was stuffy and crowded. Giuli – Giulietta Sarto, trainee private investigator, clinic receptionist and dogsbody, it sometimes seemed to her, to one and all – staggered a little as still more people jostled in. Among them she glimpsed a familiar face: Chiara, looking around for someone. They were already standing. The few chairs had been first ignored and then shoved aside.

On tiptoe Giuli strained to find Chiara again, to see if she was alone or if, like Giuli, she was with someone. Daughter of a policeman, fresh-faced, eager, nineteen years old: what was she doing here? Just the kind of new recruit they needed, actually. But she didn't reappear. Perhaps, Guili thought, I was mistaken.

A window would have been a blessing; the evening air had been soft and just warm as she and her boyfriend Enzo had walked here, hand in hand. Instead, the overhead strip lighting and absence of any natural light were combining to give Giuli a headache. She didn't suffer from claustrophobia, and she was resolutely disinclined to panic in any given situation, which was one reason why Sandro – Sandro Cellini, policeman turned private investigator and, as it happened, old friend and former colleague in the force of Chiara's father Pietro – had decided to trust her with more work. Yet as the crowd once again shifted her on her feet, Giuli felt her gut tighten all the same and she groped for Enzo at her side. Looked for emergency exit signs, of which there were none.

Enzo took her hand firmly in his and she turned her head towards him. His broad, homely face framed by the old-fashioned haircut looked back at her, absolutely reassuring.

'Not your idea of a romantic evening?' He ducked his head shyly under her gaze, looking at her sideways. She squeezed his hand.

It was not an attractive venue, but then the Frazione Verde – its membership an eclectic, impoverished assortment of intellectuals, ex-communists, fervent greens, peaceniks and all the considerable variety of those, like Enzo and Guili, disillusioned with mainstream politics – couldn't afford anything better. Access was via a passage that, if the smell was anything to go by, was used as a latrine by the local rough sleepers and ran behind a deconsecrated church on the Via Sant'Agostino, a hundred metres from the Piazza Santo Spirito. Constructed as a makeshift dispensary for charity following the war, it was crammed between two other buildings; it might have been above ground, but being inside the place felt like being buried.

At the back someone began to stamp and holler. Other feet and voices joined in a ragged chant, which then petered out. The strip lighting flickered briefly and Giuli felt a sweat break out on her forehead: she'd worn a jacket, thinking September could be treacherous, and she pulled it off with sudden violence. Enzo lifted a hand to her bared arm, to calm her. 'It's fine,' she mouthed, trying to make her smile reassuring. Was she turning squeamish? Was Giulietta Sarto, ex-offender, ex-addict, dragged up on the Via Senese by a whore, turning bourgeois? Never.

And it *was* fine. She believed. She believed in this place, however suffocating and crowded and ugly. She believed in the chants raised behind her. For to her surprise, Guili had found the first time Enzo had brought her to one of these meetings that she believed in protest. This was her voice, the voice she'd been waiting to hear come from her own mouth.

Heads were turning now, and the sound had changed, a kind of jeering applause, angry and approving at the same time. Movement set up again in the crowd, then almost magically it calmed of its own accord, a hush fell over them, an attentiveness, as though St Francis had come among the beasts.

Giuli frowned at the comparison that had suggested itself to her despite a godless upbringing, despite the fervently anti-religious stance of the Frazione Verde. But there was something of the saint about him. About the man whose arrival in the meeting room – absolutely punctual as always, the harshly ticking clock over the door showing eight o'clock to the very second – had turned heads and quieted the fray. Craning her neck, across the room Giuli could only see his narrow temples, the hair just turning grey, the deepset, dark eyes behind thick glasses, his head turning this way and that as he made his way towards the stage. Hands from the crowd went out to touch him as he passed.

Niccolò Rosselli: the Frazione's leader and figurehead, thrust unwillingly into the limelight, humble, unassuming, but once on that podium a different man. Once on that podium, you believed he could do anything. He would be a deputy, he would take his place in the seat of government, he would battle for them.

At the front of the crowd now, Rosselli bent his head to climb the three steps to the stage, and at the sight of the vulnerable back of his neck, at the head bowed as if in humility, the narrow shoulders in the dusty jacket, they quieted.

Another man waited for him, at the edge of the stage. Rosselli moved across the bare scuffed boards – no lectern, no props – he turned, he raised his hands, and they were absolutely silent. Behind the glasses his eyes burned. The planes of his face, it seemed to Giuli, were sharper than before. His voice, when he spoke, was deep and cracked and fierce.

'Do you think it will be easy?' A murmur, as though he was frightening them, that died away as quickly as it had come.

'It won't be easy.' His hands came down, as if in a blessing, and the upturned faces were rapt and still: he spoke to them and silently they gave him back their faith.

'There are forces ranged against us, we know that. You must be ready for a fight, but you must be ready to fight fairly. Because if once we falter in that determination then we are become what we are here to sweep away. Once we take a bribe, once we give preferment, once we dig dirt or pass false information. Instead we pay our fines, we deliver our taxes, we work as hard as we are capable of working and we fight to protect those who need our protection.'

Giuli held her breath: she couldn't move her eyes from him but she listened to the room around her, her heart in her mouth.

He raised his chin, and in the small movement issued a challenge. 'So we do not falter. We fight without resting. That is our understanding.'

And, pausing, Rosselli watched, his narrow shoulders very still and only his eyes behind the glasses moved, counting them all in, and they were with him. Every heart in the overheated room was lifted; they rode a magic carpet with him. But there was something else. Giuli felt with a palpable prickle of dread that as he held their attention, while they were all looking his way, something else had crept into the room.

Niccolò Rosselli held up his hands, palms out. 'You do this with me,' he said, 'and I will bring you your reward.' And as it began, the response he demanded, the growling of approval that might at this early stage have been mistaken for dissent, it was then that Giuli saw it coming, saw as if in an instant of foresight. Because something happened.

A hand came out, from the big man beside him, and touched him on the elbow. Was it a warning? Or the anticipation of what was to come? And in response Giuli could not have said what it was in Rosselli – a slip, a faltering, or just a moment's hesitation – but his whole stance changed, for a fraction of a second, the set of his shoulders, the turn of his head, as if he were bewildered by where he found himself, as if he were at a loss as to what to do next. And she was not the only one to see it: the roar the crowd wanted to deliver shifted like a wind, dying in their throats.

And then, as if he heard the warning note, because he knew the crowd better than he knew himself, Rosselli stiffened, stood straight. The hand on his elbow drew back. And the voices went up, the noise was suddenly deafening, a stamping and catcalling that must have been heard out in the piazza. Giuli gave in to it, eyes closed in relief for a moment before she opened them again.

Before them, swaying, on his face that habitual expression of fierce distress, of anguish, partly on behalf of his people, partly personal discomfort at the nakedness of their approbation and the loudness of their praise, Rosselli waited for quiet. And quiet came: they waited in turn. On tiptoe Giuli gazed at his face, willing him to speak, unable to breathe because she knew that the something wrong that she had seen, was still wrong. Behind the glasses his eyes looked to one side then another; his mouth moved, but no sound came out.

And then he fell.

Chapter Two

AT HIS KITCHEN TABLE, Sandro Cellini pushed the newspaper aside with a sound of exasperation. There was a fuzzy photograph on the front page of people grouped beside a swimming pool; inset was a studio glamour shot of a seventeen-year-old girl – a dancer was what they called her. The story was about a man who allegedly arranged for women to entertain their prime minister, some of them under-age, all of them described as 'beautiful'. He glanced over at his wife. Not a prude, nor a man of the world either, married thirty-five years and faithful – though there'd been moments of temptation, more than one – Sandro would have found it difficult to describe his response to the news story. '*Bunga bunga*' was how the sex was described.

Unease, Sandro supposed, would be his predominant emotion, if emotion it was, closely followed by weary despondency: it went deep, this stuff. When the lawyers went after the head of state, ranks closed. The last time they'd spoken, even Pietro, Sandro's old partner in the Polizia di Stato, had been tight-lipped on the subject. 'He's not the only one,' had been all he would say. 'There are ramifications.'

Something was happening, over his head, behind his back, in the force where once Sandro had been a brother-in-arms. Now he was exiled and it seemed that there really were no-go areas. Could he no longer talk politics with his old friend? He folded the newspaper so he could not see the photograph or the headline – 'NEW ALLEGATIONS! LARIO SPEAKS!'– then pulled the paperwork on his latest job towards him.

Gloomily Sandro stared at the typed page, details of a traffic accident from a medium-sized local insurance brokers. An ex-colleague had given them his name, a man neither he nor Pietro had ever had any time for, a not-very-bright police *commissario* who'd told Sandro about the recommendation with a gleam in his eye that said, You owe me one. So this was what Sandro had to look forward to as his main source of income; it seemed to him as he stared at the page to be all of a piece with the newspaper reports of men in high office booking prostitutes. There was something profoundly depressing about spying on claimants faking injury in car accidents: the insight into his fellow man, his brother Italian, the unease at representing the big company against the little guy. Even if the little guy was, in plain language, fraudulent.

It was eight in the morning, the sky was blue and the September air fresh through the open window; the gust of it that had come in with his wife Luisa from her dash to the market smelled of fallen leaves. She'd set a bag of bread and a butcher's packet of something, stained pink, on the table. A small box of mushrooms, the yellow trumpet-shaped ones, with shreds of moss still clinging to them, and a plastic carton of green figs, the last of them, oozing sweeter than honey.

Now Sandro sat back in his chair, closed his eyes and allowed September to soothe him. August was over, that was something to celebrate in itself. They'd had a holiday this year: after last year's terrible, suffocating month in the city, they'd made an unspoken agreement, never again. So this year they'd borrowed someone's mother's place in Castiglioncello, an old lady's house smelling of mothballs and damp, and gone there for three weeks. Not an unalloyed success – neither Sandro nor Luisa was good at idle holiday pursuits, she would rather cook than be served at table, whiling away the hours playing cards seemed nothing but a waste of time – but five or six days into their confinement something had come over them, something almost like the holiday spirit had taken them by surprise.

They had found themselves going out for an *aperitivo* together at six, first one night, then the next, then every night as if it were the most natural thing in the world, rather than something they'd last managed more than a year before. They had gone to the little outdoor cinema tucked away in the old town between whitewashed walls, with weeds growing up through the cracked paving, and watched an ancient Fellini film with half a dozen other couples. They had walked along the beach in the cool early morning, watching the sun come up, not hand in hand because it wasn't their way, Luisa a little in front and holding her hem out of the water.

Three old women in flowered housecoats had walked ahead of them in the pale dawn doing the same, slow, apparently aimless, talking around in circles about grandchildren and church and the baker's wife's affair. Apparently aimless but actually restoring order to the world... this was the revelation that had come to Sandro as he found himself slowing his pace, realizing that as he wasn't actually heading anywhere, there was no point in going there fast. Holidays: perhaps there was something to them, after all.

They hadn't worried about Giuli either, minding the office for them in the city after taking her own two weeks at the end of July, because she had someone of her own, now.

A neglected child, an abused adolescent, Giuli had ended up in prison for taking a violent revenge on her abuser. It had brought her into Sandro's life – he'd been her arresting officer – and had indirectly led to his premature departure from the police force. Not disgraced, no one thought that any more, not for passing information on the abuser to a bereaved father, but rules were rules, always had been. Giuli had been released from prison more or less into Sandro and Luisa's care. All parties being adults, no one had had to ask anyone's permission or sign any papers, but it had been an unorthodox arrangement for the couple, childless and now too old to have children, to decide to love and protect Giuli, in so far as they were capable of doing so. And now after forty years and more of having to fight her own corner, Giuli had Enzo, too.

Reading her husband's mind, Luisa called over her shoulder from the fridge where she was putting the meat: *involtini* stuffed with sage and ham, four sausages, only the two of them to feed.

'You know we're supposed to be eating with them Saturday night?'

Today was Tuesday. She hadn't even needed to say who *they* were. Brushing herself down in an unconscious and familiar gesture that made Sandro smile and want to take hold of her, she ran her hands under the tap and sat down at the table with him.

'Yes,' he said mildly. God only knew what Giuli would cook: it wasn't her forte. Her mother would never have made housewife of the year even if she'd lived to see Giuli hit fourteen. The girl had been fed on packet cakes and fizzy drinks then her mother had died and she'd stopped eating anything at all.

'I said I'd bring something,' Luisa said. Mind-reading again.

And he looked down once more at the letter from the insurance company. Fraudulent: it was a nasty word for something everyone did. 'Who isn't fraudulent?' he said out loud.

'Me,' Luisa said. 'I'm not fraudulent. Never took a piece of stock home, nor even a paperclip, never cheated my taxes.'

'No,' Sandro said. 'Why is that?' And she'd turned her back on him with the ghost of a smile.

'He's claiming post-traumatic stress stopped him working,' Sandro added. Luisa made a sound of deep cynicism and he raised his head to monitor his wife, his infallible moral compass. Sometimes it was tricky, living with a moral compass that accurate.

'Weren't you ever even tempted?' he asked. 'To steal just one paperclip? Or something more appealing maybe. A pair of shoes. . . a pair of stockings. . . way back when.'

Way back when the store Luisa worked for, now a gleaming white and steel palace of fashion, had been principally an old-fashioned haberdasher's with wooden drawers filled with stockings and cashmere and lawn nightdresses, hand-embroidered.

But he knew the answer. She didn't even have to smile and shake her head: it was one of many differences between them. Sandro, like all his colleagues, would borrow stationery from the office, nip out on errands on police time, turn a blind eye. There were plenty worse than him, plenty. 'So, why?'

She put her head on one side, thinking. 'Because you don't know where it would end,' she said. 'You have to have rules for yourself.' And straightened, haughtily. 'Where was post-traumatic stress after the war? In 'sixty-six after the floods?' And snorted.

'Well, yes,' he said. 'I know. But it was an accident, not his fault, woman shunted him on the motorway. Someone in the car behind her died.'

Sobered slightly, Luisa had pursed her lips. 'Still,' she said.

'He's got psychiatric reports, and everything,' Sandro said.

'That in itself. . . ' Luisa said. 'That's not someone whose life has been knocked for six. Commissioning psychiatric reports? Looking for compensation.'

'Catch-22,' Sandro said, groping mentally for a faded image. He'd read the book, thirty years before. 'Isn't that the situation?

If you're really crazy, you wouldn't be asking for the psychiatrist. Something like that.'

Luisa ignored the reference: she hadn't read *Catch-22*. It would, Sandro realized, have annoyed her too much. 'Still,' she said, 'I suppose that's not your job. To make a judgement.'

'Fortunately not,' Sandro said. It hadn't been his job to make judgements as a police officer either, not really: then, too, his job had been to gather the evidence and hand it on. Not that it had stopped him: taking judgement into his own hands had been what got him kicked out of the force.

He shuffled the papers into some kind of order, slid them into his briefcase. Checking this insurance claim was looking like the worst kind of job. Fiddly, small-scale, and already it seemed to be requiring him to examine his own conscience into the bargain.

'It's all money, though,' Luisa commented, although he'd said nothing. 'It's all work.' Sandro got to his feet, tempted to laugh at himself, or at her, for the precision with which she could read his expression. Extraordinary that she could still be bothered, after all these years, to make sense of him.

He smiled. 'Giuli's place on Saturday,' he said, hefting the briefcase. Was he looking forward to it?

'Their place, now,' Luisa said.

'He's good for her, isn't he?' asked Sandro, feeling the need for confirmation. 'Enzo, I mean?' That was why they were going for dinner, to keep tabs. Giuli didn't look vulnerable – in fact, she looked as far from it as was possible, with her fierce little face and her spiky dark hair and her cheerful recklessness on her battered army-grey *motorino* – but she was. Enzo had been around for more than a year now, but Luisa wasn't going to let up.

That grudging nod was what he had expected, but Luisa's expression was more complicated. 'Yes,' she said eventually.

Sandro was at the door before he responded to the note of doubt: wanting it not to be there. Wanting to get off to work leaving everything fine behind him.

'What d'you mean?' he asked, with reluctance, standing in the doorway.

'Well. . . ,' said Luisa, standing motionless at the kitchen table, the September light falling on half her face. Frowning. 'I'm not so sure about this political business. She – they – seem very caught up in it. I don't understand this Frazione Verde. It seems – extreme to me.'

'Oh, that,' he said with relief. 'Extreme? Aren't they a bunch of hippy, green, Rainbow Coalition types? Very soft-centred, I'm sure. And it'll just be a phase. Young people, you know.' He clasped the briefcase to him in an unconscious gesture of protection, but of what or whom, he wasn't sure.

'She's not young, Sandro,' Luisa said. 'None of us is young any more.'

The telephone rang.

*

Chiara Cavallaro, curly-headed, small for her age and slender – too slender, her mother had begun to fret, just lately – emerged from the great doorway to the Università degli Studi into the broad sunshine of the Piazza San Marco, weighed down with books. Worse than school, she'd grumbled to her mother on her return with the reading list, but she hadn't meant it: the knapsack you carried to school represented something quite different. The pink backpack embellished with friends' signatures, the childish exercise books, the *quaderni* with their doodles and their covers decorated with cartoon characters, filled with the diligently neat handwriting of a girl child, easy to please.

What expression would come over her father's face if she reminded him of that? Her father the stern policeman, soft as a pussycat at home, the man who wanted an easy life, to be indulgent to his daughter and be loved in return.

'You were never easy to please, angel,' he'd say, with that wary smile, wanting her still to be his little girl.

'No,' her mother would agree, watching her more closely. Round-hipped, good cook, red hair. No fool. Chiara loved her mother.

She loved both of them, of course she did. Blinking into the sunshine, Chiara raised a hand to shield her eyes. It wasn't just being an only child – most of her friends were only children. It was to do with – with the old order. The old ways of doing things. Cutting corners, sitting it out till retirement in the comfort of the corrupt state sector. She wanted to lean down into her father's armchair in the evenings, take him by his elbows and shake him. 'Wake up, Babbo,' she wanted to say. 'You're only fifty-six. Do something to change the world, before it's too late.' Start the fight from within.

Political science. That had got him started.

'At least she's staying home,' her mother had said, on Chiara's side in this one. 'You know, there are kids who go to the other end of the country, these days, for their *laurea*.' Neither of her parents had a degree. Her mother should have had one: she was more intelligent than her husband, which was why she had done so well in the bank.

The truth was, Chiara would have gone to the other end of the country to do her degree, if she'd had a choice. But the course in Florence was an excellent one – among the best. And she'd have had to go to her parents for the money to live away from home. Until now she would, anyway.

'But political science,' her dad had groaned, head in hands. 'Where's that going to take you?' It was going to take her away from him, her conservative old dad, and he knew it. She could see it in the face he raised to her, weary, dubious, that he only wanted her to be like him, or her mother, to get a safe job, to have a child, to live in comfort.

'Comfort's not what it's all about, Babbo,' she'd said.

Was there a word for the expression he'd worn after that? A kind of blankness had fallen over his face, as if he genuinely didn't understand what she meant. As if he gave up. At the memory, Chiara frowned.

And thank God he hadn't been there when she got up this morning, because it would have been on the local news, perhaps even in *La Nazione*, the terrible right-wing rubbish Dad read. It's got local news, though, he'd plead, as if regional loyalty was enough. As if. She loved her city, of course she did, she was Fiorentina through and through. Which was precisely why – damn, damn, thought Chiara. She felt sick at the memory, last night coming back to her.

Dad would probably say Rosselli was on drugs, or something. His answer to every evil, drugs. Chiara had never touched a drug in her life, but she wasn't even sure if he knew that. The fact that Giulietta Sarto had been there last night would only have confirmed his conviction that where left-wingers were gathered, there would be ex-convicts, junkies and prostitutes, and Giulietta Sarto qualified on all counts.

'I know she's clean now,' her dad had said a few times. 'I know Sandro loves her. But once a junkie, always a junkie.'

For a brief second of doubt Chiara did wonder if he might be right, though, as she remembered it. . . remembered Niccolò Rosselli's face as blank as her father's in that moment before he'd toppled headlong like a felled tree, on the stage in front of them all. It had been so – catastrophic.

They'd carted him off in an ambulance, dead or alive, no one knew. Rumours flew before the stretcher even left the hall, then the place had gone crazy in the aftermath, complete chaos, the hardliners setting up a chant, people talking wildly about conspiracy, some drunk singing 'Bandiera Rossa'. A fight had even broken out on the pavement outside as the ambulance moved away. Inside the meeting room Chiara had been frightened. Properly frightened, wanting her dad kind of frightened, just for a moment there, just when it looked like there might be a stampede.

In the sunshine she was hot, suddenly. Maybe she should just do it. Maybe she did need to get away from her parents, like he said. Her man.

She'd been first out of the introductory lecture and most of the others – she knew some of them from school, again had felt that pang, of wanting to start again in a new city – had hung around, to talk to the speaker, a well-known figure in the city, a left-wing historian and journalist, and something of a hero. He'd spoken openly against the current government, had told the new intake they were the only hope for their country. Chiara had found herself wary of him, of the hero-worship thing at least, and when she saw the crowd gather around the speaker she'd turned and gone, suddenly uncertain, her father's cynical voice in her head. The man probably said that to every year's new students: You are your country's only hope, knowledge is the key. And of all people Sandro Cellini, her father's best friend and ex-partner in the police force, had come into her head again then: she could almost see his expression, his frown, at the gaggle of eager students, and their hero.

They were streaming past Chiara as she stood there in the doorway, then one detached himself from the crowd, stopped. Smiled.

'I suppose you were there last night?' he asked, head tilted, between her and the sun. He lifted the books from her arms. 'Let me take those.'

She looked into his eyes. She'd tell Dad tonight.

*

Eighty miles out east, on the seafront at Viareggio, the sun that shone on Chiara Cavallaro in the Piazza San Marco sat high over the flat-calm silver sea, still strong enough to warm the few morning bathers on the groomed sands. Less groomed than they would have been a month ago, the striped umbrellas and wooden loungers depleted, the bathing stations closing down one by one as September cooled and drew to a close, but the town was still busy. Plenty of the hotels, indeed, were still booked out, the cheaper, more discreet ones, lovers stealing a last few illicit days at the end of the summer without the need for a sea view.

The Stella Maris had vacancies, but then it was expensive for what it was. A faded place one street in from the front, its blue-washed stucco no longer the deep cobalt it had been in better days, an overblown garden of unpruned magnolia and laurels, and twelve old-fashioned, under-decorated rooms, fewer than half of them occupied this sunny Tuesday morning.

'It's "Do not disturb",' said Vesna, coming out to shake her dusters among the laurels and addressing herself to her employer, Signore Calzaghe. His seedy, overweight bulk parked in a grubby swing seat on the Stella Maris's verandah, his chin rough with at least a day's white stubble, Calzaghe was the hotel's owner, manager and holder of any other self-appointed position that did not require him actually to lift a finger in its service. He frowned back at her.

'Number five?' Unfortunately for Vesna, her employer might be lazy but he had an excellent head for detail, for numbers and names and quantities (of guest soaps, for example, which he required her to dry out in the airing cupboard if barely used, or linen washed, or rolls ordered for the breakfasts). He rubbed his chin thoughtfully. 'So? Less work for you, I'd have thought. Fewer towels to the laundry, too.'

Vesna saw that crafty glint in his eye and could see he was wondering how he could somehow recoup that unused labour for himself, that twenty minutes she would have spent in number five setting the guest's toiletries straight, closing her wardrobe door, making her bed.

She tucked the dusters into the belt of her maid's uniform, a pink as faded as the hotel façade's blue, made for a larger woman. Better that than too tight: Vesna had had her fill of too-tight maid's uniforms, and the male guests' response to them. The female guest in number five had bothered her from the day she walked in, pale and breathless as if she'd run there all the way from the station. Vesna opened her mouth to say so, and closed it again: her instinct was that the last thing the woman in number five needed was Calzaghe on her case.

'Did she say how long she was planning to stay?' He was chewing his fat cheek now, his piggy eyes contemplating the possibility that he was going somehow to lose out on this deal.

'She wasn't sure, she said,' said Vesna. 'But she'd be gone by the weekend.'

He sighed, a sound he made self-important, impatient, accusatory all at once.

'Give it another day,' he said. 'She's only herself to blame. If the linen's not changed.' And he settled back into the swing seat and closed his eyes.

Chapter Three

'Y OU'VE HEARD OF HIM, right? Have you even seen the papers this morning?'

Giuli was waiting for him in the office, even twitchier than usual as Sandro came past her into the sunlit room. A tiny cup of takeaway espresso sat on his desk, kept warm by a twist of paper napkin over the top, two newspapers folded beside it. His priorities set at caffeine rather than news, Sandro dropped the briefcase down heavily in his seat and downed the coffee in one, standing beside his desk.

'Not enough, this morning,' he said. 'Shall we go out for another?'

Giuli gave him one of her looks.

There was something about her this morning: he'd got used to the new, put-together Giuli, he realized, lipstick, clothes neat if not always conventional, groomed. This morning she was wearing scuffed boots and hadn't brushed her hair.

Hold on, he thought. It's Tuesday: she's not even supposed to be here.

'Aren't you supposed to be at the Women's Centre?' he asked.

'Rosselli,' she repeated impatiently. 'I was at that meeting last

23

night. You've heard of him, right?' When Sandro just watched her, trying to make his brain shift a gear, she said impatiently, 'I'll go out and get you another, if necessary, but I don't think this is something we can talk about in a bar. Not in San Frediano, at any rate. This is his turf.' She took a breath. 'I said I wasn't well,' she said. 'I'm going in after lunch.'

Sandro frowned. She took the Women's Centre very seriously, as a rule: it had been her lifeline when she'd come out of prison.

But he said nothing. 'Rosselli,' he repeated, instead. Yes, he knew him. 'He's your guy. Your leader. The – what's it? – Frazione Verde.'

Heard of him? Yes, Sandro had heard of him. On every street corner in the Oltrarno, it seemed, the little designs had appeared, spray-painted through a stencil, rather neat and clever: *Frazione = Azione*, in fluorescent green. They were creeping north of the river too. One had even appeared mysteriously on the corner of their building in Santa Croce, riding the tidemark of street dirt that rose higher every summer. Under it the impassioned scrawl, in sprayed black: *Niccolò Rosselli è nostro Gandhi.*

'Niccolò Rosselli is our Gandhi.' What man would want that? Look how it ended. And what was this about the papers?

He studied Giuli's face, feeling the beginnings of a headache, then following her gaze down he broke off, the front page of the newspaper getting his attention at last. Giuli unfolded the newspaper in front of him with exaggerated care.

There was an inset photograph of an unshaven man in thick glasses, handsome once perhaps, now too gaunt and intense for good looks, staring fiercely from the page. And the bigger photograph was a fuzzy night shot of an ambulance parked on the Via Sant'Agostino outside an old church, something being loaded into the back and a blur of faces staring from the pavement, the ubiquitous elderly woman rubbernecking as she walked her dog.

'ROSSELLI COLLAPSES AT RALLY' was the headline.

'He's in hospital?' Sandro frowned down at the bleak photograph. The ambulance on the pavement, the curious bystanders. 'Is he all right?'

At the innocuous question, gently put, Giuli sat down quite suddenly at his desk, her spiky, determined little face collapsing into anxiety. She tugged the briefcase out from under her and shoved it on to the desk. Sandro pulled up the chair reserved for clients, although Giuli seemed not to notice the reversal in their roles, she was so distracted.

'They let him go,' she said, twisting her fingers together on the desktop. 'No one thinks he's all right.'

'Giuli,' said Sandro gently, prising her hands apart and holding them. 'What is this political thing of yours? You were never into politics. What is this man to you?'

She looked up and he could see she was all prepared to go into battle, eyes burning, but then it seemed to dawn on her that she was talking to him, to Sandro Cellini, the closest thing to a father and protector she had ever had, and the blaze went out of her. 'Is it – Enzo?' He tried to sound reasonable, friendly. 'Has he got you into this?'

'No,' she began indignantly, pushing his hands away and shoving herself back in the seat. 'No! Do you think I haven't got a mind of my own?'

'That's the last thing I think, *cara*.' He could see her frown at the endearment: he never called her by anything but her name. And saw her decide not to feel patronized. She was growing up, his Giuli. She let out a breath and her narrow frame collapsed a little more in the chair.

'I just don't understand this – this Frazione Verde thing.' He could hear the unease in his own voice. 'And I don't like to see you like this. All fired up, all emotional – I don't know. I like – an even keel. The middle of the road, a quiet life. What do they stand for, after all? Your party.'

Giuli was staring at him. She knew what he was saying, all right. 'I'm clean, Sandro,' she said distinctly. 'I'm not in it for the rush. I love my place, the city, Santo Spirito, the people. And it's all going to ratshit, isn't it? This government... I want to – do something for other people, to be part of something. You ask what the Frazione stands for?'

Sandro lifted his head, listening.

'Change,' Giuli said defiantly. 'Concentrating on the local, and working up. Just – change. It feels good, yeah. But it's the right kind of good.'

Sandro shoved the briefcase with the insurance claim away from him across the scuffed leather of the desktop. Reluctantly he leaned over and turned the computer on under Giuli's gaze, her arms folded as she waited.

'What are you, my conscience?' he said irritably. 'Bad enough with Luisa at home. I've got work to do, you know,' nodding towards the briefcase. 'I'll manage better without you looking over my shoulder.'

'I'm nobody's conscience,' she said stubbornly. 'I'm just worried about him. Nobody's telling us anything.'

Sandro leaned back in the chair and examined her fierce, frowning face. 'Who is there to ask?' he said.

The frown relaxed, just marginally. 'That's the trouble, really,' said Giuli. 'The Frazione – well, it's grown, kind of, organically.' Sandro winced at the word: even Giuli seemed embarrassed saying it. What did it mean?

'Because of that, there aren't any – any structures,' she said uncomfortably. 'Power structures, hierarchy. It's all very – democratic. The office is a little box room behind the hall, with a couple of computers. We all turn up to the meetings, everyone who

26

wants to can have their say, and Rosselli – well, he kind of listens, then sort of puts our thoughts into order. Reinterprets them.'

'So what's the – um – manifesto?'

Giuli shifted, uncertain. 'It's to do with local people, and resistance to city hall decisions that affect lives. To do with asking questions.'

'For example?'

'Rubbish collection,' she said, 'education, local health provision, the clinic. Money pulled for a new nursery and put into roadbuilding for some retail park instead. You've heard of the development on the edge of Scandicci? Business interests are being set over people's interests.'

Sandro looked at her mildly. 'Isn't there an argument about economics in there too? Jobs being provided – for local people? Aren't you being a bit simplistic?' He was unprepared for the answering flash in her eyes.

'This country,' she said. 'You know as well as I do, those jobs will go to someone's cousin, someone's nephew. We might pick up the drudge work. But our community will be changed, invaded. Houses and gardens will go.'

Sandro blinked at her certainty. 'Maybe you should stand yourself,' he said. 'You're good at this.' But he felt unaccountably anxious for her: it wasn't that simple, in the end. She went on staring at him.

'So who's in charge?' He pulled the computer back towards him, and typed the words 'Frazione Verde' into the search engine.

'There's Rosselli.' She chewed her lip. 'There's a lawyer, too. Was at college with him, I think, his name's Bastone.' She hesitated. 'He was on the stage with him last night, he – well, I don't know if he knew what was coming, but before Roselli went down, his friend put out his hand, like, to keep him steady or something.'

She took a breath: Sandro scrutinized her, holding his peace.

'So he's literally the right-hand man. Otherwise, it's all very – makeshift still. There's Rosselli's wife, of course. She used to be the kind of secretary, taking the minutes, administration, only she's taken a step back since – are you listening?'

A gaudy page had come up, bright green and ill-designed. Giuli leaned down, beaming. 'That's Enzo,' she said. Sandro frowned: he could only see the same shot of Rosselli that the newspaper had used. 'I mean, Enzo designed their webpage,' she said shyly. 'Democratic, you see.'

Sandro had to restrain himself from shaking his head at the limitations of democracy. 'I didn't know he was a web designer,' was all he said, mildly. Knowing quite well that in fact Enzo was a computer engineer and that design, quite clearly, was not his forte.

'No, he's—' Giuli's face dropped a little as she broke off, understanding.

'There's a number,' he said, peering down at the page. Giuli shook her head. 'That's Rosselli's home number,' she said. 'No one's answering, or it's engaged – or off the hook most likely, because people will be calling, won't they? They must be loving this. Wanting him to fail. Wanting us to fail.'

'Who?' Sandro asked, impatiently. 'Who is this *they*?' The look she turned on him almost made him smile, it was so full of pity and contempt. He opened his mouth, then closed it again. Feeling that they were at an impasse that could only get worse, he looked back at the screen.

'He was going to stand as a deputy, with no – no structures in place? No nothing, leaving aside this college friend, this lawyer? No advisors, no manifesto, no platform?'

'If you can elect a porn star, why not Rosselli?' said Giuli savagely. 'Did she have a manifesto?'

'I believe she did,' said Sandro drily. They were talking about La Cicciolina, elected in the eighties, though plenty of other jokers had been elected since. 'Hers involved something about cuddles.' He shrugged. 'That's democracy in action.' Giuli said nothing, her expression darkening.

Turning to the window, Sandro saw that the air outside was clear and soft and blue. He needed another coffee, and the briefcase on his desk reproached him: real work. 'Giuli, I don't know what you want me to do,' he said.

She perched like a schoolchild on the edge of the chair, hands white-knuckled as she clasped them together. This really had got to her, and he still didn't know why. 'What?' he said gently. 'Tell me.'

She looked up. 'Them,' she said mulishly. 'Whatever you say – they're out there. He's a threat to them. Rosselli – Niccolò. He's got too powerful, his voice has grown too loud.'

'Niccolò,' repeated Sandro. First-name terms, was it? What was this man to Giuli? She looked into his face, imploringly, and he tried not to think that way. Tried instead to think back to a time when he'd been idealistic, had believed in – something. Had he ever? 'You think he's in danger? You think there's some kind of a conspiracy.'

He couldn't keep the dull scepticism out of his voice. It sounded wrong to him: it sounded false and melodramatic; it didn't sound like Giuli. 'But you don't know who's behind it. Is this you talking, Giuli? Or some kind of mass hysteria?'

For a long moment they stared at each other and Sandro felt a shiver of foreboding, saw the breach ahead. Had he seen Giuli through so much only for some tinpot little bunch of green zealots to steal her from him?

And then she spoke. 'You don't know what it was like,' she said, her voice cracking, the fervour gone, and with a relief he dared not show Sandro knew he still had her.

'To see him go down like that.' Her eyes were wide at the memory. 'Keel over, like he'd been shot, or poisoned. And I saw it coming, you know? Had like a – a premonition. It seemed like – like all those assassinations: we really thought that's what it was. It means something, Sandro, I just don't know what, yet.' And he could see that she was holding her hands together tight so that he wouldn't see that she was shaking.

'All right,' he said. 'All right. We'll see if we can get to the bottom of it, shall we? We'll see what we can do.'

And for now the insurance claim and the briefcase and even the second cup of coffee receded beyond hope of return.

'We start with the college friend,' he said. 'The lawyer.'

*

In the café opposite the post office – where she had just dropped off a parcel – Luisa stood at the red marble bar and hoped it was going to be all right. The kind of involuntary thought she tried, actually, not to have: Luisa preferred to take the position that it *would* be all right. One doubter and fretter in the family – if you could call it a family – was enough. Slowly she stirred the coffee that sat in front of her on the bar, saw the barman glance over.

And what exactly did she hope was going to be all right? Well, a number of things, that was the trouble. One problem at a time, then. Fine.

Sandro would forget that it was her annual check-up next week, she was pretty sure of that.

It didn't worry her. It wasn't the check-up, it hadn't even been the breast cancer itself, when it came, that frightened her, only what came with it. The look on other people's faces was what it boiled down to. Even three years later there was still the ghost of that look. Furtive, guilty, evasive.

If truth be told, Luisa rather hoped Sandro *had* forgotten about the check-up, because she'd prefer to slip off there on her own without having to look into his anxious face in the waiting room. She remembered last time. His expression when she came out of the cubicle in the backless gown, as if she was already in her shroud: after that she hadn't let him in for the mammogram for fear he'd faint dead away. It didn't count as an invasive procedure but it sure enough felt like one, and looked like one, being cranked and squeezed and manhandled into a machine.

'Signora?' The barman was peering into Luisa's face with concern: she must have been grimacing. Did he know? She couldn't remember if he knew about her missing breast, this young man who served her coffee a few times a week. He probably did. Sometimes it seemed to Luisa that everyone in Florence knew, and it irritated her. She raised the coffee hastily to her lips. It had gone quite cold, but it was still good. She gave the barman an imperious look.

Dairy products were bad for you: so was coffee, so was wine. Luisa had never smoked, although both of her parents had; she must have absorbed more nicotine than a fly-paper as a kid. She had pored over the risk factors and causes, and had emerged none the wiser. It had made Sandro angry to see her frowning, and refusing a glass of wine: 'What's the point?' he'd say. Not like you can go back and change it now. And even if you could, Luisa had concluded after a month or so of useless fretting, perhaps you wouldn't. Life is for living, for tasting the things you like to taste. And it seemed to Luisa that even if it meant living five, ten years longer, it wouldn't be worth losing sight of what brought pleasure.

Outside a beggar stood on the steps of the post office. He swivelled to follow each customer in and out, his cap held before him, and she could see his mouth murmur those few words. *Uno spicciolo per mangiare*. Quite a respectable-looking beggar: white moustache, dark wool jacket shiny at the elbows, baggy serge trousers. An old-fashioned sort of beggar, deferential and formal. She could see he was quite successful; people responded to tradition. Meanwhile, at the other end of the arcade the Roma women would be working their pitch, long braids swinging, often a baby held across the body carelessly in a sling of flowered fabric. Luisa, who had no children although she had given birth once long ago, to a girl who died two days later, set her face against these women even if she knew, at bottom, that they – and their babies – probably needed her pity. Needed her loose change more.

Luisa's mother had given to beggars, as a protective measure, a superstition. Luisa took out her purse and looked in it, fingered a two-euro coin and put it in the pocket of her jacket. She would not do it out of superstition, though.

So what else did she hope would be all right, if not the damned check-up? Well, that first, get it out of the way. The bus to Careggi, the stuffy waiting room, the gown and the examination. She could get through that just planning what she would cook for dinner and, at a pinch, what she would wear to work the following day: her own perfectly well-regulated strategies.

On the small high table beside Luisa was a newspaper. Not thinking, she turned it towards her, stared at the headline without registering what it said.

That morning she had arrived at the shop half an hour early, as she often did: she had gone into the stock room where there was a small mirror, removed her blouse and her slip and her brassiere, and looked at herself.

Why she could not do this at home she didn't know. On one side a round breast, well proportioned, slightly low under the weight of years and gravity but a good shape. On the other side a curved and puckered scar, faded now to silvery-white. It had been first an angry red, purplish, and a rash had come and gone.

They would ask her again about reconstruction, next week. Luisa didn't know what she would say: even the question seemed an intrusion too far. She had stood there perhaps two, three minutes, looking at herself. She'd caught her own stern expression as she put the bra back on. Sandro did not discuss it: he gave no sign, in fact, of ever having noticed that her body was any different, although to Luisa it was as different as if she had had her leg removed. They did not mention it. Perhaps they would never have to. She told herself the thought should be reassuring, but somehow it was not.

Now in front of the window in the Caffè della Posta, Luisa looked away from the newspaper and down at herself. The place was crowded, no one was watching her, but she didn't much care anyway. The blouse was loose, so you couldn't tell, unless you were really looking. And who really looked at a woman in her sixties? In a sweater she could tell: the prosthesis sometimes slipped a little. But who looked? Quickly Luisa shifted her gaze aside, back to the newspaper: she unfolded it in a pretence of reading to distract herself.

She should get back: half an hour to post a parcel was more than enough. They gave her leeway, since – but she didn't want leeway.

'ROSSELLI COLLAPSES'. She frowned at the headline and as she did so the hum of conversation in the bar behind her sharpened, voices became distinct. This was what they were talking about. The tone of the newspaper article, like the conversation, was snide and hostile.

'I heard, drugs,' said a woman's unpleasant, needling voice. Luisa didn't need to see her to know what kind of woman she was: Luisa could have told you where she got her hair set without turning round.

'Oltrarno do-gooders, that green nonsense. They're all lowlife. Drugs. And they're telling us they're above taking backhanders?' The man spoke automatically: her husband, her lover, whatever, placidly agreeing with everything she said. They lived in a ground-floor apartment in Le Cure, with a garden – they complained about the mosquitoes; they had his mother's expensive silver and a house in Porto Ercole for the summer months. They complained about how much it all cost, they both fiddled their taxes and they both cheated on each other.

'Well, of course, the marvellous thing is, this should do for his chances.'

Luisa read the report at speed. Niccolò Rosselli: she knew his mother, who was fifteen years older than Luisa. Her mother had known Rosselli's grandmother, in the days when the city had been really a village. As if it were yesterday she could remember the mother and grandmother wheeling the precious child out in his frilled pram. An only child, fussed over and doted on: the father a *contadino*, the mother from the city, with ideas.

Luisa knew the precious child in the handknitted bonnet had grown up, of course she did, she knew that he had become a teacher, then an agitator, she was aware that this Frazione Verde had something to do with him. She looked at the photograph of the ill-shaven man in thick glasses staring off the page: he had been taken to the Pronto Soccorso of Santa Maria Nuova, she read, but released after tests. Luisa thought of his mother pacing the corridors of the hospital, haranguing nurses; she had always been a forceful woman. She must be seventy-five now. At least.

But there was a wife, wasn't there? Or partner, was that the term? She frowned back down at the small print, holding it at arm's length so as to focus. Luisa had glasses but didn't like to wear them. No mention of a wife: enough. Enough gossip, enough idle speculation. Folding the newspaper, she laid it down with a slap and turned to leave. The barman lifted his head to follow her progress across the small, crowded space, and she inclined her head just a little in acknowledgement.

The woman who had talked about drugs Luisa did not acknowledge, although her face was less than twenty centimetres from Luisa's and staring openly as she turned. Luisa let her eyes slide over the woman's handsome, arrogant features – younger than me, she registered, and stupid – and without bothering to look at the woman's interlocutor, she turned her back.

She stepped out through the door into the fresh, cool, September morning that smelled of woodsmoke and chrysanthemums from the flower stalls, took a deep breath and held it.

One problem at a time: and she had the uncomfortable feeling that here was another.

Chapter Four

THE MARKET STALLS WERE crowded around the southern end of the Piazza Santo Spirito, and under the statue of Cosimo Ridolfi was slumped the emaciated figure of Stefano the resident drunk, oblivious as always to Ridolfi's agrarian reforms or his sad, resigned gaze into the middle distance. Stefano raised his head and mumbled as they passed: the words were indistinguishable but from the way his faded eyes brightened as they lit on her, he knew Giuli. Sandro took her arm.

'It's all right,' said Giuli, wriggling in his grasp. They came past trestles laden with second-hand clothes, off which rose the stale smell of closeted apartments, mothballs and unwashed bodies. The customers were a surprising mix: scavengers picking through the stuff and grumbling to each other, some old women but men too, and a girl with dyed orange hair.

'So the lawyer's a Santo Spirito type too, is he?' said Sandro, for something to say. He wasn't looking forward to this encounter: perhaps it was his years in the police, perhaps it was being Italian, or just human, but he'd never met a lawyer he liked. Two years back he'd been employed by one, a so-called human rights lawyer who turned out to be one of the least moral men Sandro had ever encountered. And Sandro's whole working life had been spent among criminals.

Giuli nodded to the far end of the square, where the soft pale stucco of the church rose, undefiled and lovely in spite of it all, to meet them. 'Just round the corner,' she said. 'Off the Via Maggio.' They escaped the stalls and walked around under the steep and beautiful façade of the Palazzo Guadagni, under restoration and not before time.

There was Liliana on the vegetable stall, arms folded across her sweatshirt, chatting to a nun in the grey habit of the Franciscan mission in the Piazza del Carmine. Married for thirty years to a useless drunken husband but silently heartbroken all the same when he died, standing in the marketplace six hours a days, six days a week, all year round, Liliana couldn't in theory have much in common with an eighty-year-old nun who'd spent her life cloistered away from men and the world. But to Sandro there was something almost identical in their faces, although he couldn't identify it. Not happiness, exactly, not resignation: their eyes as they talked, peaceably exchanging opinions on who knew what, seemed separately to be fixed somewhere far off, contemplating something invisible. Perhaps God, for the nun, or heaven.

Did Liliana believe in heaven? Did he?

'Liliana was backing Niccolò,' said Giuli out of the blue, watching him. He stopped.

'Really?' So Liliana wasn't waiting for the afterlife for justice, then. 'She was at the meeting?'

Giuli nodded, a guardedness in her expression that he couldn't quite identify. For a moment Sandro felt a twinge of something, almost guilt, mixed with envy. Everyone who was anyone, it seemed, had been at this meeting.

'Well, Liliana's no fool.' He mused on this fact. Giuli folded her arms across her chest. She did seem better: outside was always better, with Giuli. She was still sometimes like a feral cat, turning around and around in any confined space, looking for an exit.

'Were they all right about it, at the Women's Centre?' he ventured cautiously.

She eyed him. 'They understood,' she said. 'They're behind him, all the way. The Centre's funding's been slashed, you know that? Half of us are volunteers, they're even asking the doctors to work free a day a week.'

Sandro, who had not known, nodded. He was perturbed by the news. They were a bunch of tough cookies at the Women's Centre and no mistake; ballbreaking, chainsmoking women doctors, most of the auxiliary staff ex-cons on community service, he always felt they were somehow eyeing him up for the chop – redundant as a man, as a useful member of society – every time he went in there to pay a call on Giuli, but there was something about the place nevertheless. He'd seen them sitting on the plastic chairs, pacing the corridors, women turning up there ready to top themselves because they were pregnant again or sick again or had been punched unconscious by a punter again. The doctors with their nicotine-stained fingers patched them up and got them back out there again. Short-term measures, maybe – but Sandro knew, and Giuli better than most, that for some people, short term was all there was. Better than no term at all.

It was beginning to dawn on him, how much was vested in this man.

'They live over there,' said Giuli, breaking in on his thoughts. 'Rosselli lives over there.'

He followed the nod of her head across the square through the feathery canopy of elm leaves: the western side was the humblest: three- and four-storey houses, plain, modestly pretty stucco frontages, no cut-stone corners or window surrounds, shallow eaves. 'That one,' she said. 'Next to the restaurant on the corner.'

The shutters to the apartment she was indicating were all closed.

They could just knock on the door, they both knew that. But they both knew, too, that even if it was the thing the journalists or the lobbyists or even the police might do, they couldn't do it themselves. They knew too well how it would be behind those closed shutters, the distress, the anxiety, the dark.

Back in the office, without thinking too hard about it, Sandro had asked Giuli if she knew where Rosselli lived. His unspoken thought had been that they could just go round and ask – what? How things were? What was wrong? Could they help? Because all that had happened as far as they knew was the poor man had been taken ill. But even as Sandro had found himself frowning at the white-faced, tight-lipped little shake of the head Giuli had given him in response, he'd understood that it wasn't going to be that easy. And Rosselli hadn't collapsed at home, but in front of an audience, at a crucial point in a controversial career. It had given Sandro a chill to think that Giuli's unease about the whole situation might be well founded: could it really be a coincidence? Could it be so easy to bring a man down?

Feeling Giuli's eyes on him, he stroked his chin. 'If you know where he lives,' he began, thoughtfully, 'how many other people know?'

'A fair few, I suppose,' she said guardedly. 'I mean, he's known in the *quartiere*.'

'No one's knocking at his door,' said Sandro. 'You'd think – there'd be a newspaper guy or two.'

Giuli glanced around quickly. 'There are journalists hanging about, but – there's a lot of respect for him. If they started doorstepping him – well, people would intervene.'

Sandro's gaze wandered over the stallholders, the drunk. 'I see,' he said. So the press were only biding their time, staying away out of pragmatism not respect. He puffed out his cheeks. 'I'm sure they'll turn up, eventually,' he said.

And they would: sooner or later there'd be a camera crew on the doorstep and all hell would break loose. He scanned the foot of the palazzo on the far side of the square, Rosselli's building, the one next to it, further along to where the carabiniere post stood. There was a little gaggle now, three men looking down at something between them, notes passed from one hand to another. Was it them? Had there been enemies at that meeting last night? Despite himself, Sandro was beginning to understand Giuli's paranoia, and Luisa's too. Politics was a dangerous game.

And it was time to talk to that lawyer.

Sandro turned his back on the piazza. 'Let's go,' he said.

*

The shop was busy all morning, and Luisa didn't get to eat until after two. *Orario continuato*, non-stop shopping, the curse of the modern age. The old two hours for lunch gone for ever, thanks to the hypermarkets. It wasn't civilized.

Sandro phoned at one, full of something, wanting to talk but she couldn't because a tour guide had just ushered inside three well-dressed German women in search of wedding suits, and Luisa, apparently, was the only saleswoman who would do. They had been told about her.

An hour later Luisa wondered if she wasn't getting too old for this as she showed an exquisite Japanese girl – a quarter of her age, half of her size and resembling a cartoon with her pink hair and long black socks – handbags costing the average month's salary. Her stomach complained: the Japanese girl gave her a politely blank look as its grumbling became audible, and Luisa looked down at the handbags.

Black French calf with silver studs, leather soft as cashmere, made in Italy; a velvet one, *testa di moro*, with distressed leather handles and brass fastenings. The girl indicated, in a kind of semaphore Luisa had long learned to understand but which did not contain one discernible word of Italian, that she would like them both. It was only when Luisa had wrapped and tied and processed the credit-card transaction – finding herself gazing into the girl's smooth, wide, placid face and wondering how it could seem so calm when its owner was spending so much, wondering at the life so distant from her own – that she was free to escape. The newspaper tucked under her arm, Luisa hurried down to the *magazzino* to remove her carefully wrapped sandwich from the fridge, pull out a stepstool and sit down among the boxes and plastic-filmed party dresses.

As she ate Luisa could see herself in the same mirror she'd stood in front of half-dressed that morning. She averted her eyes, and thinking of Sandro's call she got out her mobile and contemplated it. There was never much of a signal down here, she thought, knowing that she was postponing something. The newspaper sat on her knees, a copy of *La Repubblica* she had bought for herself to find out their take on Niccolò Rosselli's collapse. The sandwich had already left an oily mark on it.

There was a clomping on the stairs and Giusy peered around the corner.

'All right?' she said, hurrying on down. 'Gone quiet up there now, and Beppe said he could manage. I'm starved.'

Luisa put the mobile back in her pocket.

There was a bell that went if anyone came into the shop upstairs, and a CCTV monitor, but they couldn't both stay down here long. Luisa sighed. So much for the lunchbreak. Her head in the fridge, Giusy kept talking, self-absorbed as ever. In spite of it, Luisa was fond of the girl – or no longer a girl, though Luisa had known her since she was nineteen. Close to fifty now and looking it, liplined and deeply tanned after a lifetime's summers staked out on one beach or another. She'd been to the Maldives this year; she and her husband had no children, and enjoyed their leisure. Good for them, was the conclusion Luisa had eventually come to. Live and let live, though Sandro would laugh if he heard that.

Pulling up another stepstool, Giusy opened her tub of salad. 'No carbohydrates,' she'd announced proudly to a customer that very morning, on being congratulated on her figure. And the cigarettes, thought Luisa. To her eye Giusy could do with a bit more weight on her: after a liftetime of frowning over her own tight waistbands, when she'd lost close to fifteen kilos herself on the chemo, Luisa had lost the taste for skinny. Giusy was poking around in the tub with dissatisfaction. Luisa put her crusts in the bin and unfolded the paper.

La Repubblica had it on page five, hardly front-page news for them. Luisa frowned at the picture of a fuzzy Via Sant'Agostino under street lighting, and the same mugshot, only smaller. Dimly the thought of what else she had to worry about chimed and faded as she concentrated on the story about Rosselli. The hospital was running tests: what did that mean? If she had an only son, and they were running tests on him. . . even the thought of it made her stomach contract as it never had when she'd been the one being tested. What if it were Sandro? Luisa straightened abruptly, startled at the thought, one which had never really occurred to her before, that he might predecease her. Giusy raised her head from her salad bowl at the movement.

Looking from Luisa's preoccupied expression to the page open on her lap, Giusy's face cleared. 'Oh, right,' she said, and from her tone Luisa knew what was coming next. 'Communists, aren't they?' With disinterested contempt. 'A rabble, that's what Antonio says. No backbone. Catch the *cavaliere* keeling over in front of an audience.'

At the reference to their great leader Silvio Berlusconi, Luisa opened her mouth, then shut it. Berlusconi might not have passed out in front of his public, but he'd humiliated them in the eyes of the world, that was her view. She hadn't voted, and had incurred a penalty as a result: she had a nasty suspicion that Sandro, in a weak moment, might have voted for the man, though she'd never asked him outright. He was occasionally to be heard saying, 'Well, he gets things done,' in a gloomy sort of way.

In her pocket Luisa's phone chirruped, to indicate a text message: surreptitiously she looked down. *Looking into Frazione Verde*, it read. *Lawyer with Giuli. Missed call from Pietro.* What did that mean? She looked back at Giusy with resignation.

That Giusy was a *Berlusconiana* did not surprise Luisa: the girl was as empty-headed as candyfloss on a stick. And plenty of people had voted for him, no doubt a few decent ones among them, or he wouldn't be in power, would he?

'I know his mother,' said Luisa, and Giusy had the grace to look uneasy.

'Right,' she said, busying herself in the near-empty plastic tub, eyes averted. Then raised her head again. 'Actually,' she said in a different voice, 'I think I went to school with him. The Scuola Agnesi, behind Santo Spirito. Before we moved out.'

So the burning-eyed left-winger had been in a *scuola elementare* – and a notorious hotbed of firebrand teachers – with Giusy. That was a turn-up. By the time Giusy started work in the shop, her family had lived in a comfortable modern apartment in Scandicci, and she was engaged to be married. Luisa had never known she grew up in the grimy old streets of the Oltrarno – and forty years ago, they really had been grimy. Looking at her now, with her eight-hundred-euro jacket and her long pink nails, it was hard to imagine.

'What was he like?' Luisa said mildly. Giusy sat back in her chair and her face took on the expression – so unusual for her that for a moment Luisa couldn't work out what the problem was – of effortful thought. 'Grubby,' she said eventually. 'Untidy, always a rip in his coat, trousers too big. Nobody liked him.'

'Huh,' said Luisa, remembering the bonneted baby and wondering how it had escaped that attentive dictator of a mother so far as to become a scruffy child. But then again, she was surprised at the mother sending him to that school; she'd have thought the woman would have scrimped to send him to the nuns in Piazza San Felice, where the children wore little pinafores.

'Nobody liked him,' Giusy repeated.

Well, Luisa could see that fastidious Giusy wouldn't have: she was still frowning, though. 'Not just me. Not just – really nobody. He was odd. He didn't care what people thought of him. And he was – that kind of clever, you know. The kind that keeps people out.'

It was character analysis of a kind Luisa had never heard from Giusy before, and she stared. Giusy put out her hand for the newspaper, and as Luisa conceded it the electronic squeal of the door upstairs sounded. Giusy paid no attention, staring instead at the page.

'I thought he'd had a kid,' she said slowly. 'Where did I hear that?'

'So someone didn't mind the holes in his clothes,' said Luisa drily, getting to her feet. Sometimes, working in a place like this with someone like Giusy, she wondered about whether a lifetime of looking after her appearance – not to mention her customers' – might have been a little misguided. Even if such a suggestion might shake some sectors of society to their foundations.

'Yeah,' said Giusy absently, tapping the page with a long pink nail. 'Someone. Who did he marry, then?'

From upstairs Beppe was calling: still Giusy gazed down at the page.

'I'll go then, shall I?' said Luisa, turning away without waiting for an answer.

On the stairs she could hear a voice she recognized talking to Beppe, although in an unfamiliar register. Higher than usual, with an anxious politeness in it.

'Yes,' the woman was saying distractedly. 'And how is your sister, Giuseppe?' No one called Beppe 'Giuseppe', at least not for twenty years they hadn't.

'Gloria?' said Luisa, with disbelief, stepping on to the shopfloor.

Pietro's wife, round, red-headed Gloria Cavallaro, who never shopped for clothes anywhere but the old-fashioned place on the road where they lived, with its window display of lace nighties and sensible sweaters. What could she be doing here? Gloria turned helplessly towards her.

Luisa held out her hands without thinking; there was something more in Gloria's expression than unease at how out of place she was in the dress she obviously wore for cleaning the house, here on the dove-grey carpet and amongst the expensive black cocktail wear.

'What is it, Gloria?' She was ten years younger than Luisa but her pretty, usually animated face looked worn and pale, freckles standing out against the white skin. She was clasping her hands together and turning them over distractedly.

Tactful as ever, Beppe stepped back from them, nodding towards menswear upstairs, and with a flick of her head, Luisa said, 'Yes, go.'

'Has something happened, Gloria?' Pulling her hand gently, folding the other woman close to her on instinct. She thought of Sandro's impenetrable message, and of more things that might go wrong. 'Pietro?' she said, faltering. She had spent enough years fending off anxiety during Sandro's time in the force to know how that felt.

Gloria looked up: she smelled of violets, this close, her face only centimetres from Luisa's. 'Not Pietro,' she said. 'It's Chiara.'

Chapter Five

T HE LAWYER'S OFFICE, LIKE the lawyer himself, was unexpected. In the untidy room, heaped with papers, the bookshelves overflowing into teetering stacks on the floor and chairs, Giuli watched Sandro for his reaction.

The man himself – Carlo Bastone, the prop and right-hand man – suited the room. Short, stocky, rumpled, a substantial belly pushing at the buttons of a knitted waistcoat over which a badly knotted tie sat skewiff. He held out his hand hesitantly to Sandro as he came around from behind a desk mostly hidden under the same landslide of paper that looked as if it had only recently come to rest in the room.

Looking from one face to the other, Giuli saw both men take each other in and relax, in Sandro's case only fractionally.

Carlo Bastone looked uncertain, as well he might. Giuli had been garbled in her explanation, on the phone, of why they needed to talk to him. 'Niccolò's fine,' he'd repeated over and over again. 'Why do you need to see me? There's nothing to worry about.' She'd said something about wanting to help, about strategy for the press, and he'd gone quiet. It was only when she'd told him she was Enzo's girlfriend that he'd agreed.

They loved Enzo, the Frazione. Perhaps for the same reasons Giuli loved him.

Because he was good. Because he thought only of others: of his mother's catalogue of minor complaints, his father's emphysema, of Giuli's night terrors. When she'd sit up straight in bed, gasping for air, trying to remember the thing she'd forgotten, or left behind to die.

And when Rosselli had gone down like a ninepin on the stage it was Enzo who, having established that Giuli was all right and safely at the edge of the room, had worked his way doggedly through the crowd until he reached the man lying motionless on the wooden platform. It had been Enzo, earnest under the daft haircut that Giuli had learned to love, who'd laid him on his side in the recovery position, and had cleared a space around him and loosened his shirt. Checked his breathing until, after what seemed like hours, Niccolò Rosselli had begun to move.

It had been Enzo, fretting all night afterwards, who had impelled Giuli all the way here, nagging Sandro along too, calling and begging the lawyer to see them.

'A strategy for the press?' On the telephone Bastone had seemed surprisingly unworldly, for a man who'd gone all the way through law school and written learned papers on all sorts of things. He didn't even have a secretary to field his calls. But the words did seem to be getting through. 'Do you think we need that?'

Now he turned from Sandro to Giuli, his expression brighter. 'Miss Sarto,' he said, and an eager note entered his voice. 'I did wonder – what you said about the press. As you know, we don't have a press office—' And at this he looked around himself at the shambles of his office as though wondering how it had all got there. 'Perhaps you – perhaps we do need one.'

'I'd say,' Sandro broke in, 'I'd say that right now you do. You – I mean your Frazione – you need someone to tell people what's going on.'

Giuli saw Bastone's face cloud. 'Well,' he began hesitantly.

'Or don't you know yourself?' said Sandro, and it was quite apparent by the despondency with which Bastone sat down abruptly, in a small puff of dust, that Sandro had hit the nail on the head.

They stood, waiting, until eventually Bastone looked back up and said, 'Oh. Yes. Do sit down.'

They extracted two rickety chairs from the mess and sat with him around a table overflowing with paper. Giuli sat on the edge of hers. 'Is he really all right?' she said. Sandro sat back a little, arms folded, watching Bastone. In a silver frame on the shelf behind the lawyer was the portrait of a sweetly smiling elderly woman: his mother, presumably.

Bastone stood up again, and went to the long, dusty window. He stood there a moment in the soft late-summer light, looking down into the street.

'They told us it's something like nervous exhaustion,' he said, the pouchy, olive-skinned face he turned to them sagging with worry. 'The tests were all inconclusive. He's just been overdoing it.'

He ran his hands through hair that lay in oily waves high off his forehead. These idealists, thought Giuli with reluctant disapproval. Grubby, disorganized, chaotic. Does it have to be this way? Enzo was the neatest man she'd ever met, so she knew it didn't.

'Overdoing it,' Sandro repeated. 'Is that what you think? You know him. You're – what? His campaign manager?'

Bastone puffed out his cheeks, ran his hands through his hair again. 'Yes, I suppose I am, something like that.'

'How long have you known each other?' Sandro asked, and Giuli leaned forward over her knees at the sound of the careful softness in his voice. She wanted to know how to do that.

The lawyer brightened visibly in response. 'Oh, a long time,' he said, and as he smiled, his whole face changed. 'Since high school, as a matter of fact. We attended the Liceo Machiavelli together. And then we were both at the university, although Niccolò stayed on after I graduated, to get his PhD.'

'The Machiavelli,' mused Sandro, and Giuli knew what he was thinking. It had to be the Machiavelli.

The high school was no more than a hundred metres from where they were sitting. One of Giuli's favourite buildings in the city, a nice palace on the river, a sunny spot, and the school to go to if you were into protest, that was for sure. Its frontage always decorated with graffiti, sheets hung up with painted slogans announcing one student sit-in or other, and a bunch of eager kids running up and down asking passersby for money. They made her laugh. . . just their youth made her laugh. When Giuli had been seventeen she had been on the streets, but there was something about these nicely dressed, well-nourished teenagers who thought they were fighting for change that she loved. Because they might just be glued to Facebook now or eating ice cream or shopping, but they really were fighting for change – even if they weren't always sure what they wanted things to change to.

'Someone has to,' was what Enzo had said when he'd first talked to her about the Frazione and she'd looked sceptical. 'You know? Someone has to stand up and get change started. You can't rely on other people to do it.'

'So,' Sandro was saying. 'You're close.'

Bastone's head seesawed in reluctant agreement. 'Yes,' he said. 'As close as – well, as close as it's possible to be to Niccolò.' He moved away from the window and sat back down at the table, in shadow, his head between his hands. 'I'm beginning to wonder, though. If it's a matter of politics – yes. I know everything about him – where his beliefs came from, what his ideas are on local urban development or fuel emissions or foreign policy or the preservation of the city's parks or museum entry or prostitution. . .' He sighed. 'But the rest?'

'So in other words, you *don't* know what's going on,' said Sandro.

'I know he's been working hard – politically, yes. For the last six months, yes, I suppose there's been more pressure on him, since things took off. A huge amount, battles to fight already, going to city hall with petitions, lobbying the military to delay the permissions on the new road: he likes to get down to the detail. To be hands on. We weren't exactly prepared. He's always thrived on it, it didn't occur to me to think he was overdoing things. But—' And he stopped speaking again.

In the silence, from below them somewhere in the building, came the bang of a heavy door and the sudden cacophonous echo of raised voices.

'In his private life, though?' And Sandro leaned forward on the table that lay between them.

Uneasily Bastone looked towards the solid panelled door, and for the first time Giuli saw that there were things he wasn't telling them: as Sandro glanced towards her, she could see that he knew, too.

'I can't—' said the lawyer. 'I can't—' And then the door was opened abruptly. A woman stood there in an unbuttoned coat, seventy-five if she was a day but tall, upright, almost masculine in appearance, her white hair pulled back from a strong, raw-boned face and deepset eyes. Bastone started to his feet, his oily hair flopping untidily with the sudden movement. 'Maria,' he said, sounding panicky.

'Carlo,' said the woman, and Giuli heard impatience and contempt in the way she addressed him. This was a woman used to being cleverer than those around her, even lawyers. She was staring at Sandro and Giuli with undisguised hostility.

Carlo Bastone was looking from the new arrival to his seated guests as if he had no idea how to proceed. Sandro stood up. 'Sandro Cellini,' he said stiffly, with a tiny bow.

And the woman folded her arms across her strong, spare body as if to reject absolutely the possibility that she might shake Sandro's hand, should he prove rash enough to offer it. Watching the two of them size each other up, Giuli saw the tiniest glint of watchfulness come into the old woman's eye. She knows, she thought: she knows Sandro's not stupid.

'I'm sorry,' stammered Bastone in a panic. 'This is – this is – Niccolò's—'

'Maria Rosselli,' said Sandro. 'Yes. I know.' And again he bowed. 'I believe you know my wife.'

*

The shop, mercifully, remained quiet for the entire forty-five minutes Gloria stayed. A nice-looking pair of men in young middle age – a gay couple, Luisa thought with a professional reflex, from the Southern states of America – came in at one point, looking around them with smiling anticipation, but Beppe was there to usher them away before she could even open her mouth.

The younger man glanced back from the stairs as they went up with Beppe, a slightly puzzled look on his face at the scene on the shopfloor: Gloria, plump and pale and tearstained on the velvet stool, twisting a scrap of paper tissue between her hands, and Luisa back at her side protectively. She smiled at the man to reassure him, and the little group moved on upstairs. She heard the soft murmur of their voices start up and kneeled down again beside her friend.

'I'm sorry,' said Gloria, biting her lip. 'You've got enough on your plate, Luisa. Check-up must be due around now, I know.'

Luisa frowned. 'You know?'

Gloria shrugged. 'We can count, you know,' she said, bowing her head over the scrap of Kleenex. 'Pietro remembered, actually.'

Three years ago, on a rainy weekend in November, Luisa and Sandro had waited for her appointment while he distracted himself with a girl gone missing. It was not exactly that Luisa did not worry about the cancer returning – certainly somewhere buried away in her brain it had registered as a possibility. She did not know how, but she had managed a trick of faith: faith in the doctors and the statistics that were on her side. They told her she was old enough for her body to have slowed down, young enough to tolerate the treatment, the cancer was sluggish and it had not migrated to any other part of her. Faith even in doctors was irrational, she had decided, but one could choose to be irrational in one's favour; to be irrational in expecting the worst went against reason.

She had never explained this to anyone.

'They're only going to talk to me about the reconstruction,' she said easily.

Although it was not true: of course there would be the usual body scan and blood tests too. Over the tissue held to her small, reddened nose, Gloria's eyes widened, and Luisa saw her try not to look.

'Chiara, then,' she said gently. 'You're not saying it was totally out of the blue?'

Gloria shifted on the velvet stool and Luisa saw with unease that she'd lost weight recently. When had they last seen the Cavallaros? 'Well,' said Gloria, 'I don't know. She's been different for a month or so. She didn't want to come away with us to Elba last month.' The curly, faded red head bobbed down again. 'She's never done that before, never, she's got so many friends there, you know? The whole gang of them, every year since they were born practically, going to the beach together, out for pizza. '

She was almost crying again. 'But, Gloria,' Luisa tried lamely, 'it does happen eventually, you know. Children leave, in the end.' She felt uneasy, because it was something she'd consoled herself with, childless as she was; she might have had a child but by now the child would be long gone. She didn't really want to trot it out for poor Gloria, as if they were both in the same boat.

But the expression on the face Gloria raised to hers was not what she'd expected. The tears were drying, the mouth set. 'But moving in with a – with a boyfriend? At her age? She's nineteen. She's my baby. I don't even know him.'

Luisa noticed her determination. 'Yes,' she said slowly, 'I know. I suppose – I suppose I'd be worried too. But you'll meet him?'

'I don't even know that,' said Gloria, her mouth trembling. 'She said she'd come and get some things this evening. She didn't say he'd be coming with her.'

In the silence that followed Luisa could hear the hushed, happy voices of the men upstairs, exclaiming in their soft foreign accents over something nice Beppe had shown them. Was that why she stuck this job, enjoyed it even? The little pulse of pleasure observed, the satisfied customer, the sly smile when a woman or man was pleased with the way they looked? It didn't seem much, sometimes. That with such things a life was kept stable, until you found a lump in your breast, or your only child upped and left.

'You asked?'

Gloria sighed. 'She got – angry. Said she wouldn't bring him for inspection.'

Luisa could imagine Pietro, pacing the room with this – boyfriend in front of him, interrogating him, reading him the riot act. She wondered what the law said. If Chiara was nineteen – well, she was an adult. Although when Luisa had been a girl, she could have got married, had kids at nineteen, that had been how things were done then. In fact they'd lived with her parents for close to a year after they'd got married – that had been how things were done then, too. And like Gloria, she thought of Chiara as no more than a baby still, unformed.

She tried another tack. 'What do her friends say?'

'They came around in Elba, asking for her. They didn't know anything about this – this boyfriend. Well, I didn't either, not then. But they had just assumed she'd be there, like every year.' Gloria got to her feet, distractedly. 'I should go. You're – you're—'

'I'm not busy, Gloria,' said Luisa gently. 'Sit down.' But Gloria stayed standing.

'You've talked to Pietro?'

Gloria looked down at her hands. 'I tried his number, left a message.' She fumbled in her pocket in a sudden panic and got out a battered little phone. Gloria had never been one for gadgets. 'No signal in here. He might have—'

'Calm down,' said Luisa. 'Half an hour won't make any difference.' She took Gloria's hands in hers. 'Look,' she said. 'Go home, make the dinner, breathe deeply. When Chiara comes to pick up her things, be normal. Don't panic, don't get hysterical, give her a chance to prove to you, calmly, that she knows what she's doing. She might see sense, you never know. If you give her the chance.'

Chiara had always been a sensible girl, that was the thing.

Gloria gazed at her as if hypnotized. 'And Pietro?'

Luisa puffed out her cheeks. 'I don't know,' she said. 'Try and get him to see it the same way. Failing that, tranquillizer dart? Or just keep him out of the way.' Was this the right advice? In the pit of her stomach Luisa felt unease stir. But what else could they do?

'I'll talk to Sandro,' she said. Clinging to straws. 'OK?'

Hesitant, Gloria clutched her bag. They stood, facing each other: it didn't feel as though anything had been resolved. Just move forward, one step ahead: it was Luisa's only strategy.

They crossed the shopfloor. 'Will you do it?' said Gloria, her hand on the door.

'Do what?'

Pale-faced, Gloria nodded down at the careful folds of Luisa's silk blouse. 'The breast,' she said. 'Do you want it back?'

And Luisa opened her mouth, fully intending to say, robustly, 'No, no, I'm fine as I am, all fine,' but the way Gloria had phrased it meant she found she couldn't say anything at all.

Chapter Six

ON THE CROWDED TERRACE of the restaurant Sandro prodded despondently at his salad.

Luisa had her mind on something else, too. 'Why did you order it then?' she said with distracted impatience. 'You hate salad.'

Sandro forked it into his mouth. *Insalata Fantasia* was what they'd called it: it had lumps of rubbery cheese and maize kernels in it, and he chewed with stolid disgust. He had wanted *pici* with hare sauce and some beans in oil followed by a slice of cake, but had decided that he needed to look after his health. He put the fork down, pushed the big gaudy bowl away and stared into the soft warm dark of the Piazza del Carmine.

This square, the breadth of it, still as untidy and car-choked as it had been when he'd been a boy, the grand *palazzi* along one side with their ornate balconies, faded and crumbling, the big church with its jewel of a chapel: he loved it, if pushed to admit it. But the restaurant was a mistake. It had been a favourite once upon a time, an old-fashioned place with excellent food, but it had embarked on a half-baked programme of modernization that involved uncomfortable aluminium seating and neon and loud music. The menu was now too long, the quality of the food too patchy.

This was the problem with eating in restaurants, he thought gloomily as he forked a piece of cheese into his mouth – worrying about the cost. Their few weeks in Castiglioncello, it seemed to Sandro now, had only lulled them into a false sense of carefree security, persuaded them that they were the kind of couple who could do things spontaneously. Or perhaps it was just the day he'd had.

It had been Luisa's idea: she'd called that afternoon and said perhaps they could go out to eat. He'd had the impression then that she had an agenda: his head full of Niccolò Rosselli and what his mother had said in that strange, dark untidy lawyer's office, he'd thought, why not?

A distraction. The whole situation was a mess, all right: he didn't hold out a whole lot of hope for the Frazione Verde, not since this afternoon and Maria Rosselli's revelation.

Had he known what she was going to say? An inkling, just like Giuli said she'd had when Niccolò Rosselli had stopped talking and swayed on the stage. From the moment the door opened there'd been an unusual dynamic between the two people, the lawyer and the fierce old woman, that had made Sandro stop and observe and wonder. Giuli had looked at them, bewildered by the strange, crackling energy Maria Rosselli brought into the room with her. Of course, thought Sandro to begin with, the old woman's known this lawyer since he was a kid, coming round to play with her son, of course there's a lack of respect, of course she still sees him as the overweight, bumbling child struggling to keep up with her odd, sharp, determined Niccolò.

He didn't even know where these thoughts came from. He could be quite wrong about all sorts of things, and Carlo Bastone might have been a skinny child. But there was something else, too, something else consuming the woman; he could see that right from the beginning, and it infected their host. Carlo Bastone had looked from his new visitor to Sandro in a pleading panic.

'You know each other?' he'd said as Sandro had got formally to his feet and, despite – or perhaps because of – Maria Rosselli's hostility, had deliberately held out his hand.

'My wife,' he had repeated to her. 'You know my wife.'

'Luisa Venturelli.' The old woman's hard-set mouth had moved, using his wife's maiden name quite deliberately, but did not soften in a smile. 'Yes. Of course.' Then she had turned to Bastone and had spoken as though Sandro was an irrelevance.

And now Luisa sat, staring into the darkness away from him, and whatever she might have wanted to say remained unsaid. Sandro wished he could put Niccolò Rosselli's mother in a room with Luisa and see which of them came off worst: like getting blood from a stone, getting anything out of either of them.

He looked at his wife's stubborn profile, still beautiful to him, as she stared away. She knew he was looking, he could tell from the set of her jaw.

'Carlo Bastone,' she said without turning. 'Yes. Old family: old money. Plenty of fancy *palazzi* but no cash. I knew that mother too.' Sandro shook his head.

'It's nobody's business but his,' was what Maria Rosselli had snapped at the lawyer as though they were alone in the room, but Sandro and Giuli had both at once moved forwards in their chairs, listening. The lawyer had immediately begun to fiddle anxiously with something, head down. Signora Rosselli leaned both big-knuckled hands on the table in front of him. 'Why would it be? It's nothing to do with his work.' Bastone had darted a nervous look at Sandro, and the old woman had turned on the visitors.

'What *are* you still doing here?' she'd said.

'I – they – we—' Bastone had seemed quite helpless.

'We had an appointment.' Sandro had stared: Giuli had spoken with quiet courtesy. She had got to her feet and stood facing the terrifying old woman. 'I am Giulietta Sarto,' she'd said, her hands at her sides. 'My fiancé Enzo works for the Frazione. We came to see if there was anything we could do to help.'

'Giuli was great today,' said Sandro, without thinking, and at last something in Luisa unbent and she turned towards him.

'Yes?'

And he told her. As she sat and listened, nodding, she was still looking faraway, that same look he'd seen on Liliana's face, and the old nun's. Trying to fit the story into a bigger scheme: perhaps it was what women did.

'It was Giuli's thing, of course, her case. If it is a case. But she took the responsibility. She faced down Niccolò Rosselli's mother.'

'Well,' said Luisa, 'that takes some doing, too.'

Sandro nodded. 'You're telling me. And in that lawyer's office? We could have gone on for days, trying to find out anything. She's a tough nut, that old woman.'

'Are you getting paid for this?' Luisa said abruptly, leaning forward across the restaurant table. 'This Rosselli investigation, whatever it turns out to be?'

Sandro grimaced. 'Well, that's the weirdest part of it,' he said slowly. 'You know what? We might even get paid.'

That had been strange: the old woman abruptly deciding to trust them had been startling enough, and then the offer of money. He'd have said she'd be the last person to offer hard cash to a private detective.

Not that he'd had the impression that Maria Rosselli had given in: she'd looked at Giuli, at Sandro, at the lawyer, and had made a calculation. Sandro imagined that it was hard for her to admit that she needed help, but she was too clever not to.

'All right,' was what Maria Rosselli had said, addressing Sandro directly as she treated the lawyer's room as though it were her own, jaw still set hard as iron. 'All right. She's left him. That stupid girl has left him. *Beh!* Not even the excuse of being a girl. . . at her age, it's ridiculous. I tell him, it makes no difference, we can manage without her. She hardly knew what she was doing with the child anyway.'

Giuli and Sandro had been openly staring at her at this point. Sandro had found himself wondering how this woman had earned a living, brought up her only child on her own. He imagined there wasn't much that Maria Rosselli wouldn't be capable of, if she wanted it badly enough. Her certainty was frightening.

'You mean his – his wife?' Maria Rosselli had turned her deepset dark eyes on Giuli when she'd spoken, assessing her all over again. Giuli had raised her chin and bravely continued. 'Niccolò's – your son's wife has left him?'

'They were never married,' the mother-in-law had said with blunt contempt. 'She has no rights. I said that to him.'

Sandro had turned his head to ease the stiffness he'd felt building up as he'd tried to take in what Maria Rosselli was saying. 'The selfishness,' she'd said coldly. 'The neglect of duty, the weakness. It's unforgivable. You can see what it's done to him. He can't sleep, he doesn't eat. The child cries.'

The child cries. In the dim, dusty room the words had hung in the air, changing things.

Sandro felt a chill now as he felt Luisa's eyes on him: gave himself a little shake. In the wide Piazza del Carmine something was going on, over beyond the church. Banners bobbing up and down in the soft darkness, and a groundswell of voices.

'She left the child behind,' said Luisa slowly, and Sandro saw something in her face he didn't want to see. The conclusion he didn't want to draw, about the only thing that would keep a mother from her child.

Their waiter – a slightly stooped, elderly man with shiny patches on his ancient black trousers – was circulating between the tables on the crowded terrace; abruptly Luisa nodded to him, and he shuffled over in a parody of haste. Luisa brought that out in people.

'Coffee,' she said, in response to his ingratiating recital of desserts. 'And the bill.' The sound of the demonstrators in the square was getting louder; they were singing the '*Internazionale*', to Sandro's astonishment.

'How old is the child?' Luisa said when the waiter had gone.

'Young,' said Sandro, suddenly unwilling to think about Niccolò Rosselli's situation, and unwilling also to evoke the nearly newborn for Luisa, who for years – more than a decade after her own child died – had not been able to look at babies. But clearly in this case the presence of a newborn was the key: the unanswered question. 'A – a baby.' Luisa turned her hard stare on him. 'Six weeks,' he said obediently.

'Six weeks.' Her face was calm, immobile. 'That's a dangerous time.' He looked at her. 'Isn't it supposed to be? A difficult time for a woman, they can behave uncharacteristically. Become violent, all sorts of things. For those first weeks after a baby's born.'

Sandro hardly dared speak: after their daughter had been born, with a syndrome that had meant she lived a bare thirty-six hours, Luisa had descended into a state of bleak, impenetrable withdrawal from which he had feared she would never emerge. For some time he had thought that his vivid, energetic, sharp-tongued wife might sit with dull eyes at the kitchen table for the rest of their life together. He still marvelled at her recovery, one spring morning, when she'd got out of bed, put on lipstick and gone back in to work.

Calmly, she went on. 'Post-partum psychosis, isn't that what they call it? You should get Giuli to talk to the woman's midwife, the people at the Centre.'

'I don't know if she was treated at the Centre,' he mumbled. 'I'd have to find out.'

Luisa nodded, apparently still serene. Could it be that she no longer connected that phrase – post-partum – with herself? She spoke.

'Giusy – in the shop. She knew he had a baby, a wife. She was at school with Rosselli. Can you imagine that?'

'They were never married,' said Sandro. 'Rosselli's mother seemed to think that was significant.'

'More significant than the child? They'd been together how long?' He was surprised by her calmness, her tolerance; for some reason he had thought Luisa approved of the institution of marriage as much as Maria Rosselli seemed to. But then he was regularly prepared to believe that he could assume nothing at all about his wife of thirty-odd years.

She smiled at him. 'If you ask me, I don't think Maria Rosselli ever wanted them to get married. No one could be good enough for her Niccolò.'

'It sounds like they've been together more than twenty years,' said Sandro. 'That must have been tough.' Remembering the curl of Maria Rosselli's lip, as though twenty years might still count as an aberration. As though she'd spent all that time waiting for her son to extricate himself from an unsuitable relationship.

'Yes,' said Luisa.

The coffee was set down in front of her just as the untidy rabble of demonstrators came alongside the restaurant terrace, chanting cheerfully now. Most of the diners smiled back: it was all very amicable. Sandro tried to see what it said on the posters: LEAVE SCANDICCI ALONE. NO TO MORE ROADS. Hardly contentious stuff. The banners had the crude insignia of the Frazione Verde pasted to their corners, a green lightning bolt across a representation of the Duomo's cupola. He smiled to himself: the protesters all looked so young, so disorganized, they could hardly even chant in time. Had they just assembled themselves, in the absence of Niccolò Rosselli, their figurehead? How long ago had this little march been organized? He wanted to take one or two of them by the elbow and ask about the Frazione, what it meant to them. But it wasn't part of the case: the case, now, was finding Rosselli's wife, and never mind his political activity.

'She's obviously taking charge,' said Luisa. 'The mother. She's the one who's paying? For you to track the wife down.'

Sandro shifted anxiously. 'We need to talk about it,' he said. 'I don't even know – she hasn't even talked to her son about it yet. She seemed just to decide, on the spur of the moment.'

Out of spite: he'd seen the look Maria Rosselli gave Carlo Bastone as she made the announcement. 'Get her back,' she'd said, drawing herself up under the high, dark, coffered ceiling of the lawyer's office, looking down at them as though they were all pygmies. Focusing on Sandro. 'Find her and bring her back to face the music. I won't have her treat him like this. I'll pay.'

'That could be tricky.' Luisa spoke thoughtfully.

'She said, come round tomorrow morning,' Sandro said, his eye drawn back to the square as the demonstrators moved on. 'She said I could talk to him then.'

'Better make sure she's out of the way first.'

'Hmmm,' Sandro said, evading the issue. He couldn't imagine how one would go about telling Maria Rosselli what to do. 'I might need you for that,' he said vaguely.

'And what about the insurance claim?' Luisa said, eyeing him with exasperation. 'When are you going to fit that in, a bit of proper paid work?'

Sandro passed a hand over his forehead and found it moist: the evening was still warm. She was right, of course. 'I'll fit it in,' he said. He'd probably only need to clap eyes on the man to know if he was scamming them. You could tell trauma, real trauma. Talk to the neighbours. 'First thing maybe, get the lie of the land.'

Luisa made a sceptical sound, and he looked out into the darkness, avoiding her eye. An army vehicle was following the demonstrators slowly around the wide piazza, between the parked cars. A tiny thing, the soldiers inside it seemed to fill it right up, heads knocking on the roof, the driver hunched awkwardly over the wheel, like something out of the Keystone Cops. Not in their brief surely, though Sandro vaguely remembered something Bastone had said about Rosselli lobbying them over road permissions: he must have got their goat. Watching it all come to a halt, the procession and the vehicle in its wake, Sandro wondered: if the military had turned up here, who else could be keeping tabs on the Frazione Verde. . . the carabinieri? . . . the Polizia di Stato?

A movement along the terrace alerted him, he couldn't have said why. A big man was sitting there smoking: he'd raised his hand for the waiter. On the little table in front of him, next to an untouched glass of grappa, lay an open notebook. A journalist? Did reporters still use pen and paper? The waiter was leaning down to him now, they were exchanging a joke, the tall man gesturing with his cigarette at the crowd. Sandro wondered if this man had written the article on Rosselli's collapse that he'd read this morning, had been responsible for the amused, sly tone of the piece. The man seemed to detect the interest from their direction, and Sandro looked back at the soldiers.

When he had been a police officer they'd kept files on certain extremists, mostly right-wingers but once a communist who had a record for arson. It could only be justified if there were evidence of any criminal activity, in theory. As for AISI – Agenzia Informazioni e Sicurezza Interna, the secret service – well, they were a law unto themselves. Would they bother with a little bunch of Oltrarno hippy agitators? You never knew. If they thought those same hippies were in danger of actually getting something done, they might.

The door of the army vehicle opened and its occupants emerged untidily, crumpled by their confinement, adjusting their caps. . . three, four. One of them lit up a cigarette, holding it discreetly under his palm as he leaned against the car. Sandro couldn't remember if that was allowed these days. He got to his feet, stretched.

'Where are you going?' asked Luisa, sitting back in her seat.

'Nowhere,' he said. 'Just *due passi*, a little wander. I want to see what this is about. Hang on.' He stepped down off the terrace.

There was an air of lazy ease about the small group of soldiers as he approached them: the procession seemed to have diffused into something harmlessly amateurish and had in fact stopped proceeding anywhere. Sandro felt a stab of pity for Giuli and all her passion. Roads had to be built, didn't they? He assumed that the tallest soldier, turning at his approach, would be the senior officer, and so it turned out: he recognized the badge of a colonel. The man looked at him with that air of stern seriousness he knew well, cultivated in the army, city hall, even the police, to disguise the fact that one's time was largely spent doing not very much at all.

'Good evening,' said Sandro easily, with a little nod in deference to the man's uniform and token authority. He had, in fact, almost no respect for the army, but they could be decent company. 'Sandro Cellini,' he said. The officer barely inclined his head, and didn't bother to supply his own name: why would he?

What the hell? thought Sandro. 'I'm an investigator,' he said, and the colonel frowned. 'Looking into the Frazione.'

'Really?' said the man, and Sandro was taken aback by his eagerness, a sudden lively amusement in his eyes. 'Well, that's interesting. We're looking into them ourselves.' He smiled lazily. 'Daft bunch, really, but it's part of the job.' This with a sidelong defensive look. 'And there's some – well – some funny types in the Frazione, I can tell you.' The colonel put his hands in his pockets. 'If we can be of any help,' he said vaguely, turning back to look at the demonstration, which had now dwindled into no more than an affable crowd, their placards placed on the pavements while they chatted amongst themselves.

'Well,' said Sandro. Perhaps the offer had been no more than a courtesy, but that was no reason to let it lie. 'That's very kind of you.'

'Of course,' said the man, without turning back, eyeing the heads in the crowd again. 'Honoured to be of help.' Irony in his languid voice that Sandro couldn't help but find appealing. 'You know where we are? Behind the Botanic Gardens.'

Feeling himself dismissed, Sandro turned away, thinking. From the restaurant's terrace Luisa was looking at him with mingled impatience and anxiety. What's up now, he thought, what have I done now? Raising a hand in apology, he hurried back.

Picturing himself turning up at the barracks, his heart sank. What would they really tell him? Nothing. But the colonel – why hadn't he even asked the man's name? Since when had he been so timid in the presence of a uniform? – had offered possibilities. Sometimes these officials were bored enough to let stuff slip.

He sat back down beside Luisa, and again he wondered, if the army were monitoring the Frazione out here in the open, who else might be involved?

He could ask Pietro.

'I'll have to ask Pietro,' he said, hardly aware that he was speaking out loud.

'Pietro?' said Luisa, setting down her coffee cup with sudden agitation. He looked at her expectantly.

'What?'

'I think you'll find Pietro's got other things on his mind,' she said.

'Oh, yes?' said Sandro warily. So there *was* something going on. Some secret police operation and Pietro couldn't talk about it. God knew, it could even be surveillance of this bunch, the Frazione. It all made sense to him now. There'd been silences: he'd always known the time would come, and the wedge would be driven between them. He couldn't expect—

'Gloria came to see me today.' And Luisa sighed.

*

In the small bright white kitchen, Enzo was cooking. It was late, but it had taken both of them a while to realize that this was their life now. They could eat when they wanted. Fresh from her shower, Giuli leaned out over the waist-high balcony and looked into the trees around their apartment building. They'd moved in three months ago, at the beginning of the summer, and Giuli still couldn't quite believe it.

From behind her the hissing of the frying chicken, the smells – lemon and thyme, Enzo had told her patiently, Giuli knowing nothing about what smelled of what in the kitchen – Enzo's slow, considered movements around the compact space, the steamy warmth, all represented a kind of comfort Giuli could never quite bring herself to believe was hers. It was why she was looking out of the window; she could hardly contemplate the new life that had arrived for her, out of the blue, for fear it would disappear. But leaning out into the feathery canopy of acacias, she could smile and smile and smile into the evening air at her good fortune, and no one would see.

'Oh,' Enzo announced to her. 'He called. Sandro called. While you were in the shower.'

Giuli turned back into the room, frowning. In his white apron, his idiot's fringe pushed up and out of the way, as he smiled at her Enzo looked – perfect. His looks had never worried her: he was an oddball, for sure, round-faced, earnest, wore clothes his mother had bought him ten years ago just like he still let her cut his hair.

(Let me do it, next time, Giuli had pleaded, and he'd just looked shy and mumbled something.) But over their year together, and particularly since they'd moved in together, he'd begun to look positively handsome to Giuli. She liked his ears, for example, neat and funny. She liked his eyebrows. She blushed. Enzo frowned.

'What?' he said.

'Nothing.' The small fold-out table was laid for the two of them, mats, glasses, napkins. 'Sandro,' she said. 'What did he say when he called?'

Carefully Enzo turned off the gas under the chicken, and stirred something in a big saucepan. 'He said had Flavia – Niccolò's, um, wife – did you know where she'd been seen during the pregnancy, and after? Her doctor, for example, the hospital. He said he'd call you back in the morning.' Enzo looked serious.

Giuli sighed, turning away to look back out into the trees again. She'd told Enzo the bare bones of it. It had shocked and upset him, she could tell. *How could it happen?* his anxious face had said to her.

'Flavia and Niccolò have been together for ever,' he'd actually said, faltering. 'And the Frazione – could it really destroy the whole thing? A – a misunderstanding. It must be a misunderstanding.' He'd gone round and round in circles, trying to make sense of it.

Behind her she could hear him dishing up the food. As it happened, Giuli did know where Rosselli's wife had received her ante-natal care, because she had been seen at the Women's Centre. About as far as you could imagine from the expensive private care most public figures' wives would expect: a public clinic whose remit was to treat anyone who walked in off the streets, which was where most of them did come from. Sexually transmitted diseases and unwanted pregnancies outnumbered happy families by about twenty to one.

'*A tavola*,' said Enzo, just an edge of anxiety to his cheerful voice: he could sense her holding back. *Hungry*, Giuli told herself, you're hungry. Forcing herself to smell the thyme and lemon again, to look around the kitchen, at the set of coffee cups hanging on their little stand, the kitchen towel on its roller, the brushes and folded cloths on the sink. But instead of the reassurance she usually got from checking off these things, Giuli felt a little pulse of panic. Is this me? she thought. Do I belong here? She sat down.

'Wow,' she said, after the first forkful. It was good. She made herself taste it properly, she pushed the panic away. 'You're a genius, Enzo. How d'you do that?'

Giuli saw him relax, just fractionally, but she stayed tense. She wanted to ask him about Flavia and Niccolò Rosselli, together for ever. Had he seen any cracks? Together since they were at school, surely there must have been stress points? But she couldn't ask him, not now he'd wound down.

'So he thinks it's something to do with the baby,' said Enzo, frowning down at his plate as he diligently dissected his *scaloppine*.

'Flavia was treated at the Women's Centre, as a matter of fact,' Giuli said as lightly as she could. 'I'll see if I can find out who did the post-natal care tomorrow, maybe. It could be she's stressed out, you know? It's so common, women often run home to their mothers when a baby's born. Rows about who bathes the baby, who gets up at night, all those hormones.'

Giuli heard the soothing note in her own voice, the *there's nothing to worry about* note that was particularly important when there was, in fact, something to worry about.

Head still bowed over his food, Enzo nodded. He wasn't stupid. 'She doesn't have a mother,' he said. 'Flavia doesn't.' He looked up, chewing methodically, his homely, thoughtful face completely absorbed in the problem. 'Nor a father either, long dead, cancer. Niccolò's all she's got.'

He knows a lot about them, Giuli registered. 'How did you first meet them?' she said, surprised that she hadn't asked before.

'Oh, I was twenty-five or so.' Enzo applied himself to another forkful, still worrying diligently at the problem. 'They led a sit-in. The first Gulf War, ninety-whatever. We got a group visit to the army barracks in Piazza San Marco when they opened it to the public and then refused to leave.'

The first Gulf War. Giuli had hardly been aware of it, as she'd been out of her head from the late-eighties on. Only realized the first war had happened when the second one came along. She felt an uncharacteristic flush of shame: Giuli was not given to regretting her past; it only led to relapses. But the truth was, sometimes you did have to wish things had been different. She might have met Enzo then. They might have had – time. Stop, she thought. You don't know. You can't change it.

So Flavia had no parents? Giuli should have known that, somehow. The woman used to come on her own to her Centre visits, scans and all. Not that that was anything unusual for the Centre, whereas in those private clinics or in the big modern hospitals there'd be four or five family members to most mothers-to-be, hovering over the technician, cadging extra scan photos. Giuli could just see her now, waiting patiently on the hard plastic chairs among the chaos and the other women and their badly behaved toddlers – the bad-tempered, resentful, unhappy, desperate women. Why hadn't Niccolò come? It seemed obvious; he wasn't a man for sentiment, she wouldn't have wanted to seem needy.

If it were me. If I were pregnant – the thought sprang, unwelcome, into Giuli's head because after the life she'd had, the age she'd reached, it just wasn't going to happen – *if I were pregnant I'd want Enzo there.* Enzo would be there come hell or high water. And he wasn't a man for sentiment, either. Having allowed that observation in, as it was relevant, as it seemed significant, Guili shoved the whole scenario out of her mind. *I'm not going to be pregnant.*

'Delicious,' she said, cutting up the food on her plate into smaller and smaller pieces. It might as well have been cardboard, now, as she put it in her mouth. Enzo put the salad on the table, looking at her from under a worried frown. Beside it he set the cruet with oil and vinegar and salt and pepper. Throughout her childhood Giuli had only ever seen such a thing through the window of a restaurant. The surfaces of her mother's *angolo cottura* in the two-room walk-up off the Via Senese had been strewn with things that did not belong in a kitchen, and almost nothing that did.

No mother to run to for Flavia, just like Giuli. So where would she go? And at the memory of that patient figure sitting alone in the corridor waiting for her appointment, Giuli felt something, a chill, a darkness, move more assertively into the bright little room with them. It was something that sat in corners just out of sight and waited for her to turn and look at it.

But Giuli didn't turn: she finished her chicken, she finished her salad. She cleaned her plate.

'How long has she been gone?' Enzo asked, setting his knife and fork side by side. They faced each other over the empty plates. 'Flavia? When did she – disappear?'

'The mother – Rosselli's mother – said three days ago. Sunday morning he got up when he heard the baby crying, at seven. . . seven-thirty and she was gone. No note. Nothing.'

'Nothing,' Enzo repeated, looking around the room as if to reassure himself of something, that everything was still in place. The place in the bed would have been empty when Niccolò Rosselli had woken up. He would have assumed his wife was in the bathroom, the kitchen. He would have walked around the apartment holding the crying baby. And then what?

Where would Flavia go, if there were no mother to take her in? But when Giuli opened her mouth that wasn't what she said.

'Flavia will turn up,' she said to Enzo, wanting it to be all right. And when he looked back at her at last, reaching for her cleaned plate, she knew that he knew, that they both knew, that it would not be all right at all.

*

In his sitting room as it grew dark and the only light came from the flickering television, showing the late news, Pietro Cavallaro leaned forwards on the sofa with the remote control clenched in his hand. He wasn't moving, nor was he really taking in what was happening on the screen. A demonstration in Naples gave way to scenes from a suburban development on the edge of Rome, a brothel where government ministers had been secretly filmed. His grip tightened on the remote.

In the kitchen Gloria was hovering, pacing anxiously from stove to sink to refrigerator, unable to think about what she was doing. Making coffee: the little machine on the stove began to bubble and the familiar, comforting smell filled the room. Mechanically she took down the cups, the sugar, the coffee spoons.

It wasn't that Chiara would be there every evening drinking coffee with them in front of the weather report anyway. More often than not there would only be two cups on the little tray; she'd be out having ice cream with her friends, maybe at a club or a bar at weekends, maybe – lately – a university gathering, a political meeting. The details volunteered had become hazier. Gloria set the tray down, glanced at Pietro then at the lamps, decided not to switch on the light. She didn't want to see the fear and anger and confusion on his face: it was enough to see as much of the set of his pale features as the light of the television allowed her.

Had it been down to work, to distraction? Had Pietro been too busy with whatever his latest investigation was, taking him out of the house two evenings a week, to talk to their daughter?

He'd got home from work halfway through Chiara's packing:

she'd been coming out of her bedroom with a holdall, in the middle of asking Gloria, too politely, if she could borrow it. There'd been a stand-off, Chiara falling silent mid-sentence, Pietro staring with mute, pointless rage from the bag in her hand to the bed behind her, piled with CDs and clothes and stuff from the dressing table they'd bought for her fifth birthday. Nobody told me, Gloria had wanted to cry, this is what you get when you only have one child. Half an hour's packing and your house is suddenly empty. And Luisa trying to take back what she'd said, *They have to leave sometime.*

But did it have to be like this?

'You won't tell us where you're going?' Pietro had said, as Chiara had turned back and silently begun to fill the bag from the heap on the bed.

'Babbo,' she had muttered, and Gloria had heard the anguish in her voice. 'Of course I'll tell you. Just – look, I need to get settled in, to be sure it's going to work. I don't want you turning up and shouting.' Crushing things heedlessly into the holdall, when she used to be such a careful child. Folding and wrapping and ordering, every time they went on holiday, socks rolled up in pairs, larger garments in tissue paper. Zipping it up and stepping around her father in the doorway, setting the bag next to her wheeled suitcase by the front door.

'You're not – you're staying in the city?' Pietro had muttered, humbling himself. 'You're not going far?'

'Dad,' she said again, impatient – but affectionate too, Gloria told herself, surely affectionate too? 'I'm enrolled at the university, remember? I'm not going far. I'll – I'll be in touch. I will.'

Had there been something evasive in the way she'd said that? They'd both heard it. And the way she'd slid out through the door, leaving them staring at it as it closed, Gloria trying not to cry, Pietro with both fists clenched in frustrated fury, listening to her footsteps on the stairs.

They hadn't even asked, until it was too late, how are you getting there? Wherever *there* was. Just stood unable to talk to each other until suddenly Pietro had said, 'Did she go on the bus, or what? How did she come? She'll never get that stuff on the *motorino*.'

They'd bought her the scooter for her eighteenth, because she'd begged. And because they could trust her, she was a careful girl. Risk-averse, they'd trained her that way, sensible, orderly, intelligent – until now. But she couldn't have got the suitcase on the *motorino*. Pietro had started away from Gloria then, in the hall, ran in awkward haste through into the sitting room and flung open the long windows that opened on to the busy street over a small stone balcony. They never opened those windows, for some reason, though the view was nice. Incongruously, following in Pietro's angry wake, Gloria found herself noticing as the warm air came in, smelling of some flower, that it was a lovely evening. He hurled himself at the balcony and for a moment she was seized with terror of what he might do. But he was only looking down into the street.

'He must have brought her,' Pietro muttered, raging over the low parapet. 'Damn it. He was probably outside all along. When I came in the front door, he was probably waiting. Bastard, bastard! What kind of man doesn't make himself known to a girl's father? What kind of world—' He looked down then, at Gloria's restraining hand on his arm, and reared his head away in a kind of agony, she could tell, at women, women who didn't understand, and why did one have to explain everything to them?

He'd never been like this before. Throughout all their marriage, Pietro had been kind and mild and thoughtful and patient. Old-fashioned? Gloria knew this was what Chiara had come to think, she had read it in her daughter's face. *Silly old dad, who doesn't know*. But old-fashioned seemed to Gloria now only to mean experienced, sensible, cautious, all they had wanted to pass on to Chiara, the qualities she had seemed to possess in admirable abundance – until now.

Timidly Gloria pushed the coffee towards Pietro in the darkened room. Were they simply over-reacting? She wished it to be true. Why didn't the man come up, whoever he was? Why could he not come up, so they'd know at least what he looked like, they could judge him? Would they have always found him wanting, irrespective of his intelligence, good family, anything? Was that what Chiara felt? Was that why she didn't allow him up for inspection? It was what she'd said. Over-reacting? Deep down, what Gloria thought was the same as Pietro. A decent man would have insisted he meet the girl's parents.

'You told Sandro.' The words were spoken flatly, without hope.

'I told Luisa,' said Gloria. 'I knew she'd talk to him about it. Yes.'

And Pietro put his hands up to his face, the remote control still held tight in his fist and crushed against one ear. 'My little girl,' he said.

They sat there a long time without talking. Outside it grew dark.

Chapter Seven

THE SHARP, CLEAN EARLY sun slanted through the great circular window on the Stella Maris's first-floor landing, casting a golden disc on the door of number five. It was early to be doing the rooms – eight-thirty – but the hotel had only four guests remaining and three of them had been in the dining room by seven o'clock sharp.

Vesna didn't need to be doing number five. She'd done the others already, but as she'd finished up in number nine, the third-floor room immediately above, and had paused, mid-hum, as she made a last pass with her glasscloth over the bathroom mirror and listened to the near-perfect silence, something had chilled her. Vesna was neither prone to the sixth sense nor a believer in it but she'd had a grandmother who read the Tarot and could feel disaster coming. Had known, for example, when her youngest son, Vesna's uncle Maciej, was no more than fifteen minutes late for Sunday dinner that he was dead under his motorbike beside a motorway bridge. They'd all known he was reckless, and motorbikes weren't safe and the bridge was the least safe part of the journey, that was how they'd explained it to themselves. But the fact remained: *I saw it*, her grandmother had said. *The wheels spinning.*

'Hello?' Hesitantly Vesna rattled the doorknob, the morning sun on her back. A sweat broke under her arms in the heat. 'Signora?' She couldn't even remember the woman's name. Had they bothered with the passport? She thought not: it came to her by the same gift of – what? Foresight, hindsight, or just call it intuition – that this woman hadn't used her real name, anyway. This woman was not on a late holiday, recharging the batteries with a few days by the sea. She hadn't been out of her room since Monday.

Louder, Vesna called again, rattled harder. From downstairs she heard Calzaghe's voice raised in disgruntlement. *What on earth are you up to?*

Vesna felt in her pocket for the pass key. One last time she called, pleading now. '*Signora.*' She fitted the key in the lock, and the light flooded in from behind her.

*

Parked in the mild early morning outside the anonymous apartment block to the north of the city, it took Sandro less than an hour's surveillance to conclude that, for once, he was right and Luisa was wrong. At least about post-traumatic stress, and in this specific instance.

Of course, he'd have to come back, he'd have to have something to put down on paper, but he'd seen the man's face, while he was coming out on to his concrete balcony and lighting a cigarette, and that had been enough. Sandro, never usually satisfied, might almost have been pleased with himself, only it wasn't that kind of outcome.

And it was mostly down to luck. He'd arrived at eight in the battered Fiat, dusty with fallen leaves and sticky with whatever lime trees gave off, had stepped out of it just as a young woman was leaving the apartment block, jaunty with her new autumn wardrobe and a job to go to, scooter helmet hanging from her braceleted wrist. She had been in a good mood, or pitied the state of his car, or Sandro must have chosen the right form of words when he approached her or had the right expression on his face, because she dimpled back at him obligingly, and answered willingly.

'Yeah, poor guy,' she'd said, lowering her voice, transferring the scooter helmet to her other hand while she got out her keys. 'Up there.' And she'd indicated the balcony on the first floor. 'It really did do something weird to him, you know? Not that I knew him well. But they row, him and his wife, and they never did before. I thought I heard him crying once.' And she stared briefly into Sandro's face at the uncomfortable thought of that, a middle-aged man crying, before briskly turning on her heel.

He'd climbed back into the car, pausing briefly to register that it could go either way, this benign neglect of his vehicle: either it was so filthy it had become invisible and therefore perfect for surveillance, or else someone would register a complaint about it.

Window wound down, he had sat back in the driving seat and looked up. A middle-aged man crying: to Sandro it seemed the most unsurprising thing in the world. Failure, disappointment, age, boredom: never mind trauma. Plenty to cry about, even if he'd never done so himself, trained out of it in the pointlessly busy corridors of the police station, just fill in another form instead. And then the man had come out on to the balcony, a woman's voice calling querulously from behind him. He'd patted the pocket of his dressing gown and got out the almost empty pack of cigarettes, leaned heavily on the parapet and lit up. His face as fallen as a bloodhound's, unshaven, the man would have been looking straight into Sandro's face that was staring back at him from the car's open window, if he hadn't been so utterly unfocused, so completely lost to the world around him.

How could it do that to you? The woman had died two cars behind him – not even his fault, or had it been? Sandro had got out the file, and looked at the details of the accident again. He studied the traffic-analysis diagrams: a familiar enough story. Witnesses: police had been quick on the scene and they'd managed to get a few statements. The claimant had braked late and hard when a car had hit the crash barrier in front of him, and the car behind had gone into him and the one behind that had been crushed by a truck, a big shunt. Tricky to disentangle who'd been at fault: the coroner's court certainly hadn't managed it.

But the man would have lain in bed afterwards trying to sleep with the details of the dead woman's family circling in his head, their faces in the paper, at the inquest, the schools her children attended, her colleagues at the travel agency where she'd worked. He would have gone over what he had done, what he had seen, how it had felt as the first car impacted. What he might have done differently.

Up on the balcony, the man lit another cigarette from the stub of the first. Sandro put the files away and started the engine: two storeys up, the man didn't register any of it, continued smoking with a hand whose tremor was visible even from the pavement below.

The wife would have made him claim, or some lawyer friend, thinking they were helping.

Indicating carefully, Sandro drew on to the expressway that would lead him to the Viadotto dell'Indiano, and back south to the Oltrarno.

Some people were able to sidestep a death as if with a practised movement – nothing to do with them, they were alive. But for most it stood in their path a long time, like a beggar with his hand out. And when they managed to edge past death, even if they never turned around they knew that it would still be there, watching.

The trees below the old flyover were still green but turning just slightly seedier, the bamboo and rushes along the Arno still flattened after a late-August storm. They'd experienced the same storm in Castiglioncello, at the seaside: he and Luisa had holed up in the old lady's musty front room among her heavy old Mussolini-era furniture and watched the wind whip the bright sea into a grey lather.

Sandro's phone rang and he answered, tucking it under his chin as he negotiated his descent from the viaduct.

'I'm taking her out.' It was Luisa's voice. 'Maria Rosselli. I told her you should talk to her son alone, and would she come and have coffee with me? He's expecting you at eleven.'

His head still filled with the insurance claimant's hopeless face and the memory of the seaside storm they'd watched in silence, Sandro took a moment to make sense of what Luisa was saying. Eleven: he could just fit in a half-hour with the colonel first. 'Yes,' he said, swinging on to the roundabout and the four lanes that would lead him through the Isolotto and to the bridge leading north across the river.

It clamoured at him: fit it all in. 'Thanks – I—' He shifted the phone. Ridiculous, he thought, sliding between lanes, grappling for the gearstick as another car cut across him, horn blaring. The phone fell to the floor of the car, Sandro pulled in to the side of the road and felt his heart pounding. Luisa's voice squawked up at him from the footwell. A mixer truck thundered past, jolting deafeningly in a pothole.

Breathe. Sandro leaned down and picked up the phone. An ominous silence.

'Sorry,' he said. 'I was driving.'

Luisa exhaled, but still said nothing; *I've told you over and over, switch it off when you get in the car.* 'I'm parked up now,' he offered. Still silence.

He was on the edge of the Isolotto, a green residential rectangle between the Via Pisana and the Arno. It was a quiet, respectable neighbourhood. He had parked in the lee of a big development of apartment buildings, a row of shops set in below the living accommodation, bakery, laundry, electrical supplies. Nothing more innocuous, but after his slide across the traffic and Luisa's grim silence, he felt jittery, ill-at-ease: the big trees between the apartment blocks, the balcony screens and expensive shutters could be hiding anything. Strung-out trauma cases like the one he'd seen this morning, for example.

'I went up to check on the insurance claimant,' he ventured.

'Yes?' said Luisa tersely, unwilling to let him off the hook.

'Useful,' he said, figuring now was not the time to tell her she'd been wrong about him. As if there was ever a right time for that conversation with Luisa. 'I saw the guy, and a neighbour. It's a start anyway.' He breathed out. 'Thanks for calling the old lady. That's going to make things an awful lot easier.'

They hadn't even discussed it this morning, he and Luisa. But she was someone who always liked to have things straight in her head, to get right to the point. If something needed doing, then don't talk about it, just do it.

It had been a fretful night for both of them. Sandro had lain awake a long time: beside him he'd heard Luisa turning over, and back, and back again. Pietro, of course, had been foremost in Sandro's mind, and never mind the Rossellis or the post-traumatic stress case.

'Should I call Pietro?' he'd asked Luisa anxiously as they'd left the restaurant, brushing through the demonstrators and paying them no attention now. 'What d'you think?'

'He's your friend,' Luisa had said. 'Don't ask me.' Then she relented. 'Leave it for tonight,' she'd said. 'It might blow over. They might have met the boyfriend, Chiara might have changed her mind about moving out – just leave it a night.'

As a result breakfast had been a hurried, silent affair, both of them preoccupied. They hadn't even bothered to turn the light on in the kitchen but had each drunk a cup of coffee hastily in the early-morning gloom and then Sandro had left.

'And Giuli called,' Luisa said now. Outside the car window a woman was arriving to open up the laundry: as Sandro watched she pulled up the shutters with a loud rattle. 'Lavanderia Verna', read the sign. 'Right,' he said.

'She's in the Women's Centre this morning anyway, she said, and she'll ask around. About Flavia – Rosselli's wife. About the post-natal care.'

There was something in her voice, or perhaps in the abruptness with which she fell silent, that stopped them both. A woman had disappeared, leaving her baby behind, and now they all circled anxiously, each with their separate reasons for wanting her back. The husband, pacing his apartment with a crying baby, Giuli, who would probably never have a child, he and Luisa, who'd had one and lost her. *Come back*, Sandro heard the words in his own head. Come back and everything will be fine, the world will settle back on its axis, the child will stop crying.

And if she didn't come back?

*

Shouldering her way through the swing doors of the Women's Centre at eight-thirty, Giuli's heart sank. You couldn't even see the reception desk for the rabble – queue was too orderly a word for it – that had already clustered around the sign informing them to take a ticket, sit and wait their turn, to leave dogs outside, not to eat or drink or use mobile phones in the lobby. Giuli could see at least one dog.

Three generations of a Roma family, with a girl who looked

to be about eleven and was visibly pregnant, were hanging off the desk itself, claiming their place in the queue. They were talking fiercely amongst themselves in their language, of which Giuli didn't understand more than a word or two, and she couldn't tell if they were having a furious argument or this was just normal. Behind them an overweight, defeated-looking woman leaned on a vast all-terrain buggy so dirty it might have come out of a skip and probably had, with a grubby baby in it, eating a doughnut, and a toddler hanging off either side. Backed up against the wall, a skinny girl who looked like she'd been crying was standing next to an acne-scarred boy, moving from one foot to another as if desperate to run, anywhere but here. Just when I need the place to be quiet, thought Giuli. More chaotic, noisier, more hopeless than ever.

As she edged past the buggy, the baby threw the doughnut on the floor and began to scream and thrash about. Sighing, Giuli lifted the hatch that allowed her behind the reception desk, and became officially responsible.

They all began to jabber at once, the Roma family crushing themselves against the counter and reaching out their hands to her.

'Right,' she said, one arm still in her jacket, the other tapping on the computer keyboard to boot up the system. 'Who's first?'

It turned out that the young gypsy girl was thirteen not eleven, and not only pregnant but in early labour. The woman with the buggy wanted surgical sterilization *and* was pregnant again; the skinny girl had symptomatic gonorrhea but her boyfriend didn't. Yet. It took Giuli forty-five minutes to process them and by that time there were others. And then miraculously, abruptly and certainly very temporarily, the reception area was empty, only the lingering smell of dirty nappies and unwashed clothes in the overheated air.

The noise, however, had merely moved on further inside the old building, where the patients were dispersed among the various clinics: contraception, STD, maternity. The Roma girl had gone in an ambulance to the Meyer – the children's hospital, the mother-to-be being still a child herself.

Peering through the glass doors that led out on to the dusty trees and swings of the Piazza Tasso and seeing the outside world bright and for the moment empty of new customers, Giuli lifted the counter hatch and came out. As she did so, little Maria the cleaner came around the corner, leaning on her wide soft broom to push it ahead of her. Maria looked ancient – she had only two remaining teeth and was as wrinkled as a walnut – but she spent all day in motion and had all her marbles, even if you couldn't always understand what she was saying. No one knew how old she actually was.

'Can you watch the desk for me a minute, Maria?' asked Giuli. The cleaner set her hands one on top of the other on the broomhandle's end and considered, head cocked like a little bright-eyed bird. 'Just a minute, honest? I'll hear if the door goes.' Then Maria nodded, face creasing briefly in her guarded version of a smile. And Giuli flew, skidding down the red-tiled corridor.

The Women's Centre was in an old convent that had also served as a foundling hospital, and the corridors were whitewashed with niches for the *tondi*, little round plaster representations of the Holy Child, swaddled, with his arms held out, on a blue background. The obstetrics clinic – two consulting rooms with one harassed doctor between them and a rota of midwives – was the quietest part of the Women's Centre. By the time a mother was decided upon having a baby, it seemed, the fight went out of her. Some of them were even happy. But not many: most of the pregnant women who came to the Centre 'pursued other options'.

One consulting room was empty of patients or professionals, and the door stood open; the neighbouring one was in use. Damn, thought Giuli, sitting down abruptly on a flimsy plastic chair and beginning to fidget. From behind the door she could hear Farmiga's voice. A tough, bullying woman. Good-looking, but if you looked closely it was all painted on, and her eyes were hard and she seemed to have only contempt for her colleagues and patients alike: the latter would emerge looking whipped and scurry away, never to return. 'Good riddance', was all Farmiga would say, loudly, as she changed into her high heels at the end of the day. As if saving the state money was her only priority. She'd voted for Berlusconi.

Fortunately, the midwives dealt with most of the care. Where were they? Giuli didn't know who was on duty today as they'd already got in by the time she arrived, and she didn't know which of them had seen Flavia either. Or if they'd agree to talk to her. The door to the washroom opened.

Clelia Schmidt. The German, or half-German, midwife: she'd been here a year. She was quiet and modest, and as a result Giuli didn't know her well. Plus she had the mild, unmade-up face and braided hair of the idealistic, the back-to-nature, alternative-lifestyle sort of person for whom Giuli had never had any time. She got to her feet hesitantly.

'Um, Clelia,' she began, glancing back over her shoulder in the direction of the reception area. 'Miss Schmidt?'

Standing in the corridor in her green scrubs, Clelia looked at Giuli with mild enquiry, then held out one arm towards the open consulting room. It was only when they were inside and the door closed, the midwife seated at the desk in front of a computer, that Giuli understood Clelia thought it was herself she'd be talking about; that she, Giuli, had some personal obstetric emergency. The realization made her jittery, and it took her a while to explain herself.

'Ah,' said Clelia, frowning, when eventually the question was asked. Giuli, perched on the narrow vinyl bed, leaned forwards attentively. 'Actually, yes,' Clelia said, 'I dealt a great deal with Flavia, I signed off the post-natal care last week. But I'm not sure if I'm even supposed to tell you that.'

Her Italian was exceptionally good, with barely a trace of an accent, but Giuli could have wished – fervently – for a fellow Italian, who would be more likely to bend the rules, and to understand the situation for what it was. Or would they? Giuli didn't even know if she understood the situation herself. Would she want other people to know things she'd said, hoped, regretted, imagined – or even done – to professionals? There had been plenty of professionals at the rehab centre when she'd been on her way out of prison to the outside world – shrinks of one kind or another, nurses, doctors, social workers – and it had taken a lot for her to speak to them at all. She took a deep breath.

'I know,' she said, 'I don't understand the rights and wrongs of it myself, Clelia.'

Far off through the bowels of the building she heard the mechanical squeal that indicated someone had come in at the front door.

Ignoring the sound, Giuli went on. 'I know there has to be trust in the system, or it fails. I don't want to breach the trust – I work here too, after all – but Flavia's disappeared. She left the baby behind and disappeared, and we need to find her.'

The fair, kindly, unadorned face gazed back at her, with dawning horror.

'There's something, isn't there?' said Giuli. 'She wasn't well, was she?'

As if mesmerized, Clelia Schmidt moved her head, indicating no, as though if she didn't actually say the words, she could not be held responsible. Giuli slid from the high narrow couch and stood stiffly close to Clelia Schmidt, hands behind her back. 'It's a difficult time for mothers, everyone knows that. But was there anything in particular in Flavia's case? There was, wasn't there? Something more dangerous than the hormones and all that?' The midwife's distress deepened visibly.

'I don't know why you are saying these things,' she said, shaking her head furiously. 'The hormones are dangerous enough.'

'So she was finding it hard?' Giuli tried to keep the sense of urgency she felt out of her voice, heard herself sounding earnest.

Clelia Schmidt's hands fiddled with nothing in her lap. 'I was not her only caregiver,' she said, and looked towards the cloister, out of the window, as if someone there might rescue her.

'But you formed a relationship with her? As midwives do.' Giuli knew this: it was part of their charter, to support women in childbirth and afterwards, the continuity of care, or something. The midwife bobbed her head reluctantly. 'The hormones,' prompted Giuli. 'I mean, generally, can you tell me? The effect on them of giving birth.'

With half an ear she was listening out, now, for old Maria shuffling down the corridor to fetch her, but so far nothing. She leaned forward, attentive.

'If we are speaking generally.' The midwife seemed to relax, frowning, unfocused, at her computer screen. 'There are certain conditions that can be brought on by the trauma of birth, by unregulated hormones and chemicals in the body, and by the emotional upheaval of birth.' She was warming to her subject now, almost eager. 'In some women – abused women, and we do see them here – the physical act of giving birth can—' And she stopped short, staring at Giuli and stuttering, 'Not that – not that I'm saying Flavia was – no, no—'

Damn, thought Giuli, composing her expression. 'Of course not,' she said, calmly. 'You're talking generally.' Clelia Schmidt looked desperate. 'Really. Please go on.'

'The conditions that may be brought on by the birth are first, and most commonly, post-natal depression.' She spoke as though reciting from a textbook. 'This can be hard to detect. New mothers are aware that they are supposed to be happy and they feel ashamed when they are not, so they pretend. There are specific questions we can ask, but they are not always useful. Intelligent women in particular—' And the midwife stopped again.

The one thing everyone knew about Flavia Matteo was that she was an intelligent woman. A degree in one thing, a master's in another, a doctorate in something else. What other kind of woman would Niccolò Rosselli have wanted? But Giuli smiled blandly as if she hadn't made the connection and Clelia went on doggedly.

'Then there is post-partum psychosis,' she said, raising her eyes to meet Giuli's. 'Much rarer, more – well, I don't know if it is more serious. Post-natal depression can have very serious consequences. But more extreme. Mood swings, delusions, violence. . .'

'Violence,' said Giuli. Holding her gaze, Clelia nodded. 'Towards – others?'

'Often in psychosis,' the midwife replied steadily. 'In the deluded state the violence is employed against others.'

'Such as?'

'Such as the child,' said the midwife, holding her gaze. 'Most often, the child.'

Giuli said nothing.

'Flavia left her child behind, you said.'

So we're not really talking generally any more, thought Giuli, are we?

'She did,' was all she answered. But Flavia might have left the child behind to prevent herself from harming it.

'I'm sure she wasn't psychotic,' blurted Clelia Schmidt, as though she'd read Giuli's thoughts. Then she would say that, wouldn't she? She wouldn't want to admit she hadn't detected it – but midwives weren't psychiatrists. Detecting mania seemed to Giuli to be quite a responsibility.

'What about depression?' she said gently. 'I mean, the behaviour pattern, speaking generally. Those serious consequences you were talking about.'

Clelia looked at her, her expression taut and anxious. 'Any kind of depression can lead to family breakdown,' she said. 'Insomnia, inability to communicate, hopelessness, apathy, anxiety, panic attacks. And the failure to bond,' her frown deepened, 'can be very serious for the child and the mother, can lead to lasting psychological problems for both. And of course where in psychosis the violence may be directed outwards. . . ' Here she stopped.

Depressives killed themselves.

And Giuli heard her name, called down the corridors from the outside world. 'Sarto?' Maria's croak. 'Signorina Sarto?' A man's voice further off, hectoring. Sounded like a wife-batterer, come for his woman: it wasn't uncommon.

'Look,' she said gently to Clelia Schmidt, 'you've been a great help. I know how things are. But if you could talk to your colleagues. If there's anything more—'

'She might have been depressive, yes,' the midwife said urgently, head bowed over her desk so she need not meet Giuli's eye. 'I watched her closely. She was anxious, yes. She was trying so hard – I didn't want to demoralize her. I should have – should have done more.'

'You're doing plenty,' said Giuli, her hand on the doorknob. 'We still don't know for sure.'

There was a rap. 'Signorina Sarto?' Maria must have heard her voice through the door.

'Coming,' called Giuli. And as she turned back she saw Clelia Schmidt's eyes fixed on her, as if she represented hope. Don't, she said in her head. Don't look at me like that.

Chapter Eight

VESNA, WHO NEVER CRIED, found that she wanted to cry. Standing beside her outside the hotel, among the magnolia and laurels, Calzaghe had his greasy hand on her shoulder, not so much to comfort as to detain her; she knew that he was thinking about the effect this would have on business and how he could thrust Vesna ahead of him into the scandal of it. She pulled away.

Calzaghe turned at a sound, lifting his big head like a jowly dog scenting the air. It was the ambulance siren at last, coming closer but not quickly, not hurrying. It was, after all, too late for that. In a part of her brain Vesna knew that she should change. Her maid's uniform was soaked, even her hair was dripping wet; she shivered suddenly. Was this shock? She felt numb, she wanted to cry but she could not. She remembered the dripping deadweight in her arms, slipping through them, impossibly heavy.

With her hand on the door, even before it opened, Vesna had known. The cool, moist air, the sudden sensation of emptiness like a kind of dying exhalation. The shushing draft from the open window, the neatly made bed; and the drip of a tap in the bathroom, splashing into a full tub. Vesna had set down the plastic basket in which she carried her spray detergent and her glasscloths and her duster on the floor by the door: it was still there to trip her up when – was it five, ten minutes later? – she ran – *ran* – dripping into the hall to shout. '*Ambulance*. Call an ambulance.' And Calzaghe's fat ugly face, rough with white stubble, scowling at her furiously up the stairwell.

She hadn't looked for a note. Everything had seemed so orderly, so composed. The woman in number five had made the bed and packed her small bag. Or perhaps she had never slept? Perhaps she had never *unpacked*? She had looked out on to the distant sliver of sea from her balcony, she had at least done that, opened the windows and walked out into the air, looked at the world. Oh, God, thought Vesna as another shiver overtook her. On the gravel of the drive Calzaghe took a step away from her, as if shock might be contagious.

Must I go back up there? thought the maid with horror. To look for the note or the – the weapon, or the passport, to examine the bed to see if she'd slept there?

'We don't even know who she was,' she murmured, and Calzaghe turned to her.

'What?' He spoke sharply.

'I – well, she gave a name, in the register.' Vesna couldn't remember if she'd even looked at it, her mind a blank. 'But I hadn't got around to taking her ID,' she mumbled, knowing she might as well take the blame now, it would come her way sooner or later. He glared at her and she took some satisfaction from the fact that the police would hold him responsible, ultimately. His hotel: she was just the Eastern European help. Calzaghe didn't even know which country she came from, but she was legal.

The police. And they'd want to know when the woman died, wouldn't they? When she'd done it. And Vesna wouldn't be able to tell them. How long the thing had been there, and they going about their small business, the breakfasts and the laundry and the drying out of guest soaps.

She had walked towards the bathroom quickly, crossing the large bedroom, looking around, slowing unconsciously as she approached the door of the en suite. One of the earliest en-suite bathrooms, Art Deco, was how she'd been told to introduce it to guests who might be more familiar with shiny modern chrome and glass. 'No shower?' some of them would say incredulously, looking around at the original fittings, the cream rectangular tiles with black border, then down at the vast, yellowing marble tub.

The tub was in fact so big that she had fitted inside it, full length, like a child's drawing of a woman. A woman underwater. A woman whose legs were too thin, though her stomach was softish, very pale skin with a dark line running up it. Vesna knew what that was: the *linea nigra*. The toes turned in, the dark red hair floating out around her head in water stained pink, the hands palm up and the wounds across the wrists frilled and blanched from immersion. The woman in number five, lying dead in the bath, was wearing her underwear.

Taking it all in – the sink, the toothbrush, the chemist's paper folded, the open packet, the white palm of the woman's hand marked like a schoolchild's – Vesna wondered if she would ever be able to erase it now, like the pink stain to the tub. How would you go about cleaning blood from marble? And then with that thought in her head she had dashed for the bath, plunged her arms in and grappled for the body – the woman – felt her bob and slip under her hands, grabbed and pulled and hauled until the woman's weight shifted abruptly, up and flopping across the bath's edge and on top of Vesna. She still felt the spongy flesh between her fingers.

'I'm going to be sick,' she said to Calzaghe, turned aside and vomited into the laurels, just as the ambulance pulled up at the rusting gate.

'For the love of God,' he said with disgust. 'Jesus.'

And, head down between her knees, the sour smell of her own stomach contents in her nostrils and something wet on her cheek, Vesna felt a different hand on her shoulder, a gentle touch.

There's a baby, she thought, head down. The *linea nigra* means a baby. Where's her baby?

'All right, kid,' a woman's gruff, comforting voice said. Still crouched Vesna turned her head just a little and saw the sleeve of a paramedic's uniform. 'It's all right now, sweetheart.' And Vesna put her own hand to her cheek and found that she really was crying.

*

Damn, damn. Parking up illegally behind the Botanic Gardens, Sandro was late, and sweating like a menopausal woman. What was he even doing here, now they knew it was. . . ? Well, domestic. Messy, miserable, relationship stuff, no conspiracy after all. Sandro couldn't have said, except there'd been something about the soldiers last night that had interested him. And maybe after all he was trying to wrest it back, to prove to the monstrous Maria Rosselli that there might be bigger forces at work here.

Opposite the army barracks he passed an old-fashioned bar, and glanced up at the original signage in tarnished gilt; the Bar dell'Orto was just the kind of place that would have tempted him in if he'd had time or excuse. Standing in the window a lad in camouflage fatigues, raising a glass to his lips with a tattooed hand, gave him a look; a couple of men in the dark berets and sand-coloured uniform of the higher ranks watched the new arrival curiously. Ten-past ten, and he had to be back down in Santo Spirito by eleven.

And when you were pushed for time, everything else slowed down. Somewhere in the bowels of the ancient shabby building, someone took an age to respond to the intercom that Sandro pressed repeatedly. The vast heavy doors took an impossible time to open electronically and then, once he'd found his way inside the converted convent that housed the logistics unit, to the gloomy little reception area, he encountered only obstructiveness. An attitude so guarded and obtuse it amounted to naked hostility.

It was the thing he hated more than any other. Having himself been a part of an organization like this, Sandro knew the mentality: keep close, give nothing away. And now he was on the wrong side of the glass screen, it made him want to commit murder.

A male and a female soldier in camouflage fatigues behind the armoured glass – who were they afraid of? A new Red Brigade targeting a sub-section of the administration of the smallest standing army in Europe? – went on chatting for a good two minutes before the seated man turned and eyed Sandro.

'Yes?' He was about thirty-five and exceptionally good-looking, which for some reason annoyed Sandro even further. That and the fatigues, irresistible to women, no doubt. A certain kind of woman, anyway: he tried to picture the expression on Luisa's face if she saw the man. A name displayed on the desk – in a concession to the age of openness and accountability – read Canova. In theory Sandro could complain about his rudeness. Practice was a different matter.

Sandro didn't even know if it was worth opening his mouth. Why hadn't he taken the colonel's name?

'I spoke to one of your officers last night,' he said, without much hope. 'This is the Regional Command? Tall guy. Colonel. He said to come and see him if I wanted.' Reluctantly he fished out his card and slid it under the glass screen. 'It's – about the Frazione Verde.' The soldier took the card and turned his back on Sandro again. He said something to the female soldier, and her expression, lip curled, gave Sandro a good idea of what it was.

'It is concerning?' Sandro saw that the woman's eyes never left Canova: he imagined there were rules about relationships that in this case, and probably plenty of others, were being ignored.

'To do with roads,' Sandro offered, leaning closer to the glass again. The soldier didn't turn back for a good thirty seconds, but when he did Sandro, mastering himself, smiled.

'Stupid of me not to take his name. I didn't want to detain him, you see.'

'Yes,' said the soldier. Next to him on the reception desk was a newspaper. Reading upside down Sandro saw a headline: 'ONE DEAD, ONE INJURED IN AFGHANISTAN'. That made it easier to control his impatience somehow: they were just boys, out there. This one might be a bastard, but. . . 'Sorry,' he said again.

The soldier looked at him, expressionless. 'It would be Colonello Arturo,' he said, with an exhalation of impatience. Slowly – still slowly – he lifted a telephone. Sandro stole a glance at his watch, and had to suppress a groan. Ten-twenty.

By the time the female soldier left him, having led him in ungracious silence to the man's office in a high and distant corner of the old convent, it was ten-twenty-five. Sandro guessed that he had perhaps twenty minutes. What a waste of time. He knocked.

Arturo's office was surprisingly small and dingy; he sat behind a wide desk covered with scratched imitation leather, surmounted by a computer and a small wire document tray into which, on Sandro's arrival, he deposited a folded newspaper. Legs stretched languidly to one side of the desk, the tall officer, raising his head to examine Sandro in the doorway, seemed out of proportion to his surroundings, his limbs too long, attitude too relaxed. On the wall above his head was a crowded shelf of books and a small plaster bust.

'*Permesso?*' said Sandro awkwardly.

'Ah,' the colonel said, stretching. 'It's you. Mr Private Eye.' He gestured to a chair against the wall. 'Pull up a seat.'

As labyrinthine Italian bureaucracies went, Sandro reflected while he sat, the army probably had to be the weirdest. Forbidden by the constitution actually to go to war, sporadically dumped in some war zone or other under NATO's aegis, to be shot at or, as now, blown up by the Taliban, most soldiers seemed to Sandro to spend their time either taking potshots on rifle ranges by the seaside, in endless convoy on the motorways, or else holed up in offices like these, twiddling their thumbs. Heirs to the Roman legionaries.

'You said I could come,' began Sandro tentatively. 'It was about the Frazione Verde.'

Arturo looked at him as if working out whether there'd be any amusement in it for him. He smiled lazily.

'D'you think they'll last?' he said, leaning abruptly over the desk towards Sandro and taking him by surprise, his long legs folding up like a grasshopper's. He was bored stiff, Sandro realized: might well say more than he intended to, just out of ennui. How old was he. . . fifty? Ten years off retirement. There was a photograph of him on the shelf, in full dress uniform, hand on the pommel of a sword.

The soldier pursed his lips. 'The party, I mean? It's interesting, I can see. But after the other night, when Rosselli passed out on stage. . . ' He gave a little exhalation of contempt. 'Who's paying you?'

Sandro shifted uncomfortably. 'Ah – it's complicated,' he said. Because he could hardly say 'the vengeful mother-in-law'. He improvised. 'The party's administration realize that things are at a delicate stage. They want to clean up their act – that is, get more organized. Make sure there's nobody inside working against them, that kind of thing.'

'Or outside the party?' Arturo set his fingers together as if in prayer, regarding Sandro over the top of them with the same mild amusement.

'Well, yes,' he said, startled. 'I suppose. Do you know anything about that?'

'You mean us?' The lazy smile. 'We're keeping an eye on them,' he said, 'no more than that. You have to admit, they're a whole arsenal of loose cannon. What do they believe in? Sabotaging power stations? Stopping the functioning of the city, obstructing progress?'

Sandro recognized an uneasy kinship between him and this man: a shared weariness at the thought of idealism, at its disconnection from the practicalities.

'Well, there's the road on the edge of Scandicci,' he said, reluctantly. 'The new shopping mall. I happen to know that there are obscure permissions to be obtained from the army for road-building. It may be how things work in Italy, but do we really need that? Aren't they entitled to raise their objections? Don't they have – a democratic right to do so?'

'Of course,' said Arturo, who seemed to be enjoying himself. 'They have rights. Just as we – the bureaucracies they so object to – have duties. We gave permission for the road because all the technicalities had been observed, the signatures obtained, the fees paid. It didn't happen overnight, it's taken five years. You can't just deny on a whim a business consortium the right to the lawful exercise of commerce.' He smiled. 'And as I'm sure you're aware, we aren't so important; it's just a formality, the army's permission for roads. One of those things.'

Sandro did know. The colonel seemed completely relaxed: he was in the right, after all. They were going to be so delighted, thought Sandro, the lot of them: the *Berlusconiani*, the *comune*, the vested interests, when they found out. The road would go through and they wouldn't have to lift a finger to finish off the Frazione. The sudden disappearance of a post-natally depressed woman, the partner of the movement's leader, would do their work for them.

Still Sandro persisted, Maria Rosselli's grim, triumphant face haunting him. He realized he'd agreed to take this on to defend poor Flavia Matteo, not to hunt her down.

'But even if Rosselli doesn't get to parliament,' said Sandro. 'If he becomes – let's say – *assessore* for roads in the *comune*? Wouldn't that put a spoke in it for you lot? He could cause trouble.'

Arturo just shook his head a little. 'We're used to that,' he said. 'It keeps us busy.' He smiled again. 'Keeps us out of Afghanistan. Some of us.'

Sandro felt his shoulders sag, and despite himself he let out a sigh. He gazed despondently at Arturo's bookshelf. Russian literature. He squinted at the name on the bust: Aristotle. Sandro wanted not to like this man, but it was difficult.

'Look,' said Arturo then, almost kindly. 'It seems to me that if anyone's got a reason to have a go at the Frazione, it'd be some business interest or other, wouldn't it? Or at a pinch, the secret service boys. But to be honest, the amount of time I've spent watching the Frazione Verde mill around aimlessly at one rally or another, they're just not a threat to anyone. They don't need – what? Sabotaging?' He laughed. 'They're going to fizzle out of their own accord.'

And with that he straightened up and glanced at his watch.

Damn, thought Sandro, checking his own. He's right, isn't he? And I've got to go.

*

Luisa hadn't expected it. Why not? What else was the woman to do with her grandchild? It was the practical solution, not to mention better for Sandro: he could talk to Niccolò Rosselli without interruption.

'You brought the child,' she said blankly.

Maria Rosselli, stern as some kind of governess rather than a blood relative, stood at the door holding the baby, swaddled to a stiff cocoon, in her arms with a faint air of dislike. It – he – was asleep, upright, his plump face flushed pink, with a small spike of hair protruding from under a woollen hat. Round and rosy and healthy, he did not, thought Luisa, look like his father.

Irrationally, Luisa hadn't expected the baby only because babies did not feature in her life. No children of her own, no nieces, no nephews, no grandchildren. Cousins had children, but Luisa had stayed out of their orbit, consciously or otherwise, in the thirty years since losing her own. She leaned towards the baby, saw his mouth work at an invisible milk source in his sleep.

'I left the perambulator downstairs.'

Perambulator. It would be the huge old thing Maria Rosselli had gone to Milan to buy when Niccolò was born, fifty-odd years ago. Where could you keep such a thing, in this day and age?

'He's put on weight since she went,' said Maria Rosselli coolly. 'It's the formula milk. It's marvellous, these days. All there is for mothers, now.' But there was still that expression of distaste. Although it was warm the old woman was wearing an ancient winter coat of very good quality, and a hat.

Luisa found she wanted to offer to take the child from her but she did not. 'Come in,' she said, and stepped back to allow the old woman into the apartment.

She'd taken the morning off work at Frollini: Beppe had, as always, been laidback about it but Giusy had moaned. Luisa almost never took time off. 'I'll be in at midday,' she said when Giusy had finished. 'That's precisely an hour and a half.'

With a heavy sigh that indicated she was here very much against her will, Maria Rosselli deigned to enter. She looked around as she passed through the hall, right to left, for something to disapprove of, a big plasma screen perhaps, or a marital bed with satin and flounces and cushions, but she found nothing and remained silent, reserving judgement. Luisa ushered her into the *salotto*, the big sitting room with its small, ancient television, where they spent almost no time at all. But she didn't want Maria Rosselli in her safe cosy kitchen, silently criticizing her spice rack and the contents of her draining board, and putting her on edge.

'Here,' she said, and suddenly she could stand it no longer; seeing the old woman holding the child as though he might be a bomb or a hostage, she took the baby with one quick movement before Maria Rosselli could say anything, and set him down on the sofa. Like some sort of chrysalis, he didn't stir in his swaddling. 'Coffee?' she said.

Maria Rosselli looked at Luisa as if she did not believe for a moment that she would be capable of producing a decent cup of coffee. 'Water,' she pronounced. 'Just a glass of water.'

'It's a long time since we spoke properly,' said Luisa, when she returned from the kitchen. As if they ever had spoken properly, she and old Signora Rosselli, nothing but guarded niceties concealing a standoff, but the elderly had to be given their due. She set the glass down warily in front of her guest, on a coaster on top of a hand-crocheted snow-white doily, everything she might want in deference to her status. But the old woman made a sudden, explosive sound of frustration; beside her on the deep sofa the baby started briefly.

'I don't see why I had to leave them alone,' she said angrily, ignoring the overture, leaning forward over hands that were clasped in her lap and thrusting her strong chin at Luisa instead. 'I'm Niccolò's mother. There are no secrets between us. I know more about that – that relationship than anyone.'

I'm sure you do, thought Luisa, and she nodded seriously. 'But still,' she said easily. 'It's not that we – that Sandro thinks there might be secrets, not at all. At least, not between you and your son. But, professionally, it's simply easier for him.' She smiled gently. 'He's not a young police officer any more, after all. He needs all the help he can get, concentrating. One person at a time, you see?' And silently apologized to him for the slander.

Maria Rosselli, who obviously prided herself on faculties undimmed by the passing of time, leaned back into the sofa, mouth pursed in satisfaction.

'How's the baby, then?' Luisa said, knowing she'd have to keep the woman here as long as possible. 'You're managing?'

'Managing?' said Maria Rosselli, and snorted. 'It's hardly work, is it? Hardly a complicated business. One small baby. Only interested in the next feed. And six weeks – well, in some ways it's the ideal age. None of that separation anxiety nonsense, more or less anyone will do. I mean – if she never comes back. . . ' She broke off, shrugged coolly, and Luisa stared in frank disbelief.

'But you want Sandro to find her?' she said, before she could think about it.

Maria Rosselli's eyes were like grey stones. She looked at Luisa for a long moment before eventually she spoke. 'Don't think it's for myself,' she said. 'I can deal with the raising of this child. Niccolò – well, God knows why, but he's beside himself. It's his intelligence, you see. Not having any explanation for it.' And at last she seemed to falter, her expression showing incomprehension, frustration, doubt. 'He seems to feel the need to know why. To understand. Personally I don't believe such a person is worthy of understanding.'

Lifting the glass of water to her lips defiantly, she took no more than a sip. 'And the child's clearly thriving on this formula. Sentimental nonsense, all that nature-knows-best rubbish.'

'She – Flavia – was breastfeeding?' Luisa said. She cleared her throat. When her own baby had died, of course they had told her the milk would come in, but that if she were lucky it wouldn't last more than a day or two, and it had not. She tried to amplify the terrible sensation that had dogged her for those thirty-odd hours – of something having been lost, left behind, gone missing, and even in her sleep she must search for it – and apply it to a woman leaving this warm, rosy living child for not hours but days. Days that might stretch to weeks. Or for ever. She stole a glance at him down there between them on the sofa, and strained, against the sudden fury that rose in her against the absent mother, aligning herself with Maria Rosselli, heaven forbid. Strained to understand.

'What do *you* think?' she said, giving up. 'Why do you think Flavia's gone?'

And the big pale stone-eyes rested on Luisa as Maria Rosselli leaned forward again over her large bony hands, white-knuckled now, and Luisa could see all the fury wound tight in her big, spare frame.

'She's weak,' she said, and Luisa found the level calm of her voice more unsettling than rage, hissing, or spitting or shouting. She made Luisa think of a beast of prey, lean and strong and evolved into preternatural control, like a cobra or a hawk. Maria Rosselli straightened herself. 'She's a weak, silly woman, I knew she would fail him and she has. I told him. Long ago, I told him. Weak but stubborn.' She looked down. 'Like a baby: like this baby, strong-willed when he's after something.'

'After something?'

'She wanted the child.'

Like a baby wants his feed: an imperative. Luisa waited, and Maria Rosselli, steely calm now, went on. 'She wanted to secure Niccolò, she kept on at him, on and on, and never mind his ideals. She had to prove that she was more important than the party. The personal relationship was more important than his work.'

'The personal relationship,' said Luisa. 'You mean love.' She was surprised at herself; she didn't like the word. But something about Maria Rosselli made her contrary. And sometimes love was the right word.

'If you like,' said Maria Rosselli stiffly.

'Come on,' Luisa said. 'Of course personal relationships are important. They're what make the world go round.'

'He never wanted a child.'

'But once he was born—'

'All right, all right,' said Maria Rosselli, and Luisa saw the force of her jealous rage.

'They loved each other. They were happy about the child.'

Maria Rosselli's mouth set in a stubborn line. 'Yes,' she said tersely. Blood from a stone. 'Fools, both of them. There are more important things.'

Luisa hadn't consciously been intending to mine the old woman for information, but as Maria Rosselli's mouth clamped shut she knew she'd had all she was going to get. Beside them the child stirred and struggled in his swaddling; raised his small, strong chin, tipped his head back, opened his mouth and wailed.

His grandmother didn't even seem to notice.

*

Niccolò Rosselli looked terrible. Ill-shaven, gaunt, shambling as he moved ahead of Sandro further into the apartment – his and Flavia Matteo's apartment on the Piazza Santo Spirito – and Sandro walked with his hands instinctively held out as though he might need to catch the poor man if he fell.

Worth a euro or two, Sandro couldn't help thinking as he looked around himself furtively, even on the modest side of the square.

The apartment was not large, but comfortable. On the second floor, running from front to back of the building, which was more unusual than it might sound for a city where the old stone palaces, regular enough in their symmetrical front elevations, turned into twisting, turning labyrinths inside. Divided and subdivided and added to like termite mounds, some of them. This was not a palace, though: Sandro understood quickly that these people would never live in a grand or noble building, not even a dilapidated one. Against their principles.

Niccolò Rosselli was standing now as if uncertain of what to do next. Waiting, Sandro glanced around himself.

They were in a *salotto* at the front of the apartment with all the walls but one covered with bookshelves, more books than Sandro had ever seen in his life outside a library. A desk stood between the windows with a battered computer on it and a pinboard behind. The furniture consisted of a low, brown corduroy-covered set of two armchairs and a sofa, shiny with age. An Indian-looking embroidered cloth lay over the *divano*, another was hung on the back of the door, and a beaded string of brightly coloured cloth birds and bells chinked against the door jamb.

Finally Niccolò Rosselli gestured at the brown sofa and Sandro sat down. Rosselli sat in one of the matching chairs and thrust his hands under him, as if to keep them out of harm's way, thin arms taut, shoulders hunched. He looked hamstrung, as if he might at any moment begin rocking like the straitjacketed inmate of an asylum. No wonder the mother was worried: no wonder Giuli and the rest of the Frazione Verde were too, if this man was their new bright hope.

'You know why I'm here?' said Sandro, and slowly Rosselli focused on him. His dark eyes were magnified by the thick, old-fashioned glasses he wore; a boy who'd ruined his eyes through over-studying, that would be the old-school diagnosis. Tentatively Sandro persisted. 'Your mother—' And Rosselli sighed.

'My mother wants to help,' he said. He spoke hurriedly as if everything was urgent, running the words together: Sandro imagined it might be rather effective in front of an audience, but in this confined space it seemed like a kind of shyness, awkwardness. 'Do you need help?' he asked gently.

Rosselli frowned. 'My – my – Flavia's gone,' he said. 'My

partner. The mother of our child.' How many words to describe it, thought Sandro: it would be easier if you'd married. My wife. He opened his mouth.

'Yes,' Sandro said. 'Your mother said she – you haven't seen her since Sunday. Or heard from her, I suppose. That must be hard.'

He glanced around, only now remembering the child. Asleep? Or out with the grandmother? Yes, of course: he shied from the thought of Luisa entertaining them on his behalf.

There was a silence which Sandro interpreted as agreement. Uneasily he shifted on the brown corduroy, levering himself up out of its yielding depths. It was not the way he would have chosen to sit, asking questions like these. 'She went before you woke? That's what your mother said. In the night?

Then Rosselli raised his head and frowned, as if at last Sandro had asked something new.

'Early in the morning,' he said. 'She was there during the night itself.'

'Right,' said Sandro, waiting.

'I don't sleep well,' said Niccolò Rosselli wearily. 'I often don't get to sleep until two, three in the morning – I mean, I go to bed, but I don't sleep. I – Flavia says, I think too much. I sleep deeply only between three, perhaps four and seven or eight in the morning. That night she was still there beside me when I got to sleep, and she was gone when I woke up. I always said to Flavia I should do the night feed as I was awake anyway. She said I could when she stopped breastfeeding.'

It felt like a long speech, somehow. If Sandro and Luisa had had a child, would he have got up in the night to feed it? He couldn't imagine so.

'So when you woke that morning. . . Sunday morning?'

'It was eight, just before eight. Flavia had fed him in the night but still it was a long time for him to sleep. He was crying, and

I woke. I don't know how long he'd been crying.' Niccol Rosselli stared unfocused at some point beyond Sandro. His hands came out from under his thighs and briefly went to his face. Finding them there, he pushed them under the glasses and rubbed his eyes hard.

'It's usually Flavia, you see. I wasn't conditioned to respond. To the crying.'

Conditioned to respond. 'What's his name?' Sandro found himself asking. 'Your son's name?' It had just been 'him' so far.

Rosselli frowned as if unable to make sense of the question, or to remember the child's name perhaps. 'Luca,' he said eventually. 'I – we only decided recently.' Sandro fought against what he knew to be prejudice: this man was odd; this set-up was odd. So clever, and so helpless, and so weirdly cold – *conditioned to respond*? – was this man or his partner even capable of looking after this child? Yet there were soft touches too; there were the brightly coloured cloths, and the bells and birds, and the photographs and postcards on the pinboard. All hers, thought Sandro.

'Did she take anything? A – a bag, clothes? Money? Passport?'

Again Rosselli sighed. 'My mother asked that,' he said. He seemed to sigh, Sandro observed, whenever he said anything about his mother. 'She – I let her look, my mother looked. In the wardrobe, the drawers. The suitcase is still there, pretty much all Flavia's clothes. She doesn't have a passport. It expired: we don't travel much. We were going to – we did talk about a holiday. After he was born. We were going to renew her passport – and mine for that matter. We got them together, they had both expired. When we got one for him, we would—' And here he seemed to run out of steam, stopping abruptly.

The suitcase – a family with only one suitcase between them. Modest in all things. Luisa, thought Sandro, would probably approve.

'She took her handbag,' offered Rosselli, 'so she would have had her *carta d'identità*. And I suppose money.' He passed a hand over his forehead. 'Should I have thought of these things? Her purse. . . but she never carried much money. There's a bank card for taking money out, and a credit card, but we don't use it.'

'She has her own bank account?'

'A joint account,' said Rosselli. 'We don't have much, and we don't spend much. We're – the same, really, there's no question of not trusting – I mean, we have the same feelings about money, it's not important to us.'

Easy to say, thought Sandro. When there is money to be had. Furtively he looked around him again; nothing expensive, it was true. The furniture shabby, but everything clean, ordered. The photographs on the pinboard behind the computer drew him. There was a picture of a woman's face: she had the dark red hair and freckled white skin common in the Abruzzo. She was looking away, to the side, no make-up at all. She seemed very beautiful to Sandro.

'She worked?' He realized he'd used the past tense and scrambled to catch himself up. 'I mean, before the baby?'

'She's a teacher,' Rosselli said, and looked down at his hands. He had heard the past tense, for sure. 'Before the baby she taught mathematics at the Agnesi.'

'You've looked to see if any money's been withdrawn?' Sandro asked. 'I assume you can see online? Has the credit card been used?'

Rosselli looked blank. Had he done anything at all? Had he just sat and waited?

'You've tried calling her?' Sandro asked: because of course Rosselli would have done that. But, of course, he was wrong.

'Calling her?' The man looked bizarrely confused. 'But I don't know where she is.'

'On her mobile? The *telefonino*?' Sandro pulled his own out by way of demonstration – that new magic phone he'd finally been talked into getting – and when he touched it, the screen brightened. Missed call, it said. Pietro. How long had it been since he'd spoken to his old friend? A while.

'Oh,' said Rosselli, frowning fiercely. 'We – she doesn't have a mobile phone.'

For a moment Sandro was stumped. Everyone had a mobile. Even he could hardly remember a time when he hadn't had one, and he wasn't exactly a technophile.

Rosselli took off the glasses: his eyes, Sandro saw, were red-rimmed, small and weak without the magnifying effect. 'I mean, we have one, between us,' he said, in that same shy, urgent voice. 'For emergencies, that kind of thing. If we're out in the car. My mother made us get it. To tell the truth, I don't even know where it is.' Still Sandro was lost for words. One between them? For emergencies? Only ones that occurred when they were together, clearly. Were they never apart?

'But you've called it?' Rosselli just stared. His own phone still in his hand, Sandro said, 'What's the number?'

'You think she might have taken it with her?' the man asked wonderingly.

'The number?' Sandro tried to restrain his impatience.

'It's – it's—' Casting about, from his back pocket Rosselli pulled a small, battered, leather-bound book, stuffed with scraps of paper and held together with a rubber band. He leafed through to the back and peered down, replaced his glasses. Sandro dialled as Rosselli read out the number, tracing each digit with a thin finger.

'But it won't be switched on,' the other man said.

Both of them listened, Sandro with his phone held to his ear, one finger held upright to silence Rosselli. And there it was, the message. *This number cannot be reached, please try later.* Sandro breathed out hard, defeated, and pressed End Call.

So Flavia probably hadn't taken it with her. After all, she didn't want to be reached, did she? Or to reach anyone else. Sandro tried to imagine her setting off alone at dawn, cutting loose from the world. Only a handbag? Against hope he thought, there might have been a change of clothes in there.

Or she might have been meeting someone who would take care of everything.

It was the first time Sandro had seriously looked at that possibility: it might have occurred to Luisa before. Had it been hovering at the back of his mind for a while? But this set-up, these two serious, politically committed people – an affair seemed remote. Pleasure, self-indulgence, didn't live here. An affair would be better, wouldn't it? Than the other.

At least she took the handbag. Was that a woman's reflex, even if all she was planning to do was lie down on the train tracks somewhere? Or was it the one bridge not burned, containing the credit card that would get her to her new life, among the handful of possessions she'd take with her in an emergency. But no phone? Lipstick, a diary, a book, a photograph? A purse. She'd left her baby behind.

And then Niccolò Rosselli's landline rang, a loud, clattering, old-fashioned ring from an ugly telephone on the desk next to the computer, resounding in the apartment that at this instant, like its two occupants, seemed to Sandro to be holding its breath. And all that happened next seemed to happen in slow motion. Sandro watched, hypnotized, from the brown corduroy sofa as Niccolò Rosselli pronounced his own name carefully into the receiver and then grappled, as though blinded, for the chair behind him when finally he understood what it was his interlocutor was trying to tell him.

'Where?' Sandro heard him say, sounding breathless, disbelieving, doomed. 'She's where?'

Chapter Nine

ENZO'S WORRIED FACE UNDER its helmet of hair appearing at the smoked-glass doors, his finger tapping insistently while she fumbled for the admission code, aroused complicated feelings in Giuli. He pushed in, eyes fixed on her, heedless of where he was or who else might be there. The reception area of the Women's Centre was mercifully quiet, just one thin middle-aged woman whose daughter had not wanted her to accompany her inside the doctor's room, who was waiting patiently, head down.

'I can't go yet,' Giuli said to Enzo, desperate. 'She hasn't arrived.' It was five-past one. Giuli was supposed to work till one, when bad-tempered Valerie would turn up to take over. Valerie was English and always late, especially when it mattered.

'I can't stay more than half an hour,' Enzo said. He was working in some big office on the northern boulevard, the Via dei Mille, the other side of town. An insurance company. 'What did Sandro say?'

'Maybe you'd be better spending the time at the Frazione,' Giuli said, her mind racing. 'I mean, God. What's it going to do to Niccolò? It'll destroy him.'

Enzo stared at her, white-faced, and Giuli could see, her heart softening so she thought she might actually cry, for the first time in about a hundred years, that he was wondering what he'd do. If it were him. 'What did Sandro say?'

And then the middle-aged Englishwoman was there, thumping in the entry code, square-shaped and furious. She was bad-tempered because she'd married a chauvinist pig of a man from Campania, and she'd left it too late now to jump ship and head back to England. 'Christ,' she said apropos of nothing as she barrelled through the glass doors. Giuli grabbed her bag and her jacket.

'Let's go,' she said.

Out in the Piazza Tasso she took a deep breath, of September mist and car exhaust, and it smelled wonderful after the inside of the clinic. She'd have to go back in and break it to Clelia eventually. She fished in her bag for a cigarette. Enzo frowned.

'I'll give up,' she said. 'I am giving up. Just not today.' They sat on a bench. She lit the cigarette and took the smoke into her lungs, held it there a long moment before exhaling.

She leaned forward on her knees, the cigarette in her hand. 'They found her in a hotel in Viareggio; she took pills and cut her wrists and got in the bath. No note, not yet anyway, but they're in no doubt it was suicide. The chambermaid, a Bosnian girl, found her. A handbag had Flavia's address and phone number, and the local police called Niccolò while Sandro was right there with him.'

Enzo eyed the cigarette; following his glance, Giuli saw it was down to the filter and about to burn her fingers. She flicked it into the grass and stubbed it out with the toe of her boot.

'He'll need to identify – ah, the body.' Enzo was looking down at his hands as he said it. He sat stiffly, looking anguished. Tentatively Giuli slipped an arm through his and pressed herself against his side, and he stayed stiff. She could smell the smoke on her own breath, on her clothes. I'm not good enough for him, she thought.

'I suppose he will,' she said. 'Awful.' It seemed quite unbearable, impossible in fact. She thought of Niccolò Rosselli's thick glasses, his uprightness, of him bending awkwardly to look down in some police mortuary. 'Maybe his mother will go with him.' She stopped. The mother: cold comfort there. She could hardly voice the thought that came next into her head. This was no longer their business. The mother had commissioned Sandro to find Flavia, and Flavia had been found, even if not by him. End of story, or end of their involvement in it anyway.

Suicide. Giuli shouldn't have been shocked for she'd known plenty of suicides. Any number of addicts, including her own mother, slowly killing themselves, and during the year she'd spent in prison three had done it the quicker way. One of whom had still taken four days to die, from a paracetamol overdose leading to liver failure: unwitting relatives had supplied the stuff for supposed back pain, and the woman – mother of five, four of whom had been removed from her care – had stockpiled it for three months, biding her time.

It wasn't a pretty way to go, and Giuli knew what was required to get to that point: the knowledge that life held nothing for them. Guilt and pain and self-hatred and that meltdown in your head, neural pathways dying, capillaries collapsing or whatever, what might be called your soul being destroyed, assuming you believed in a soul, so that anyway you no longer knew where happiness came from. So dead looked good: it looked like sleep, like peace.

Yeah. Giuli knew: it was why she'd never done it, because luckily for her, even though it hadn't felt like it at the time, some little pathway in her head had stayed open. She could just see down it back to the world, back to life. Standing at the end of it there'd been Luisa and Sandro, and now there was Enzo, and she wasn't looking down a tunnel at it all any more, she was back in the world. She knew where happiness came from. Giuli shivered suddenly, and reflexively Enzo's hand came out and rubbed her arm.

'I just can't – I can't believe it,' she heard herself murmuring. 'I didn't think – I never thought she would be someone—' Impulsively she took Enzo's hand, warm in her cold one. 'You knew Flavia properly,' she said, staring into his worried face. 'She had so much in her life. Believing in – in things. In Niccolò, in the politics, in ideas, all those things. Do people like that kill themselves?' Looking into his face, she saw it was too difficult a question for him to answer.

'Roman philosophers were always doing it,' he said, frowning furiously, trying not to put his face in his hands and cry, thought Giuli, not daring to hold him tighter, or to kiss him, for fear he would pull away. 'Taking poison. People of ideas.' He shook his head stiffly.

She spoke up tentatively. 'Not Flavia, though, not once the baby was there, surely?'

He didn't look at her. 'I don't know,' he said. 'Where I come from – no one I know would do that.'

Where Enzo came from: a hardworking peasant family was what he meant, rather than the Casentino. You worked, you pushed on, you provided for your own. Giuli saw the gulf open up between them. Where she came from, it happened all the time.

'And where was Flavia from?' she murmured, to herself.

'Pigneto,' said Enzo promptly, literal as ever. 'Rome. Not a nice bit of Rome, especially not then.'

Giuli, who had hardly left Florence her whole life, was none the wiser. She looked at Enzo.

'I asked her about her childhood once,' he said slowly. 'She said, it wasn't a place you'd want to go back to. Not Pigneto and not the upbringing either, was the impression I got. She moved here when her mother died, straight to university, *Scienze Politiche*.'

How old had Flavia been when her mother died? What had happened to the father? There were plenty of unanswered questions: Giuli sensed the dark contours of a story like her own. A childhood you didn't much want to revisit.

'I've got to go,' said Enzo. He looked desperate, and Giuli didn't know if it was for her, or for Rosselli, or for the Frazione. 'Will you be OK?' he said, on his feet and hands jammed in his pockets.

'Oh,' she said vaguely, wondering if this sudden feeling she had, that Enzo was taking a step back, meant anything. There was nothing she could do about it if so. She looked down at her boots, the cigarette stub in the grass. 'I'll be all right.'

She watched him go, watched him half turn, lift a hand. She stayed on the bench. Sooner or later she'd have to go inside the Centre and tell them that Flavia was dead.

*

'Another half-hour,' said Luisa, not bothering to plead with the idiotic Giusy, not even registering the whine in her voice. She hung up.

What did she need half an hour for? The old woman was gone, at last, thank Christ she was gone, out through the door with Luisa having to restrain herself from shoving her through and slamming it behind her. And once the door was closed the place seemed to expand, to breathe again, as though the oxygen Maria Rosselli had seemed to suck from the air while she was in the room had rushed back.

How would the child survive? Luisa thought of the baby, struggling to get a fix with those weak newborn's eyes on the hard old face turned away from him, as his round pink cheeks turned red with frustration and the crying turned desperate.

'I'll get his bottle,' Maria Rosselli had said, leaving him to strain against his wrappings on the sofa. No sooner was she out of the room than Luisa had the child up and against her shoulder, the left shoulder, what she thought of as the empty side, but the child didn't seem to mind that there was no breast there. And then she was walking with him, jiggling, shushing, patting, feeling the hiccuping distress under her anxious hand. What on earth did she think she was doing? She knew nothing about babies. And then the phone rang, so when the old woman returned, bottle in hand, Luisa had the receiver jammed between one shoulder and her ear and the baby howling in the other.

The look Maria Rosselli gave her was rich in contempt, and lasted a full half-minute before she stiffly extended her arms for her grandson.

'Hold on,' Luisa had said into the receiver, keeping her grip on the child. 'What?'

'They've found Flavia Matteo,' Sandro had said into a temporary lull in the howling, and it was a long time since she'd heard him sound so flat and low. A long time. 'She's dead.' Luisa had felt Maria Rosselli hauling on the baby; his small face had looked up at Luisa in panic. 'I need to talk to the old woman.'

'It's my husband,' she'd said into Maria Rosselli's face, setting the receiver flat against her shoulder. 'It's you he wants to talk to.' She had experienced a fleeting spasm of triumph as the old woman relaxed her hold on the child and instead thrust the bottle into Luisa's hand in disgust.

'What?' Maria Rosselli had snapped into the phone.

Don't talk to my husband like that, Luisa had thought, turning away to disguise her sudden loathing. The bottle of milk had been ice-cold: the baby had made small, desperate, panting sounds at the smell of it. She'd gone into the kitchen, trying to unscrew the bottle as she went, well aware of Maria Rosselli wagging a finger at her. 'He'll take it cold,' the old woman had hissed after her.

The hell he will, Luisa had thought, turning her back resolutely. He has no mother. The hell he will.

She walked into the empty kitchen now, and it was as though the air still resonated with the child's crying. Luisa rubbed her eyes. He'd struggled and hiccuped and choked in his desperation to get at the teat, and Luisa had murmured to him, words she didn't know she knew. *All right, darling. Little one.* And at last he'd taken a great shuddering breath and settled to it.

It was how Sandro found her ten minutes after she'd hung up on Giusy and twenty minutes before she should herself be back in the shop, leaning against the kitchen counter and staring at nothing. She collected herself only partially when he spoke, looking around as if she'd just woken up.

'What a mess,' he said, setting his bag down angrily and sinking beside it at the table. 'What a fuck-up.'

Luisa blinked at that, because Sandro hardly ever swore. 'Preventable,' he said as if to himself, 'totally preventable. No one has to kill themselves.' He put his face in his hands. Gingerly Luisa set a hand on his shoulder. 'You want a coffee?' she said. He grunted.

'How'd the old lady take it?' he asked as she unscrewed the little aluminium machine, put water in and meticulously began to load the filter. Work would have to wait another half an hour. By then the sound of the baby's crying might have gone from her ears.

'You talked to her,' said Luisa. 'What do you think?'

She'd only seen the woman's reaction to what Sandro was telling her through the kitchen door, the baby's cries drowning out the tone of Maria Rosselli's voice as well as her words. But the expression on her face had been contemptuous, unsurprised, cold.

'She sounded like she couldn't care less,' said Sandro. Setting the coffee pot on the stove, Luisa turned back to her husband. 'Yes,' she said, eyeing him. 'But why does that matter? Suicide. It's not like you're looking for suspects.'

'No,' agreed Sandro glumly.

'And if it wasn't suicide – well, it's not as if you're a police officer any more, is it? Murder's their job; murder, manslaughter, all that.'

'The woman's found,' said Sandro. 'So in theory none of it's my business any more, not even her suicide.' He darted a glance at her. 'Our business.'

The coffee soon bubbled up. Luisa set a cup before him and leaned back against the counter, arms folded tight against her chest.

'So why,' she asked, 'does it still feel like it is?'

*

Not much of a place, thought Chiara, setting out her books tidily on the table in the sitting room, but it's ours. In theory anyway: it would take time, she supposed, before it felt like it. Trees outside the apartment window, old-lady furniture she supposed the last tenant had left behind, the kitchen dingy with age. She felt a sudden anxious tug of nostalgia for the bedroom she'd had since she was born and the smell of her mother's cooking. Homesick.

She'd tried her best. Not a wife, exactly – how could she be a wife, at her age? – but then a housewife wasn't what he wanted anyway. The nostalgia changed just fractionally, became tinged with panic. It was so quiet, that was all, in the leafy suburbs, a part of the city she'd never known well.

She'd get to know it, she'd use the local shops, she'd take the bus to the university and get on with her studies. . . and he'd come home from work and ask her how her day had been. She'd be able to talk to her friends again, the girls: would she be able to tell them what it was like, this kind of – love? She imagined telling certain people, there were those who'd understand. Just – not the girls she'd known since she was in nursery. And not her parents.

'He travels a lot.' She practised saying this to her mother and could picture her face: *Doesn't this man value my daughter that he should leave her alone, for days on end?* Mortified, wounded, angry, just as Chiara had last seen her.

'It means I can come home and see you and Babbo,' she would then be able to explain peaceably. 'While he's gone.' Meaning it would all settle down and they'd have the same kind of relationship most offspring have with their parents after they've moved out. But it didn't have quite the right ring to it; it sounded, as she rehearsed it in her head, as though she was saying she'd have to sneak away behind his back if she ever wanted to see her parents again. And that wasn't what she meant, was it?

She didn't know. She didn't know how to explain what this was. Only that from the moment he'd touched her on the shoulder as she'd emerged from the Frazione meeting in the heat of early summer and made her turn to him, his long cool fingers on the exposed skin, and she'd looked into his face, Chiara had been his. His to do with as he wanted.

How did you know, feel, instinctively, that someone understood you, understood those things you had always secretly wanted and imagined would come to you when you were grown-up? Murmuring to herself while she waited in the heat for him to get home, rehearsing how she might try to explain it to her mother, Chiara could only say it was nothing like that little, uncomfortable thing you felt in school when a boy first showed interest. There'd been no small talk, no going for a *gelato* or to the swimming pool. He'd given her books, he'd said, tilting his head in that way he did, because he knew she had the intelligence for them. His touch was light but strong. We wait, he'd said, his hands on her hips as she yearned up towards him, as if he knew what was in her heart. For that, we wait. For sex.

Sometimes, when he was gone, the thought would come into her head that she hardly knew him at all.

*

'The damned police!' said Calzaghe belligerently. 'After a season like this. That's all we need.'

He was glaring at Vesna as if it were her fault.

'I just found her,' said the chambermaid, setting her jaw mutinously. 'I didn't ask her to top herself, did I?'

She felt cold, although the sun was high now and shone straight on to the verandah where they sat. In the swing seat Calzaghe was sweating profusely into his vest: Vesna found herself wondering if this was his stress response, like hers was to shiver, or if he was just a fat pig.

Parked out on the street for all to see was a police car that had contained one male and one female officer – Vesna recognized them both from around town, where there was little for them to do aside from reprimanding beach vendors and moving on foreign students sleeping under the promenade and in the park. They had looked bored and disdainful as they took her statement and moved in and out of the hotel. Was suicide really so far beneath them? Maybe they cultivated that look, and underneath they were feeling something else: it was a characteristic Vesna had noticed among all officials everywhere, among soldiers and military police and those who sat behind counters and passed judgement on who might stay and who might go. The male police officer had, it was true, looked a little pale, but the woman maintained an expression of disgust, talking into her lapel microphone to summon someone else.

Behind the police car was a small van, modified with a boxy extension on the back and containing forensics equipment. As far as she could see it was unmarked but Vesna imagined that every nosy old woman who passed – in turn looking from one vehicle to the other then across to the open front door of the Stella Maris and the two of them sitting fidgeting on the verandah, she and Calzaghe, quite the odd couple – every one of them would put two and two together, adding the sum to an earlier sighting of the ambulance and coming up with an approximation of the grisly truth.

'That's all we need,' repeated Calzaghe at her side, staring off into the laurels. 'This is the end.' No one ever sat on this verandah, with no view of the sea, only the unkempt garden. It came to Vesna that he was right. The place was doomed: the two guests in the dining room this morning had already paid up and fled, and although a third had gone early to the beach and was therefore oblivious, they'd be gone by the evening, she'd bet on it.

Overpriced and shabby and obscure, the Stella Maris had been dying on its feet long before the police turned up. Why had the woman come here? Because it didn't matter to her where she died?

The ambulance had not taken her away. There'd been nothing the paramedics could do, and so they had packed up, left her for the forensics team and then the coroner's office. She was still up there.

They'd phoned someone in Florence. The male police officer had paced the gravel talking gently – or as gently as he was capable of doing, Vesna could tell it was an effort. That must be a hard job. You'd be hoping you were wrong: *Oh, right, your wife's sitting beside you, I'm so sorry*. But if you'd reached the right person, what were the right words?

'I'm so sorry,' she'd heard the policeman repeat through gritted teeth, over and over. 'You're going to have to come and identify her.'

Chapter Ten

WELL, THIS WAS A turn-up.

Standing at the centre of the crowded Piazza Signoria where he had just watched Luisa head away from him towards Frollini and work, Sandro thanked the man and hung up. It was hardly appropriate to feel anything like exhilarated, but nonetheless he did feel a sense of challenge, the knowledge that something was required of him, and that was better than the way he'd been feeling before.

His *telefonino* had rung in his pocket while he was kissing her off, a hand on each arm, his handsome, frowning wife. Looking into her face and seeing – from the way she would not quite look back – that something was worrying her that she wasn't saying, at least not yet. She'd pulled away from him at the sound of the phone, raised a hand and gone, away from him through the busy square. It was a beautiful, warm September midday, and on the terraces of the Signoria's bars lunch and *aperitivi* were being ordered and enjoyed. Sandro could see at least four pretty women from where he stood, all with men, all at least twenty years younger than him. That was all right: some days, age didn't seem to matter.

'Hello?'

It was Niccolò Rosselli: Sandro made a mental note to put the man's name in his phone's address book. Why? This was unfinished, that was why.

'I need someone to go with me,' Rosselli had said without preamble. 'I can't do it on my own. I – my mother doesn't even think I'm safe to drive.'

Right. The situation clarified abruptly. If he had to choose between Maria Rosselli and a washed-up private detective on such a journey – the hour and a half on the atrocious Pisa superstrada to identify the body of his wife at a seaside morgue – well, even if Maria Rosselli were his own mother, he, Sandro, would go for the man. So she'd be lobbying him to take her, and Niccolò Rosselli, possibly for the first time in his life, was standing up to her.

What about the *avvocato*? Rosselli's oldest friend, from university? Sandro thought about Carlo Bastone in his dusty office, podgy, distracted by book-learning and fine principles, disorganized. Would he come good in a crisis? It occurred to him that the Frazione had to be more vulnerable than he'd thought, if the only man Niccolò Rosselli wanted at his side in this situation was Sandro himself.

There was something heart-rending about Rosselli's extreme agitation. About his transparent not knowing – not knowing what he should be doing or feeling or saying, a man who had relied on books and intelligence and the rational, and had never before come up against the unavoidably real. 'Do you think it'll be all right?' Rosselli had asked. 'I mean, they won't wonder why I'm bringing you?'

'You can say I'm a friend, if you like,' Sandro had said. 'But actually it's none of their business; you can bring whomever you wish in this kind of situation.'

A friend. Was that what Rosselli wanted him to be? For the first time Sandro's gut stirred with the realization of what he'd probably have to do. He wouldn't just be a chauffeur, he'd have to go in there, see the body of the woman on the mortuary slab, smell the chemicals, drive home with the sharp stink still in his nostrils.

And wonder why. Why a woman with a newborn child and a loving man had killed herself.

'I'll be there in twenty minutes,' he said. 'We can go in my car.'

Nonetheless, when the mobile almost immediately rang again he could feel it, the pulse of adrenaline that came from being needed. It was Pietro this time, and Sandro sobered instantly, guilt lowering his voice.

'Sorry, old friend,' he said. 'I should have called you.' Only Pietro hadn't called him either, had he? Not in months – until today. 'It's been – there's been a lot on.'

'I heard,' said Pietro, and Sandro detected the coolness in his ex-partner's voice. 'You're involved in this Rosselli business.'

Sandro wondered how much he'd know: most of it, was his guess. Something like that happens, the jungle networks light up with it. A politician's wife commits suicide. . .

'Yes,' he said hesitantly, and suddenly the most important thing seemed to be to get that chill out of the atmosphere between them. 'But what about you? Luisa told me. . . Or at least told me what Gloria had told her. Chiara's moved out?'

There was a silence and then Pietro exhaled, a sound of frustration and unhappiness and anger mixed.

'She has,' he said. Another silence, then it burst from him. 'Is this the modern world? I thought we'd have another five, six, maybe ten years. And she doesn't even introduce us to the guy?'

'I'm sorry,' said Sandro, feeling helpless. What would he do if it were him? His daughter? 'Have you asked around? Asked her friends about him?'

The next silence was different, thoughtful. 'You think – no,' said Pietro, with growing determination. 'What, snoop on my own daughter? Ask those kids I've known since they were in nappies for help with my own child?'

Stubborn, thought Sandro, taking Pietro's point all the same. 'She been in touch?'

'Not with me,' said Pietro shortly. 'I haven't talked to Gloria since I left this morning. We've been busy – like you.' Rebuked, Sandro stayed quiet. 'So. You were looking for Rosselli's wife, were you?' his friend went on. 'And now you've found her.'

'He wants me to go with him to Viareggio this afternoon,' said Sandro, aware of wanting pathetically to sound to his ex-partner like he still had something useful to do with his life, even if he wasn't a policeman any more. 'To ID the body.' He found himself checking his watch. 'In a half-hour or so. I said I'd pick him up.'

'Don't envy you that,' said Pietro, and Sandro didn't know if it was his imagination but was there something wary in his friend's voice? Some combination of probing and evasion, as if they didn't know or trust each other enough to ask a straight question? 'He's an odd one, isn't he? Does he even know you?'

'I was there when he got the call,' said Sandro. 'You know how it works. They fix on you, if you're there when the news comes in. It binds you. Like that imprinting thing.' It was true, though it had only come to him as he said it. Pietro's silence seemed warmer now: Sandro hesitated, then took the risk. 'Look, how about a drink when I get back? Or even something to eat? Or – or we could just sit in the patrol car and talk.'

Sandro could hear himself, like a discarded lover, begging for a chance. He ground his teeth, turning on the spot in the big sunny piazza, taking in the happy crowds around him. Couples arm-in-arm under the great green statue of Neptune in its fountain, bathed in the clear blue September light, a tall man sauntering through them with not a care in the world. There was something familiar about the man, but it took a while for Pietro to recognize him: journalist? No, soldier. Out of uniform.

'Maybe,' said Pietro, sounding distant. 'I don't know. I've got – things to do.'

'I'll call you,' Sandro said, trying to sound concerned but not panicked. 'Look, it'll be a phase, it'll be a brief rebellion, she'll come back. You'll have your five years. You're good parents. The best.'

'I've got to go,' said Pietro abruptly. 'Good luck this afternoon.' And then he hung up.

It wasn't on his way to where the car was parked but Sandro made the detour, past Frollini's big plate-glass windows, full of padded jackets and fur-lined boots when it was twenty-five degrees in the shade and winter seemed a long way off: the craziness of fashion. The mysterious side of his Luisa: that she took it seriously, even now she was long-since an adult woman and sensible with it. He remembered coming here to call in on her when they were newlyweds, and how she would look so delighted by the sight of him in his uniform. Sandro slowed to look in and there she was. She still stood like a young woman, with her shoulders back, proud even when serving, and he saw her bend to get something out of a cabinet and then straighten gracefully. Setting down some knitwear on the glass counter, her hand went quickly to adjust her own sweater.

As he turned to go, she was alerted by the movement, raised her head and looked at him. They didn't need to wave, or smile: he moved off, and she turned back to her customer.

Ask her later, he told himself.

*

'I don't understand,' Guili said to Sandro when he called as she sat there on the bench alone in the Piazza Tasso. She was watching a tiny child wedged into a swing and being pushed by a woman who was not its mother, a Filipina. Did nannies bring children down here? Would Rosselli get a nanny for his now-motherless child? 'I thought it was all over.'

He sighed. She'd understood from the sound quality that he was in the car, his voice muffled from holding the phone under his chin.

'It is and it isn't,' he said. He was going with Rosselli to identify the body apparently. I knew that, had been Giuli's first thought on hearing him say it. 'I see,' she said. 'Is he with you now?'

'I'm going over to get him,' said Sandro, and she heard him shift the phone. 'Did you talk to them about her? At the Centre? I don't know what to say to him.'

'No,' said Giuli, thinking of Sandro and Niccolò Rosselli squeezed together into his scruffy little car, the fact of Flavia's death hanging between them. Thinking too of Clelia Schmidt. 'I did talk to one of the midwives earlier.' But then she hesitated: what had she learned, exactly, from that conversation? 'Flavia wasn't a happy bunny, by the sound of things – but the woman was pretty shocked all the same to hear she'd disappeared. Clelia, the midwife, I mean. And now I've got to go back in and tell them she's dead.'

'Ah.' Sandro's voice changed and she could tell he was acknowledging that burden: they'd feel guilty, that little team of overworked medical professionals. We should all feel guilty, thought Giuli out of nowhere, when someone kills themself. 'She was depressed?' he asked.

'I don't know,' said Giuli slowly, turning her conversation with the midwife over in her head. Something had been missing, something had been withheld. 'Not exactly. Maybe the professional discretion thing. I don't know, I just had the impression I didn't get the whole story.' She sighed. 'I guess it'll come out at the inquest. I guess they'll talk to people -- about all that.'

'I suppose so,' said Sandro, and thinking of the inquest they both fell silent. Then he spoke again. 'Still,' he said. 'I don't know that you don't have a better chance than a coroner's investigator of finding out – well, the whole story. More of the whole story.'

'Right,' said Giuli warily, watching the Filipina nanny haul the child out of the swing and clasp it against her with rough tenderness. Was that enough, paid-for love? Having had considerably less herself and survived, she thought, maybe it was.

Sandro cleared his throat. 'And finding it out quicker.'

'Do you think there's more to this?' she asked.

'Don't jump the gun,' he said. 'We're not being paid. Call it *pro bono* for the moment, but if you care about that Frazione of yours – it's as well to know the extent of the damage. To learn the whole story.'

'Not always,' she said before she could think. 'It must be worst of all for him, don't you think? For Rosselli. Because if the midwives are feeling guilty – if we're feeling guilty, for God's sake – then how must he be feeling? Living with her, sleeping next to her...'

'All right,' said Sandro, interrupting. 'All right. You leave him to me.' She heard a change in the background sounds and understood that he had come to a stop. 'I've got to go.'

Hanging up, Giuli sat there a long moment, watching the empty swing move with the memory of the child's weight in the pale smoky air. The trees were still green, the big mediaeval wall glowed pinkish-grey. She looked at the handsome building that housed the Centre and thought, do I have to? And as if in answer, the tinted-glass door swung outwards and there was Clelia Schmidt in sensible shoes, broad in the hip, fair and frowning, handbag clasped against her chest. Giuli got to her feet and Clelia stopped. There was something in the midwife's face that said she knew what was coming.

Giuli waited until they were both sitting down side by side on the bench.

'I was going for my lunch,' said Clelia vaguely. 'But I'm not hungry today.' Giuli took her hand.

'She's dead, isn't she?' said Clelia, and let out a long, ragged sigh. 'Poor girl.'

Girl. 'Forty-two,' said Giuli. 'Same age as me.' Clelia's eyes widened and Giuli could tell she'd thought Giuli older. 'And me,' she said wonderingly.

'Some of us age quicker,' said Giuli wryly. They both looked down at their hands entwined.

'It's so hard to tell, with educated, intelligent women,' said Clelia, as if picking up a conversation halfway through. 'They feel the need to hide more. They require more privacy. They can see what the questionnaire is trying to discover, and they can evade answering.' She faltered. 'But there was absolutely no sign in her answers to the questionnaire or to my questions that Flavia was depressed. How was I to know?'

'But you now believe she was?'

Clelia frowned, looking up directly into Giuli's face with her blue eyes. Giuli felt as though she herself – her thinning skin, her dry lips – were being examined by those clear eyes. 'I believe – perhaps with hindsight – I do believe she was very unhappy,' she said finally. 'Is that the same thing? Don't we have a right to our unhappiness without some professional diagnosing it as depression?'

'I see,' said Giuli, although she wasn't sure she did. 'Unhappiness – well.' She thought hard. 'I think of that as – as something with a specific reason, a clear source, and as a temporary state. If you're lucky.'

'Exactly,' said Clelia, suddenly energized. 'I think that was what worried me. That if Flavia's feelings were diagnosed as depression she might think it would last for ever—' And her voice broke off. Her face fell. 'Or that was my excuse. That was why I didn't push it with her. I was wrong.'

A specific reason. Giuli remembered something. *A clear source.* 'You said – back there – you said you weren't the only professional she was seeing. There was another midwife?'

Clelia didn't speak for a moment, and when she did, it was hesitantly. 'Well, I didn't deliver her,' she said, and Giuli heard caution in her voice. 'The child was born in an ambulance, on the way to the hospital. Flavia stayed at home too long, sometimes women do – the child was delivered by the paramedics, in the ambulance bay as a matter of fact.' She breathed out. 'But it was all fine. Textbook delivery. Flavia did very well—' And again she broke off.

An old man shuffled towards them on the gravel of the little square, eyed the space on the end of the bench, looked at the two women and shuffled on past. Thinking better of it.

Giuli waited till he was out of earshot: this seemed suddenly the most delicate ground imaginable. Although the woman was dead, Giuli didn't want to invade her privacy more than she could help. She frowned. 'So the other caregivers – you didn't mean the paramedics?' Clelia said nothing, not daring even to look Giuli in the eye. 'Was she – was she seeing anyone else at the Centre? In the other clinics?'

Birth control. Addictions. Sexually transmitted diseases. Jesus God, thought Giuli, catching her breath, thinking of Niccolò Rosselli. Then thinking of the Frazione.

'I – I don't know,' said Clelia, desperately casting around. 'I can't say.'

'The coroner's officials will come and ask you,' said Giuli, taking Clelia's hands again. 'You know that, don't you? And you'll have to answer them.'

'Will I?' She looked terrified.

'Well,' Giuli said, 'people have been known to lie to officials of the state. Even in Germany. But I don't know how advisable it is.'

Clelia pulled her hands away and buried her face in them. 'I want to help her,' said Giuli urgently, not realizing until she said it that it was true. 'She's dead, I know that, but – if there's anything I can do to help Flavia, now, then I want to do it. Do you understand that? The coroner's office has no interest in that. In helping her.'

'They just want the truth,' said Clelia Schmidt dully. 'Poor Flavia. Poor Flavia.'

The truth, thought Giuli with sudden dislike of the whole concept. What good did the truth ever do? She saw the old man on the next bench, fishing for something in a battered shopping bag. A newspaper, a plastic tub, a fork. She saw his anxious old face soften into an expression of contentment as he peeled the lid from the tub and began to eat, eyes half closed in the soft late-summer air.

'You need food,' she said suddenly. 'We both do.' She nodded across the square to the small old-fashioned restaurant tucked into the corner. 'Let's go and sit down and eat, and you don't need to talk if you don't want to.'

The two women stood and made their way through the swings to the far side of the square. The old man paused in his enjoyment of whatever the plastic tub contained, and watched them go.

*

At least, thought Luisa as she stood patiently, hands behind her back and waited for her customer to emerge from the changing cubicle, she had not thought about her check-up and her damned breast for a good five hours. On the negative side, she was sure the boiling rage she felt at the memory of almost everything about Maria Rosselli could not be good for her. It was a bit like having the menopause back: poor Sandro, those had been bad years. It was a surprise to her sometimes, even now, that he had stuck it out.

Of course, the years of declining communication preceding it following the death of their only child hadn't helped. Perhaps it was because they were still of the generation that stuck it out, that didn't ask for happiness but only stability. She had never thought of leaving Sandro: she had thought of death more often than that. She was pretty sure he'd never thought of leaving her, either.

'All right, madam?' she asked brightly into the curtain. 'Another size?'

The woman was one who was in denial about her measurements: common enough. This one, middle-aged and too thin, thought she was two sizes bigger than she was in reality: most often it was the other way. The answer through the curtain was muffled and non-committal.

Luisa smiled, not thinking of the customer but of Sandro, but when the woman emerged she caught the smile and tentatively returned it.

'Oh, madam,' said Luisa in involuntary despair at the gaping neckline that revealed the bones of the woman's chest, and the customer's face fell. 'Please,' said Luisa, reaching behind her for the smaller size she'd kept ready. 'For me, try this one.'

How old was this woman? Luisa had known her ten years, off and on, a rare but regular customer, not one to treat herself. She came in when her husband gave her some cash and told her to make more of an effort; Luisa tried to picture the husband, and failed. The woman was probably only forty-five but looked older: almost anorexic. It didn't seem right to Luisa that women of forty-five could still have the insecurities and eating disorders of an adolescent. They should feel strong. When Luisa had been a child those women of middle years had held all the power; even she, Luisa, with her silent marriage and lost child, had not been as cowed as this woman seemed. What had changed?

Mutely, the woman took the dress and retreated back into the cubicle. Luisa closed her eyes briefly at the memory of the visible ribs where a cleavage should have been.

She'd looked on the internet during a lull. They had a computer in the shop now – had done for five years – with a program showing the stock levels, and a website for customers to look at catwalk shows and the like. Luisa still marvelled at the way you could type in something like, say, 'breast reconstruction' and get pages and pages. Pictures and everything, detailed explanations of what they called the gold-standard procedure, which involved moving skin from your back and took months. She marvelled at the women they photographed, brave enough to stand there in front of the camera for the before and after, some of them ageing like her, their flesh softened and pale. Some of them young, *young*, and even lovely. Truth to tell, made lovely again, in some pictures, brave enough, too, to get themselves rebuilt without fear of the cancer coming back, should they have the boldness to allow a new breast to appear where the disease had been.

That fear was irrational, she knew. But Luisa had to admit, it was one of the things that frightened her.

The curtain opened again. 'There,' she said with satisfaction. 'Didn't I tell you?'

The woman was still too thin, but the smaller size made the most of her. Luisa appraised her robustly, the woman's eyes never leaving her face to actually confirm what Luisa was saying by looking in the mirror, timidly trustful. Perhaps she has no mother to tell her, thought Luisa. Doesn't her husband say anything nice to her?

Not that her own did so much, but there was a way he looked at her that was enough.

I'll get the reconstruction, thought Luisa suddenly, out of nowhere.

'Your husband will be very pleased, I should think,' she said, but when she turned to look at the woman she didn't seem to be listening, was in that reverie that fell over insecure customers at the moment of purchase.

'Poor cow,' said Giusy ruminatively as the door swung shut behind her. 'There is such a thing as too skinny. It just looks unhappy, don't you think? At a certain age. Or ill.'

Luisa, ready to disagree on principle with Giusy, said, surprising herself, 'Um, hmm, well. Yes.'

'You're getting it done then,' Giusy went on cheerfully. 'The breast thing? Reconstruction?'

Luisa stared. Could it be that this late in her self-absorbed life, Giusy had taken to empathizing to the point of being able to read her colleague's thoughts? Giusy licked a finger and turned a page of her magazine. 'I saw you looking it up on the computer. I've heard it's a piece of cake these days. Our surgeons, they're the best. Good on you, I say. Life's too short to shrivel up and hide.' They were both still turned in the direction of the door through which the skinny woman had left.

'Yes,' said Luisa.

She thought she might not tell Sandro straight away.

Chapter Eleven

THE EXIT FROM THE city seemed interminable. Who were all these people, changing lanes at random on the superstrada? The superstrada itself was a joke, too; thirty years on, the Firenze-Pisa-Livorno road still seemed only half built and was potholed to extinction: Sandro felt himself boil up with useless anger. Crawling around temporary barriers and traffic cones through the Isolotto, still crawling on the overpass through Scandicci, the multiplex cinemas and shopping centres crowding in. The grey prison to the left, built like a concrete stadium. Sandro hated Scandicci.

At his side in the battered little car Niccolò Rosselli blinked through his glasses at the road leading away to the west. If you looked far enough ahead, the castles and cypresses came into focus, San Miniato and Vinci, and then umbrella pines and forested hillside. Perhaps that was the trick – and sure enough, as Sandro refocused his gaze, the traffic around him seemed to ease and shift and they were moving again.

He'd found Rosselli more or less where he'd left him, standing in the shuttered gloom of his sitting room, as bewildered as though he'd forgotten who either of them were. It seemed to Sandro that the room was dimmer, as if dust had already settled over it all, dulling the photographs on the pinboard. Had his woman been all that had been animating Rosselli? It fitted with Sandro's ideas on women, though he was uncomfortably aware that they were old-fashioned views, and Rosselli and Flavia would no doubt have dismissed them.

Although Rosselli had responded to Sandro's name so far as to buzz him up, he'd stood silent once his visitor arrived. Waiting for the man to say something, Sandro had stepped around him and rested a hand on the chair at the desk. Not quite casually, he had looked again at the photographs pinned behind the computer's silent screen, the pale, sensual face of the woman being the one that stood out.

You never could make sense of partnerships, was the thought that had come to him. A beautiful woman might not need to be told she was beautiful, or she might crave it. A plain woman might be fearless.

He didn't wonder much about men; Sandro thought of them as simple creatures, motivated by sex – or call it love – or money, or power. Niccolò Rosselli didn't seem to fit the rule, though.

A meeting of minds: Sandro supposed that was – had been – the key to Rosselli's relationship; intellectual companionship, was that it? He found himself covertly considering his own marriage: his and Luisa's minds met these days, more than they used to, knowing what each other was thinking, but that was a matter of growing into each other, like plants twining together until their separate beginnings are no longer visible. It was more a physical thing, in a way he could not explain, than an intellectual one: a matter of simple proximity, of feeling one's way in the dark. Even in his short exposure to the partnership of Rosselli and Flavia Matteo, this was not how their relationship seemed to him. There were distances in this apartment, there were shadows.

There was a photograph of Rosselli, frowning intently behind his glasses, under an umbrella pine on a beach with hills behind, looking like he didn't belong. There was a photograph of Flavia Matteo with a woman with short dyed blonde hair, both smiling broadly. Another of Flavia Matteo in a woollen hat pulled down hard and unflatteringly over the red hair, under a *loggia* he vaguely recognized from the city, a red slice of the Duomo's cupola visible behind.

The baby was still absent, Sandro had registered. It had come to him then with painful suddenness that if he and Luisa had had a child that lived, if Luisa had died and left him with a newborn, he would have held on to it every minute he could. And as Sandro had the thought, Rosselli had suddenly taken off his glasses and polished them as he spoke, head bowed. 'I found it,' he'd said.

'You found it?' Sandro hadn't known what he was talking about.

'I found the mobile phone. Our mobile phone.' He'd spoken flatly.

'Right,' Sandro had said slowly. Rosselli had made no move to produce it. Would the police want to look at the phone? Was it anything to do with Sandro, any more?

'Could I see it?'

He'd not been able to help himself, had he? This isn't your business, you aren't being paid, the woman's been found, he told himself. But he'd had to see. And like Luisa said, if it's not our business, why does it still feel like it is?

Rosselli had replaced his glasses and scrutinized Sandro as though he were a new species. Then he had crossed to the desk, pulled open a drawer and taken out the phone. Sandro had been able to tell by the way he handled it that he had no interest in the thing, that it was not, as it was to almost everyone else these days, a talisman and lifeline and fetish. He had handed it to Sandro.

It had been an ancient model, but in good condition; the first thing that had been surprising about it was that it was fully charged. Even if it had been kept turned off, this had seemed improbable for an elderly mobile phone that was almost never used. Sandro had wiped a thumb across the small screen reflexively. Giuli would be the one to look at it and find out its secrets: all Sandro knew how to do was to scroll quickly through the phone book: doctor, lawyer, dentist, mother-in-law, a few miscellaneous names, all women. *Wanda, Maria, Anna K.* Flavia did use it, then, to keep in touch? So she had friends, old schoolmates, perhaps the teachers she worked with at the school?

Sandro had been halfway through thinking he'd send Giuli to the school, to the Agnesi to find out who might have been her friends, when he'd had to tell himself again, None of your business – not any more. But he'd kept the phone in his hand, had felt it warming from his touch in secret communication.

'We'd better go,' Niccolò Rosselli had said, half turning towards the door. 'Yes, right,' Sandro had said, and without thinking, or at least without thinking much, without the appearance of thinking, had slipped the mobile phone easily into his pocket.

As they'd wound their way through the clogged backstreets of Santo Spirito, Rosselli had gazed out of the window with a kind of fervour, a kind of longing, or so it had seemed to Sandro as he'd snatched a sidelong glance. They had passed a greengrocer's Sandro knew to be the best in the city, a shabby little shop, an old woman picking through a tray of figs on the pavement. A huddle of streetsleepers of all varieties, with the knotted and dreadlocked hair of the young revolutionaries, with the bound and battered feet of the seasoned traveller, with the trolleyful of bizarrely assorted possessions of the mentally ill – all queuing outside the side door of a church. Christian charity still existed, then.

'How long have you been going?' he'd said to Rosselli. 'The Frazione?' He'd asked more by way of distracting them both than with any clear intention of gathering information, but as he'd spoken it had struck him again as weird to find himself in close proximity to this man, this hero. All those followers, all those acolytes, but no one he could trust to come with him to identify his wife's body.

It had to be her, didn't it? It did. Rosselli had seemed to be sure, which Sandro supposed was a blessing. Not a man given to denial or self-delusion.

With reluctance Rosselli had shifted his gaze to Sandro from his contemplation of a pair on the corner of the Via dei Serragli and the Via Mazzetta, outside a bar, a man in a hat and shabby camel coat giving some folded notes to a drunk: more charity.

'They're good people, round here,' he'd said. 'It functions. We can function, at the level of the street, of the village, we can function informally, we can be generous, we can care for each other.'

'We?'

The ghost of a smile had appeared on Rosselli's face, mirrored on Sandro's. 'That's the point, isn't it?' Rosselli had said. 'The people of Santo Spirito? Of San Frediano, the Oltrarno? We Florentines, we Italians, we members of the human race. You have to work outwards, from your own doorstep.'

Like when children wrote an address. Third floor, Via dei Macci, Florence, Italy, Europe, the World, the Universe.

'It's the same everywhere, isn't it?' Sandro had said. 'Charity begins at home. Close to home, anyway.'

Rosselli had shifted his position, turned towards Sandro, and it was as if a spark had kindled inside him.

'Yes, but you have to work outwards,' he'd said, and his voice had been different, stronger, more certain. 'We start with the roads. We start with people's homes and livelihoods and the environment in which they bring up their children, we stand up against those who want to push the ordinary people aside in the pursuit of big business.' He'd taken a breath, a practised speaker. 'First home, then the *quartiere*, then the *comune*.'

'Then parliament?' Sandro had understood from the web-page that the Frazione's primary intention was to have Rosselli in the *comune*, the city hall. To have him appointed as an *assessore* – a councillor – with responsibility for roads. It seemed a solid, unglamorous, honourable ambition, but in this country was anything straightforward? He'd thought then of their prime minister's broad, jovial smile. No.

Rosselli had frowned. 'I don't look that far ahead,' he'd said, and had shifted again, turned his head back to look out of the window. 'In answer to your question, the Frazione was formed – officially formed – two years ago. Carlo Bastone and I decided it was necessary.' Sandro had stolen a look at the man's quarter-profile, the jaw set. 'Of course, like all things, it becomes more complicated the bigger it gets. More people, more opinions, more debate. It's healthy. It's democracy.'

'Right,' Sandro had said, registering the grim note in the other man's voice. 'Did you think it would get so – big?'

'No,' Rosselli had said shortly, and Sandro had understood that the man had no personal ambition at all. Which left him vulnerable, in Sandro's book, because all that went with it, pride and greed and worldly understanding – well, Sandro had thought uncomfortably, they weren't pretty, but they were essential, weren't they? He'd fallen silent then and Rosselli had volunteered no more, staring out of the window instead.

It took an hour and a half to get to the floral roundabouts that marked the outskirts of Viareggio: all the way Sandro had held his peace, not wanting to intrude on the other man's silence, and all the way the questions built in his mind. If he were investigating this. . . There was something curious, though, about Rosselli's silence; Sandro felt it not as an absence but as something that grew and multiplied, containing possibilities. He had the feeling that the man wanted to say something, but could not. Wanted to ask, but could not: strange for a man with a reputation for oratory, for persuasive speaking, for articulacy. Yet perhaps not strange at all. It was one thing to talk about world peace and roadbuilding and health-care facilities; quite another to talk about one's grief with a stranger.

Strangers, though, were sometimes the only ones who'd do. As they negotiated the first roundabout, Rosselli asked the question Sandro had been asking himself.

'Why here?' he said with painful bafflement, looking at the first of the prim, stuccoed villas, the Art Deco apartment blocks, the shady avenues. 'Why did she come here?'

Sandro cleared his throat. Interesting that the man hadn't asked, *Why?*, full stop. 'You don't have any idea?' he asked cautiously. 'Not a place where you came on holiday?' He thought of the odd beach photograph he'd seen on the pinboard: not Viareggio. There had been a rocky hillside in the backdrop, and Viareggio was as flat as a pancake.

Niccolò Rosselli shook his head. 'My mother had a place on Elba,' he said. 'We went there, if we went anywhere. But—' He frowned. 'We're not really holiday people.' And realizing he'd used the present tense, let out the awful sound of one unused to emotion, a kind of muted groan. 'Weren't.'

'Nor us,' said Sandro hastily, because until this year it had been true. Not wanting, suddenly, to have anything in common with Rosselli, he willed the memory of Castiglioncello into his mind. Life is to be enjoyed, he told himself, surprised to find he believed it.

'Anyway, my mother decided to sell it this summer,' Rosselli said with weary bafflement. 'She said we'd need the money for the child.' He passed a hand over his forehead. 'I told her we had enough money.'

Do you? Sandro wondered. And if so, where does it come from?

'I mean,' elaborated Rosselli, who seemed, even without turning his head to look at Sandro, to have understood what he was thinking, 'I mean, we don't need much. As I said. We live – we lived a quiet life.'

Sandro made a non-committal sound, but it occurred to him that a politician with that kind of following could not hope to lead a quiet life for much longer. 'But no connections with this place?' he asked.

'I don't think so,' Rosselli said. They had come to a halt at some lights – at the end of the road the sea was just visible, a narrow band of deep blue – and at the uncertainty in Rosselli's voice, Sandro turned to look at him.

'I mean,' said the man, and hunched over as if he were in pain, 'I didn't know everything about Flavia, that is clear. I just – I suppose I just assumed I did, because we have been together practically since we were children. But her family were poor, and she was orphaned young. They had no connection with Viareggio.'

'Did she – did you do everything together?' Sandro put the car into gear and moved off. The street opened up to the seafront abruptly, the windscreen filled with blue and light, the glitter of the waves, the stripes of the beach umbrellas on the combed sand below. Red and white, blue and white, green and white. What a place to come to die. Happy memories, or no memories at all?

Damn, he thought. What are we doing here? The police mortuary was nowhere near the sea. Running on autopilot, he had arrived at a seaside town and instinctively headed for the water. You're not on bloody holiday, are you? he chided himself. 'Sorry,' he said. 'We've got to turn around.'

Rosselli just looked at him in vague distress. 'I don't really know what you mean,' he said, and his voice firmed into indignation. 'Flavia was an independent, intelligent woman. She had her work. We weren't married, you know, although my mother didn't like that.'

Hauling on the wheel, Sandro gritted his teeth and said, 'Well, yes, I suppose that's what I meant. Social life, too? Independent in that way?'

'We weren't social creatures,' said Rosselli. 'Dinners and parties, you mean?' He shook his head, took off his glasses again and polished them.

Sandro wondered if there was meaning in this gesture. A response to high emotion? A desire not to see, or not to be seen? Sandro himself had never worn glasses; even now he didn't need them, not even for reading. He couldn't feel much satisfaction at the thought. What must it be like to be as shortsighted as Rosselli? To know that a thousand years ago, maybe two, he'd have been helpless, easy prey, an evolutionary dead end? Yet shortsighted genes persisted. As Sandro turned into the car park of the police morgue, this was the last-ditch digression he conjured up for himself, wondering whether there was indeed a connection, as in popular myth, between shortsightedness and intelligence.

Makes me dumb, was his dismal conclusion, with my twenty-twenty vision.

They pulled into the cramped parking area behind a series of low, ugly buildings with blinds at their windows, and stopped.

'This is it,' said Sandro, and for a moment they sat without moving, staring through the grimy windscreen, neither of them wanting to climb out and confront the end of Niccolò Rosselli's private life.

Chapter Twelve

BADIANI'S WAS FULL TO bursting, another warm September dusk bringing in the customers. Back from their holidays and wanting to prolong the summer just another day or two, they were pressed four, five deep against the long glass cabinet filled with bright-coloured mounds of ice cream. Mango, fig, raspberry, chocolate – thirty flavours or more, along with the celebrated vanilla custard and cream Buontalenti for which the place was famous. Giuli hovered in the doorway, waiting for Enzo.

She hadn't had the heart to say she wasn't really in an ice-cream mood. One of the big advantages of a job on the roaring Via dei Mille, according to Enzo, was its proximity to Badiani and what he held to be the best ice cream in the city. There was something of the big kid about Enzo, only child of doting, hardworking parents, but it was also a serious matter, his ice-cream fetish.

'I'll bring a kilo or two back on Saturday,' he'd said eagerly on the phone 'For dessert. For Luisa and Sandro.'

She'd hardly dared say that Luisa couldn't eat ice cream, it hurt her teeth. 'And maybe some of their little cakes,' she'd ventured, but her heart wasn't in it, not after her lunch with Clelia Schmidt.

A restrained sort of scuffle broke out at the glass cabinet, following a bit of flagrant queue-jumping. An elderly woman – dressed, bizarrely, in a fur coat – was the culprit, and Giuli watched as she effortlessly defeated her rival for the attention of the unflappable *gelataia*, and marched away with a towering concoction – marrons glacés, chocolate and Buontalenti in a big sugar cone. Some people, she reflected, were born to win.

The woman strutted like a small, fur-clad bird, out on to the pavement and the roaring *viale* in the twilight, tucking in to her ice cream with unashamed pleasure. She'll live for ever, that one, thought Giuli, and her thoughts returned, as they had all day, to poor dead Flavia Matteo.

It wasn't even as if Giuli had known Flavia: she'd seen her around in the ten years or so she'd been a Santo Spirito resident herself, she'd exchanged a greeting with her on occasion. She was what you'd call distinctive, even if – and this gave Giuli pause, she hadn't formulated the thought before – there was something about Flavia that was the opposite of the old woman smacking her lips in her fur coat and not caring who saw her. Flavia Matteo had not wanted to be distinctive, had not wanted to be beautiful, had played it down to the point of dowdiness. She had wanted to be invisible.

She'd worn a headscarf like a woman of her mother's – or grandmother's – generation, hiding the flaming hair. No make-up, the amber-coloured eyes indistinct in her freckled face – indistinct, that is, unless you got close, which Giuli had once or twice, when you could see the flecks of gold in them. At a metre or so's distance she could look plain, even ugly. She could hide.

Why did a woman do that? Giuli, abused child and ex-hooker from the Via Senese, knew one or two reasons to refuse the male gaze in the street. Did they apply to Flavia? It seemed to her that this woman – more like a nun than anything else, she reflected – could not have anything in common with Giuli herself. So her diffidence wasn't born out of shame, nor out of guilt or rejection, but perhaps modesty, or political principle, feminism and the like? Her mind simply set on higher things. Still, Giuli mused, and didn't feel quite convinced. Felt her frustration rise that she had never known Flavia Matteo, and now it was too late.

'Sweetheart!' Enzo's voice broke in on her thoughts, anxious and out of breath. 'Sorry I'm late.'

Giuli refocused, and his broad features were there, filling her frame of vision, his arm was right around her and squeezing. Then she felt him stop, mid-squeeze. 'You all right?' Taking in her expression his face fell, and she felt guilty.

'I'm fine.' And stopped herself from sighing and spoiling it all. 'There's just – well, I'll tell you later. Let's get your ice cream.'

Enzo looked miserable. 'No need. It was stupid of me. It's been an awful day, awful news. I – I—' He was examining her face earnestly, trying to make amends, trying to work her out, poor guy. And she understood: no one was more distraught than he was about Flavia Matteo. He was trying to soothe himself, all this kids' stuff, ice cream and normality, and he was looking miserable because he suspected it wasn't going to work, this time.

'No,' she said. 'We're here now.' And shoving with gentle insistence, shoulder to shoulder at the long counter, she did feel better. A bit better.

On the street, they leaned against the shopfront and watched the evening traffic, eating in silence. Six o'clock, and the sun was already down. The air was still warm, but cooling, and Giuli experienced all at once that mixture of wistfulness and relief that comes with the end of summer. The end of those seemingly endless months of heat, the unbearable nights without sleep, of the long days of pleasurable boredom on the beach, skin warm and rough with sand and salt, the feeling of a body peeled and new after a week by the sea. The ice cream *was* delicious, and Giuli felt a moment's sisterly feeling for the greedy, selfish old lady. Sometimes it was fine to enjoy something.

'It's pretty good,' she said, lifting her tiny plastic spoon in tribute, and although Enzo smiled she could see that he was down, that the ice cream hadn't quite done the trick. She didn't know if she should tell him. But how could she not?

She eyed him as he ate with a slight frown of contemplation. He was wearing his work clothes, trousers and a short-sleeved shirt, plus a vest now that summer was almost past; his pristine nylon laptop bag at his feet on the pavement. Enzo was a magician of the laptop: she loved to watch him work on the computer, any computer, their workings as natural to him as breathing. Giuli might be more computer-savvy than Sandro, to whom the machine was a goad and a torment, but she still had regular moments of panic when she pressed the wrong button on the neat little laptop Enzo had bought her last Christmas, or it started making a weird noise. Enzo had grown to recognize her panic in the ether and would be there before she had made a sound, a hand on her forearm to calm her, his voice carefully explaining.

If only, she sometimes thought, there'd been teachers like him at school. If only there'd been someone like him when she'd hit fourteen and a very different sort of boy had come around. Of course she had him now, but now might be too late.

'Clelia Schmidt told me something,' she began carefully. His frown deepened; carefully he stuffed the paper napkin inside the remains of his cone, took Giuli's paper cup and put them both in the swing bin outside the *gelateria*. He took her arm and they began to walk along the wide pavement, the traffic roaring and honking beside them. 'The midwife,' said Giuli, feeling herself unbend just a little at the feel of his arm in hers. 'I had lunch with her. I wanted – well, she felt guilty about Flavia. I had to break it to her gently.'

*

'I know it's difficult for you to talk about this,' she'd said as soon as the waitress was gone, trying to catch Clelia's lowered gaze across the table. 'I know it feels wrong, but—'

'I shouldn't have known about it myself,' Clelia had said quickly, interrupting her. 'There's confidentiality between – well, between certain specializations, unless it's pertinent.' She'd frowned then, as though something had only just occurred to her. 'And it should have been – actually. I should have been told. Although. . .'

Giuli had grappled with her meaning. 'Certain specializations?' Then she'd understood. 'Oh. You mean, the other clinics?' Obvious. 'Right,' she'd said. 'Like, the STD clinic, for example: you'd need to know if a pregnant woman had something that might be transmitted to the baby.' Clelia lifted her face abruptly. It was white.

'Flavia didn't have an STD,' she'd said, horrified. 'I do that testing, if the woman's pregnant. With permission, of course. She gave me permission.'

'I see,' Giuli, who did, had said. She knew about that stuff. But something had occurred to her. 'She reacted – how? When it came up? The testing, asking for permission? What d'you check for?'

Clelia had frowned. 'She – she was fine. Composed.' The frown had deepened. 'We test for syphilis routinely, HIV on request, other stuff on request. She had the test most people have, just the syphilis. Negative, obviously.'

'Obviously,' Giuli had said mildly. The waitress had come back then, with the two thick white bowls of pasta. Clelia had taken a gulp of the wine Giuli had ordered for her and stared down at the food until the waitress was gone. And then she had said it.

*

Now, in the humid dusk, Enzo took Giuli's hand. They were walking to where he knew she'd have left her *motorino*, a spare helmet for him in her pillion box. He came in on the bus.

'So what did she tell you?' he asked, disengaging his arm when they reached the scooter and facing her.

Could she be sure? Could Clelia be sure? Giuli didn't want to see the look on his face when she said it. She told herself, a disease would be worse, surely? If Flavia had a disease. And all Clelia had seen was Flavia going into a consulting room.

'She was visiting the Addictions clinic,' Giuli said, holding his gaze. 'Flavia was seeing somebody about an addiction.'

The truth was, she didn't know what would be worse. She'd been there herself, and it wasn't straightforward, it wasn't just a matter of poisoning the body. It was the whole package: it was the dealers, it was the desperation, the going to places you shouldn't go, it was the brain cells dying and the danger disregarded and the friends lost and the self-respect – if there'd ever been any. She saw Enzo looking at her and that gulf was there between them again. She knew – she knew too much – and he didn't.

Giuli was the one who looked away first.

*

He rang as she was locking up. Luisa could tell from his voice that it had been grim. It didn't escape her that worse was to come.

Locking up wasn't a five-minute affair. There was so much stock in the shop at this time of year you had to be extra careful, and there was a set routine. Steel shutters had been fitted on the bays in the cellar stockroom, where the high-value items were kept:

padlock those, then double-lock and bolt the back door. Shut the electrically operated metal grilles on the windows. Set the alarm and, finally, attend to the three locks on the front entrance, Beppe waiting behind her on the pavement since the raid seven years ago when Luisa had – stupidly – been on her own one wet November night, reaching up for the top lock, when someone grabbed her from behind and held her while an accomplice pushed into the shop and snatched a couple of thousand euros' worth of handbags from the window display. They'd just been opportunists, but crime levels in the city had hardly improved since.

No chance of that this evening. It was eight o'clock and the Por Santa Maria was busy. As she kneeled down to turn the last key, Luisa could hear laughter behind her in the street; there was a good mix of people, locals happy to be back in the city after the tourist-haunted desert of the summer.

Then the phone rang, her heart jumped in her chest and the laughter behind her sounded suddenly wrong. Luisa scrabbled in her bag and Beppe kneeled beside her with a questioning look: she gestured to him to finish off and stood up, stepping away with the phone held to her ear. She could see the girl who was laughing in a small group – young, underdressed, breasts gleaming under the streetlighting – slyly registering the look she was getting from a boy in the little gang as she laughed. The young used to make Luisa smile, but some days now, the sight of a kid like that only made her feel anxious.

'*Caro,*' she said, knowing it would be him. She tried not to sound worried, and failed. 'How's the traffic?'

Sandro sighed, long and heavy, and something about the quality of the background sound told her that he wasn't in the car. 'I'm not coming back,' he said.

'What?' For a single, lunatic second Luisa heard her husband tell her he was leaving her: she saw herself alone in the hospital waiting room, not out of choice but because she had no one.

'I mean, we're not,' Sandro added, correcting himself but oblivious to any possible misintepretation of what he'd just said. 'He can't face it, not tonight. We've got a hotel. He says he'll pay.'

Luisa's world now righted itself. 'Don't let him pay,' she said quickly. 'So it was her. Was it – how awful was it?'

'Pretty bad,' said Sandro, and she heard the strain in his voice. 'Rough. It was her, all right.' He stopped, she heard him swallow. 'She cut her wrists and lay in the bath. She'd been there probably two days.'

Luisa's mouth dried. She blinked. She turned slightly and saw Beppe looking at her, his neat-bearded, handsome face furrowed just a little with concern. She shook her head in a gesture of smiling impatience she knew he'd recognize. Bumped a kiss from her fingers to wave him off and held out her hand for the keys. *Sandro*, she mouthed. After a second's hesitation he dropped the keys in her open palm, straightened his waxed jacket fastidiously and, with a wave, headed off towards Gilli where he would, she knew, enjoy a Campari topped up with prosecco, and a handful – no more – of salted nuts. Beppe looked after his figure. She thought with longing of that other world, where people had routines and lived by rules, and were content with small things.

Two days. 'Oh, God,' she said. 'Poor man. Poor man.' She thought of that beautiful woman softening to nothing but water-swollen flesh in a bathtub; she thought of the rosy swaddled child.

'Yes,' said Sandro. Luisa thought of the night he was going to have.

'You got two rooms?' she asked, and there was another sigh. 'There was only a twin left,' he said. 'I didn't know the seaside was so lively in September.'

'When the weather's still this good,' Luisa replied, but her mind was elsewhere. Sandro had booked himself into the same room because he didn't want to leave the grieving husband alone, she could read him like a book. Even though he wouldn't get a wink of sleep himself. 'Don't let him pay,' she repeated.

'He wants to – to engage me now,' said Sandro, his voice leaden.

'Engage you? As a detective? What for?'

'I don't even know,' said Sandro. 'Look, he doesn't know what he's doing. It's a kind of denial or a distraction, or something. I expect in the morning he'll have changed his mind. People do. I was there from the beginning, he's leaning on me. It's difficult.' Another sigh. 'But of course I won't let him pay for the room.'

Under the uplit vaulting of the Straw Market, where the stalls were packing up and being rolled away, something caught Luisa's eye: a profile. The smooth crow's wing sweep of shiny black hair. Then a little bobbing group of Japanese tourists all talking in their own language, all nodding and turning their heads with that distracting foreignness of theirs, came into her line of vision, and whatever it was – whoever it was – was obscured. Absently Luisa stepped to one side to avoid a market trolley and get a better look, but someone barged into her and awkwardly she had to disengage herself.

'You all right?' said Sandro, hearing her intake of breath, her fumbled apology.

'Yes, yes – I just thought – I thought I saw—' She stopped. Best not.

'So,' he went on, filling the silence. 'I'll keep an eye on him tonight. I think – well, it depends. I'll be back some time tomorrow, for sure.'

He didn't sound sure. 'I suppose he's spoken to his mother?' Luisa was thinking out loud. 'She'll have the baby for the night.'

'I – I don't know.' She could almost hear him cogitating: a puzzle. Sandro liked a puzzle to solve. When he spoke again, his voice was just a little brighter. 'He doesn't have a mobile phone of his own, can you believe that?' She couldn't. 'But he did wander off a while back, after we'd checked in, went downstairs. He might have called her from the lobby.'

'I'll give her a ring,' said Luisa decisively. 'Offer – oh, I don't know. Help, or something.'

'Right,' said Sandro, and she could tell he was still in puzzle-solving mode. 'I wonder if the old woman's got anything to do with it.'

'What?' said Luisa, startled.

'Well, would you fancy being her daughter-in-law? But no, you're right. She's an old bitch but she's not bad enough for – for that.'

Luisa didn't know what he was suggesting. That the woman deliberately drove her daughter-in-law to suicide? 'I don't suppose she helped matters,' she said. Sighed. 'Have you talked to Giuli and Enzo? They knew Flavia, didn't they?'

'Giuli,' he murmured, and she could sense him receding. 'She – I think Enzo knew them better. But Giuli was asking around. The midwife.'

He petered out: *Christ*, thought Luisa. *It's thirty years ago, I can stand the word midwife.* She said nothing.

When Sandro spoke again his voice was different. 'Right, look, yes. I'll call Giuli.' And for a second she thought he was going to hang up on her without saying goodbye. But he caught himself in time. 'Don't worry about me, sweetheart. I'll call later, before you go to sleep.'

After he'd gone Luisa stood there a moment, feeling oddly dazed, people moving past her in a blur. She hadn't even asked him if the police had spoken to them. Rosselli wanted to take him on as a detective and she had the strongest feeling, quite suddenly, that no good would come of it.

But then, when the one you love chooses to disappear without explanation – and with that thought Luisa raised her head, a small herd of tourists moved en masse out of her way, and she saw Chiara.

Luisa opened her mouth to call but she made no sound. Because what would she say? Chiara was on the far side of the small square marketplace with its high vaulted stone roof. Talking to someone Luisa couldn't see because a stall was in the way. Chiara looked – different.

Partly it was the clothes. Every time Luisa had seen Chiara since she hit thirteen, she'd been in jeans. Skintight or loose and low-slung, darkwash, stonewash, there'd been a black phase. . . but it had still been jeans; Gloria had smiled indulgently and Luisa had despaired. They sold jeans in the shop and Luisa knew you couldn't fight it, but as it moved down the generations she wondered what feminity would come to if women grew old wearing jeans. And not to mention it encouraged fat on the hips, it lost them their waist, they just let it all hang out – but no one listened. Beppe could never hide a smile when she started her rant about jeans.

Framed in the arch, one hand on her hip and a proper handbag slung over her arm, Chiara was wearing a dress. Not just a dress but a pale silk dress, the colour something between cream and peach, with short fluted sleeves, a tie at the neck, a nice fit over the waist that only came, Luisa's practised eye recognized, at a price. And heels: four-centimetre heels in pale flesh colour: even at this distance Luisa could tell they were good shoes. Where did she buy all that? was Luisa's first thought. And, why didn't she come to me? was her second. But wherever she'd got the stuff, Luisa had to admit, she'd made good choices. Or someone had.

The girl's hips swayed just a little as she talked, the handbag swung. She was different, and it wasn't just the clothes. The pose, the unselfconscious sensuality, even the way her hair had been done, they belonged to an older woman than the Chiara Luisa knew. A man eating a filled roll at the tripe stall behind her was eyeing the girl's legs appreciatively. Then whoever it was Chiara was talking to shifted position and she saw him, or at least the quarter-profile and a back view of a stocky youngish man. They made an odd pair because although he was decently enough dressed and probably a couple of years her senior, the boy seemed too young next to her, too gauche, his hands stuffed in his pockets.

The street was emptier, quieter now, and Luisa took a step forward, but just as she did so Chiara's gaze shifted a fraction away from the man, and Luisa's movement drew it across the thoroughfare, and their eyes met. Chiara froze.

Raising a hand to greet her, or delay her, or to calm the sudden panic in the girl's eyes, Luisa took a step towards the market. Chiara, all her new poise departed, took a step back, half stumbling in the heels. Luisa saw the man put out a hand quickly to catch her arm before she went over altogether, saw him begin to turn to see what had alarmed Chiara, and then a trolley laden with cheap leather goods rounded the corner at reckless speed and came to a stop in front of Luisa, almost on her toes.

'Hey, watch it,' bellowed the beefy stallholder, hauling on the iron handle, his swarthy face in Luisa's. 'Some of us have work to do.'

Where were they?

Leaning on the soft pale stone of a pillar for a moment, Luisa wondered if she'd crossed over to the wrong bay: in front of her now the market was almost cleared away, but there was no sign of them. Not of Chiara, nor of the man she'd been talking to. She was in the right place, all right; there was the tripe stall. The man who'd been looking at Chiara's legs was pushing the paper wrapping of his sandwich into the refuse bin and reaching for a paper towel.

'Excuse me,' said Luisa, breathless from hurrying towards him. 'Did you see where she went?'

Had she ever been bothered by losing male interest? The look the man gave her was a world away from the look he'd been giving Chiara. Why would Luisa care? One breast down, but still alive. 'The – the girl in the dress? Did you see which way she went?'

He studied her, wiping his hands, wondering if he could be bothered, whether he cared if this woman had seen him eyeing up a girl young enough to be his daughter. But then he jerked his head towards the narrow alley that led south, down to the Via delle Terme. Raising her head, Luisa thought she heard the click of heels on the stone: they could hardly have got far.

'Thank you,' she said, but he was already turning away.

Almost immediately Luisa knew it was a lost cause: that gloomy alley – and perhaps, she thought in a paranoid moment, the man at the tripe stall had chosen it for that very reason – had four possible exits. They might have slipped left and back to the Por Santa Maria while she was distracted, right and right again to the marble arcades in front of the post office, along the Via delle Terme to the Via Tornabuoni, or through a crooked alley crossing down to the dark, high-sided canyon of the Borgo Santissimi Apostoli.

Luisa plumped for the last option – it was the most sneaky somehow – but once she was on the Apostoli, it became obvious she'd got it wrong. The street was empty bar a dumpy tourist couple holding hands and looking in a jeweller's window. In vain Luisa listened for that particular sound of high heels on rough Florentine flagstones but instead the air seemed to be full of all kinds of other noises: scooter engines, raised voices, the wooden wheels of the traders' trolleys.

The tourist couple were looking at her with interest. Luisa knew what she must look like, for this frowsty pair to wonder about her: jacket unbuttoned, wild-eyed, pale and panicky. But she didn't much care.

'Chiara!' she shouted, ignoring them, instead turning in a circle on the spot and looking – down the Santissimi Apostoli, back up the alley, towards the Por Santa Maria. 'Chiara, it's all right.' She waited as the muffled, uneven echo from the rough stone of the tall façades died away, mocking her. 'I just wanted to say hello.'

There was no answer.

Chapter Thirteen

RELUCTANTLY, SANDRO HUNG UP: at least, he thought as he put the phone away in his jacket pocket, Luisa understood. He wasn't ambulance chasing, and he wasn't angling for a day by the seaside. He didn't want this job, but it seemed to want him.

The hotel was more expensive than he'd hoped, and without wishing for one they'd been granted a sea view – to bump the price up even further, was Sandro's suspicion. Clean and cool, speckled terrazzo flooring and twin beds with pale blue covers, a single long window at which now, in a breeze that had come with the failing light, long, fine cotton curtains drifted and blew as if they were somehow being breathed in and out.

Even this modest level of luxury seemed incongruous. What had the woman at the front desk, with her blandly neutral expression and her neat suit, thought of the pair of dusty stragglers, of the dingy little Fiat they eventually left in the private underground car park? Niccolò Rosselli sat on one of the beds with his back to Sandro, barely seeming to make a dent, his shoulders dropped, still as a statue.

Rough didn't even begin to cover it. When they had emerged

from the police morgue into the fading silvery light of the seaside town on a balmy evening, Niccolò Rosselli had looked about a hundred years old.

Were there human beings who would be able to identify the dead body of their lifelong beloved companion with equanimity? Oh, yes: in his thirty years in the police force Sandro had accompanied perhaps fifty men and women to the morgue, and among those there had been a good few unable to muster up more than a dry, insincere sob; then there had been the others whose operatic breakdowns were simply a matter of going through the motions, doing what was expected. Of those, half a dozen perhaps turned out to have caused their partner's death themselves; some had been in shock; most had simply lost any proper feeling.

He had stood at the door while Rosselli identified his wife's body, pulled on rollers from a drawer, not yet autopsied: he had seen the marble-white arm laid alongside the torso, and the contrast between pale profile and rusty red hair, life unmistakably, irretrievably gone, though the ghost of her humanity was still there, in the gleam of her fingernails and the softly freckled plane of a high white cheekbone. Rosselli had become still then, frozen in the attitude of looking down on his dead wife, as if his life had stopped there too and he would need to be led by the hand through the rest of his days.

When he had spoken, his voice was no more than a whisper. 'Yes,' he'd said. 'It's her.' The mortuary assistant had waited, looking anxiously from Rosselli to the policeman attending the identification, whose name was Tufato: eventually the officer had nodded curtly and the drawer had been slid back in.

You could never tell a hundred per cent from the reaction, because even murderers often experienced genuine emotion – remorse, yes, but also grief, horror, disbelief, shock – when confronted with what they had done.

Catching himself looking at Niccolò Rosselli with this thought in his head, Sandro had stuffed his hands in his pockets in shame. It was a reflex. Perhaps he should be grateful he still had it, for professional reasons, but at the moment it was inappropriate, to say the least. Niccolò Rosselli's wife had committed suicide in a hotel room: she had checked in alone for that purpose.

All the same, as they had emerged from the low ugly complex of buildings – a temporary solution to the town's expansion, Tufato had informed them apologetically, and more like a light industrial unit than anything else, a place where catering ovens or light fittings might be produced – Sandro had found himself wondering whether this provincial police station would pursue any other line of inquiry. Certainly it would be their duty to establish that the woman had died by her own hand, and up to a point, to determine why. Up to a point: Sandro was uneasily sure that they would not pursue the *why* any further than was strictly necessary, and certainly not as far as would satisfy her grieving husband.

Why was a huge question. . . why leave this world, the blue sky, the sea, a newborn child? Any answer, it seemed to Sandro, that would rely entirely on a scientific solution – chemical changes in the body following childbirth, say, depression – would never be sufficient. But it did not follow that it was the duty of the police to provide philosophical truths as well as simple facts.

Tufato, thickset, bullet-headed, had seemed a decent enough sort, and not stupid: he had not looked at Rosselli with anything like suspicion. Not as far as Sandro had been able to tell, anyway. Tufato had outlined what they knew. Flavia had checked into her room on Sunday at midday, had come out of her room only for breakfast on Monday and since then had remained in it, with the 'Do not disturb' sign up.

'Did she have any visitors?' Sandro had asked and Tufato had frowned, moving his head in a small, stiff, negative motion that to

Sandro did not indicate anything but a reluctance to answer the question, at this point. Was Rosselli a suspect? Sandro had glanced swiftly at the man he supposed was now his employer, but Niccolò sat there, his eyes dull, lost. He seemed to have registered neither the question nor the implications of Tufato's reticence.

The investigating officer had cleared his throat, and when Sandro's question had faded into the silence, had stolidly taken a brief statement and punctuated his questions with scrupulously proper expressions of sympathy and regret. *When did you last see your wife? What was her state of mind?*

It had not felt much like a formal interview: they had allowed Sandro to be present. 'I'm a friend,' he'd said, when they asked, and looking at Rosselli's pale face and shaking hands, they had agreed that he might sit in, if he kept quiet.

Shifting in his seat as his questions were answered, the policeman had been as uneasy as Sandro, to whom the burden of explanation seemed to have been passed, now felt. Sandro had seen his eyes slide away from Rosselli's bleary, magnified brown gaze. Rosselli, he'd noticed, had not taken off his glasses to polish them at any point in the brief interview.

He'd been able to tell them when he last saw his wife – but then Sandro could have told them that. To everything else he had seemed only to be able to repeat, 'I don't know,' in a mumbling monotone, and Sandro had felt a surge of sympathy. Unpicking those last days or weeks, disentangling them from the tidal wave of remorse and guilt at not having seen this coming: no wonder. *Dangerous*, he'd thought, stop identifying with the man. And then, *Why not?* You're not the investigating officer. You're meant to be on his side.

'Did she leave – any explanation? Any message?' Rosselli had waited patiently until the policeman's questions had finished before posing his own. 'A note?' He'd frowned as he pronounced the word, with a kind of distaste for it, as if it were a melodramatic prop from a cheap thriller.

The policeman had shaken his big head, taking off his cap and running a hand over his shaven scalp. Sandro had been fairly sure from the questions the man had already asked that there had been no suicide note, and it hadn't surprised him. For every scrawled *sorry* or rambling litany of grievances and accusations, there were plenty who left only stony silence behind them. Who could, in extremis, find an adequate explanation? An intelligent person would, he supposed, find suicide harder to justify than a fool, and besides there would be the same distaste, he imagined, in Flavia Matteo as in her partner for the detective-story cliché.

'There was some evidence that your – that Ms Matteo – that your partner sat down to write something,' the officer had said carefully, staring at his cap on the desk between them. 'But for whatever reason, she failed. There was a piece of paper on the desk, and a pen. The chair behind the desk – it would appear she had sat at the chair, she picked up the pen – but she didn't write anything. It isn't uncommon.'

Now, with Rosselli motionless on the bed with his back to him, Sandro felt a sudden, overwhelming desire to have seen that other hotel room, that chair, that desk with its single sheet of paper. He wanted the chance to examine the apparently inconsequential things, to get down on his hands and knees in that room and look under that desk, to take the unused sheet of paper in his hands: he wanted to lean close enough over the bed to see the impression of a head in the pillow, to know what scent Flavia Matteo wore. Damn, thought Sandro, grinding his teeth in frustration as much at the persistence of his detective instinct as at his powerlessness. How had he come to find himself here, with this man, having these thoughts?

Coming out of the morgue, Rosselli had looked bad.

'Are you all right?' Sandro had asked wearily. Stupid question. 'Perhaps we should be heading back.'

The man had stared at him. 'Back?' he'd asked. 'Back where?' He'd shifted, looking behind him at the morgue, and for a moment there in the car park he had seemed to Sandro no more than a dusty smudge in the afternoon sunshine, a mirage created by the heat haze, a grieving ghost made out of the city's soot and sin, out of place among the striped parasols and the ozone. Without his wife, he might just disappear altogether, Sandro had thought, and then he had realized he was thinking as much about himself.

'Well, home,' Sandro had said, clearing his throat.

'Home,' Rosselli had said, still looking at the morgue, turning the word over as though trying to understand it.

'Florence,' Sandro had elaborated, shifting from foot to foot. 'Back to the city.' He had longed for its shadows and cool stone streets: it had seemed bizarre to him now that he and Luisa, Enzo and Giuli, had separately come out to a place very much like this only weeks ago – holidays seemed an aberration. Bizarre too that the summer still seemed to be going on without them.

'I'm not going – home,' Rosselli had said. 'I can't go home. I'm staying here.' Sandro had waited, and as he'd watched something began to kindle behind those thick glasses. 'Why did she come here?' The focus, smouldering now, had come to rest on Sandro. 'You can help me find out, can't you?' He'd frowned as if trying to remember how Sandro had come to be there, as if he had quite forgotten that he had asked him. 'You're an investigator. That's what you're for.'

'Well, I—'

'I didn't ask him if I could go there,' Rosselli had said. 'Can I go?'

'Go where?' Sandro had asked gently.

'The hotel,' Rosselli had said, and his eyes behind the glasses looked cloudy and dark. 'Where she died.' Sandro had taken him by the elbow and tried to guide him back towards the car, but felt a resistance. Rosselli had stood his ground, and seemed to grow momentarily taller, more substantial. The smudge of dust had become a man again.

'One night,' he had said. 'We stay here one night. That's all.'

And so here they were.

Sandro stood in the window of the hotel room, holding the drifting curtain back with one hand, and looked out across the sea. The sky was a dark electric blue, a few scattered high clouds luminous in the last of the light, and the sea turning black in the shadow of the headland. The sight was beautiful, he supposed, even though Flavia Matteo would never see it. It would still be there after they'd all gone and the world had turned back to jungle and desert, but would it still be beautiful with no one to see it, or to say that it was? Sandro closed his eyes to stop himself wishing Luisa were there with him, and the image of that dark headland, somehow negative, imprinted itself on his closed eyelids.

Below the window, the evening *passeggiata* was starting up on the wide boardwalk. Languidly a handsome woman was pushing an elaborate double perambulator containing twin newborn babies, her slow walk deliberate so as to garner the maximum praise for that clever trick of fertility. She was nodding gracious thanks to the admiring comments, though Sandro found himself reflecting, by way of distraction from the silence behind him in the darkening room, that twins, these days, were very often down to science. The woman pushing the pram looked much the same age as Flavia Matteo, forty odd, one of those miracle mothers. Of course, she might be their grandmother.

'Let's go and get something to eat,' he said abruptly. 'A bit of fresh air.'

Obediently Rosselli stood up.

At the desk, a portly middle-aged man in a striped waistcoat was now on duty: he looked up and Sandro saw an inquisitive glint in the man's eye before professional discretion made him bow his gleaming head back over the evening newspaper. There were few people, Sandro reflected, as curious as hotel staff, and fewer still as nosy as those in his country's seaside establishments. And for some reason, the thought perked him up.

'Need to get a toothbrush,' he remarked, thinking aloud as he held the lobby door for Niccolò Rosselli to go ahead of him. 'Before the pharmacies close.'

The concierge's head was immediately raised. 'The nearest pharmacy is on the Via Roma,' he said. 'Left, then left again. He doesn't close till eight.'

Sandro stopped, hand still on the door and Rosselli out on the street, waiting, ever obedient. 'Thank you,' he said. 'That's very helpful, um—' Unlike the surly soldier at the barracks' reception desk the concierge had no identifying tag: instead he seemed prepared actually to be forthcoming.

'Salvatore, Signore Cellini,' he said, eyes bright with interest. 'If there's anything else, I would be glad to assist.'

The streets were not packed, as they would have been a month back, but they were busy. It was a family place. Grandmothers were the dominant group, middle-aged and elderly women with a toddler or an infant in tow, some widowed, some with grumbling husbands along for the evening air and the chance to get out of cramped accommodation and to complain to another man. Gradually the feeling that Sandro had at first, that he and Rosselli were like a pair of ghosts moving among the living, diminished. Just keep walking.

He wasn't particularly hungry when they set out, it had to be said, but there was a market strung along the boardwalk and the air was full of the smell of street food, pizza slices and basil and *schiacciata*, peanut brittle and frying fish. Sandro stole a glance at

Niccolò Rosselli; his hollow cheeks warned that Sandro would have to force the man to a table and stand over him like a parent. An old-fashioned baby carriage passed them, a child in a knitted bonnet sitting upright.

'They think it was the child, don't they?' said Rosselli. 'The child brought it on. Flavia's – depression.' He was motionless, staring after the pram.

'I don't know,' said Sandro, hedging, then deciding to be straight with the man. 'Yes. Probably. It is – ah, statistically – the likeliest cause. And it's – well, I don't know, we've – we didn't – I have no children. But it can be – what's the term? – a life-changing event.'

'Ah, yes,' said Rosselli. 'Life-changing.' He sighed, and for a moment Sandro wondered if he had even wanted the child. He was surprised by how horrified he felt at the thought.

'What do you think?' he said carefully.

'I never – felt it would be right for us to have a child,' Rosselli said abruptly. 'I always thought she didn't either. But then – out of the blue, or it seemed out of the blue to me – she decided we had to have one.' He twisted his neck in a gesture of discomfort. 'And then it seemed – to be too much for her. No sleep, she found it hard to eat. She wouldn't talk to me about it.'

He turned to look at Sandro. 'But this began before the child was born,' said Rosselli, and Sandro was startled by a different note in his voice. 'Long before.' Behind the glasses the misty brown eyes seemed sharper, and then as swiftly as he had divulged this new fact, he swerved and changed tack. 'Remind me,' he said. 'How you came to be involved with – this? With us.'

Now he asks, thought Sandro, taken aback by this sudden display of sharpness, very different from the cultivated professorial vagueness. Was this the real Rosselli? Was this what explained his – and the Frazione's – steep rise to prominence? 'I – um – well. You did ask me to come,' he said.

'No,' said Rosselli sharply. 'First. Before. When my mother encountered you, you were in Carlo's office, yes? Asking him questions.'

They were facing each other in a kind of stand-off, an island parting the stream of the *passeggiata*, some of the evening boardwalk-strollers already giving the two men curious glances. Sandro raised both palms, in a conciliatory gesture. 'Giuli – you know Giuli? – asked me to help,' he said. 'Her boyfriend Enzo got her involved with the Frazione.' Rosselli unbent a little at that, giving a slight inclination of his head at Enzo's name.

Emboldened, Sandro went on. 'You're their great white hope, if that's not the wrong expression. She was worried about – about, well, she had all sorts of ideas, after you collapsed at the rally. Assassination attempt foremost among them. Sabotage. Poisoned umbrella. That kind of thing.'

He tried a smile: Giuli's conspiracy theories had been off the mark, after all. Nonetheless, he recalled the rally he and Luisa had seen in the Piazza del Carmine, and the comedy uniforms in their little military vehicle, his own musings about the secret service. Before Flavia Matteo's body had been found: before everything changed. The world of men and their roadbuilding and machinations and bureaucracy somehow seemed tissue-thin by comparison with what that woman's pale corpse represented. Grief.

Rosselli frowned at Sandro's tentative smile. 'And you think she was wrong?'

Sandro stared at him, bewildered. 'I don't understand,' he said helplessly. 'You – what do you mean? You think – you were poisoned?' He grappled with the absurdity of the suggestion.

'I wasn't poisoned,' said Rosselli, and he seemed to collapse a little as he spoke. 'No. I hadn't eaten for days, I was under stress. As a matter of fact, the doctors in the hospital did all sorts of toxicological tests, and there was nothing.'

'But you were – you thought it was a possibility?'

'I don't know what I thought,' said Rosselli, looking grey with tiredness. 'Carlo – Avvocato Bastone – had been very jumpy. The bigger the party grew, the more he kept saying we needed to stay small, not to attract too much attention. To bide our time – but how does one do that? If the people come, then they come. Perhaps you don't – perhaps you aren't in sympathy with our cause. But this country needs us to stand up, that man – our prime minister—' He broke off.

Sandro didn't know whether to agree with him, to state his support, Yes, the country's going to the dogs. But a lifetime's vehement distrust of politics and politicians – even politicians like this one – kept him silent. Like the rest.

Rosselli was still talking. 'And then I was – very anxious, about Flavia's going, about the child, being alone with the child, about the rally. I hadn't slept, I hadn't eaten, and the *avvocato* saying – well, I wasn't thinking very intelligently.' He frowned hard. 'It all came at once. Anything seemed possible, there seemed to be danger everywhere.' The look he gave Sandro beseeched him to understand. 'I don't know.'

There was a moment's silence, the two men looking at each other in a kind of truce.

'You need a square meal,' said Sandro, and thought, you sound like Luisa. 'That's the first thing you need, if you're going to get past this.'

'Food,' said Rosselli vaguely; for a moment Sandro tried to imagine him ever eating, even as a child, the only offspring of a single mother, her hand extended grimly with a loaded spoon in it. Perhaps to him food wasn't the source of comfort it was to those with easier childhoods.

Over Rosselli's head, mounted above the boardwalk, there was a brown state sign announcing the hotels in the vicinity, one-star, two-star, the graphic of a bed – always a single bed. Among them the Stella Maris, three-star. If the man turned and saw it, he would be back at square one, there'd be no evening meal, no semblance of normality, he'd have Sandro standing outside the hotel where his wife had died and recreating every terrible detail in his imagination.

'A square meal and a good night's sleep,' said Sandro, and firmly he took Rosselli by the elbow and steered him past the sign. He could call Giuli later, and Luisa; he could wait for the man to sleep, but just now Rosselli was too close to the edge, he had to be the priority.

'Everything else can be dealt with tomorrow.'

*

In the small, square room, too hot, not dark enough, the whine of a mosquito approaching and receding despite the plug-in and the spirals and the roll-on, Giuli couldn't sleep.

Beside her Enzo was dead to the world: intimacy had that effect on him. Not just the verbal kind, although there'd been some of that and it did wear him out – but what women's magazines called intimacy. By which they meant sex. She had worried about it, at the beginning of the relationship – she worried about it still, if truth be told, the weight of her experience against his innocence. There'd been something about Enzo that made even virginity a possibility, but she hadn't needed to worry about that, in the end. He'd waited a long time – months of patient, constant waiting while she backed off and then returned – and in the event it had been Giuli who'd felt like the ignorant one. Never having been in love before, she had not known what to do at first.

She turned over, wide awake: intimacy had the opposite effect on her, it seemed to activate a particularly acute wakefulness full of restlessness and regrets. It prodded her, saying, 'A whole life lived before you got to this? All your youth, all those pointless men, all that blundering cruelty and stupidity.' So intimacy kept her awake, that and a day too full of bad news.

On this side, facing Enzo, she could at least breathe in the healthy smell of him and feel the steady warmth radiating off his solid, motionless presence, flat on his back. If she could just stop fidgeting. If she could just stop thinking about Flavia Matteo.

Flavia wasn't on drugs. No. Giuli wouldn't believe it – couldn't believe it. Actually, in the airless room, with the harsh light of the street filtering through the blinds, as her head sifted and cleared, she *didn't* believe it. Giuli had been an addict, she'd lived most of her youth among addicts, and she knew that they came in all shapes and sizes, all classes. They weren't always toothless hookers or vagrants, there were playboys and businessmen among them – there were doctors, and lawyers, and mothers. Giuli pulled her hands up and laid them flat on top of each other, between her chin and the pillow. But Flavia Matteo's child had been born plump and healthy, Clelia Schmidt had been adamant on the subject, she'd have known if the mother had been using drugs. It had to be – had to be something else, she'd said, fervently. Wanting to believe it. It was why she hadn't wanted to say anything at first.

It had been a while ago that Clelia had seen Flavia in the – the other clinic. Before the baby.

What other kinds of addiction were there? As many kinds as there were human beings, as many as there were fetishes. Gambling, exercise, online chat, clothes. Love; money; pornography. To each his own: was there anyone, Giuli wondered, with no weakness, no chink, no wound whereby the craving might enter the bloodstream? And what had been Flavia's?

Behind her on the bedside table Giuli's mobile hummed, set to silent, in receipt of a text message. Swiftly and silently she turned over and reached for it. Sandro.

Despite herself, Giuli smiled. Sandro would never be a master of the text. He went on too long, rambling: he wouldn't use abbreviations, but he was even in this cramped form fully himself. Bad-tempered, despairing, kind, persistent. Worrying at this problem she'd got him into like a dog with a bone, seeking out the marrow, working into the crevices. Lying awake, like her.

He'd forwarded her a list of names, friends, or at least ex-colleagues, from the Scuola Agnesi where Flavia had worked: she'd stopped work at Easter, and the baby had been born in July.

She'd had friends... that was interesting. Of course, most people did: Giuli was the exception, too wary, too much of an outsider, and although she supposed that Luisa and Sandro counted, she thought of them more as family. Of course Flavia Matteo had had friends. Still, Giuli frowned at the word in the text, unable quite to picture the nervous woman she'd known among a group. *Go to the school tomorrow, maybe*, said Sandro. The text stopped short: he'd overrun his limit, or had sent it by mistake. As she held the little phone between her hands, intent, another text came in.

He was, he said almost as an afterthought, still at the seaside with Niccolò Rosselli, staying overnight: suicide confirmed, identity confirmed. Giuli's eyes widened at the thought. Then – *Rosselli wants me to look into her death.* She could hear the despondency in it as if Sandro had spoken the words aloud. *Why me?* it seemed to say. Giuli clicked the mobile phone shut and lay on her back with it clasped to her chest between her folded hands like a talisman.

Because you're clever, she thought as she fell asleep, at last. Because you're the best. Because you've got a heart.

*

As her head shifted restlessly on the pillow, the memory of the look Chiara had given her across the emptying market weighed on Luisa's chest like a stone. Should she have called Gloria and told her she'd seen her daughter? Gloria's first question, of course, would be, How did she look? Did she look all right? And the honest answers respectively would have been, *Beautiful*, and, *No. She didn't look all right to me*. Questions needed to be asked: tomorrow, in that market, Louisa would ask them. Someone must know that man Chiara was with.

Luisa reached with both arms across the empty space to where Sandro should be and left them extended there. When he got back, they'd – they'd do what they always did when he got back, and everything would be fine. His broad fingers wouldn't falter as they passed over the place where the breast had been, they'd be as warm and certain as they always were, his skin would smell the same. Sandro would come back to her, even if their friends' daughter had disappeared, even if another man's wife was dead. He was the one who'd come back.

*

A kilometre from Giuli, four kilometres from Luisa and six from the apartment in which she'd grown up, Chiara lay wide-eyed in the dark in the double bed, thought about the man who had lain beside her, and then thought, there are some things you can't tell your parents.

Tonight, he'd told her, he would have to go, he couldn't stay. Where did he go? She knew her mother would ask the question, her friends – were they still her friends? – would ask it, but Chiara didn't ask. She knew it was part of a game he was playing, a test he was setting her: a woman, he seemed to say as he got up from the bed, a real woman doesn't have to ask. Men go about in the world and they don't have to account for themselves. And she knew, he said, she knew he'd always be back. Because he said so.

He'd shown her photographs, of things men and women did. He said, 'You need to be ready, of course. We'll wait.' She had had to control a reflex of disgust. No, she'd thought, never, that's not love – but after a half-hour of his long fingers on her calf, stroking, she'd just thought, perhaps it could be love. Yes, it is. And then he'd said, But you're not ready yet. And he had got up, and gone, and left her with the hairs still on end, where he'd touched her.

Chapter Fourteen

T HE NEEDLE-SHARP LIGHT SHONE early through the slats of the unfamiliar room's shutters, but Sandro had no need to remind himself where he was. He felt as if he hadn't slept more than an hour the whole night.

Carlo Bastone had called at two a.m., when Niccolò Rosselli, under the influence of the sleeping tablets Sandro had given him, had been snoring the deep, harsh snore of the heavily medicated, an untidy sprawl on his bed. On the other bed, Sandro had been dozing, no more than that. He'd texted Giuli, he'd called Luisa, later than she'd have liked but she was glad to hear his voice, she said. He smiled now in the pale early sun at the memory of his wife's impatient *Yes*.

Dozing at most – but enough to befuddle him when he'd heard an unfamiliar ring tone and only realized too late that it was Rosselli's mobile. Retrieving it – eventually – from the jacket pocket into which he'd slipped it, Sandro had seen it still had a good charge on it. These old phones had a lot to be said for them: what he called the 'magic phone' Giuli and Luisa had talked him into, with its touchscreen and 3G and whatnot, died after an hour on the road. You had to carry any number of chargers around with you.

Missed call, Avv, it had said on the screen. He had frowned at that, then his own phone had begun to ring and when he'd answered it, and heard Carlo Bastone's voice, he made the connection. Sitting up, he'd cleared his throat.

Avv for Avvocato.

Niccolò was still snoring now, his face grey as marble. Sandro's phone told him it was six-twenty-two. On impulse he swung his legs over the bed and pulled on his trousers.

Looking fresh and spruce at the front desk with the sun flooding into his foyer, Salvatore smiled at Sandro as he emerged from the lift, as though it was the most normal thing in the world for a guest to go out for a stroll, unshaven and looking like death, at half-past six in the morning.

'All right, sir?' he said, raising his eyes from another paper – the early edition of the local rag, by the look of it. *Il Tirreno*, the holiday newspaper, full of complaints about the beach disco and cuts in ferry services. There'd be nothing in there about it.

'All right,' said Sandro warily, his eyes scanning the front page.

'You're here about the girl, aren't you?' said Salvatore. 'If you don't mind my asking.'

It was there on the front page. 'WOMAN FOUND DEAD IN HOTEL BATH'. A large photograph of a hotel frontage; a smaller one beside it, a headshot.

'Girl?' In death Flavia Matteo receded from them, the middle-aged men who would grow older and more hangdog, the red-headed woman still beautiful, the young mother. 'Yes,' he said. 'You mean Flavia Matteo. Yes. I'm here with her husband.'

The grieving widower: Sandro thought of him lying like the dead on the bed, and covered his face briefly with his hand.

Bastone had wanted to talk to him in the early hours.

'I can't wake him, no,' Sandro had said. 'After the day the man had yesterday? Please. Tell me what it is, Bastone.'

'There's been a break-in.' The lawyer had sounded terrified. 'At the Frazione's offices. A lot of mess. I don't think anything's gone – but I don't know. The police called me at midnight.'

In a low voice Sandro had told him to calm down. Another mummy's boy, this one, another only child. Sometimes it escaped Sandro's memory that he was one himself: this younger generation seemed, though, to profit less by all that exclusive parental attention.

'Nothing's gone? Well then. Someone'll have been looking for valuables. This kind of thing happens when you hit the headlines. Or – well – someone trying to capitalize on the confusion maybe. It's possible perhaps a businessman doesn't like you, sends in a goon or two, some right-wing loner, drunks – could be anyone.' He had sighed in the dark, warm bedroom, with the unfamiliar smells, another human being in close proximity. A weird time of night.

'Two in the morning's not the time to think straight,' he'd said. 'Has it been secured? The office?'

'I got someone out to board it up,' Bastone had said. Sandro had been surprised the man would even know where to start finding a handyman in the middle of the night. 'Good,' he'd said. 'Look – get some sleep. I'd call Enzo in the morning, if I were you, he's a sound lad. But not too early, eh?'

It had been impossible for him to get off to sleep after that.

'She was a good-looking woman,' said the concierge, studying the newspaper with concentration. Sandro angled his head to get a look at the photograph they'd found of Flavia Matteo; it looked like a passport picture. They must have been quick off the mark. 'Distinctive.' The man looked up at him. 'It's not a nice business, suicide.'

'No,' agreed Sandro, and with the receptionist in his striped waistcoat in front of him, for the first time found himself thinking about whoever it was – bellboy, chambermaid – who'd found Flavia's body. 'It's rough on everyone, that's for sure.'

'Never understood it myself,' Salvatore said, clearing his throat uncomfortably. 'Leave the world behind? Never.' Together they stood in the sunlight, feeling its warmth. The street outside was empty, bathed in that clear pale brightness of the seaside, where the streets all end at the water.

'Nor me,' Sandro said. 'Just lucky, I suppose.' He straightened. 'When do you go off duty, Salvatore? It is Salvatore, right?'

He inclined his head, acknowledging Sandro's courtesy. 'I go off at eight,' he said. 'And breakfast is between eight and ten, sir.'

'Is it a good breakfast?' asked Sandro. He had never had a good hotel breakfast – it was one reason for staying in hotels as little as possible. Packet croissants and filter coffee. Salvatore gave him a conspiratorial look.

'Not bad,' he said, without conviction. 'Considering. But if I were you I'd head down to the Bar Cristina, on the front, two blocks that way.' He nodded to the left. 'They make their own pastries. The coffee's good. Has the added advantage of Cristina herself.' And he smiled to himself.

The bar was spacious and bright, filled with the light off the sea. It would have been modern in perhaps 1932 but had been nicely maintained, fitted out in pale green glass. Cristina turned out to be a bustling little woman perhaps five years older than the concierge – Sandro suspected some not inconsiderable history there – with high-piled dark hair and small, shrewd brown eyes.

As she set a *caffè macchiato* and two pastries in front of him, the woman rested her elbows on the counter and regarded him. 'You're here with the husband,' she said. This was a smaller town than Sandro had suspected, for all its sprawl inland; Salvatore must have phoned ahead. 'Of the suicide. Friend of the family?'

Sandro downed his coffee and took a bite of the pastry. It

was stodgy but delicious: he tasted butter and vanilla. 'Sort of,' he said.

'That's nice,' said Cristina, watching him. 'A time like that you need friends. Poor kid.'

There it was again, Flavia, who would never grow old. 'Yes,' he said, and deciding on impulse to trust her with more than platitudes, 'we're trying to work it out. What happened.' He imagined Luisa in the corner of the room eyeing him and this attractive older woman with sceptical amusement.

'She must have been desperate,' said Cristina, and there was something in her voice that made Sandro look into her face, trying to fix her meaning. She started to look away but Sandro held her gaze.

'She'd been here before,' Cristina said quickly, and smoothed her apron with a hurried, anxious gesture. 'I've seen her before, in the town. Girl like that? You don't mistake her. I said to my husband: She's been here, I don't know when, don't know where I saw her...'

Husband? Sandro wondered fleetingly where Salvatore fitted in. 'She was hardly a girl,' he said, obscurely trying to retrieve the real, living Flavia Matteo, with that madonna's pale face, weighed down with worry. He pictured her on that mythical ferryboat, over the dark river, dwindling into a child, when she'd left behind a child of her own. 'She was forty-two and recently a mother.'

'Dangerous age,' said Cristina, frowning.

'Do you have children, Cristina?' asked Sandro. The woman raised herself, pulled her apron tight, her bosom – high and round for a woman of her age – seeming to become more prominent.

'No,' she said shortly. There was a story here, one that Sandro would never be told. 'But for any woman – dangerous,' she insisted, daring him to challenge her. 'When you know you're getting – not just older, but old.'

A silence fell: Sandro picked up his second pastry and contemplated it. Luisa was always warning him about diabetes: his own father, wiry into his seventies, had developed it, and no one would call Sandro wiry. He adjusted his waistband downwards and took a bite. Life was too short. There was a contradiction there somewhere.

'You think she'd been to the town before.'

'I'm sure I've seen her before.'

'Not in Florence? By all accounts she didn't get away from the city much.'

Cristina made a face. 'Florence? I wouldn't go there if you paid me.' Out here they were basically Pisans, and the centuries-old hostility between the kingdoms held good. She shook her head. 'No, I'm here all year round. There's nothing like it, the seaside. Nothing like it.' She looked over his shoulder through the wide glass window, where the water glittered in the early light.

'Might she have come in here? In the bar.'

'I suppose so.' Cristina frowned, dubious. She reached under the counter and brought out a cloth. She passed it in a wide arc over the pale blue-green glass, buffing it to a shine. She must have to do that a thousand times a day, thought Sandro, marvelling at the industry required, all for a glass bartop. A woman of standards. The door swung open and a weary-looking woman came in with two small children, chattering insistently. They tugged their mother over to a glass cabinet full of coloured plastic balls and began to wheedle for a coin. Cristina didn't pay them any attention.

'It wasn't in here,' she said slowly. 'I'm pretty sure of that, I'm – well. It's different when you're at work, you don't quite have the leisure – and I remember the sunshine. On her hair. Isn't that peculiar? To remember that,' she marvelled.

That hair. He'd seen it dull red against the laundered sheet of the morgue. 'You work every day?'

'Except Sundays. We're closed Sundays.' She brightened. 'So

it'd have been a Sunday, wouldn't it?' She looked at him with grudging respect. 'That's clever.'

'Not really,' said Sandro mildly. 'Sunshine. How long ago, do you think? A warm day?'

'We have a six-, seven-month season,' said Cristina proudly. 'There are a lot of warm sunny days.' Behind Sandro the door opened again and he felt the cool early air, heard the shush of waves. Could he and Luisa retire to the sea? People did.

A man in overalls came up to the bar beside Sandro and took off a cap: he brought the whiff of dustbins in with him but Sandro held his ground. Cristina bustled back to the coffee machine and filled a glass with warm milk. A dash of cold coffee from a jug. The man ladled teaspoons of sugar in: two, three, four. A small glass of brandy, and only then did Cristina look back at Sandro.

'It was a while ago, that's all I could say. Time does funny things, doesn't it? As you get older. I think it wasn't this season. I think—' She put a hand thoughtfully to her hair, spun like candyfloss. 'I think I was blonde. Which would make it the end of last season.'

Sandro nodded, careful not to smile. 'Brunette's good on you,' he said, surprising himself.

'What was she at the Stella Maris for?' Cristina asked, absently brushing off the compliment. The dustbin man looked up at the name, then back to his *latte macchiato*. 'What a dump that place is. Digusting old Calzaghe, one chambermaid for twelve rooms and her not even an Italian. Not that many are these days.'

You couldn't stop people saying things like that. It was a small town and even in Florence, the big city swarming with all nationalities, people said such things.

'And pricey with it. No wonder he can only scrape a handful of guests.'

'Who knows?' said Sandro thoughtfully. 'When you're planning – well. Perhaps it doesn't matter.'

'If it didn't matter, why didn't she just lie down on the tracks in Florence? Or walk into the river, if she wanted to spare the train driver. Or the chambermaid, even if she is a Croat. It's an ugly business, however you do it.'

My sentiments exactly, thought Sandro. And Croats are practically Italians, aren't they? Spit from Venice and it lands in Croatia.

'Where is the Stella Maris from here?' he asked. Cristina drew herself up behind the bar, bosom lifted. She nodded along the seafront. The dustbin man set down his empty brandy glass and wiped his mouth, but didn't make any move to leave, standing motionless in the full blessing of the sun.

'Five hundred metres that way,' said Cristina. 'Take the right fork down behind the promenade, one street back from the front.'

Sandro nodded, pensive. 'I don't know if you'll find anyone up at this hour,' she went on, curiously, sliding his empty cup and plate towards her and turning to stack them into a wire basket to go into the dishwasher. 'Gaetano. . . that's Gaetano Tufato, he'll be the policeman you talked to, can't keep up with his rank, you'll have to excuse me on that one. I've known him since he was thirteen. . . Anyway he told me they'd closed the place up for the meantime.'

'I think he's a *vice-commissario*,' said Sandro mildly. 'Tufato, I mean. I wonder why they did that? Are they not sure it was suicide, after all?'

Cristina smiled. 'I would say,' she said after a judicious pause, 'that there's more than one reason: you know how these things work.' Sandro seesawed his head. Provincial police? Yes, he knew. 'First, they don't like Calzaghe – no one does. They won't do him any favours. It's a blot on the seafront, that place, and should be closed down. Then, the woman's married to a politician, so they're covering their arses.'

'Yes,' Sandro said, almost enjoying this. 'Who knows when some big cheese might come down to make sure they've done things properly?'

'That's it,' said Cristina, head on one side. 'And – I suppose there's always some doubt. A girl – young woman – dying like that. Do you think it was suicide? I mean, you knew her.'

'I didn't know her,' said Sandro, and suddenly he felt sad. 'I didn't know her at all.'

It wasn't until the dustbin man cleared his throat that Sandro realized he was still there. 'I'll show you where the Stella Maris is,' he said. 'It's on my way.'

*

The day had dawned cool and bright and it was still early when Giuli found herself standing on the pavement outside the small primary school – the Scuola Elementare Agnesi, tucked behind Piazza Santo Spirito – where Flavia Matteo had worked. Term, Giuli calculated, would only just have started, and the place had the air of barely having woken up again after the long summer's desertion. A battered double door stuck with posters and a peeling wall daubed with graffiti, a railing above it through which the green curls and tendrils of a climbing plant wound themselves. The children hadn't arrived yet and it was quiet, but Giuli often passed this way during the day and if she paused and listened she could hear them behind the elegant building's thick, five-hundred-year-old walls, through the long windows with their flaking paint and battered shutters, the unselfconscious piping voices of small children.

She could picture their hands up, eager for attention. Giuli had been to one school she'd loved, before it all went wrong – the first, the nursery. *Scuola materna*, the right sort of name. There'd been a teacher whose breast she'd once – aged four perhaps – brushed against and been so startled by its warmth and fullness that she'd pressed harder. Her own mother being so thin from self-neglect, Guili had marvelled at the feel of it, not daring to move away, and the teacher, if she'd noticed, had not moved away either but instead rested an arm lightly on her shoulder, keeping her safe. Giuli still marvelled at it, sometimes, the yearning persistence of that small physical memory. She wondered what kind of teacher Flavia Matteo had been.

The poster-stuck door opened abruptly outwards and the bristles of a broom emerged behind a small cloud of dust. As the dirt settled on the pavement a broad-faced woman in a janitor's coat appeared in the doorway, big hands resting on her broomhandle. She stared levelly at Giuli and it occurred to her that the janitor was primed to watch out for child molesters. Something Clelia had said blinked in the back of Giuli's mind, something about abuse.

'Yes?' said the woman. 'Did you want something?'

Giuli pulled from her pocket the paper where she'd scribbled the half-dozen names Sandro had texted her, from Flavia Matteo's phone. 'Um – are any of these in yet?' she asked, holding the paper out to the janitor. The woman stared.

'Her,' she said, eventually, pointing with a work-roughened finger to a name halfway down the list. 'Teaches maths, first floor, room fourteen A.' And grudgingly she stepped back to allow Giuli past and inside.

There was a gloomy *terrazzo*-floored passage with doors off it, ending in a broad flagstoned hall, and a wide, dusty staircase. Giuli's heart sank. A maths teacher. Wanda Terni. It would be maths: Giuli's worst subject at school. And Wanda sounded like a northerner: bullying, angry, hardline.

But she turned out to be nothing of the kind. A small, rounded woman with dark roots showing in short blonde hair and a harassed expression, sitting at a desk in a dusty classroom in front of a pile of dog-eared workbooks. She looked up and Giuli saw she was red-eyed with tiredness, or something else.

'Can I help you?' she asked blearily. And when Giuli hesitated, she said, 'Is it about a pupil? Are you a mother?' Looking at her watch: not yet eight. School started at eight-thirty.

'No,' said Giuli. 'It's about Flavia. Flavia Matteo. You're – you were a friend of hers.'

'Yes.' The woman's mouth tightened into a line.

'You've heard,' said Giuli. She'd only been officially identified last night – but the Oltrarno was a tight little place. News spread fast.

There was a wooden chair beside the desk, and unbidden Giuli pulled it up next to the woman and sat.

'You were her friend,' she said. 'There was barely a handful of numbers in her phone, and yours was one of them.'

'What were you doing with her phone?' said Wanda Terni, almost savage: Giuli saw tears in her eyes. 'What business is this of yours?'

Giuli spoke quietly, wanting to soothe her. 'I work for a private investigator called Sandro Cellini. He's – he went to identify the – he went with Flavia's – with her partner—' Spit it out, she told herself.

'I know Niccolò,' said Wanda, still tight-lipped.

'Were you close?' said Giuli, leaning towards her. 'You and Flavia. I'm sorry to ask. I really am.' She looked into Terni's eyes, and unwillingly the teacher looked back. Some of the fight went out of her.

'We had been close,' she said, with weary misery. 'They found her at the seaside.' Her voice was flatly uncomprehending.

'You don't know why she would have gone there?'

Sandro's text messages, rambling though they were, had mused on this point. *Why did she go there and not in her own bathroom?*

Reasons presented themselves. She didn't want her husband to find her body. Who could commit suicide with their baby sleeping in the next room? Choose a hotel at random, at the end of a train line? Giuli didn't believe in the random argument.

'She never mentioned a connection with Viareggio to you?'

Terni shook her head, wordless.

Giuli spoke gently. 'You were – her best friend?'

'I suppose,' said Wanda slowly, examining her hands. 'She wasn't one for big gangs of girlfriends. Not really.'

Giuli hesitated. 'She didn't – confide in you? Talk about personal things. Lately, particularly, I suppose. But ever?'

Wanda looked up at last. 'Over eleven years she maybe talked to me – in that way – a handful of times. About her family. You couldn't ask, or she'd clam up straight away.'

Giuli nodded: she knew that feeling. People asking questions you didn't know how to answer. She felt Flavia's presence in the room as she met the teacher's gaze. 'Her father was a violent man,' said Wanda. 'And her mother failed to protect her. Not uncommon, thirty, forty years ago; probably not uncommon now. She ran away from Rome when she was sixteen and enrolled in the university.' There was a gleam of pride in her eyes.

'Abusive? You mean—'

'I mean he hit her,' said Terni, her face set and pale. 'Her mother didn't want to know. That left its mark too. And when the mother died – well.'

'She came to Florence, and she met Niccolò Rosselli.'

'It was a great love affair,' said Wanda. 'They were two halves of the whole.'

'She said that?'

'You could tell. Their beliefs, their ambitions, their politics. They were absolutely committed to each other. He gave her the strength she needed, and she gave him the – sweetness, I suppose.'

'She needed strength?'

Wanda shrugged, uncomfortable, and didn't answer.

'Depression?' Giuli spoke gingerly. The shitty childhood, then the fallout. The cycle of abuse: she knew the terminology. From outside she could hear the chanting of children gathering before school, counting in some game, then a jubilant clamouring as they were released to run, and her heart lifted at the sound.

'I thought she managed it.' Terni looked away, evasive. 'She had her techniques. She had Niccolò. She had her walking. She'd say she knew every park and garden in Florence. We used to go together.' The voice dropped.

'Used to?' Terni examined her hands, and Giuli pressed a little harder. 'You fell out? Grew apart? What? Was it – the baby?'

'The baby,' repeated Wanda, as if she'd never thought of that before. 'I – I don't know.'

Giuli shifted, uncomfortable. 'People change, I don't know. Busy with other things.'

Wanda went on. 'Perhaps,' she said, frowning. 'I wasn't aware of it – but I suppose it's possible. I've known for a long time I can't have children.'

Shit, thought Giuli. Outside the chanting had changed, someone's name was being repeated. *Olu, olu.* It wasn't clear if the child was being persecuted or urged on.

'It's possible I was jealous.' Terni looked up. 'I didn't even know Flavia wanted a baby,' she said, and there was a tinge of something – offence, injury, outrage. 'They were always rather – offhand about that kind of thing. Well, Niccolò certainly. I always had the impression they thought babies were – for people who didn't have a world to save. Plus you couldn't imagine them. . . we all know how babies are made, and it wasn't like Flavia was prudish or anything but . . .'

'You mean you don't think they had a sex life?' Giuli was blunt.

Terni was flustered. 'Oh, God, I don't know. You never do know, do you, about people? It just seemed like it might be a factor. Anyway, I always thought they were agreed on it, one way or another, and with her background – after all, so many years together and she never got pregnant. Does that happen by accident?'

'There might be reasons,' said Giuli. 'As you get older. Things change in the body.' Terni didn't meet her eye: she shifted ground. 'So it was around then, around the time she got pregnant, that you – didn't see so much of each other?'

The tired, dark eyes flickered over Giuli, weighing her up. 'Flavia changed,' she said finally. Giuli waited.

With a sigh Wanda put her face between her hands. 'It was before she got pregnant. The baby was born at the end of July, so I suppose she got pregnant in – October? It was earlier than that I noticed something different. She'd been on some training course in Bologna. . . when was that? First weekend in September. And we – the teachers – we always have a meal at the end of summer, a week or so before term begins, get back into the groove, you know?' Giuli nodded. 'So we went to the usual *pizzeria*. There was something different about her then.' Giuli tilted her head, waiting. 'She was – up.'

'Up?'

'Happy, I suppose.' Wanda frowned. 'In another person, I suppose you might not have noticed. She hardly ate a thing. Jittery. Happy – high, almost. Maybe she and Niccolò – oh, I don't know. I hadn't seen her all summer – they'd been away in July then in the city in August, when I was away. She'd lost weight, that was all I noticed. She said she'd been doing more walking than usual.'

Giuli's heart sank: she thought of the Addictions clinic.

Wanda sighed, absorbed in her memories. 'At school we did speculate about it – about them. She could have been happy just because of the baby, couldn't she? She'd got him to agree on a baby and she was happy.' Again Wanda frowned. 'Except that it wasn't the kind of happy you'd associate with pregnancy. . . you know, comfortable, contented, placid. She's – Flavia had always been lovely to look at, though she didn't know it: when she got thinner she was something else, that fragile kind of beauty – you worried for her. And at our age. . .' She shook her head, colouring. 'I don't know if you know what I mean?'

'I do,' said Giuli, who'd spent her youth starving herself.

'And people commented. She didn't like that.' Again the lips tightened.

'Did *you* comment?'

Terni nodded, and breathed out, a long sad sigh. 'We went for a walk after term started and I started to wonder if she was ill. I said I was worried about her. She stared at me, like she was frightened of something, and she wouldn't answer.' Wanda's face clouded and she looked away quickly, avoiding Giuli's eye. 'That was the end, really.'

'Frightened?' Giuli leaned forwards, intent. 'You don't – you never thought it might be drugs? Anything like that? She didn't start hanging out with – that kind of person?'

Terni made a sound, an incredulous laugh. 'Flavia? Never. No. She was a vegetarian, she barely drank coffee. Two cigarettes a day, and gave those up when she got pregnant. No way. Substances scared her to death.'

There was a silence. 'Do you remember when you saw her last?' said Giuli quietly, leaning back. 'How she was?'

'It was last week.'

Giuli gaped: she hadn't expected that.

Terni took a deep breath. 'I'd hardly seen her in months: I called in to see the baby but she was too tired for visitors. That's what *she* said, the mother-in-law.' She grimaced. 'Then last week Flavia came into school, came up to see me, brought back some textbooks she'd borrowed, some excuse. . . I hadn't lent her any books.' She put one hand to the side of her worn face that was crumpled with regret. 'Clearly she must have wanted to tell me something, or ask me something, I don't know. It was busy – I was about to go into a lesson—' She broke off. 'This place. My God, this place.'

The noise level from downstairs was increasing almost to a din in the echoing stone labyrinth of the building: older children's voices, and footsteps now on the stairs. The maths teacher's gaze strayed to the door, then back, despondently, to the pile of unmarked work on her desk.

'So she said nothing?'

Wanda shook her head. 'I didn't have the time. She ran off. Just dumped the books and bolted down the stairs.'

'It's all right,' said Giuli, without any hope that it was.

Wanda looked at her despairingly. 'Half of them don't have a wage-earner in the family in this school,' she said. 'They speak ten different languages. It got Flavia down too, but never seriously. She thrived on it, helping these kids.'

A head appeared at the door, a cheeky-looking North African kid with a backpack as big as himself. Wanda held up a hand. 'In the corridor a minute,' she said, with weary kindness, and the boy disappeared.

'Right,' said Giuli hurriedly. 'But Flavia said nothing, no clue that – something was going on? Sometimes people give clues. They can't quite come out with it but they drop hints.'

Wanda's face, still directed towards the empty doorway, changed, clouded, and she turned back to look at Giuli. 'I – I don't know,' she said, putting a hand to her head. In the corridor outside more children were arriving, shouting cheerful insults to each other.

'No, she said wait,' the African kid was insisting, just the slightest tinge of a richer accent to the Florentine Italian. Amazing, a kid from Tunisia or Morocco, turning into a Florentine. It seemed to

Giuli in that moment to be a good thing, though she couldn't have said why.

'You think about it, will you?' She got to her feet, carefully laid a card on the desk in front of the teacher. 'If anything comes to mind, you can call me, yes?'

Wanda took the card in both hands. 'But – won't it just – isn't it—?' She stopped for a moment. 'They think it was post-natal, don't they? Isn't that the most likely explanation? Isn't it the least – problematic?'

'You mean, let sleeping dogs lie?' Guili said.

Heads were reappearing around the doorway. Wanda sighed. 'All right, come in,' she called, and the children began to jostle through the door.

'You might find,' said Giuli, leaning down to the woman and speaking quietly but clearly, 'that the problem is, sleeping dogs don't lie still after all.'

The maths teacher looked from the business card to Giuli, their faces only centimetres apart. The children paid them no attention, dumping bags on desks, pulling out chairs. Wanda said nothing. Giuli thought back to the beginning of their conversation, to almost her first question, still unanswered.

'Why Viareggio?' she said softly. 'Why leave your baby and take the train to a seaside town full of happy families, and kill yourself there?'

'I don't know,' said Wanda in a strained voice, leaning around Giuli to focus on the children. 'Carlito,' she called, 'stop that.'

Her gaze lingering on the woman's averted face, Giuli straightened.

Time to go.

But as she paused fractionally in the doorway Giuli saw that the teacher was looking back at her, pleading silently as if she wanted something, or had something to give.

Chapter Fifteen

As Luisa kneeled on the pale carpet in front of a German teenager and pulled patiently at the lacing of a pair of high suede boots in a dark red colour they called *merlot*, the thought sprang into her head that she was close to not wanting to do this for a living for much longer.

Under her right arm there was an ache: it didn't worry her, it had been there on and off for two years. She was more or less intact apart from the breast going, they'd said, all that complicated mesh of tendon and muscle under the arm should function all right; the lymph had been minimally disturbed by the operation but it still might play up, and it did. Her own fault: they'd told her over and over she need only have the lump removed. Too late to start regretting it now. And she didn't regret it.

Luisa sat back on her heels and smiled at the girl, whose mother sat beside her, stiff and anxious with a handbag on her knees. The boots were very expensive. The father, in a Loden coat and hat, was pacing on the pavement outside. The girl was eighteen or so, younger than Chiara. Looking into her eyes Luisa wondered if she was an only child, if she had a boyfriend. The girl gazed back and

Luisa could see that she was on the verge of tears. Family arguments were so common on holiday: were they trying to make something up to her with this present? And for some reason Luisa thought of Viareggio, and red hair in a bathtub.

'Do you like them?' she asked, and the girl nodded slowly. 'Stand up,' said Luisa. 'Walk about.' She gestured down the length of the shop: mirrors everywhere. The girl walked away slowly and, still on her knees, Luisa studied the mother's expression.

'They're expensive,' said Luisa with the girl out of earshot; she grasped for her smattering of German. 'Does she look after her things?' The mother turned towards her eagerly. 'Yes,' she said, 'she's a good girl.' She glanced through the window towards her husband, standing now in his smart coat with his back to the window, hands clasped behind him.

'Well,' said Luisa. 'I expect her feet won't grow any bigger.' The mother smiled sadly. 'And the quality is very good.' Luisa spread her hands and said no more: together they watched as the girl reached the end of the shop and stared at her reflection solemnly. Her back was to them so that she thought herself unobserved, but they could see her in the mirror, eyes fixed on the dark red boots. Luisa wondered if the mother could remember, even faintly as she herself could, a time when it seemed that anything could be solved by a new pair of shoes.

Then they both looked towards the window and as they did the husband turned, looked, nodded, and at last the mother smiled.

Luisa got to her feet, feeling a painful tweak under the arm as she supported herself, an ache in the back of her legs as the tendons straightened. Not young any more. But her earlier despondency had lifted.

Shepherding the small family – three now as the father, having come inside, was standing between them, his hand tentatively on his daughter's shoulder – to the till and Giusy's tender care, Luisa looked out of the window, and saw him.

'Excuse me,' she said, and the four of them, Giusy and the German family, stared after her as she turned and bolted through the shop door. 'Um, right,' she heard Giusy improvise, 'so. . . the boots,' as the door swung shut behind Luisa.

Was he there? The stalls were crowded under the high vaulting of the market's roof, cluttered with racks of purple and tan cheap leather, ugly scarves; stupid, dithering tourists hung about with cameras and backpacks. Luisa dodged and shuffled, desperate to get a view down the aisle, between the packed stalls. Which one had it been? She glanced back at the shop, trying to work out her line of sight, saw the faces staring at her, in the street in her cardigan. Turned back: and there. . . there he was, at the far end of the central aisle of the market, just where she'd seen him before. Looking straight at her, puzzlement dawning.

Luisa stood on tiptoes, to make herself more visible, raised a hand. Realized quite suddenly that she felt absolutely alive, something coursing in her veins that banished the weary anxiety of her morning; of her life. 'Hey!' she shouted, and although a number of heads turned, the young man knew she was addressing him. He shrugged, turned to someone next to him obscured by a tower of handbags, and said something. 'Wait there,' she called, and he laughed. She saw him laugh.

The quickest way, other than a parting of the Red Sea of tourists, was to run around the outside of the colonnaded marketplace past the bronze statue of the little boar, past the tripe stall. Luisa dodged and hurried, holding her breath until she was there and came up short right in front of him. She could smell his aftershave.

'Hello,' she blurted. He looked at her with faint amusement. She saw that the person beside him was not, as she had fleetingly hoped, Chiara, but a stocky, bearded young man. They were both dressed in the casual uniform of kids, market traders and students alike: hooded sweatshirts, plaid shirts on top, jeans.

'Hey,' he said, warily. Luisa became aware of the colour in her cheeks: she pulled her cardigan across her front.

'You know Chiara,' she said, straight out with it. 'Chiara Cavallaro. I saw you talking to her yesterday. Here. '

The two men exchanged glances. Neither looked like trouble to Luisa, she had to admit: young, cheerful, open-faced. But what did she know?

'You ran off,' she said, holding her ground.

'Ran off?' The man shook his head slowly. 'No. I didn't run off anywhere.'

'Listen,' said his companion nervously, 'I'd better—'

'Sure,' said the first man, jerking his head in a gesture of dismissal, 'you get going.' But as he reached the end of the next aisle the bearded young man turned back, and Luisa saw anxiety in his eyes.

The other young man stepped back off the raised stone of the market floor and thrust his hands deep in the pockets of his hooded sweatshirt, his back half turned to her. He turned back. 'If I might ask, Signora. Is there a problem?'

'I'm Luisa Cellini,' she said, sticking her hand out stiffly. Nodding across towards the shop. 'I work in Frollini. I'm a – a friend.'

'Gianluca.' He took her hand curiously, in a brief soft handshake, as if he didn't understand the gesture. The young. 'You're a friend of Chiara's?' He looked dubious.

Luisa sighed. 'I've known her since she was born.' She felt weary suddenly as the adrenaline ebbed. 'I'm a friend of her mother's.' She hesitated, knowing that the information might set her on the wrong side of the fence. 'We're – worried about her.'

'Worried?' Gianluca smiled warily. 'I thought she was looking great.'

Luisa blinked: this was not the response she'd expected. 'You —'

'Didn't you?' He tipped his head on one side. 'I mean, it's a change, sure. But it seems to suit her.'

'Yes,' said Luisa. 'But – you're not – with her? I mean, you're not her—'

'Her boyfriend? No.' Gianluca nodded in the direction in which the bearded man had disappeared. 'I'm *his* boyfriend, Signora.' Eyeing her for a reaction. Luisa was too tired, suddenly, to bridle, to say, You can't shock me, young man. I work in fashion. And he seemed to see something in the drop of her shoulders.

'Look, I'm sorry, Signora Cellini,' he said, hands thrust guiltily back down in his kangaroo pockets. 'I didn't mean to be rude. D'you – I don't know, d'you want a coffee or something?' He chewed the inside of his lip, eyes darting. 'I'm a friend of Chiara's, yes. And I guess – well.' He looked at his watch. 'I've got a class at eleven.'

'All right,' said Luisa impulsively. 'All right. I'll – I've just got to tell them, in the shop. Caffè La Borsa? Five minutes.'

Be there, she thought, meeting the anxious eyes of the departing German family as she pushed her way back inside the shop. As if somehow this kid with his hooded sweatshirt and his sexual freedom turning up meant everything, meant people looked out for each other and kids respected their elders and the world was on its axis still.

Be there.

*

The two men ambled up to the rusted iron railings in the cool bright morning as if they had all the time in the world. Vesna watched as they exchanged a handshake, and the dustbin man in his fluorescent orange jacket leaned down to look at the small handmade sign on the gate that informed the clientele that the hotel would be closed briefly for renovations.

Clientele: that was a joke. She'd made precisely two phone calls for Calzaghe to put off customers: that was the sum of their bookings for the next three weeks, never mind three days. And anyone who could be bothered to look as closely at the sign as the dustbin man had, would probably reckon that any renovation work was long overdue.

'Just a couple of days,' the policeman, Tufato, had said reassuringly. Not knowing whether to address himself to Calzaghe the sleazebag, puffing in his string vest with sweaty outrage, or to Vesna the foreign chambermaid. 'You know, suicide – it's a crime. Evidence must be gathered. A formality, in this case.'

She didn't know where Calzaghe was: he had not appeared this morning. He was probably sitting on the sofa in his dead mother's apartment, watching porn. He'd made enough remarks to her about how he liked to spend his spare time for her not to need to apply her imagination to the subject. Vesna in her turn had perfected a look of dead-eyed disinterest in response to such remarks: it seemed to work, for the moment.

The dustbin man looked up at her before walking away: at least *he* was a decent bloke. The man knew everyone and everything, and she'd never heard him make an unpleasant remark about foreigners. Quiet in his habits, modest: she liked them quiet.

The other man, however, remained; he was wearing a battered hat. Vesna stayed where she was on the porch, leaning on the railing. He held his head up, looking steadily at her, and the longer he looked, the more she thought, who are you? Come to ask questions, she decided.

The police had asked questions. Did anyone visit the dead woman? Did she make any calls? They had looked in her bag and found her identity card, a change of underwear.

No one had called for her. She had not phoned out using the hotel landline, but then who did these days? People had mobiles, only they hadn't found hers. On the verandah, Vesna shifted uneasily. Should suicide be a crime? It was already a mortal sin, and if you believed in mortal sin, wasn't that enough? But in her heart she knew there were reasons not just to let it go. To ask questions, to know – what? If a life might have been saved, restored if the right thing had been said or done at the right moment. Or not.

She stepped off the porch.

'Can I help you?'

It was very quiet: from the other side of the boardwalk behind Sandro came the sound of a trailer being wheeled down to the sea, the slap of halyards against an aluminium mast, the slow, happy voices of the rich, indulging themselves.

'Hello,' he said, hands up at the railings as though holding on to prison bars.

The girl – woman, he saw as she walked towards him down the weed-clogged gravel, close to thirty – did have the pale look of someone confined inside all day. Slight but strong, in a maid's button-through housecoat washed almost to whiteness from what might once have been pink.

'The owner's Calzaghe,' the soft-spoken dustbin man had told him, his quiet voice betraying only the slightest hint of distaste, but it was enough. If a man smelling of the week's fish-heads and rotten potato peelings looks like he wants to hold his nose when he says your name – well.

'I feel sorry for the girl,' the man had said. He spoke quietly, out of respect perhaps because they hadn't got to the railings yet and the girl – woman – wouldn't have been able to hear. 'She's a hard worker. I hope he keeps his hands off her, anyway. From Bosnia, I believe.'

Not Croatia then: an easy mistake to make, though possibly an unforgivable one if you were the Bosnian in question. Muslim? Sandro couldn't tell: she had dark eyes but then so did an awful lot of Catholics. He took a step back from the high railings, took off his hat and waited.

'We're closed,' she said, eyeing him, hands thrust defensively in the pockets of her overall. 'For the foreseeable future.' Her Italian was clear and uninflected.

'I know,' Sandro said.

'You've come about her, haven't you?'

They all knew. It comforted Sandro obscurely to be reminded that Flavia Matteo's unnatural death sat at the heart of this small community and would not be ignored. *Just one of those things, none of our business, she was only passing through. . .* She had not passed, she had stayed, she would never leave this place. It was everyone's business, it seemed, and that was as it should be.

Of course he would have come about the dead woman, he told himself roughly, guarding against sentiment. They must have had all sorts already: journalists, nosy parkers, ambulance chasers. Making something your business doesn't mean you care, not these days. Everyone was everyone else's business these days with the internet, and no one cared a damn. But leaning down, the maid tugged at a rusted bolt, straightened and let him through. She walked ahead of him without a word, straight-backed as a dancer.

Stepping behind her inside the hotel's dim lobby, Sandro detected bleach, ancient cooking smells, and a grittiness under his feet on the speckled grey stone of the *pavimento*. If the question *Why here?* had seemed the significant one as he and Niccolò Rosselli had approached the seaside town, it grew even more insistent inside the Stella Maris itself. Why *here*?

'*Permesso?*' asked Sandro reflexively as he crossed the threshold, but there was no answer.

'Like I said,' said the chambermaid, 'we're closed. There's no one home.'

The lobby was wide and shallow, in a wide, shallow building, two doors to left and right standing open in sunshine, a third in darkness behind a vast cracked Biedermeier reception desk. Above the desk was a row of dark wood pigeon holes with keys hanging inside them, and above that a broad staircase curved upstairs. They stood together in the gloom.

'What's your name?' asked Sandro, and she almost smiled.

'Vesna,' she said, and he heard her surprise. He supposed people didn't bother to ask: Americans might do, he supposed, they were friendly. But then, he couldn't imagine Americans staying here.

'Sandro Cellini,' he said, and then, sacrificing subtlety for clarity, 'I'm a private detective.'

She betrayed no response, only lifted a hand to indicate one of the sunlit doors. 'Please,' she said.

It was the dining room. Chairs were upended on a dozen small tables. She'd been in the middle of cleaning: greying muslin curtains were folded on a buffet table along one wall, a broom leaned against the long bare windows and dust motes sparkled in the clean sunshine. She's probably not even going to be paid, thought Sandro, but still she's working. With a swift movement Vesna took a chair from the nearest table and set it down for him.

'I would offer you a coffee,' she said. 'But I am not permitted.'

'Ah,' said Sandro. 'Not permitted by. . . ?'

'By my boss,' she said. 'Signore Calzaghe. One meal every day. If I require coffee I may have it on my break, in the town.' She shrugged, eyes veiled. 'It's nice to get out anyway.'

They both remained standing: Sandro leaned forward and took another chair down. 'Please,' he said.

After a moment's hesitation, she sat. 'A private investigator,' she said, turning the words over. There was, after all, some trace of her foreignness in the accent, a little sharp edge to the rolling 'r'. 'They already asked questions.'

'Yes,' said Sandro, 'I've been there. To the – police morgue. I spoke with the officer.' He put his head on one side. 'You think it was a suicide?'

Vesna drew in her lower lip and her eyes widened, seeming darker. 'You saw her?' she said, very quietly. 'Of course, suicide. What else?'

Sandro nodded. 'What else indeed?' he said, almost to himself. 'Perhaps she didn't mean to do it.' Vesna drew a hand quickly across her cheek, wiping at something, but she seemed dry-eyed.

'No one came,' he said. 'The police said you told them she had no visitors. But – forgive me – are you the only person working here? The only staff member?' Vesna shrugged, holding his gaze. 'And you're here all the time? What about when you – get away? For your coffee. Or anything.'

Did she have a boyfriend? She was pretty enough, but perhaps she had no time for boyfriends, or no patience. 'I don't get away so often,' she said, with the air of admitting something shameful. 'There is Signore Calzaghe, of course,' she went on, frowning. 'He's always there, sitting on the verandah. He watches. I can't go for any break without checking with him first.'

'Always there,' repeated Sandro. 'Only not now.'

Again she shrugged, putting a hand out to the surface of the table and raising her palm to inspect it for dust. 'He locked the kitchen,' she said with the ghost of a smile. 'So I can't steal anything. No guests, no one to watch any more. He's probably at his mother's place.'

Sandro nodded. 'But they asked him too, anyway?' he said. 'The police asked him about visitors?'

She nodded, still watching him intently. 'You think someone else is involved?'

'There's always someone else involved,' he said. 'In my experience. Where unhappiness is concerned.' He spoke with deliberate care, because she was foreign, but he saw a watchful understanding in her eyes. 'I'm here with her husband, you see. He needs to know why, of course. It's a terrible thing, to feel one did not see, did not feel, so much unhappiness.'

'And a child,' she said, pain evident in the dark eyes now. 'She – had had a child. Just – recently.' It was not a question.

'You read that in the newspapers?' He couldn't work it out otherwise. But had the paper mentioned it?

'I don't read their papers here,' she said with an edge of disdain. 'I didn't read, I saw. I saw on her body, she had had a child. I saw—' And she broke off.

'You saw?' Then he understood, or partially he did. 'Ah. You found her.'

Reflexively Vesna – and in that second he wished he knew her surname, out of some desire to award her more respect – brought both arms up across her chest, hands resting on her shoulders, and she nodded.

'She was up there two days alone, dead. Or thinking of doing it,' she said. 'And we were down here. I wish I had known.'

'You might have saved her?' said Sandro gently, leaning forward on the hard chair, elbows on his knees as he looked up at her. 'I think there are others closer to her she might have talked to, and she didn't. It seems unlikely that you would have been able to help her.'

You never knew, of course. To look at her, Vesna might have been just the woman to talk to. But he couldn't say that.

The maid glanced down at the floor 'I know,' she muttered. 'I know, I know.' Shutting him up.

Sandro could see her unfocused stare, and he knew she was remembering something terrible. It was an awful moment, seeing what was left when life had gone; Sandro had seen enough of it himself. There's so little in a human body, when the brain's stopped working, the lungs, the heart. He would not ask her about that. Not yet.

'Did you talk to her at all?' he asked. 'Did you – I don't know, I expect it's hard, guests come and go. But did you form any impression of her at all?'

Vesna raised her head and looked at him curiously, as if this was something she had not been asked already. 'Impression?' She straightened, leaned back in the chair and looked up at the dusty plaster cornices of the ceiling, her bare legs stretched in front of her; he could see the downy hairs on them. She wore ugly rubber overshoes like a medical orderly, but her ankles were fine-boned. Sandro averted his eyes.

She brought her head down and looked at him. 'She was frightened,' she said, sounding surprised. 'That's the impression I had of her.'

'Did you say that to the police?'

Slowly Vesna shook her head. 'No – I – no. They didn't really ask me – that. And I don't think they would understand what I mean.' She chewed her lip, eyes dark.

Frightened. Of what? Of whom? 'The room *was* locked,' said Sandro quickly. 'When you found her? No one could have—'

She stared at him. 'The door was locked, yes,' she said. 'From the inside. I had to use my pass key to get in.' She passed a hand over her face, and Sandro shifted in his chair at her discomfort. 'Her key was on the dressing table. The police took it.'

There was a brief silence. Then: 'Why do you think she was frightened? What gave you that feeling?' He wondered: if Flavia Matteo was planning suicide, she might well have been afraid.

What would that fear have looked like? He felt something, in the bright clean sunshine, he felt the presence of darkness through the door that led back into the lobby, at his back.

He must have moved, turned his head, because Vesna said tentatively, 'Do you want to see? Her room?' Sandro almost shook his head, because the truth was he dreaded even going back into the lobby.

'I know what fear is like, perhaps,' said Vesna when he didn't answer, and for a moment he thought she was talking about him. 'I know how people smell, when they are afraid. When you are in a room with fourteen people in a house, not knowing whether you will be shot if you come outside?'

Sandro remained silent. This was beyond his experience. 'When your mother does not return when she's only gone to buy bread and you go to look for her? You can smell your own sweat, you can't stop it. She was like that, Flavia Matteo. She was like an animal, so thin under that linen blouse. I could see the sweat on her neck, and I could see her eyes, looking, looking, and her breathing, it was very light and quick.'

The maid exhaled, smoothed the skirt of her overall, her look turned inward, talking in a rush as though all of this had only just come to her, all at once. 'Her sheets were like the sheets of a child who can't sleep, a child with a fever. I would have changed them but he does not allow it. Sheets changed every three days, but I only did her room the first morning. After that – it was "Do not disturb".' Her eyes flickered.

Sandro held her gaze: there were so many people, so many potential witnesses, it wasn't worth asking a thing because they didn't notice anything. But Vesna was different. He took a chance.

'Do you think she was afraid of – someone? She thought someone might come to find her, someone was looking for her? It might be why she stayed in her room.' Even as he said this, it didn't make sense to him. Was she hiding? She got up at dawn to come here, she wasn't fleeing someone in the street. And she'd been before; this wasn't after all a random choice.

On the evidence it seemed to Sandro more likely that she had come here to find someone than to escape someone.

Vesna crossed her arms, thinking. Shook her head. 'It was more like – she was ill. Afraid of something – in her own body, in her own head maybe.'

Was that how post-natal depression manifested itself? Sandro didn't know, did he? Was what Luisa had experienced post-natal depression? She hadn't been frightened; she'd been like a dead thing. Again, he didn't know. He was a man after all.

Vesna went on. 'And she did come out, that first day.' She frowned, thinking intently. 'She didn't seem afraid to go outside. That wasn't it. She went into the town.' She raised her head and blinked.

'She did? She went for a walk?' Like me, thought Sandro, an early walk, to clear the head. And suddenly he thought, I'm not here alone, though, am I? Damn. He looked at his watch: eight-thirty. Would Rosselli be awake? Would he wait, patiently, eating breakfast at the hotel, for Sandro to return? Somehow Sandro doubted it: he stood up in sudden impatience.

Vesna looked at him, barely registering his movement. 'She went out – I thought she was. . . I thought she needed something, I heard her downstairs asking Calzaghe where to find something. He was giving her directions. I heard him tell her.'

'Really? Can you remember what she was looking for?'

Slowly Vesna shook her head, still looking up at him like a child. 'I don't know. He said – what did she say? Something about, back towards the station. Next to – yes. Next to the *pizzeria* there's one, he said. But I don't know one *what*.'

'OK,' said Sandro, thinking furiously. 'OK.'

Vesna got up, awkwardly. 'It's important, isn't it?' she said, biting her lip. 'I should have said.' She hugged herself.

'Calzaghe should have said,' countered Sandro. 'Did he – tell the police, I mean? Where's his mother's place? I should talk to him.'

The maid looked away, uneasy. 'I'm sure he didn't tell them anything,' she said. 'He doesn't like the police. He didn't want to give them any reason for blaming us – for what happened. He said, Give them the chance and they'll pin it on us.' She hesitated. 'Except he always pins everything on me. His mother's place is in the hills, behind the station. She's dead, it's her old apartment. He goes there – for his leisure time.' She studied her feet in the ugly rubber clogs.

'Leisure time,' said Sandro. 'Right. Well, I wouldn't want to disturb him. I can have a look around myself. He directed her to – the *pizzeria*, you said? Towards the station?'

'I suppose he meant the Venere.' She looked paler than before. 'It's on the way there.'

Almost to himself Sandro said, 'But there's the husband. I've got to get back to him.'

'The husband,' she repeated. 'I had a husband, once. In Bosnia.'

'You look too young,' said Sandro in an attempt at gallantry, wanting to bring colour into her face. He thought, I won't ask what happened to the husband.

'It must be terrible for him,' said Vesna with sudden feeling. 'For the child. The rejection. The child is not enough to stay alive for?' Her hand came up to her face again but still Sandro could see no tears.

'I can go,' she said abruptly. 'Why not? There's nothing for me to do here. What can he do to me? I can go and see what there is next to the *pizzeria*. If you give me your number, I can ring you. Or I can tell you if Calzaghe comes?'

She pulled a battered pink mobile from her pocket, the kind a child might own, and deftly moved her thumb across its keypad. 'You give me your number, I will call you immediately, and then you'll have my number?' She frowned, biting her lip, and Sandro understood that this was not usual for her, this kind of exchange of trust. He repeated his number to her, and felt his phone blip as she dialled it. He took it out and pressed *Reject*.

'OK,' he said. 'I have to go.' But something held him there a minute longer.

The ultimate rejection. Was that what Flavia Matteo had done? Was it rejection or love? Was she hiding or seeking? Was she afraid of herself or another? Vesna stood there in her creased and faded overall with her arms folded tight across her body, holding something in.

She watched him. 'But she was not a bad woman,' she said, when he did not make a move to go. 'She was only afraid.' He said nothing, but waited.

'In the bath,' she said, with a great weariness, and at last he saw it, a gleam at the corner of her eye, the tiny overflow on to her pale cheek but now she did not put a hand up. 'In the bath, when I found her, she – she was not naked. She put on her underwear. She did not want to be naked, found like that.'

Sandro saw her hands tremble in her lap.

'It's nothing,' she said blankly, as if this small, terrible observation had drained her.

Flavia Matteo was not a bad woman: she was afraid.

'No,' said Sandro. 'It's not nothing.'

*

When the private investigator had gone, Vesna walked slowly into the back room off the lobby, and between Calzaghe's cluttered desk and the filing cabinet and the coat rack with his old coats smelling of grease and sweat, she sat down and cried. She cried for about twenty minutes, not worrying about the noise because no one could hear, and then she stopped. There always came a moment, with tears, when you had to stop because you thought, what next? I can't cry for ever. She stood up, removed her apron and walked out into the sun.

Chapter Sixteen

'YOU TALKED TO HER?'

The phone bleeped: another call trying to get through. 'Wanda,' said Giuli. 'She's called Wanda.' She was in the cloister of the Women's Centre, pacing. Could she lose her job, skulking like this, trying to get confidential information out of people? Spying. She held the phone away from her face. *Enzo*, it said. *Hold call and answer?*

'Just a second,' she said. Then to Enzo, wary, '*Caro?* Hold on a sec. This won't take a minute, I'll call you back.' He didn't get a chance to respond before she switched back to Sandro.

'It's Enzo,' she said.

'Right,' said Sandro and his voice dropped, despondent. 'What?' said Giuli. He liked Enzo, didn't he?

'I might have landed him in it,' said Sandro wearily. 'The Frazione got broken into last night.' A heavy sigh. 'To be honest, I'd forgotten about it. Like a bad dream, you know? The *avvocato*, Bastone, he called me at God knows what time. . . two in the morning. The police had been, something about computers. I said Enzo'd be the guy to help him get things back to rights.

Bastone doesn't seem to be able to find his own backside with both hands.'

'Funny, isn't it?' said Giuli, softening. 'You'd go to Enzo with a problem rather than leave it to a lawyer with half a dozen letters after his name.'

'He's a good lad,' said Sandro, reticent as ever. 'Are we still coming to dinner tomorrow night?'

'Oh, God,' said Giuli. She'd forgotten.

'No problem,' said Sandro. 'We can do it another time.'

'No,' said Giuli reluctantly. 'It was Enzo's idea. I can't cancel for him, can I?'

'I guess not,' agreed Sandro gloomily. 'And Luisa's keen.'

There was a silence in which they each reflected on their good fortune, and the duties it entailed.

'So,' said Sandro. 'Wanda. Flavia's friend, right?'

'She didn't have many friends, is what I found out. She and Niccolò were joined at the hip. The only thing she did for relaxation was go on long walks in every park and garden in the city, she smoked two cigarettes a day until she got pregnant, no drink, no drugs.'

Giuli sniffed, there was just an edge of autumn to the wind and her nose was running. Sandro remained silent.

'According to Wanda, Flavia changed just before she got pregnant: she lost a lot of weight and was – distracted. Preoccupied. Looked beautiful, said Wanda. She put it down to hormones, maybe.' Dutifully she repeated all she'd been told: dates next because she knew Sandro would want to know precisely, his policeman's brain. 'It would have been a month or so before she got pregnant: Wanda dated it from when they went on some training course in Bologna in September.'

'Bologna.' It struck her as entirely typical that Sandro was interested in Bologna and not hormones.

'But no other friends? She didn't confide in this Wanda about what had changed? If anything.'

'The opposite,' said Giuli. 'Before, she'd started to loosen up – she'd had a hard time as a kid, said Wanda, and then her relationship with Niccolò' – how had she described it? – 'was always very high-minded, very intense, didn't allow for girly chat, was the impression I got, or maybe she just wasn't that type of woman. Flavia had started to open up in recent years – but only to Wanda, from what she said. Then this weight loss, this hormonal thing if you like, and she clammed up. Shut everyone out.'

Sandro grunted uneasily. 'Hormones,' he said. 'I suppose there are theories about women of a certain age.'

'Like me?' said Giuli lightly.

'Not like you,' he said. And cleared his throat. 'Though myself, I think after forty if a woman loses weight, people don't generally think she looks great, whatever they say. They think she's got cancer.'

Or something. Giuli realized she hadn't told him yet, about the Addictions clinic. Who was she protecting? Flavia Matteo was dead. It felt like Giuli was somehow protecting herself: don't judge me, don't judge her. People make mistakes.

But the one person she could trust was at the other end of the line, listening. And addictions didn't come out of nowhere, you had to have your need, and you had to have your dealer.

'Cancer?' Giuli said. 'I don't think it was cancer. But I think she had a – a problem.' She cast about, trying to make sense of it, the non-drinking vegetarian. 'An – addiction.'

'I thought you said no drugs?' Sandro was incredulous.

'No, she was frightened—'

Of drugs, she was going to add, but Sandro jumped in. 'Frightened?' he said, too quickly. 'That's what the girl said too. You don't think she was trying to come off something, coming out here? Cold turkey, kind of thing?'

'What girl?' said Giuli.

'The chambermaid in Flavia's hotel,' said Sandro. 'The girl – woman – who found her body.'

Giuli struggled to get her head clear. 'Withdrawal?' She shook her head, slowly. 'As far as I can tell she was seeing someone here in the Addictions clinic more than a year ago. Around the time, I suppose, that she lost the weight. She stopped going after she got pregnant.'

'That doesn't mean she came off it,' said Sandro. 'Whatever it was.'

Giuli hadn't considered that. 'But the baby. . . ' She stopped, choked.

'The baby was healthy. Is healthy. She might just have been lucky.'

Lucky. Not really: neither of them spoke.

'I'll try and find something out,' she said eventually. 'I'm a bit worried – about pushing things here, though. It's delicate, what with them being colleagues and all.'

'Tell me about it,' said Sandro, with feeling. 'Talking of colleagues—' He paused. '*Ex*-colleagues, Pietro gets in touch today, after weeks, asking about Rosselli.' He frowned. 'Something's not right, Chiara maybe. Or maybe it's me: we communicate mainly via Gloria and Luisa these days.'

Giuli heard the unhappiness in his voice and didn't know what to say. 'Look,' she said uncomfortably, 'I told Enzo I'd call him back. Everything OK there? Otherwise, I mean?' Because how could it be, really? 'How's Niccolò?'

There was a long sigh. 'Rough,' said Sandro. 'He's pretty rough. He's inside eating breakfast.' She pictured Sandro standing in the sun outside the hotel, twitchy at being cooped up with a grieving man. 'It seems pretty clear Flavia killed herself. The maid gave me a bit of background.' He paused. 'Nice girl. I suppose – I suppose we'll be back this afternoon, if he'll agree to leave here now. He wouldn't yesterday. I haven't told him about the break-in yet.' There was a pause.

'Look,' he said, 'if you see that Wanda again, can you ask her if she can look over the names in the address book of Flavia's mobile? Well, their mobile, I suppose. The joint mobile. I suppose I can text you the list of names.' He sounded vaguely flabbergasted at the idea of the technology involved. 'To identify them. There might be someone else you can talk to.'

'Sure,' said Giuli. 'Um – give him our – our best regards, will you? Our condolences.' Sandro grunted and hung up.

Giuli looked at the mobile a while. She genuinely could not remember a time when she hadn't had one; there'd always been some dodgy Chinese fake or piece of stolen goods to be had for next to nothing. Cigarettes, a little fold of cash, and a mobile. The panic if you lost it, the frantic attempt to remember the lost numbers, the messages, the people who might be trying to get hold of you. She stepped out of the cloister and into the sun that shone on the scrubby grass quadrangle.

When it was allocated to the Women's Centre, the convent had been made over to be as plain and penitential, it seemed to Giuli, as possible. No orange trees or statuary, the vaulted cloister scrubbed clean, only a fragment or two of eroded frescoes bearing sparse witness. A calming environment: perhaps the theory was that if they left any of the religion behind it might stir up negative feelings among the sinners who visited the Centre. Guilt, say.

Giuli felt the smooth, warm weight of the phone in her hand. Did she feel guilty, was that her trouble, guilty for having wasted her life and abused her body and done one or two stupid, ugly things? But wasn't guilt just – natural? In a way it made the world function. She tried to imagine a person free from it. Those well-fed politicians acting like blue-arsed baboons with teenage immigrant girls in some brothel in Rome, did they feel guilty? Maybe it was part of the fun for them.

The sun fell on Giuli's face. The cloister was quiet. She was waiting for the scrape of chairs, banging of doors and chatter of voices that accompanied a staff break. Waiting, specifically, for the nurse from Addictions to come out so that she could try and persuade her to breach her duty of confidentiality – and do so to someone such as Giuli, who was as far from being there in an official capacity as was possible. But it was still early and so she dialled Enzo, unsure if her heart was sinking because she'd spent too much time contemplating ethics, or because she just dreaded talking to him. Her own *fidanzato*, her betrothed.

Sandro would say that you only have to know the difference between right and wrong. Don't talk about guilt, don't invent sins. She could even hear his impatient voice in her head: don't indulge yourself. The phone rang three times and then Enzo answered. At the sound of his voice the dread evaporated, the sky above her seemed suddenly a brilliant blue.

'Hey, darling,' she said. 'What's up?'

'I don't know, exactly,' he said. 'But it's not good.'

Out of the corner of her eye Giuli saw movement in one corner of the cloister and she stepped back out of the sunlight.

'What d'you mean?' she said, watching. Two doctors – both women – were standing, smoking outside the door that led off the STD corridor. She shifted uneasily. 'Oh, yes, Bastone. Sandro told me he'd landed you in it.'

'He did?' Enzo sounded serious. 'Well, I guess he did the right thing. Bastone's in a proper state, God knows what he was thinking, letting them—' He broke off. 'You still there?'

'Yes,' said Giuli, forcing herself to concentrate. 'There was a break-in, Sandro said. In the middle of the night.'

'Bastone called me just after you went out,' said Enzo. 'Seven-thirty.'

'He can't have slept,' said Giuli, thinking. 'Sandro said he called at two in the morning or something. Called them at the seaside.'

'He'd got the place made secure, at least,' said Enzo. 'Not that there was a whole lot of damage, it's hardly Fort Knox. A cracked pane of glass, which was incidental. The locks are so old it must have taken them all of a minute and a half to force the door.' He sounded despondent. 'I should have said something about it months ago, just didn't get around to it.'

'And what did they take?'

'The laptop. Worth about a hundred euros, if that.'

He sounded worried, though, more worried than she could remember him being. Enzo didn't panic, ever.

'Was there a lot of stuff on it? Useful stuff?'

'Nothing that's not backed up. Mailing lists. Publicity material. Donors' details. It's not that I'm worried about, it's not lost. It's—'

'What?' Giuli said sharply. 'What is it you're worried about?'

'These weren't thieves,' Enzo said. 'They're not going to sell that laptop. They want what's on it. They want something on us, on the Frazione.'

'But there's nothing. . . ' Giuli swallowed '. . . to worry about. Is there?'

'I mean,' he said patiently, 'the names, the people; someone wants to know who's behind us, who's involved, who to target. That's my worry.'

Giuli shifted the phone under her chin. 'I thought we'd done with all that? That conspiracy theory stuff.' She spoke uneasily. 'I thought this was just a – personal thing.'

'Yes,' he said, sounding strained. 'Well, let's hope so. I mean – it's bad enough, isn't it? The personal thing.' Were there things he wasn't telling her? 'I'll – I think maybe I'll give Sandro a call. Tell him what Bastone told me, the police and all that. What they – what they said to him. What they did.'

'All right,' Giuli said hesitantly, thinking of what Sandro had said about Pietro. She lifted a hand to shade her eyes: in the furthest corner of the cloister she saw the green scrubs and white cap of a nurse appear, luminous in the vaulted shade. 'All right – look, I've got to go, angel.'

The woman stood her ground as Giuli approached across the grass, but she eyed her warily. In her top pocket was the outline of a soft packet of cigarettes: her own little addiction.

Giuli stopped the other side of the low wall and leaned against the fine pillar of pale grey stone. Under the cap the nurse's brown hair was very short and threaded with white. What was her name? Their paths rarely crossed, but Giuli put calls through to Addictions often enough. 'Sorry,' she said.

'What for?' said the woman, her voice smoke-roughened. She fished for the packet without taking her eyes off Giuli.

'It's your break,' said Giuli. 'I don't want to spoil it.' The name came to her, along with the sound of the woman's voice, and a distant echo of something else. 'It's Barbara, isn't it?'

'And you're Giulietta.'

There was something about the way she said it. 'I work the switchboard,' she said guardedly.

'I know that,' said Barbara, eyeing her narrowly. 'I put in a word for you when you applied for the job. Though I don't suppose you'd have been told.'

Giuli stared, uncomprehending. 'You put in a word for me?'

'You don't remember when the Women's Centre was in the Borgo Santa Monaca?' The nurse lit up and took a deep drag. 'I've been in this job a long time.'

Shit, thought Giuli. 'I don't remember,' she said. 'There's a lot I don't remember about those days.'

'I cleaned you up a few times,' said the nurse, blowing smoke out of the side of her mouth. 'We'd talk about rehab and treatments and I'd give you a diet sheet and the methadone and you'd disappear off the face of the earth for a few months.'

'And you still put a word in for me for the job?'

Barbara's eye was caught by something over Giuli's shoulder: she took the cigarette from her mouth and held it cupped under one hand. Officially, smoking was not even allowed in the cloister – nowhere that was technically enclosed by the premises.

'There was always something about you, Sarto,' she said drily. They were probably the same age, thought Giuli, seeing the woman's cracked lips, the fine lines around her eyes. Good-looking still – maybe more so for being close to the end of caring what men thought. Or maybe Barbara had never cared.

She inhaled the smoke rising from under her hand, and sneaked another quick drag. 'You knew what was happening to you. You kept messing up but you kept coming back, too. You never gave up. You knew the difference – and most of them never did, even when they were way back up the line compared to you.'

'Knew the difference?'

'Between behaving well and behaving badly,' said Barbara, taking a long pull on the last of her cigarette, and stubbing it out carefully in a matchbox she took from her pocket. 'Good and bad, right and wrong, you know.'

'I'm not so sure,' said Giuli, resting her cheek against the smooth warmth of the grey stone pillar, suddenly tired.

'That's part of it,' said Barbara. 'Not being sure is part of it.' She stepped closer and Giuli could smell the cigarettes on her breath.

'So,' she said. 'What can I do for you this time, Giulietta Sarto?'

*

He was there, but it looked to Luisa that if she'd been a second longer than her five minutes, he'd have upped and gone.

The Caffè La Borsa was tiny and mirrored and twinkled with golden light: it made Luisa – who'd been there only once, for the shows – think of one of those bars in Paris. It was a tourist place – that was the business they were all in, on this street – but it was fine. Giancarlo was sitting at a tiny round table in the furthest corner, as if trying to hide, a lost cause in this little, light-filled box of a place.

Luisa paused at the bar, asking for two coffees and two glasses of water: Giancarlo had nothing in front of him and she'd be damned if he got away that quickly, not even giving her the time it took to drink a glass of water.

'So you think we're shocked,' she said, setting down the water and the tiny cup and saucer. 'By what you boys get up to? There've been gay men in this city for thousands of years. And if I were prejudiced I'd be in the wrong business, wouldn't I?' She was feeling better. 'Is your mother shocked? I bet she's not.'

He bobbed his head down. 'I didn't mean—' He put two spoons of sugar in his coffee and stirred it, a flush beginning at his neck.

'So I'm shocking you now, is that it?' He laughed, and she saw him relax.

'No,' he said, looking at her directly with clear green eyes. 'It's just my ma died a while back.'

'She wouldn't have batted an eyelid.' Luisa felt the need to say it. 'Look at you! Nothing to find fault with.' She didn't know what it was in the boy that was bringing this out in her: the euphoria of finding him here, his sweet cleanness, his dead mother even – she'd no idea.

She'd dashed in and out of the shop and hadn't given Giusy and

Beppe a chance to complain. Still, she couldn't hang about.

'Right,' Luisa said. 'So what's the story with Chiara? She's moved out just like that to live with this boyfriend. She's barely twenty! Her parents haven't met the man. Is it any wonder they're worried?'

Their coffee cups were already empty. He looked over her shoulder into the street: she turned to see what he'd seen but no one was looking inside the Caffè La Borsa. No escape for him there.

'What's she said to you? To her girlfriends? You're at the university too, right? Who does she hang out with? What's this man like?'

A couple came in: a man in a suit, ruddy-faced, past his best, with a woman in very high heels. She spoke in a little girl's voice, asking complainingly for a Mimosa. Some men, Luisa reflected, wanted that bargain. Most of them wanted it, it sometimes seemed to her, after a day of serving pretty, spoiled women. What would she see in him but the wallet? Giancarlo shifted in his seat, but didn't bolt. Slowly he took a sip of his water.

'I haven't seen the guy,' he said. 'None of us has. Come to that, I haven't seen much of her lately. Since she met him, Chiara comes in less and less and she keeps a low profile. A couple of the girls were complaining she's avoiding them.' He smiled. 'But then, maybe that's down to them. A particular kind of girl, if you know what I mean.'

'What kind of girl?' Luisa didn't know what he meant.

Giancarlo leaned back. 'Oh, you know. You've known Chiara long enough – she was one of them too until now. Those girls who go on demonstrations and wear baggy sweaters and don't brush their hair.'

'Oh, those,' said Luisa drily. 'You don't approve?'

'Do you? Working in that place?' And he nodded towards Frollini. 'I'd have thought they'd drive you mad.'

Luisa eyed him. 'I think they make the world go round,' she said, surprising herself. 'Idealism? Isn't it what being a kid is all about?' She laughed. 'All right, I do wish they'd brush their hair. I don't think you have to hide yourself in a paper bag to believe in something. It's like – the burkha, isn't it? Men need to learn that just because a woman looks good, it doesn't mean she's available.' She stopped abruptly, because he was staring at her. 'Speech over,' she said. 'I'm not prejudiced, is all. I liked Chiara as she was.' And she realized it was true. 'It's too soon for that kind of dressing up.' She glanced at the woman at the bar, running her finger around the rim of her glass while the man stared at her hungrily. 'High heels and all that.'

'Right,' Giancarlo said slowly, still frowning. 'But parents never are ready for their kids to grow up, are they? They always want them to stay as they are, sweet and innocent. Life's not innocent, fun's not always clean.' He shifted along the banquette, preparing, Luisa could see, to make his getaway.

'I know that,' she said.

'You know what?' he said, calling her bluff. 'I think there's a bit of, you know, rough play involved here. I think Chiara's a bit scared of him. That can work. It's the kind of thing parents don't like the idea of, but – we like to experiment, you know? With an authority figure.'

Luisa stared. Not Chiara, she thought.

'So she's stopped talking to the girls who don't brush their hair but she talks to you? Because you understand, and they don't?'

Giancarlo didn't move off his seat but both hands were down on the leatherette, ready. His shirt came tight across his body with the movement and Luisa saw the outline of something in his top pocket, a little cylindrical shape, pointed at one end. A – not a syringe? She averted her eyes, mind working. Stop it, she thought. You're not his mother.

'Maybe,' he said uneasily, 'I mean, she did come over yesterday when she saw me. Showing off her new look.'

He rubbed a hand up and down his arm, as if cold suddenly, though it was warm in the bar.

'But it's not – I mean, it's happened all of a sudden. I don't think she wants to stop being anyone's friend, not really – I suppose it's to do with him, you know. When there's suddenly only one person that matters, everyone else has to take a back seat.' He looked away. 'Love, you know.'

'Love,' repeated Luisa. The word sounded old and false.

'Yeah, love,' he said, looking back at her, defiant.

'I think maybe you mean sex,' she said, and looked involuntarily at the couple at the bar.

'Maybe I do,' he said, and with that slid out around the table and was on his feet.

'You got kids?' he said, looking down at her, and she shook her head. He shrugged. 'Funny,' he said. 'You look like someone's mum.' Luisa stood, resisting the temptation to offer him her hand this time, folded her arms instead across her body.

'You're worried about her too,' she said. Giancarlo tipped his head.

'No,' he said. Then straightened his head again. 'Well, maybe. Maybe just a bit.'

He moved off then, and she hurried after him: they were caught briefly together in the narrow entrance to the bar. 'If you were to see her again,' said Luisa quickly, as if it might be her last chance. 'If you were to just try and find out where she is. . .'

'I've got to run,' Giancarlo said, his gaze caught unwillingly by her need. 'I'll be late for my lecture.' He stepped away from her.

'You know where to find me,' she called after him as he moved off, threading his way north through the crowds around the little market.

A woman walking past, hanging on tight to her companion's arm, turned to peer at her and then at Giancarlo's broad young back, and Luisa stepped, deliberately expressionless, into the moving throng and back to work.

Chapter Seventeen

'I WANT TO GO AND see it,' said Rosselli. Standing there beside the hotel with its jaunty striped awning, bathed in the sharp brilliance of the seaside sunshine, he seemed horribly out of place. His skin had a grey look, as though he'd been living underground.

Sandro had broached the subject of their return as they stood to leave the breakfast table. 'We can't stay here indefinitely,' he'd said tentatively. 'And there's your mother. There's the baby.' Rosselli had turned to look at him blankly, his milky brown eyes magnified behind the thick lenses.

And there's my life, Sandro had thought. There's Luisa, and Giuli, there's Pietro and Gloria and Chiara to deal with, there's the great thronging city coming back to life after the summer. Damn the man for getting him involved in this – forgetting that it wasn't the man, it had been Giuli and Enzo and Luisa feeling sorry for the baby, the whole conspiracy of emotion – but damn him anyway, and his loss and his grief. Because, for all the clean blue air and the sound of the gulls and the freedom of a wide horizon, Sandro couldn't wait to leave this place.

So when he'd said they'd better pay up and clear out and Rosselli had just nodded, Sandro had taken it as compliance. He'd paid the bill himself, on a credit card, while the man stood beside him obediently: he'd claim it back, he supposed, though he couldn't imagine the settling of accounts at the end of this case. Could Rosselli, standing there vacantly with his hands hanging at his sides, still lead his Frazione to power, any kind of power? It seemed improbable. Perhaps there were things about intelligence, and principle, that Sandro didn't understand, that drained you like this, left you used up. Or perhaps it was just grief.

'Come on,' he'd said, leaving the bags in the car, and then, as if all Rosselli had needed was that morning's hour of catatonic introversion to come to this one decision, he'd made his announcement. He wanted to go to the Stella Maris.

'I don't even know if it's allowed,' Sandro said, stalling because surely this wasn't advisable. What if the man – what if he did something reckless? 'The police have closed the hotel for the time being. There's no one there but the maid.'

'I want to go there,' Rosselli repeated stubbornly. And his eyes seemed to gain focus. 'And surely if there's only the maid it' better?'

Sandro gazed at him, and for a moment a doubt flickered. Always suspect the husband first: could it all be a smokescreen, this sleepwalking show of grief? He had to admit, he didn't like Rosselli, but more importantly, he didn't understand him. Bereavement threw everything up in the air, of course, no one could be expected to behave normally under such circumstances. But what he knew – what Giuli had just told him – about Rosselli and Matteo's relationship, that high-minded, politically committed partnership of theirs, repelled him. He couldn't understand it.

Sandro passed a hand over his face, and as he felt the patchiness of his own stubble it occurred to him that, fifteen years older and after a sleepless night, he probably looked even rougher than Rosselli. 'All right,' he said. 'Let's go.'

They could have taken the car, and gone straight on from the hotel to the superstrada. But something told him it was advisable to take this day step by step, not plan ahead even as far as that. They walked in silence: as they stepped on to the boardwalk and were hit by the full wide radiance of the sun glittering off the sea, Sandro's phone rang.

'It's Enzo,' he said, almost talking to himself, squinting down at the screen in the glare. Giuli had said – what had she said? He'd been trying to get hold of her. 'Can I take it? Is that OK?' He glanced up and Rosselli just stared at him a moment as if he couldn't remember who Enzo was: Sandro felt the vibration in his hand as it rang on.

'Enzo,' Rosselli said eventually. 'Sure.' Sandro, who realized he'd been holding his breath, pressed the accept button, exhaled.

'Hi,' he said. 'What's up, Enzo?' The night call from Bastone came back to him: the heat of the hotel room in the dark and Rosselli snoring on the bed beside him. 'Did the lawyer call you, then?'

Rosselli had sat down: there were benches along the front edge of the boardwalk, behind a railing, and some small trees turning dark after the summer. He put both hands in his pockets and then, staring out into the blue light, he lapsed into stillness.

'What?' said Sandro. 'Hold on, Enzo. What?'

This wasn't like the lad: he was gabbling. 'Slow down, start again.' Enzo took a breath and Sandro repeated what he knew. 'There wasn't much damage, they only took the laptop, right? Then this morning you met Bastone at the Frazione's offices. And the police came?'

Enzo murmured despondently and Sandro strained to get his drift. 'They came back again? Anyone – anyone I'd know?' As if Enzo would have encountered any of Sandro's old mates in the

Polizia di Stato: Enzo had led the cleanest and most blameless life of any forty-year-old man alive.

And at last Enzo seemed to pull himself together, and despite the occasional shakiness to his voice, what he was saying took shape. Sandro concentrated hard and let him talk, interrupting only once or twice.

'They didn't say what they'd found?' he asked. 'Or what else they were looking for?' Enzo mumbled again: he sounded shellshocked. 'No, well, they wouldn't, maybe. At this stage.'

When Enzo had finished, Sandro said, with as much reassurance as he could muster, 'You've done absolutely the right thing, Enzo, absolutely the right thing. You have to comply with the police. They'd have arrested you if you'd refused, you and Bastone both, even if he is a lawyer.'

Which is something I'm beginning to wonder about, Sandro thought to himself. For a highly educated man Bastone had struck him as neither competent nor reliable. Was he involved with the Frazione merely because he was, effectively, Rosselli's only friend? It didn't seem enough of a reason, for either of them.

'I'm sure he knew that. Listen—' He glanced at Niccolò Rosselli's figure, still motionless on the bench, outlined against the silver waves. 'I'll be back in the city this afternoon. Yes? And we'll go over it. In the meantime – ' and his heart sank at the prospect ' – I'll see if I can find anything out. Someone might do me a favour at Porta al Prato.'

Porta al Prato was police headquarters: he deliberately didn't say, *Pietro might do me a favour.* 'I'll call you when I'm back.' He hung up.

'All right?' said Rosselli, looking up at him now, trustful as a child.

'Not exactly,' said Sandro, hesitating. 'There's something – the *avvocato* phoned last night. There was a break-in, at the Frazione's offices.'

Rosselli stood up abruptly, his jacket crumpled. 'Thieves?' he said. 'Why?'

'Let's walk,' Sandro said. And as they set off he went over it – at least, over what Bastone had said on the phone in the middle of the night. He found himself fumbling for words. It was procrastination, he knew: the break-in on its own could be explained away, if not seamlessly. Opportunists, political or otherwise, a bit of crude sabotage or just ordinary burglars. Only it didn't ring true, not any more, not after what Enzo had just said. He stopped. Still putting it off.

'I don't understand,' Rosselli repeated stubbornly.

Sandro sighed. 'The thing is, Niccolò,' he said, 'it's taken a nasty turn, now. The police came back this morning. They called the lawyer and asked him to come to the Frazione's offices, and he called Enzo. For moral support.'

'Carlo always was a bit of a panicker,' said Rosselli peremptorily, and Sandro could see the politician in him reasserting itself. But then he frowned. 'A nasty turn? What d'you mean, a nasty turn?'

'They said – the police said they'd had information that gave them cause to suspect that there might be –' and he hesitated ' – illegal material on your computer. Not the laptop the thieves took, but the big old office computer.'

'Too heavy to steal,' said Rosselli. 'Not worth a thing.' He didn't seem to have registered the key information Sandro had been trying to impart.

'So the police removed the big computer to examine it. They had the appropriate paperwork.'

And only then did it seem to penetrate. 'Illegal material?' said Rosselli, stopping abruptly. Ahead of them Sandro could see a corner of the Stella Maris's faded sign. 'What does that mean, illegal material?'

Sandro shifted uneasily from one foot to the other, Rosselli standing in front of him as though barring his way. Slow down, he thought. Let's not jump to conclusions, let's keep calm. But at the back of his mind the possibilities – none of them pleasant – gathered.

'Well,' he began slowly. 'It could be one of a number of things – or it could be nothing. It could just be gossip, someone being malicious.' He examined Rosselli's face for fear or panic, and saw none. Not a panicker, this one. A rationalist? Or just cold-blooded.

'Is there anything,' he asked carefully, 'that you would be worried about people seeing on those computers?' Rosselli stared, and said nothing. Sandro tried again. 'Any – illegally gathered information on political opponents, for example? Any background acquired, I don't know, while gathering donations? Any names?'

Rosselli merely uttered a sound of contempt at the suggestion, so Sandro took another tack. 'Anything – personal?'

'Personal? Personal?'

Such as downloads or images – Sandro found he couldn't say it. 'Yours, or anyone else's,' he said. He thought for a moment. 'Who else is there who uses the computer? There's Enzo, I suppose. And helpers? Do you vet the volunteers?'

'We don't vet people,' Rosselli said, his voice mild but his eyes unswerving. 'We're not that kind of party.'

God help you then, thought Sandro.

'But we're not naïve. There are passwords, Enzo insisted on that: it's not chaos, just because we're progressive.'

'Bastone,' said Sandro, still thinking. 'You've known him since you were a boy, yes?'

'I trust everyone who uses those computers,' said Rosselli, and he stepped out of Sandro's path. Which didn't seem to him to answer any of his questions, but something about the dangerous set of Rosselli's mouth told him to drop it, for the moment.

'In that case,' said Sandro, 'I'm sure it's just troublemaking. It's not as if you have no political opponents. And there's the road, the mall, the financial interests there, to take into account too.'

Rosselli's hands were jammed back into his jacket now, and with its pockets already misshapen from being stuffed with keys or books or wallet, he made an untidy silhouette. He stalked on into the sun with angry, hunched shoulders, and Sandro had to hurry to keep pace. As well as being younger, the politician had longer legs than him: as he scuttled behind the man, Sandro had the feeling of things flying apart, out of his control.

'Whatever it is,' he said, 'we can sort it out.'

'We?' said Rosselli, barely looking at him. 'We? You as good as accused me—'

'Niccolò,' said Sandro, feeling his temper rise suddenly – Luisa warned him about it, particularly with clients. *Don't fly off the handle, I know you.* The only strategy he had to contain it was, the angrier he got, the more politely he spoke.

'If at any time you would like to change your mind about needing my help,' he said stiffly, 'I mean, with your bereavement or with any other matter, then you must assuredly terminate our arrangement without obligation. I would only require the expenses already incurred.'

Niccolò Rosselli stared at him, his bristling jaw set.

'And I most certainly accused you of nothing. Do you think I would have come with you unless I were on your side?'

Sandro almost convinced himself that this was true, until he remembered, *First suspect the husband.* Rosselli had been a hundred kilometres away when his wife died, hadn't he? Did he have an alibi? Once a police officer, always a police officer. Sandro fell silent.

Rosselli held his aggressive stance a second longer and then he seemed to collapse. 'All right,' he said. 'I'm sorry – I said that. All right. It is kind of you to help.' He spoke awkwardly, unused to apology.

'Are you sure you still want to go to the hotel?' Sandro asked reluctantly. Thinking, there's the chambermaid I need to talk to. I want – come to think of it, I'd like another word with that dustbin man.

We can always come back. But the last thing he ever wanted to do was to come back here again. To think that, for a moment that morning in Cristina's sun-filled bar, he'd contemplated retirement here, a little apartment overlooking the sea. What had he to do with the sea? He was from the city.

'Yes,' said Niccolò Rosselli. 'I want to see where she died.'

*

Giuli stood at the gate of the Parco Strozzi, waiting in the sun. Its pale disc was high overhead: a month ago it would have been unbearable and she knew she should be grateful for the change. But the new cool in the shadows, the edge of freshness to the breeze, seemed to form part of a soft, accumulating sadness, gathering like mist in their little corner of the city. Summer would be over soon, and it was time to knuckle down. She looked at her watch.

Barbara had refused her: the worst of it had been the look of stony disillusion on her face when she'd heard what Giuli wanted.

'I can't tell you.' She'd heard Giuli out and spoken tight-lipped, lighting her fourth cigarette from the stub of her third. 'You know I can't. Clelia will have said the same thing. I can't believe she told you – anything.'

'Oh, come off it,' Giuli had exploded. She was blowing it, and she knew it: Barbara should be on her side, but she was no pushover. 'The girl's dead.'

'Woman,' Barbara had said. 'And I'm protecting her. Dead or not. Protecting her, protecting her husband. This was over, this was no one else's business. And besides, there was never any chance of

her – her problem harming her unborn child. It wasn't like that.'
And she'd stopped speaking, shaking her head furiously.

'So what was it like?' Giuli had asked, knowing she was pushing
her luck.

'Would you want God knows who knowing about every mistake
you'd made, just because you happened to be conveniently dead?
Would you want your child growing up knowing things about you
you were ashamed of, without you being there to explain it? This
stuff gets into the coroner's court, it's out there. It's in the papers,
it's on the internet. You know that as well as I do. And once we blab
– once they know we'd break all those confidences – who's going
to come here for treatment?' And the nurse had flung the cigarette
away in disgust, all reserve gone.

Giuli had tried the approach she'd used with Clelia. 'What if
they come after you, though? The *questura*. The coroner.' She'd
realized she didn't even know who it would be. 'The police.'

Barbara had said nothing to that. The doctors had been looking
over at the sound of the raised voices. She'd kneeled to retrieve the
cigarette stub and looked up at Giuli. 'How will they know?' Her
voice had been steely quiet. 'Unless you tell them?'

Giuli had stood in shamed silence. The woman had been right,
of course. Who was Giuli to be asking for these confidences?
Weren't they right, all of them, better to let it lie? Just attribute it
to post-natal depression. Barbara had got to her feet and their eyes
had been level again.

'I'm sorry,' Giuli had said humbly. 'I know it's – difficult. I
know you can't afford to believe me when I say you can trust me –
trust us.'

'Us?'

'Sandro Cellini,' she had said. 'I thought everyone knew, I work
for him part-time. He does a bit of private investigating.'

Barbara's head had lifted at that bit of information. 'I know who he is,' she'd said. 'Knew, I should say. When he was in the police, plenty of overlap among our clientele, even before you came along.' She had given herself a little shake. 'Not that I ever breached a patient's confidence for him, either.' Her voice had been subdued, though, somehow, just the ghost of a doubt in it now. She must have got on with Sandro, even if she wasn't saying it.

'We're trying to help,' Giuli had said, sensing an opening, weaselling her way in. She hadn't liked herself for that. 'Get Niccolò back on the rails. With the kid – the baby – and everything. It's a bit of a mess.'

'You think this'll help?' Barbara had asked. 'Sincerely?' She'd sounded only depressed now, all the anger gone.

'Niccolò seems to think it will,' Giuli had said. 'What else can we do?'

'He wants to know?' Barbara had said. 'He'll change his mind.'

'What d'you mean?'

'What if he ends up wishing he'd never asked?' Barbara had rubbed her arms through the thin cardigan: it was cool under the cloister. The doctors had turned and gone inside, and she had stared after them.

Break over, Giuli had thought, feeling her chance slip away. 'Do you really think it was post-natal depression that drove Flavia to suicide?' she'd asked. 'Or do you think it had anything to do with her – with whatever you treated her for? If you think this'll only do harm, if you sincerely think –' and then she'd cast about her for the right words, frustrated ' – there's no one to blame.'

'No one to blame?' Barbara's voice had been sharp. 'It was suicide.'

'Just because she did it herself,' Giuli had said, 'doesn't mean no one's to blame. Flavia spent her whole life working to stay on the straight and narrow, to keep it together, you know that.' She hadn't really understood it herself, but it was true. 'Addiction's a lonely business. But there's always someone pushing the stuff, isn't there? They say, it's just the market forces, or whatever, don't they? The people selling the latest thing. Internet porn or plastic surgery or speed or whatever.'

Barbara's face had been pale as she'd stared back and for a moment Giuli had thought she was going to say something else. But then she'd looked away.

'I've got to get back to work.'

As Giuli had made her way slowly out through the stone corridors, lost in uneasy contemplation, someone had stepped out sharply from a side door, as if waiting for her footsteps. It was Farmiga, the consultant, hard-faced as ever.

'What are you up to, Sarto? You're not working today, are you?'

'I wanted a word with Barbara,' she'd said.

'I heard,' Farmiga had said. Had she meant she'd heard the conversation itself? She'd eyed Giuli with an expression that had said, distinctly, *I never wanted you here*, and Giuli had gazed back, mesmerized by the woman's undiluted dislike.

'I don't think I made her late,' she'd said.

'Don't poke your nose in,' Farmiga had said. 'All right? Some people get what they deserve, and do-gooders like you trying to cover their mess up just make it worse. Matteo was a frigid neurotic little bitch, not a saint, just as well people know that.'

'No one's a saint,' Giuli had said, as mildly and gratefully as she could manage. But she'd been alerted now: either Farmiga had heard her conversation with Barbara, or word had already gone out. 'But I wouldn't be here if I hadn't been given the benefit of the doubt.'

'I don't need reminding of that,' Farmiga had said sourly, and stepping back inside the room from which she'd emerged, had pulled the door sharply shut behind her.

In the sunshine now, outside the great gates with the wooded parkland stretching up the hill behind her, Giuli felt a prickle at the back of her neck as she watched Wanda Terni on the other side of the Via Pisana, round-shouldered and blinking in the sun, waiting nervously for the traffic to stop.

'There was something,' she'd said on the phone, just as Giuli had emerged, irresolute, on to the Piazza Tasso. Giuli had heard the racket of children's voices echoing in the corridors behind the teacher. 'I can't hear myself think here,' Wanda had said then, distracted.

'Where shall we meet?' Giuli had said quickly, 'Can you do lunch?'

There were people who really hadn't liked Flavia Matteo, and Farmiga was one of them. Was that surprising? People who wanted to do good often had enemies, Flavia and Niccolò both. But no one was a saint: everyone had their flaw, their chink. And Giuli was pretty sure Flavia's had been what killed her.

Wanda, halfway across the road, lifted a hand in a dismal sort of greeting.

Giuli waved back, and she thought about Sandro, at the seaside. What about Niccolò? Where was his flaw? She supposed that if he had one, Sandro, stuck with him in his little car or in a hotel room, would find it: at the thought, her spirits sank even further. The Frazione had to survive.

'I've only got half an hour,' said Wanda, out of breath as she reached Giuli. 'That'll have to be enough.' They turned and entered the deep cool between the trees.

Chapter Eighteen

VESNA MADE HER WAY slowly up the wide, cool boulevard that stretched from the sea front to the station, in the shade of the big-leaved mulberry trees. There was movement overhead through the green canopy, no more than the flick of a tablecloth, the flash of a well-upholstered pink housecoat, and a tiny shower of crumbs arriving on the pavement as Vesna passed. She heard a volley of bad-tempered domestic exchanges as she sidestepped the dusting of breadcrumbs, and was content, briefly.

Content to be single, to be independent: even the imminent possibility of unemployment meant freedom – from Calzaghe, from all the small indignities of life here as a woman, and a foreign woman at that. Vesna had a degree in biology from Sarajevo University, she had read Tolstoy, in Russian. Calzaghe had never read a book in his life as far as she knew, and his understanding of biology was strictly limited to his afternoon viewing, at his mother's apartment.

She comforted herself with the thought that she would escape this life, this awful present: he would not.

The Pizzeria Venere came into view on the far side of the road, a low, ugly and garish building with tables set outside on the broad pavement in the sun. A sunburned northern European couple were already seated: there were place-settings and tall glasses of beer in front of them. When did their holiday season end, these people? Sooner or later, they'd have to go home.

She stopped in the last of the shade and looked around, unobserved, and tried to remember what she'd heard, on Monday morning, standing on the landing above the foyer. Calzaghe had spoken to Flavia Matteo in that insinuating voice of his, the one he didn't waste on married lady guests in the presence of their husbands. Perhaps he thought he was sounding charming, kindly: to Vesna he'd sounded slimy. *Viscido,* slimy like a snail trail, that was the Italian word for a creep like Calzaghe. Had he thought he had a chance with a woman like Flavia Matteo? The thought turned Vesna's stomach.

What had Flavia been doing here, alone? The question tormented Vesna, who'd learned how to protect herself. Flavia Matteo had been an Italian woman and she should have known better, but she had no such protection. She had been, from the moment she stepped into their lives with no luggage save for a battered handbag, as irresistibly thin-skinned and vulnerable as a worm was to birds.

On one side of the Pizzeria Venere there was an expensive wine shop, with a tasting bar just visible through the open door, a vast empty champagne bottle with a pink foil top leaning across the window display. On the other side an electrical goods shop, a window full of travel irons and hairdryers, a dusty microwave. The kind of thing people on holiday or furnishing a second home would need to buy, last minute. What would a woman contemplating taking her own life go in search of – champagne, or an electric carving knife?

Perhaps she hadn't been contemplating suicide then: perhaps there'd still have been time to stop her. Vesna shivered and rubbed her upper arms briskly in the wind off the sea. A man appeared in the doorway of the wine shop and she stepped off the pavement and walked towards him in the sun.

*

Luisa was eating her lunch at Giacosa. Filled this lunch hour and every other with mature *vendeuses* like herself, wealthy Russian women, old-school Florentine matriarchs with lacquered hair and knuckledustered with diamonds. . . the old-fashioned bar was guaranteed to restore Luisa's equilibrium under any circumstances, to set her squarely back among her sisterhood.

Any circumstances, it seemed, but today's. She could hardly taste the food – which was always good – and she hardly registered the cheerful respect of the handsome barmen, or the new egg-sized sapphire on the owner's wife's hand. Luisa hadn't spoken to Sandro since last night and she didn't like it. Things were falling apart: babies left motherless, daughters not talking to their parents. And then she realized, setting her empty dish back on the counter, that the man she'd been vaguely focusing on through the side window of Giacosa, standing in a doorway on the Via della Spada and talking to another man, was Pietro.

He wasn't in his uniform, but wearing jeans: Pietro never wore jeans. And a polo shirt. There was something weirdly unrecognizable about him that explained why she hadn't seen it was him straight away. The other man – younger, perhaps thirty-five, good-looking from his profile at least and also rather oddly dressed, to Luisa's eye, in an unseasonable hooded raincoat – was moving restlessly from foot to foot, as if warming up to run somewhere.

As she watched, she distinctly saw Pietro put something in the man's hand and then, looking quickly around as if – exactly as if –

to make sure he hadn't been seen, his eyes rested on Luisa, through the glass. Immediately he raised his hand and patted the man he'd been talking to sharply, twice on the upper arm, in what might under other circumstances have been a kind of hearty greeting but in this case seemed to Luisa like a signal. Because the man turned away instantly – as he moved the sleeve of his raincoat rode up fractionally and she saw the shadow of something revealed, at the wrist – and then he was off down the street without a backward glance or a goodbye. The whole exchange was so unmistakably clandestine Luisa just stared, trying to make it mean something else and failing.

Opposite her Pietro held her gaze a moment from the doorway, and then he stepped off the pavement and was inside, bringing the cool breath of the street in with him and as instantly out of place among the jewelled women, it seemed to her, as a Nigerian street vendor with a trayful of lighters. He took her by the arm, and they moved into a corner, leaning against a small high table.

'What are you up to?' she said, bluntly. Then as something occurred to her: 'It's not about Chiara? You're not – he's not—' Pietro was staring at her, and she stopped speaking. He'd lost weight. The reliably pouchy, contented face she'd seen grow older for the preceding twenty years, had a sunken look. There were bags under his eyes.

'You're wearing jeans,' she said, changing tack. 'Who was that man?'

Pietro opened his mouth, closed it again, then signalled to the muscled barman for a coffee.

'It was work,' he said abruptly, nodding into the street to indicate the transaction she'd just witnessed. He obviously wanted to talk about Chiara even less than he wanted to discuss giving money – or something else – to some dubious character in the street.

'Oh, yes,' said Luisa. 'If you say so.' It felt strange, standing in a bar talking to Pietro: that was Sandro's job. Well, obviously not his real job, not any more. Pietro was looking at her with an odd, tense expression.

'How long is it,' she said, as it occurred to her that it had been a while, really quite a while, 'since you and Sandro last got together?'

'It's been hectic,' said Pietro, half turning away from her. 'There's a lot on.'

A lot he wasn't going to tell her about.

'He misses you,' she tried: Sandro would sooner be garrotted than admit to such a thing, but it would be true all the same. 'You know – he doesn't want to make things difficult for you, using you. Putting you in a difficult position. He knows how things are.'

'It's appreciated.' Pietro spoke gruffly, still not looking at her. 'I don't know if he does know how things are, though. There really is a lot on.' He set the cup back down carefully.

'It's not – Chiara then?' Pietro flinched – so subtly Luisa felt it rather than saw it – but he said nothing. She went on. 'You know, you could talk to him about that. That's not business, is it? If you're getting some dodgy contact to go after her and not Sandro, who's a private investigator – well. There's nothing he wouldn't do for you, you know that.'

'I told you,' said Pietro fiercely, jerking his head towards the street and the doorway where she'd spotted him. 'That back there, that was work, a – a covert operation.' He shot a glance at her from under a deep frown, gauging to see if she believed him. 'I can do my own investigating of my own daughter.'

His knuckles were white against the edge of the high table. Luisa, who had known him twenty years, had never seen Pietro like this, ever: no trouble at work had made him so much as raise his voice to a woman. He was the gentlest and most reasonable man she'd ever known: gentler than her own husband, and an awful lot more reasonable.

'I saw her, you know.' The words sprang to Luisa's lips before she knew where they'd lead her. Pietro's head jerked up.

'You saw her?' His voice cracked, and looking into his face she saw the tears in his eyes.

'Outside the shop,' she said, wishing she'd kept quiet. 'Yesterday evening. She looked so pretty. She was wearing a dress.'

'Chiara, wearing a dress?' He tried to laugh but it came out strangled.

'She looked fine, honestly.'

Had she, though? Luisa recalled the soft shade of the summery dress and the pale shoes, but also that the face itself – Chiara's strong, familiar features – had seemed blurred, as though with late nights, or tears.

'Did you talk to her?'

'I – I tried.' Should she say, Chiara took one look at me and bolted? Should she tell Pietro about Giancarlo? She could picture Pietro seizing the boy by the shoulders and trying to shake information out of him. Fathers, Luisa knew only too well, should not do their own investigating: it was a cardinal rule and breaking it had cost Sandro his job.

But no one was going to murder Chiara. In the warm fug of the Giacosa, Luisa felt a sweat break on her upper lip.

'I'd better get back to work,' she said.

It was as though a shutter came down in Pietro's face.

'Right,' he said stiffly.

There was a silence, but she didn't move, and then as if her staying put one second longer had given him licence, the flood-gates opened.

'What you mean is, you're not going to tell me. You talked to her and you're going to tell me nothing? How long have you known me, and you're treating me like this? Everyone's pussyfooting around me.' Pietro raised his hands to his temples in frustration, and as his arms came up she saw how much weight he'd lost, the torso no longer stocky, the jeans loose. Was Gloria worried?

'What do you all think I'm going to do, murder the man? He hasn't got the decency to climb the stairs and shake my hand, he waits in the car. He knows I'd see through him, that's why. Or maybe she's told him I'm some kind of Nazi.' Pietro snorted in disbelief. 'If only she knew. Why don't they trust us to be the good guys? I'm her father.' And, rising, his voice cracked again.

Luisa remembered what Giancarlo had said about Chiara's new man: an authority figure. A father figure? It made her uncomfortable: this was one piece of information she would not be able to pass on to Chiara's parents. She resisted the temptation to put out her hand to Pietro: he'd probably shove her on to the floor if she tried. People weren't looking at them yet, and Luisa didn't want them to start.

'I didn't talk to her,' she said quietly, and he stared at her with that policeman's look, searching for a lie. Not finding one, his shoulders dropped. She went on. 'I came out of the shop, and she disappeared. Perhaps she saw me: perhaps she knew I'd react – just like you.'

'Like me?'

'Worried.'

He was grey-faced: 'worried' didn't begin to cover it.

Luisa went on. 'Of course you want to look the man in the eye, get the measure of him. Of course you do. Have your permission asked even, why not? It's not being a Nazi. But kids – well.' She took a breath. 'There are times when they don't see us as we are,' she moved on before he could say '*Us?*' to remind her she didn't have kids of her own. 'She needs to know you can be reasonable, I suppose. You need to show her that.'

'You mean I need to shut up and leave her to it,' he said, and began shaking his head, and then she dared put a hand out and stay his arm.

'You're the most reasonable, level-headed man I know,' Luisa said. 'It's not me you need to convince. You need to show her you can leave it.'

Pietro looked over his shoulder, along the bright, busy street, one way and then the other, like a hunted man. Along the front of the bar the usual row of tiny round marble tables, the elegant smokers gossiping: what danger could they represent? And in the Via della Spada a handsome, ambling elderly couple, arm in arm. For an instant Luisa glimpsed the possibility that the stress had unhinged Pietro: she saw him pacing the city's cool, narrow streets after dark, looking for his daughter.

'I can't leave it,' he said, and the anger in his voice gave way to sorrow. 'She needs me. She still needs her father.'

*

'She walked here every day?'

The gravel path was steep, winding through the dark, grey-green trees with the view all behind them, and Giuli was beginning to feel puffed out. She'd have to ease up on the cigarettes: she hadn't had one yet today but she could feel last night's in her lungs.

Wanda nodded, drawing on her own cigarette. Short-legged, she had a particular walking style that seemed compatible with chainsmoking. She marched doggedly: there was nothing leisurely about it. 'All year round,' she said. 'It'd have to be pouring with rain to stop Flavia – although sometimes they close the park, in high winds and that kind of thing. Then she'd go along the river.' She shoved her hands in her pockets and raised her head, squared her shoulders, imitating a taller, more romantic figure. 'Like this, face front, into the wind.'

'On her own.'

Wanda nodded. 'Mostly. She'd ask me to come, like I told you, now and again, but she knew I wasn't a walker.' She made a face. 'Hate it. I'll walk through the city as much as you like, on my way here or there, but walking for its own sake?' She shook her head. 'And besides, I think she preferred to be on her own, thinking her thoughts, in her own world.'

What world would that be? thought Giuli. Daydreaming? Flavia Matteo was the last person you'd imagine it of, but everyone dreamed, didn't they? Of a different life, of how things might have been, or might still become. Wanda had fallen silent and Giuli wondered if her mind were running along the same lines.

'But when you did come along with her, that was when you and she – talked?'

There were footsteps approaching, coming around the winding path and down the hill towards them on the gravel: Giuli glanced up, then back at her own feet. The tall man kept on without breaking his long stride, past them and down the hill, although his head turned to watch them as he went.

'I suppose,' said Wanda. 'At school we talked, in the breaks, about this and that, mostly school work. But it's hard to say anything that means anything much in a place like that. The kids, the staff, the constant racket.'

'Flavia liked it, though?'

'She did.' Wanda frowned. 'The noise didn't bother her. The kids loved her. She was so serious with them, and so beautiful, they quietened down, just to see her.' She sounded surprised: Giuli looked at her and saw not a trace of resentment in her square, plain face. What was beauty? Giuli thought of Farmiga then, good-looking but a bitch, all the way through. She took a breath.

'You said – there was something. Flavia told you something.'

Wanda stopped, and turned. Spread out in front of them was the red-roofed expanse of the city at high noon, the sun sparking off windows, the hazy air glittering with heat and exhaust fumes. The big red dome of the cathedral off to the right, the dark green double hill of Fiesole, all the façades of the city's great churches turned towards the southern slopes, like sunflowers to the sun.

'Yes,' said Wanda, frowning. 'I – well. The truth is, I'd forgotten it myself. Like you forget your own dreams, you know?' Giuli didn't understand what she meant. 'You wake up and they're so real for a bit, you think they really happened, then – pouf!' She threw up her hands. 'They're gone.'

'Right,' said Giuli, still not understanding.

'It was a dream she told me about,' said Wanda patiently.

'Oh.' Giuli couldn't disguise her disappointment.

'Dreams have their own logic,' Wanda said earnestly. 'That's why they seem real – aspects of them *are* real. They're related to reality, they mean something.'

'Right,' said Giuli. All this way for a dream? She wiped her forehead with a sleeve.

Wanda persisted. 'But obviously their logic doesn't stand up in the real world, so they evaporate, they don't leave a trace, except maybe in the subconscious. Unless you retell them, of course, then they become fixed. They're stories, really. Stories our minds tell us to explain – the inexplicable. Or the unpalatable.'

'I thought you taught maths?' Giuli could hear herself say, the surly, boneheaded student, back of the class.

Wanda sighed. 'Yes, among other things' she said, deflated. 'But I've read Jung. He's interesting. Do you want to hear Flavia's dream? Or do you think I'm wasting your time?'

With an effort Giuli relaxed. 'I'm sorry,' she said. 'It just makes me uncomfortable, this analytical stuff. So much bullshit, a lot of it.' She picked at the chipped varnish on a fingernail. Wanda Terni didn't need to know she'd had her share of mind-doctoring, and had resisted it all the way to the wire. Guili sighed. 'You're right,' she said. 'Dreams do mean something. So tell me.'

Without a word the teacher looked around and set off for a stone bench, tucked into the trees. They sat down, half hidden from the path: below them the park was empty now, the loping figure long gone.

'In a way the most significant thing about it was that she told it to me at all. Of course, in our early days, when we first knew each other, she'd never have talked about such things.' Wanda shrugged. 'Perhaps she didn't have a lot of dreams, or didn't want to remember them, but if she did, she'd have kept them to herself. This one – well. It was like she had to get it out. Had to tell it.'

Giuli shifted, the stone cool under her backside. 'So it was when you were still talking – when everything was fine?'

Wanda bit her lip. 'It was when I asked her if she was ill. She sort of blurted it out to me, but it was clear she regretted it straight away. It might have been one of the reasons she stopped talking to me.' Wanda frowned. 'I think she must have been pregnant then, though she hadn't told anyone yet.'

'You'd forgotten this?' Giuli was incredulous, and Wanda flushed.

'Not exactly,' she said. 'It just seemed – so private. The subconscious, you know, so private you don't even understand it yourself. I didn't say because – well. It felt like I'd be betraying her.'

Giuli exhaled, exasperated. 'Why do I get this from everyone?' she said. 'Flavia committed suicide. . . privacy doesn't come into it. You were her only friend, it seems to me. Don't you want to know what drove her to it?'

Wanda gazed at her. 'I suppose you're right,' she said uncertainly.

'I *am* right,' said Giuli. 'So tell me.'

The teacher took a deep breath. 'I can't remember all of it myself,' she said slowly. 'But it was extraordinary. It had everything. It was like the perfect dream. Symbols, emotion, danger, archetypes, revelation: the lot. You might have made it up, it was a perfect narrative.'

Wanda paused. 'There was a palace,' she said then, slowly.

Giuli sat quiet, mesmerized. It was just like a story. A ghost story, or a murder story. A big, dark palace – like the Pitti Palace, set up above a city like their own. A faceless man with a sword, hacking people to pieces and leaving them in bloody heaps, finds his way inside the palace. Flavia Matteo goes running through its corridors saying she has to find her baby before the killer does. Then there was something garbled about stockings and blue glass all over the ground stopping them catching the killer, but always, even in Wanda's halting retelling of it, it was completely gripping. The chase, the terrible faceless man, then the revelation.

'He got the baby?' Giuli said. 'He killed the baby? That's pretty extreme.'

'Dreams are extreme,' said Wanda, with an effort. 'Pregnancy hormones can do pretty extreme things too. Women dream of blood and destruction all the time. We're not the gentle creatures people imagine us to be, are we?'

'No,' said Giuli, thinking of Flavia Matteo cutting her own wrists, thinking of the sinew and veins, of the deep breath you'd have to take before you made the first cut. Thinking of Sandro viewing the body. And Flavia dreaming of a baby cut to pieces.

Wanda was looking at her. 'There was something else,' she said.

'What else?' said Giuli, with dread.

'She said, "He made me dance for him, to save the baby, and then I saw his face, before he killed the baby." She said, *I knew him.*' Wanda Terni's own face was pale and tense, her eyes wide.

'And who was he?' The teacher shook her head. 'Flavia wouldn't tell me that.' She squeezed her eyes shut. 'It was as though she had to get to the end, to tell me what had happened in the end, and only when she got there did she realize she might have given something away. She said, "No, I didn't mean he was a real person, no, no."'

'But she was lying.'

Wanda nodded. 'I think she was.'

'You were here,' said Giuli, 'when she told you?'

Wanda nodded again and Giuli shivered suddenly. 'There's no palace here,' she said. 'Could she have been thinking of, I don't know, the Quirinale, of government buildings, city hall? Of what would happen when – if – Niccolò got to power?'

'There are palaces everywhere,' Wanda said, frowning with concentration 'This city's like one big palace. Have you never thought the streets are like dark corridors? You never know who's around the next corner.'

Giuli saw the raised hairs on her forearm. 'You're cold,' she said. 'Let's get walking.'

The sun, though, even at midday, seemed suddenly to have lost its ability to warm. They reached the top of the hill by dogged determination alone. Giuli realized she was like Wanda in her attitude to walking, or perhaps she just didn't like the idea of having the freedom to think her own thoughts forced on her.

'I'd better get back,' said Wanda, fretting as they looked down at the city. The river shone lazily below them, a wide green band. Some sunbathers were stretched out along the fishing weir, distant specks.

'All right,' said Giuli reluctantly. The story haunted her, its ugly meanings circling with menace, just out of reach. It could be anything: it could be hormones, chemicals cooking up their own stories in Flavia's bloodstream, the baby sending out its own warning signals before it knew anything of the world it would enter.

'There was nothing else?' she said as they set off back down, almost as an afterthought. 'Just the dream.' As if the dream wasn't enough.

Their steps crunched on the gravel, the increase in speed as they headed downhill lending a sense of urgency they hadn't felt on the uphill climb. Faster, faster they went, chasing something down.

'There was something else,' said Wanda, and she stopped abruptly. 'Actually, there was. Just a small thing.'

*

He would be angry, thought Chiara. The dress hung on the back of the wardrobe, like her pale peach ghost, crumpled, sweated in under the arms because she'd run in it, running in heels like trying to struggle out of a trap. He wouldn't like that, either, he wanted her delicate and feminine. She wondered where the iron was: wondered if she should take the dress to the cleaner's before he saw it. It didn't feel like it was hers. He'd bought it for her.

She'd had to run: she couldn't have stopped, couldn't have talked to Luisa: one word and Luisa would have her skewered. She could deflect her own mother, who so desperately wanted to believe her child, but Luisa had always been able to ferret out the truth. Chiara remembered as a child sitting on her lap, Luisa's firm hand on her heel as she extracted a splinter, straight in with the needle, ignoring Chiara's squeal, her writhing: ruthless, focused. Then holding up the splinter: there.

He'd sat in the car waiting for her when she'd gone to get her stuff: she hadn't asked him up and he hadn't said he wanted to meet the family. He'd known her dad was in the Polizia di Stato – sometimes she wondered if everyone knew – and what kind of lover wanted to be subjected to that scrutiny?

What kind of lover.

Was he her lover? Not yet. And as she lay still on the bed a sweat broke on her again. She'd run across the river to get away from Luisa and, reaching the other side, hurrying for the bus stop, she'd glanced down a sidestreet and she'd seen him. Leaning into a car window as easy as you like, as if he'd known the person inside for ever. The woman looking up at him from the driver's seat, sly and certain. He'll leave me, thought Chiara suddenly. Unless I do the things he wants.

'I'll show you,' he'd said.

Chapter Nineteen

'I'M SORRY,' SAID VESNA, looking around fearfully. 'I'd better check first. That Calzaghe's not back, I mean. He won't allow it, you see.' Although Sandro thought she seemed as much afraid of Niccolò as she was of her boss.

They'd waited fifteen minutes, he and Niccolò Rosselli, inside the rusted gates to the silent hotel, time to reflect that it wouldn't take long for nature to reclaim the Stella Maris, its flaking shutters and unkempt laurels and weed-clogged gravel. There was something about Rosselli's dark, relentless misery that muddied Sandro's own thoughts; his head was already back in Florence, pondering the significance of a police raid in the dark alleys of the Oltrarno. He had completely forgotten the errand Vesna had offered to run for him until he'd seen her hurrying along the wide sunny street towards them.

'OK,' she said now, coming back out of the hotel's dark lobby. 'He's not here.' Her eyes darted again from Rosselli to Sandro. There was something she wasn't sure she should say, in front of the husband. 'Quick, quick, come in.'

She looked different without her overall: she looked like any girl in the street, she looked free. You could imagine her just taking off, running for the train without a bag. That was what Flavia had done. Had it felt like escape? Or the opposite – capture? Running into a brick wall, the end: that would always be how someone like Sandro viewed suicide.

The staircase led up to a long, light-filled landing and rooms leading off it.

'I suppose we'd better not touch anything,' said Vesna, fishing a key from her pocket and unlocking the door. The police hadn't left tape up; perhaps they'd thought there'd be no need, with the hotel closed. Vesna pushed the door with a fingertip and, before they had a chance to decide who would be the first to enter, Rosselli stepped purposefully forward and through the doorway.

Even in the room's shuttered dimness you could tell it was a mess. Vesna had her arms wrapped across herself in distress: even leaving aside that she'd found the body, her job, supposed Sandro, whenever she came into a room like this, would be to restore order to it, and the mess left behind after a death was disorder like no other. Possessions whose owner has gone, things once of value to someone, now worthless. Meaning drained from them.

Rosselli moved through the room before them. He stood and looked down at the bed first, the sheets creased and limp, pulled roughly back up; stood there a long time, it felt to Sandro, who was averting his eyes from the imprint of a dead woman's body. The door to what must be the bathroom was ajar, but the shutters would be closed there, too. Then Rosselli moved, stepped across to the small cheap wooden desk, with its writing set. The policeman had said Flavia took a piece of paper and set it on the blotter; she'd held the pen because it had her fingerprints on it. But nothing had been written.

Behind Sandro, Vesna stepped over to the long French doors and, taking a handkerchief from her pocket, turned the handle. 'She had a balcony,' she said. 'One of the nicest rooms.' She sounded apologetic. She pushed the shutters outward and a band of light widened in the room: Niccolò Rosselli's face, grey and blinking, turned towards her.

'They were open,' Vesna explained. 'The shutters, the window, they were open when I came in.'

'Open?' Rosselli seemed galvanized, lit up by the shaft of sun. 'The door was locked, they said. The door to the room, as if that meant no one could have been in here, no one could have—'

'You told the police?' said Sandro swiftly, wanting to shut down that note he heard in Rosselli's voice, of a kind of desperate hope.

'Yes,' said Vesna, 'Of course. I told them I hadn't changed anything.'

'You're sure you didn't open them yourself?' Sandro was intent. 'Don't you do that when you go into rooms to clean them, throw open the window first?'

'I do sometimes,' she said slowly. 'But I knew something bad had happened. Even before – when she didn't answer the door. I knew not to touch – I – I don't know why. I just knew.'

'And you told them that?' She nodded uncertainly. 'I heard them round the back, afterwards. The police, I mean. They went looking to see – if anyone might have—' She stepped on to the balcony, Rosselli shoving abruptly ahead of Sandro to follow her, then the three of them were out there.

The balcony was generous but shabby, the paint on the balustrade flaking and loose, and about four metres from the ground. Rosselli stepped to the balustrade: Sandro came alongside him and they both looked down into a patch of tangled vegetation and the contrastingly neat garden of the condominium behind, where two swinging garden seats and four substantial loungers were set tidily around a handsome table. Sandro glanced at Niccolò Rosselli's face, but it registered no emotion, only a kind of intentness.

'But it's possible,' Rosselli said eagerly. 'Someone could have climbed up here.' Out of the corner of his eye Sandro could see no drainpipes or handholds: he could also see an elderly man watching them from the condominium's rear terrace.

'I don't think so.' Vesna's voice was quiet, but certain.

'Why not?' Rosselli stood straight, hands clenched. She stepped around him respectfully.

'Look,' she said, and pointed, her finger a centimetre or so above the balustrade but not touching it. 'The exterior hasn't been decorated in twenty years. If anyone had come over here, the paint would have flaked off all over the place.'

The stone floor of the balcony was dusty, but no more than that. Vesna went on, quietly determined. 'And whoever climbed up would have been covered with dust. You only have to blow on it – ' and she leaned and blew by way of demonstration, and the powdery blue distemper lifted obediently from the plaster ' – and you're covered.'

She stepped back. 'Plus the old folks next door are so terrified of being robbed by *Albanesi*, they call the police when a stray cat comes into their yard.'

'*Albanesi*,' said Rosselli, but all the energy was gone as he looked dully down into the garden next door. 'Yes, they always blame the *Albanesi*.'

The Frazione, Sandro knew, took a very liberal stand on the immigration issue for which the word '*Albanesi*' had become shorthand: they were anti-racist and all the rest, but this seemed to him no more than a reflex. Would it save Rosselli, all this politics? Or anyone else, for that matter? Sandro wasn't going to count on it.

'I'm sorry,' said Vesna, glancing back inside.

Rosselli said nothing. He turned abruptly and went back in, and before they could slow him – warn him, protect him – he walked straight into the bathroom. And stopped.

The huge marble bath stood like a tomb in the centre of the room, gleaming palely in the half-light. A crouched shape was on the tiled floor beside it: staring, Sandro realized that it was a towel.

'You found her,' said Rosselli, without turning.

'Yes,' said Vesna, and Sandro could tell it was only with an effort that she was holding her ground. And then, haltingly, as if unsure of whether she should say it or not, but in the end having to: 'She was wearing her underwear.'

And it seemed to be the odd banality of the words that did for Niccolò Rosselli because he suddenly folded in on himself like a long articulated doll and was on his knees, leaning against the bath, and making a sound that Sandro only belatedly realized was sobbing.

He knelt beside the man: it was almost a relief to feel Rosselli's back shaking under his hand. The bones: the man was thin, thin as one of those starved saints.

He was saying something over and over, trying and failing to get to the end of it. 'She would never – she would never – she would never—'

'Never what?' said Sandro gently. He glanced sideways and saw Vesna's eyes on him from the doorway, as if she wanted to say something to him but could not take one step further into the room.

'Come on,' he said into Rosselli's shoulder, inhaling his acrid scent of sweat, despair and lack of food and sleep. 'Let's go downstairs.'

Abruptly, the room seemed horrible to Sandro; even though he had no belief in any single supernatural thing, it seemed to him a haunted place. Rosselli's head turned, his gaunt face streaked with the drying tears, but something in him had been mastered. Had Sandro still been a policeman, he might have taken advantage of this opportunity to examine the dead woman's husband for signs of guilt, for some inappropriate response. But the professional reflex seemed to have deserted him and instead he waited.

'She would never let a stranger see her – unclothed,' Rosselli said. 'She put the underwear on for you.' Looking across at Vesna. 'Not to shock you.'

'Not to shock me,' repeated Vesna. Sandro felt something knot in his chest at the thought of Flavia Matteo's modesty, and the futility of it: at the note of dull acceptance in Rosselli's voice. He swallowed.

'Downstairs,' he said, and inserting his hands under Rosselli's armpits, raised him bodily from the floor. Ahead of them Vesna moved across the room as lightly as a ghost and opened the door.

They parked Rosselli in a grimy lounger on the verandah. He'd been obedient enough coming downstairs and Sandro had been relieved not to have to carry him; at Sandro's age, it would have been an undignified struggle to do more than prop him up.

He'd seen the watchful look in Vesna's eye from the lobby below as, with painful slowness, they'd negotiated the wide, ill-lit staircase with its monumental mahogany banister, and had interpreted it as her doubting his ability to make it to the bottom. But when they emerged on to the sunlit verandah, he saw she was trying silently to convey some different message.

'A glass of water?' she said, leaning down into Rosselli's face as if talking to someone very ill. 'Or perhaps – ah – coffee?' Sandro frowned. No coffee, she'd said, she wasn't allowed. She straightened. 'Perhaps you could help?' she said to him, with a meaningful tilt to her head.

'Water,' said Rosselli vaguely, looking but not seeing her gesture, and she turned to go inside. 'Perhaps a glass of water. Then we should go – home.' He looked at Sandro. 'Didn't you say that?' He spoke with a kind of blank relief, as if it had all been wiped clean. Sandro's head ached with the effort of trying to understand him, and with dread of the journey home.

'Yes,' he said. 'I'll just help the girl.' And hurried after her.

He didn't know where she'd gone: he went into the bright dining room, where the chairs were still stacked on the tables, save the two at which they'd sat when he'd been there before. He heard a chink from behind a door at the far end of the room and there she was, in a small old-fashioned kitchen with the kind of cupboards his mother's kitchen had had sixty years before. They hadn't been modern then.

'I'm glad he didn't want coffee,' she said. She looked exhausted in the sunlight. She set two glasses and an elderly bottle of mineral water on a tray. 'We refill them from the tap,' she said, seeing him looking. 'The bottles.' She didn't pick the tray up.

'What did you want to tell me?' Sandro asked, and then, 'Do you really think no one could have climbed up on that balcony?' But even as he said it the idea seemed outlandish: cat burglars, or some killer tracking Flavia down and cutting her wrists in the bath. Why? If they wanted rid of the Frazione, it would have been easier to kill Niccolò Rosselli. The certainty settled in him: she'd wanted to die, and even her husband had accepted it now. Did they really need to know why?

Yes.

'I went to the Pizzeria Venere,' said Vesna, and for a moment he didn't understand what she was talking about. 'Where Calzaghe sent her.' She raised her head, as if even the mention of her boss's name was enough to bring him to the door.

'Yes,' said Sandro, intent now. 'Yes.'

'A wine shop and a kitchen shop,' she said. 'The man in the wine shop knew who I was talking about, right away. The dead woman with red hair. Everyone in this town knows. Only he said he hadn't seen her, not on Monday morning nor any other time. He was the kind to have run straight to the police, too, if he had. Highlight of his week, it would have been.'

'Uh-huh.' Sandro knew the type. 'So she went to the kitchen shop?' He scratched his head, mystified, and caught a gleam in Vesna's eye.

'Not so much kitchen as electricals,' she said carefully.

'Ah.' A picture formed itself in Sandro's mind of the standard provincial kitchen-cum-electrical shop – alarm clocks, irons, answerphones – and he remembered pulling over yesterday morning, on his way back from observing the insurance claimant. Was it only yesterday? Pulling over and parking up on the edge of the Isolotto, where an electrical shop sat alongside a dry cleaner's, all quite normal, all quite innocuous, the domestic services provided to ordinary, decent law-abiding citizens everywhere. A possibility suggested itself. But he waited for Vesna to tell it her way.

'There was an old woman in there at first, she said she didn't know anything. A bit fuddled – I don't think she was quite all there. But I kept saying, "A red-headed woman, who was in the newspapers," and then a customer came in, a tourist, and the woman knew what he'd come for because she just said, "He'll be back in a minute, you have to deal with him. With my grandson, it has to be done on the computer," she said. Because she didn't know anything about computers.' Sandro nodded, concentrating on keeping up as the chambermaid talked without pause, knowing with ever greater certainty where she was headed.

'So I hung around,' Vesna went on, as diligent as a rookie police officer. 'Waiting behind the microwaves. I wanted a look at the grandson. And when he came, and I saw what the tourist wanted him for, I knew.'

'Yes,' Sandro said. The same thing as Flavia had gone for, but where was it now?

'She'd have had to go back to the hotel and get her ID card, you see, there's a lot of paperwork involved nowadays. You need a document, you need your tax code, it's all done on the computer.

When I got mine – well, that was before all the terrorist stuff came in.' And she raised her head and looked him in the eye, knowing he knew.

'A SIM card,' he said.

'A prepaid mobile, and a SIM,' Vesna said, raising her hand to her mouth to suppress the nervous, inappropriate smile coming to her lips. 'These days you can buy them in all sorts of places, and the electrical shop sells them. I asked the grandson, and he remembered, straight away. He must have been the only person in the town who didn't know the red-headed woman had committed suicide.' Her expression was grave. 'He seemed a nice boy. He was so shocked.'

There was a sound from beyond the dining-room door so faint he hardly registered it. But Vesna did, and she paled in recognition.

'Calzaghe,' she said, lifting the tray in panic.

'So she went looking for a phone,' Sandro said, lifting a hand to detain her, just one more moment. 'Because she'd left hers at home? But there was no phone, was there? In the room, after she died?'

'No,' said Vesna, eyes fixed on the room behind him, then with an effort shifted to meet his eyes. 'Because she didn't buy it. They told her about the registration with the authorities, the need for identification, and she said she didn't have it on her.' Vesna swallowed. 'She didn't come back. He said. . . the boy. . . that happens sometimes.'

People panic, they don't want to go through all the paperwork.

'There was something else,' she said. 'I didn't think of it before, I hardly noticed it. There was something. On her hand—'

Why had she left the mobile behind? Had she just forgotten it? If she needed to make a call, why hadn't she used the hotel switchboard?

'She had a phone, at home. She could have brought it with her.'

Sandro was more or less talking to himself now, but looking up he registered that Vesna's anxiety was still focused on the doorway behind him. He turned and stepped ahead of her through it, and there in the dining room stood a fat man of about his own age with small, suspicious eyes and an unmistakable air of hostility.

*

'*Caro.*' Luisa spoke to the answerphone uncertainly. Should she send a text message instead? They always seemed so insufficient, terse: she was too old, that was the truth of it. She needed the spoken word. 'I saw Pietro, I saw him – well, it's hard to explain. He said it was a covert operation but – oh, damn. I suppose you're driving. I need to talk to you. Are you driving? I hope you're on the way home.'

She was rambling now. Cut it short.

'Maria Rosselli came by the shop this afternoon, with the baby. She asked when you'd be back and I said before it was dark. Anyway, I'm home now. I left early.'

She clicked the phone off. The apartment was cool and silent around her: she needed to get something on for dinner.

No need to go into it all, the whys and the wherefores, not on an answerphone. Sandro was unreliable enough at checking his messages, anyway.

Pietro had walked her back, dutifully, like a stranger in his jeans as they came through the sunny, crowded Piazza della Repubblica. 'I'm trying,' he'd said, after long minutes' silence. 'I'm trying not to be too heavy-handed. But it's a dangerous world out there.'

Did all fathers think the world was too dangerous for their daughters? Perhaps all policemen did. 'Chiara was tied up with this Frazione, too,' he'd said. 'You knew that, didn't you? I don't know if this guy's connected with them, even.'

'I think he might be older than her,' Luisa had said, slowly: Giancarlo hadn't said it in so many words, but it felt like the truth to her.

They'd reached the Orsanmichele, both of them turning down the side of it, beckoned by the quiet and stillness in the tall shadow of its soft sandstone façade. With its white marble cornicing, its recesses lined in blue with silver stars, a market converted to a church, it was probably Luisa's favourite building in the city, too delicately pretty almost to be Florentine. It didn't seem to belong to the history of bloodshed and power struggles and men. They'd stopped walking.

'Older?' Pietro's voice had been dangerously quiet.

'Just an impression I have,' she'd said, realizing that she'd probably said too much already.

'I don't like it,' he'd answered, his voice ragged. 'I don't like the boyfriend – the older boyfriend, if that's what he is – and I don't like the politics. The Frazione – plenty of people want rid of it. I don't want her associated – say a demonstration turns nasty? There can be violence. I don't want her in trouble.' His voice had risen.

'But it's democracy,' Luisa had said, surprising herself. She'd never thought she had a political bone in her body. 'It's the young. You can't stop them rebelling. It's all peaceful demonstration anyway, isn't it?' She realized she'd had exactly the same conversation with Sandro, only Pietro seemed to have more information. And more than he was telling her, too.

'Do they know who's running their Frazione? Do they?'

'Do you?'

He'd subsided. 'I can't talk about it,' he'd said. 'I – it's work.'

'Do you know something about Rosselli?' she'd said. 'Is that what you've been working on? Is that why – why—?' Why you've kept away, was what Luisa wanted to say, from your oldest friend?

Pietro had shaken his head, tight-lipped. 'Not Rosselli,' he'd said. 'They haven't – no one's got anything on Rosselli as far as I know. But Bastone? The lawyer. Do they think he fought his way up from nothing? Chiara calls the police corrupt. His family owns some nice building land, a sizeable parcel down near Scandicci, as a matter of fact.' And he looked at her. 'A sale is being negotiated. I've spent a bit of time at the land registry lately.'

Where the mall was being built. Dimly she remembered the couple in the bar talking about Rosselli's collapse, the man saying something about backhanders. Bastone. Sandro had thought him nothing more than a bumbler, a hopeless idealist, out of his depth.

Luisa had tried to get more out of Pietro then but he wouldn't elaborate, and seeing him there, uneasy in his ill-fitting jeans, looking around as if he was being watched, she had let him go.

They'd been looking at her askance in the shop even before Maria Rosselli turned up. She hadn't been a minute beyond the hour for lunch, but truthfully her mind hadn't been on the job after meeting Pietro. Gazing out of the window, fighting to make sense of it, she'd tried to picture him, this older man Chiara might have been drawn to, this authority figure. Chiara had always been such a determined little thing, it had pained Luisa to think of her subdued by some – some controlling arsehole.

Language. What had got into her?

No, Maria Rosselli had just been the last straw. Parking what she called the perambulator in the busy street without a backward glance and marching her strong-boned features into the shop, looking at the colour-coordinated rails and high heels with incredulity.

'Have you heard from them?' she'd barked without preamble, and at the sound Beppe had appeared at the top of the stairs, startled.

Maria seemed to have aged ten years since she'd had sole charge of the child, and to have grown angrier.

'You can't leave the baby out there,' Luisa had said.

'Well, I can't bring him in here, can I?' Maria had said, looking around herself with a kind of contemptuous disbelief. And it was true. Even if the great, ungainly, sprung baby carriage would have fitted through the glass doors, it would have looked as out of place as a spaceship inside the shop.

At the till Giusy had made an ushering gesture: they'd gone outside.

The baby had been asleep, but judging by his flush and the dried tears on his fat cheeks, it had been a struggle. Maria Rosselli had followed Luisa's gaze impatiently.

'Obstinate,' she'd said. 'Like his mother. And look where that got her.'

Giusy had stuck her head round the door then. 'It's all right,' she said. 'Beppe says, Why don't you head home?'

Luisa had stared at her, taken aback. Affronted even.

Giusy had given her a meaningful glance. 'We can manage.' And then a quick glance at Maria Rosselli, telling Luisa, Get her out of here. Luisa had looked from Giusy to Maria Rosselli, but it had been the baby, at whom she did not look again, that had done it. How could she have left him to this woman's tender mercies?

'All right,' she'd said, and Giusy's head withdrew. Then to Maria Rosselli, 'Perhaps you'd walk back with me?' Maria Rosselli had looked at her with haughty suspicion. 'As we've both been abandoned.' And before the woman could have taken umbrage at that, Luisa added, 'I'll get my bag.'

They had walked in silence for at least half the way, side by side in stately progress. You had to walk in the street with such a baby carriage: it was too wide for the pavements. It had seemed to Luisa entirely typical of Maria Rosselli to refuse to make any concessions in the matter. A small electric bus had trundled patiently behind them the length of the Via del Corso without even a toot.

In the pram between them the baby had slept on, despite the jouncing of the springs on the paving slabs. A number of questions had occurred to Luisa as they'd walked: she'd dismissed each of them in turn. *Who will look after the baby? Will Niccolò find another woman? Or will you, Maria, move in with him?* But they had all seemed to suggest an answer that would only seal the poor child's fate.

'Carlo Bastone,' she'd said, instead. 'Have you known him all his life?'

Maria Rosselli had stopped walking, and Luisa had realized with satisfaction that she'd succeeded in surprising her. 'Yes,' she had said warily. 'He was at school with Niccolò.'

'So he came to the house? You – you approved of their friendship?'

Still wary, Maria Rosselli had shrugged. Tightened her grip on the pram's handle and resumed walking.

'He wasn't a particularly intelligent child,' she'd said. 'Not like Niccolò. I felt sorry for him.'

Luisa had found it hard to believe that Maria Rosselli had ever felt pity in her life. They'd arrived now in the sunlit expanse of the Piazza Santa Croce, pigeons strutting around the stone benches, the frescoed façades of the south side in the shade. One bench sat empty in the sun a hundred metres from them.

'Shall we sit down?' she'd suggested reluctantly. Maria Rosselli had pursed her lips, but sat.

'Is he married?' Luisa had asked. 'The lawyer, I mean?' She couldn't have said why she wanted to know, only that an unmarried man had no checks on him, no woman to moderate him. Would Rosselli – would the Frazione – survive with Flavia gone?

Maria Rosselli had looked at her with contempt. 'No,' she said. 'At least he had sense enough for that. I don't suppose any decent woman would have him anyway.' Luisa had wondered how she'd define *decent*: she herself had only been able to conjure up the image of an iron-jawed matriarch on her hands and knees, scrubbing.

She'd sighed. Get to the point. 'His family was wealthy?'

'Oh, yes,' Maria Rosselli had said. 'Very well off. But of course I wasn't impressed by his family.'

I bet you weren't, Luisa had thought, getting the picture. She would allow her bespectacled son a single friend, the class's other misfit, someone she could look down on despite his money. Condescension, of course, might be confused with pity but was not the same thing. Sandro said she'd barged into Bastone's office as if she owned the place.

'You were widowed so young,' she had said, changing tack. 'It must have been difficult.'

'My husband was always an invalid,' Maria Rosselli had said stiffly. 'My life was never easy. But we managed.'

'There was never any difficulty – with Niccolò's best friend being from a privileged background?'

Maria Rosselli's mouth had turned down. 'None at all,' she'd said. 'My son can acquit himself in any company. If you ask me, Carlo was envious of Niccolò, not the other way around. I'm sure you know how that is in those friendships? One person simply wishes to become the other, wants everything they have.'

Such as? Luisa wanted to ask but the woman had carried on. 'And Carlo's family were not of that vulgar kind, that spends freely.'

Right, Luisa had thought. Tightwads, then.

And suddenly she'd had enough of this lot, the Florentine reserve, the chilly, closed-off snobbishness of Maria Rosselli and, no doubt, Carlo Bastone's miserly landowner family too. She had stolen another glance at the sleeping child, without whose existence she'd happily never have exchanged another word with either Rosselli. They were tough, weren't they, babies? They could survive all sorts, that's what people said. She had sat, looking down at the golden sleeping face. . . and looking at its features the same thought had come to her that she'd had the day before, only more insistent this time.

'It's his, you know.' Maria Rosselli's harsh voice had broken in on her, as if its owner had read her mind. Luisa had looked from the child to his grandmother. 'Niccolò's the father. I know what you're thinking. But it's in the file.'

'In the file?' Luisa had found herself at a loss: she could only repeat the horrible old woman's words.

'In the medical file. They had to crosscheck his DNA to rule out. . . some syndrome or other. When he was just born.'

'Well,' Luisa had said, repelled. 'I suppose that's useful information.'

The other woman had said nothing more and abruptly Luisa had got up and brought their encounter to a close. 'I'll let you know,' she'd said, glancing down at Maria Rosselli's set face and noting something new in the stone-grey eyes looking up at her – an ebbing of that ferocious, hostile certainty and the beginnings of something that might be fear. 'When Sandro calls.'

The apartment was cooler now and Luisa moved through the rooms, opening windows, letting in the ripe smells of Santa Croce's restaurants and dumpsters, along with the warmer air of the streets. She was filling the coffee pot, to distract herself, when the house phone rang.

She knew before he spoke that it would be Sandro, the only person in Italy, and possibly the world, who still believed in the landline.

'You were right,' he said, and her heart filled at the sound of his weary, familiar voice. 'I was driving. We're on our way home.'

*

Slowly Enzo walked down the alley that led from the Frazione's offices to the Via Sant'Agostino. Behind him Carlo Bastone was still in there, talking among the ransacked filing cabinets and empty desks to three policemen who stood around him like sentries: from they way they'd gone on, Enzo had thought for a moment that they might detain them both. He took deep breaths.

The alley stank. It had never bothered Enzo before, he was accustomed to the smells of the city. But this evening, as the sky faded overhead, the day's heat seemed to be concentrated in the narrow space, and the staleness of the air was suffocating. He increased his pace, resisted breaking into a run. How would that look, if the police officers emerged and saw him pelting like a pickpocket for the Via Sant'Agostino?

On the corner he stopped. A tall man in a suit and tie stood against a wall opposite with his arms folded, a windowless wall that stretched between a bakery and the fag-puffing neon-jacketed drivers outside the ambulance post, the *misericordia*. There was graffiti behind the man. *Frazione = Merda. Frazione = Shit.*

Enzo weighed his mobile in his hand.

The man in the suit watched him: there weren't many suits seen down here, south of the river. He had a crew cut and a briefcase that he carried as if unused to it. There was something rough about him, something hard-edged; he might have been an ex-con trying to better himself.

Enzo felt as though the city was shifting around him, drafts and eddies, roads dug up, traffic diverted, police on the doorstep: things were moving out of focus and for a second he had the distinct impression that he might one day look up and not recognize where he was.

He began to compose a text message.

*

In Sandro's office, Giuli sat alone at the computer. She'd opened the windows when she let herself in because the place seemed stale and stuffy: she could hear the shrill sounds of children playing in the Piazza Tasso and the low murmur of voices passing in the street.

She'd typed 'Interpretation of Dreams' into the search engine, and had come up with a whole load of mystical, Tarot-reading nonsense, home-made websites referencing crystals and poltergeists. Giuli scrolled down looking for something more convincing, all the while only becoming more and more sceptical: if dream interpretation was not a science but the equivalent of palm-reading, she wasn't interested. Her phone bleeped with the arrival of a message and, frowning, she pushed it away. Concentrate. At last she got an online encyclopaedia entry, and settled back to read it.

Within ten minutes she was fidgeting on her chair, as if she was back in school. What was wrong with her, that facts just didn't go into her stupid head? Partly it was because something else was in there, bouncing around, trying to make her hear it. Her meeting with Wanda Terni: what had it meant? The dream, the park's long, empty alleys, and the rest. How well, after all, did Wanda know Flavia? Giuli had started out with a niggling envy, that Flavia had had this decent, thoughtful woman as a friend, that they'd gone for walks together: she'd had to tell herself, Luisa's your friend now. Stop dwelling on the past, stop thinking everyone's got it better than you. Even this poor dead woman. And then the envy had fallen away, because in the end Flavia hadn't been able to tell her friend about whatever it was that had been eating at her.

But she'd told the nurse.

At the computer, Giuli sat up straight with the certainty: Flavia had told Barbara. Barbara might have refused to say what she knew, but that didn't mean she knew nothing, and it didn't mean Giuli had learned nothing from the exchange. Good. She looked back at the screen but she couldn't bring it into focus; her mind was elsewhere, sifting through what she'd learned from Barbara and Wanda, deciding what was significant and what wasn't.

'A small thing,' Wanda had said uncertainly. 'But it was never something I associated with her, you see. That's why it startled me. I'd never heard that sound before when I was with her, and when she got it out and looked at it, I thought, Wow, so Flavia Matteo's joined the modern world.'

Back at the search engine, slowly, Giuli typed in, 'palace dream interpretation'. Nothing useful. She typed in, 'sword'.

Again the mystical websites: DreamMoods, WhatsYourSign. No thanks. She tracked her eyes down the page and it jumped out at her, a reference back to the online encyclopaedia:

> *Jung cautioned against blindly ascribing meaning to dream symbols without a clear understanding of the client's personal situation. He described two approaches to dream symbols: the causal approach and the final approach. In the causal approach, the symbol is reduced to certain fundamental tendencies. Thus, a sword may symbolize a penis, as may a snake. In the final approach, the dream interpreter asks, 'Why this symbol and not another?' Thus, a sword representing a penis is hard, sharp, inanimate, and destructive. A snake representing a penis is alive, dangerous, perhaps poisonous and slimy. The final approach will tell you additional things about the dreamer's attitudes.*

A sword representing a penis is hard, sharp, inanimate and destructive. Well, sure, thought Giuli, gaining confidence. But does it have to be a penis? Can't it be just – danger, say? Or a real sword? She realized that this was exactly what the entry was saying. Huh, she thought, unable to suppress a smile of satisfaction, I like this Jung. But the small glow of pleasure at understanding faded as she realized this only left her just where she'd started: needing to know more about Flavia Matteo.

Wanda. . . she rubbed her forehead and tried to get back to Wanda. Just a small thing, yes. She pulled her own mobile towards her. *Flavia Matteo's joined the modern world.*

Her mobile didn't recognize the number but the message displayed on the screen was unequivocal. *All right*, it said. *You're right, she's dead and it can't hurt her. I'll tell you.* It was from Barbara.

Giuli stared at the message thinking, but I already know. Don't I?

The mobile trembled in her hands and bleeped, another message coming in.

Chapter Twenty

THE KITCHEN WAS DIM and cool now, and they were gone: Enzo and Giuli had gone home, and Luisa was in the bedroom, putting the ironing away. Taking her time: calming herself, and leaving Sandro to think. He heard her move slowly around the room while he sat alone at the table under the light.

He'd dropped Rosselli back in Santo Spirito. Climbing back into the car, Sandro had just been able to hear the sound of the baby starting up, a monotonous repetitive cry from the first floor, where the old woman had appeared in the window at the sound of Niccolò fumbling with his keys. Christ, he'd thought with something like admiration as he slammed the door on the sound, they're programmed for survival all right. Those small bodies, you wouldn't have thought they'd have enough energy to keep it up.

After that, he'd just wanted quiet. But then the text had come in: *This is bad. I'm coming over to Santa Croce.* Enzo had sent it to all of them. Staring at it, Sandro had felt his stomach churn, acid. Enzo had arrived first, Giuli, bewildered, ten minutes later.

White-faced, he'd blurted it all out. The vice squad had been called in in the aftermath of the break-in. They'd confiscated the big desktop that had been left behind, and they were looking at it for child porn.

After a tip-off: of course. That face, those half-blind eyes behind the glasses, fixed on socialist heaven. Wasn't that just the type to download images of children being abused? It could be standard dirty tricks, someone hoping to rake up trouble for the troublesome Frazione. Sandro had glimpsed Giuli's expression, though.

Enzo had looked desperate. *Look her in the eye*, Sandro had thought, but Enzo couldn't, or wouldn't. 'I've never – I've never seen anything like that on them. But computers are – permeable. Stuff – people can download stuff in error, they can get infected.' His words had come out, jerky and faltering. 'I installed fire-walls, I clean them regularly, I monitor them, but I – I can't be everywhere.'

Sandro had seen Luisa look over at Giuli, and his wife had started talking quickly about Chiara then. Anything, maybe, to get off the subject of Enzo and computers and what he might or might not have known: anything to get that look off Giuli's face. Luisa had told them she'd seen Pietro: she was worried about him. Chiara was off the radar and he was worn down with it, and she'd seen him doing some deal in plainclothes with a man she didn't recognize. She'd hurried on with her story, glancing sidelong at Giuli as she went. Pietro – this with a worried shake of the head – had hinted his meeting was to do with getting background on the Frazione, but she was sure it was also to do with Chiara running off. Her hand to her mouth, hushing her own fears.

His wife was good, Sandro had thought, not for the first time, watching her keep a lid on her own anxiety, watching her work methodically through what she'd found out, and watching Giuli edge closer to her at the kitchen table, colour returning to the girl's face.

And Niccolò Rosselli was definitely the child's father apparently. Had it occurred to Sandro that he might not be? The relief he'd felt at the information had revealed to him that he hadn't wanted to contemplate the alternative.

Bastone, though: that was interesting. Luisa had got her teeth into him then, a subject altogether safer than child porn or Chiara. Maria Rosselli despised Carlo Bastone – but then she despised most people. A rich boy, whose family owned land down where they were going to build the new mall. A childhood friend, devoted to Rosselli – or obsessed with him? Admiring – or jealous?

But Luisa's energy had begun to falter: she'd clearly still been thinking about Chiara. And whatever they knew, or thought they understood, was not enough. What had made life so unbearable for Flavia that she'd left her child motherless? Was Pietro only looking for his daughter or did he have information on the Frazione? Or both, as Luisa seemed to think?

Sandro just hadn't liked it: he hadn't liked the implication of dirty stuff on computers his nearest and dearest were involved with. He hadn't liked a girl he'd known since she was a baby going AWOL. And he'd hated seeing that look on Giuli's pale face.

'Giuli,' he'd said, and her eyes had slid away from him. She looked down, cleared her throat, looked up again. And had begun to tell them about a dream.

*

Pietro and Gloria sat in a corner of the small trattoria two doors down from their apartment, eating in silence. The place was busy – a long table of young women were having some kind of celebratory meal – but the elderly waiter in his frowsty black waistcoat kept darting anxious glances across at them: he'd known the policeman and his red-haired wife since their daughter was a baby.

As the waiter removed their plates, Pietro spoke.

'I saw Luisa today.' Gloria folded her napkin in her lap, waiting. 'She said she saw Chiara.'

Colour flooded Gloria's freckled cheeks. 'What? Really? Really?' She stopped, helpless as tears came into her eyes, helpless at her own stupid parroting. He took her hand.

'Luisa said she looked fine. She said she looked very pretty.'

'Pretty?' Gloria felt her mouth tremble and turn down. She saw the waiter look back across his shoulder. 'Of course she's pretty, what's that got to do with it? What did Luisa mean?' She was confused: it wasn't the right word, pretty, not for their tomboy daughter, not when all they wanted to know was, where is she? Come home and eat with us, be at our table.

'Oh, I don't know,' said Pietro, despondent: she felt sorry now as his face reverted to sadness. He cleared his throat. 'You know Luisa. Trying to say something positive. Look. . . ' And Gloria did look, into her husband's worried face. 'She's on our side. They both are.'

'You haven't spoken to *him* though, have you? To Sandro?'

'It's complicated,' said Pietro, and his face closed tight against her.

*

They went home separately, Giuli and Enzo. That was only normal, she had her *motorino* and he had his little car, but this time she sped away without looking back as she usually did to check he was behind her. He would have noticed, of course; Enzo noticed everything.

The evening air was cool. She zipped through Sant'Ambrogio, the covered-market building locked up and the square quiet but not empty, a small crowd around one of the bars, a match inside on a big screen. She joined the traffic on the big, four-lane ring road and followed it down to the bridge of San Niccolò, over the river and up the curving sweep of the Viale Galileo to the Piazzale Michelangelo. The wide, flat space was thick with people: pavement artists, stalls selling soft drinks and souvenirs, the strolling crowds looking down over the glittering spread of the city. Giuli sailed on around the contour of the hill and the umbrella pines formed a canopy overhead: it was still warm enough for their resinous scent to hang in the air.

The smell of the seaside, of the plantations that led down to the sea, the silvered trunks falling over in the white sand. They'd had two holidays by the sea now, she and Enzo, but with an empty feeling Giuli found herself wondering if there'd be another.

An old woman on the top floor peered down as Giuli let herself in. 'Where's your fancy man?' she cackled. Her idea of a joke: Enzo was nobody's idea of a fancy man.

'Ha, ha,' Giuli said, unsmiling. It meant he wasn't home yet.

As she let herself into the neat apartment, with its smell still new and unfamiliar, Giuli had the inescapable certainty that something here was broken, something in their life together. She switched on the light and Enzo's orderliness gleamed back at her from the white walls, the red stools arrayed around the breakfast bar, just visible in the kitchen. All at once she could see how it would go, unreeling like a film ahead of her: into the bedroom, get a suitcase, put her stuff in it. He'd stand there in the doorway not able to say a word, she'd mumble something and run, into the lift and freedom.

But *why*, Giuli? She could see Luisa's face, stubbornly uncomprehending. *What's the poor boy done?*

Freedom. It's just easier that way.

How could she explain? She was a stray, one of those mangy cats some old lady tries to take in and it's fine for a while then it turns and scratches. Why would he want her anyway? Unless there was something wrong with him.

Enzo? You suspect *Enzo*? That's what Luisa would say. Only Giuli had seen it in Sandro's face too as they sat around the table, that flicker of doubt as his eyes passed over Enzo's frightened, homely features. As he told them what the female police officers from the vice squad had come looking for. And something inside her gathered and clenched and mastered her, the old, old panic and fear and rage she thought had gone. They never went.

'You're a survivor of abuse,' they'd told her in all those sessions, the red-faced man, the worn-out woman, the succession of weary therapists whose job it was to get criminals back out into the world again. And Giuli was a criminal still, just like she was a survivor, even though her crime had been to fight back at her abuser.

'Childhood abuse is a kind of hard wiring; you mustn't expect it to disappear. You have to manage it.' Foolishly, Giuli had thought she was the exception. Working at the Women's Centre as a kind of therapy, limited exposure, doing something positive to help women, some of whom had had similar lives to her. Working with Sandro, whom she knew – *knew* finally – would not ever let her down. These things would wipe it all out, because surely she deserved that, after thirty years?

Apparently she did not.

She should have talked to Sandro, but there'd been no time, no privacy, the four of them stuck under the kitchen light as if they were in an interrogation room. Damn it, she should have told them what she knew, now, about Flavia Matteo.

Only once the doubt was there, like the first crack in a crumbling wall, all she could think of as the panic screamed in her head was, I knew it, I knew it, I knew there was something wrong with it, I knew there was something wrong with me, he never wanted me. He's one of *them*.

Because it was all too easy, working as a receptionist, dispensing a smile and a bit of patient kindness, sorting out Sandro's computer systems for him and doing a bit of legwork on insurance fraud. All very well: child's play, in fact. But letting someone into your bed, trusting someone with your love, your future – that was different.

They'd thought about having children themselves.

Behind her Enzo's key turned in the lock and in that moment, miraculously, Giuli quieted. The suitcase was still on top of the wardrobe, this was still her home.

He'd held her hand and said, It doesn't matter if we can't have children. It's just you I want. He'd looked at her with his brown eyes. Could it have been true? Hold your ground, something said quietly inside her head: that's the answer. Hold your ground, don't panic, look for the truth. That's what Sandro would say, wasn't it?

Giuli turned to Enzo.

'I'm sorry,' she said, and couldn't believe how calm she sounded.

Enzo looked close to tears. She put her arms around his back, and she couldn't believe how easy it was to comfort him.

'I'm sorry.'

Chapter Twenty-One

CHIARA SAT ON THE concrete balcony, concealed from the neighbours by the rattan barrier. He'd told her not to lean out.

'They're so nosy,' he'd said, with that slow smile of his, fixing her with that intense, hypnotic look. They were in the bare kitchen together two days ago. He'd been getting dressed for work while she stared at him, feeling something that wound her tight, like hunger. Chiara thought, God, what must my face look like, staring at him like I could eat him? But she couldn't stop herself from staring. His long body, his arms sliding into the shirt sleeves, the wiry hairs on his strong hands straightening the pale tie. Had she been in love before? She thought of the boys at the *liceo*: it had been nothing like this. Where was he?

He was out there somewhere in the dark. He'd come home when he was ready. She couldn't control his movements, he'd told her that too, and she couldn't question him, for fear – of what? Just fear. It occurred to her that fear was one of the things that tied her to him. In the dark on the balcony she felt herself flush.

'I don't want them seeing how beautiful you are. I don't

want them jealous. You know what neighbours are like.' From somewhere above her Chiara could smell someone smoking on an upper balcony: she sensed them all around, trying to get a look at her.

The woman in the laundry had given her a funny look, Chiara was sure of it, but the flat had no washing machine, she had no choice but to take the sheets there.

'I'll get one,' he'd said easily. 'We're just like honeymooners, aren't we? These things take a while. Home-building: there's time enough for that.' And he'd smiled again. 'Aren't you pleased, that I don't think of you as a little wife? You're a lover, that's what you are. We're lovers.'

The thought sprang into her head: she shouldn't have spoken to Giancarlo. She shouldn't have said anything to him. She'd been told not to say anything to anyone about where she was. This was about them, the two of them, the lovers, it was their private world and they didn't have to be told what they could do together. She'd thought Giancarlo would understand better than the girls she'd been to school with; anyway, he was a gay guy, he had to live outside the rules, didn't he?

She was drinking Coca-Cola: the fridge was full of it. She had wondered if he thought she was a child, to be given sweet, fizzy drinks, but he drank it too. He liked two sugars in his coffee.

Perhaps it was the same in the little mini-market as it was in the laundry; did they know who she was, and who he bought the Coca-Cola for? They looked at her strangely there, too.

She remembered Luisa's face, as if from a hundred years ago, the anxiety in her dark eyes just glimpsed across the market as Chiara had stood there talking to Giancarlo, the panic. Chiara knew that face almost as well as she knew her own; could picture Luisa's dark head next to her mother's red curls, leaning down towards her, encouraging her to walk. Or sitting at a restaurant table with Luisa and Sandro and her mum and dad, trying to be good, all of them talking to her at once. Eat up, wipe your chin, no Coca-Cola, no.

Luisa would have seen the truth, straight away: *You're out of your depth, my girl.* And then Chiara was seized with panic, wanting to call out in the darkness, Babbo, I'm here! Here in that bit of town, a suburb we might have driven through a hundred times, off to the seaside, remember that? Not daring to name it, because *he'd* said not to.

What was she doing here?

She was waiting for something. He'd promised her, tomorrow. He would finish work early, he'd be home early, she should wear that slip he liked. *You wait, it'll be worth it, it'll be something special.* That was part of this love affair too, he'd told her, it had to be a surprise because you didn't always know you wanted something, till you got it.

The darkness beyond the balcony was warm and soft. She was waiting.

*

It was close to two in the morning and Sandro was out on the street, staring at something written on a wall.

From the Piazza Santa Croce came a peal of loosened female laughter, followed by the murmur of male voices. A set of footsteps not far off in the shadowy streets, wandering like a drunk's, another set more distant but sharper: the click of steel tips, or high heels. The city was a different place in the dark, an echoing labyrinth, its canyon streets full of hiding places. Sandro put a hand to the powdery stucco, wondering.

He'd been to bed once already.

'You're dog tired,' Luisa had said, the minute the door had

closed behind Enzo. 'This can wait till morning. It'll make more sense then.'

They'd listened to Enzo's reluctant steps on the stairs: it had sounded as though he was hanging back deliberately rather than trying to catch Giuli up.

So he'd obeyed, they'd gone to bed and he'd listened to Luisa's breathing ease and slow as she fell asleep. She hadn't told him whatever it was that was bothering her. Then it had all started to go round and round for Sandro: Enzo's frightened face, Giuli's closed one, Luisa's distraction. The baby without its mother, the Frazione's followers dispersing, just another leaderless rabble now, all mixing with that insurance claim he should be filing a report on. The traumatized claimant chain-smoking in silence on his balcony, who turned briefly into Pietro who'd never smoked. A man with a tattoo on his hand, in two places at once, something written – something written on someone else's hand? Who'd said that? Sandro must have lain there three hours with it whirling like a snowstorm in his exhausted brain: had he slept at all? Had he even closed his eyes?

By one o'clock he'd given up and found himself sitting under the light at the kitchen table, trying to read his own scrawled notes.

Earlier, Sandro had taken his turn to give his account of the day – close to two days, as a matter of fact – after Giuli had arrived.

He'd thought, somehow, from her excited face when she'd come into the apartment, that there'd be more to it than this dream. The friend of Flavia had obviously been interesting. He'd supposed it was Wanda the maths teacher who read Freud, or whoever: interesting but quite likely cracked. Quite likely half in love with Flavia herself, although some warning glance from Giuli had stopped him from voicing that particular theory.

Flavia Matteo had seemed ill, was the gist of it: she'd lost weight, seemed withdrawn – or more withdrawn than usual, retreating from her friends. He'd caught Luisa's eye then, remembering the way she'd looked at her own body when the cancer diagnosis and the chemo had robbed her of her appetite for most of a year. Disbelieving: she'd always thought she could do with losing a pound or two, but the only time she'd cried throughout the whole cancer thing was on coming out of the bathroom one night, having seen her thin bare arms in the mirror. Thin as a drug addict, thin as a camp survivor, thin as a cancer sufferer. No longer herself.

Was that how Flavia Matteo had seen herself, too, wasting away? Stress could do it. So the weight loss, followed by the pregnancy. An affair might have been the explanation if it wasn't Flavia Matteo they were talking about, and besides, the child was Rosselli's. A showdown with her husband? A series of rows over whether to have a baby? The mother-in-law no doubt sticking her oar in as well. Happy families.

'What about the addiction thing?' he'd said to Giuli with a frown because that was the hot trail she'd been following when he'd spoken to her from the seaside hotel, it wasn't his imagination. It was written down in big letters, too, on the notes he'd been making; he'd gone over it a few times until it stood out. But Giuli had shaken her head.

'It's a tricky one. Patient confidentiality,' she'd said, and her face closed. 'I'm waiting to hear.'

So at one Sandro had found himself sitting there in his undershirt and looking at what he'd written, to see if it made any more sense.

It would be so easy to agree with the general perception: Flavia Matteo had never been happy, she was a woman who'd denied herself, who repressed her emotions. The birth of a child was a vast thing, an earthquake in anyone's life let alone this shy, withdrawn woman's. So why was it so hard to believe that she'd get post-natal depression?

The truth was, it remained the logical explanation. And it was looking like the least harmful one, too, so shouldn't they just let it lie, like they'd suggested at the Centre?

But Niccolò Rosselli wanted the certainty: he wanted it laid bare, he wanted the hard facts and not the rumour. Rosselli, Sandro had to admit, was a brave man: he hadn't faltered at the news of the break-in last night, nor at the police raid; he wasn't frightened. Perhaps he should be.

Sandro had got dressed, and come out into the ghostly streets, and here he was with half his brain listening to the footsteps, the wandering set falling silent behind the bang of a door, the clicking feet moving in parallel to him, to the north. With the other half of his mind he was visualizing those notes made under the kitchen light, their shared thoughts.

Giovanni Bastone: a wealthy man, a landowner. Sandro had told them what the soldier had said. 'Look to the business interests.'

Chiara: he'd written down her name absently, listening to Luisa fret about her, crossed it out.

Pietro: his name had been in the notes too. You could call Pietro, Giuli had said, and he'd dutifully written it down, unable to admit that if he were to call his old friend, Pietro might not answer, he'd been so unlike himself lately. A line through it, when Giuli wasn't looking.

He'd written down the dream, too, had felt his hand cramped with the concentration of it, the murderer chasing Flavia, the faceless man who would hack her to pieces. The assassin. There had been no assassin scaling the balcony at the Stella Maris. But the bare bones of that dream haunted him now, in the street – the slashing arm, the dismemembered victims, the shadowy corridors of the luxurious palace.

He'd told them – Luisa, Giuli, Enzo, all looking back at him gravely – about the Stella Maris: for some reason found himself needing to describe it in detail. Not a palace with long corridors, he'd said: only a shabby, sunlit hotel.

And Calzaghe. Luisa's eyes had narrowed when he'd described the man. Sandro had shaken his head reluctantly. 'I don't know about him,' he'd said. 'I don't think he had anything to do with it.'

'He would have had pass keys,' Luisa had said. Sandro had thought of that, of course. The hotel proprietor could have let himself into that room any time he liked – or he could have given the keys to someone else for a backhander; the place looked like it had been losing money for years.

'I mentioned that,' he'd said to Luisa, and she'd almost smiled.

'Vesna keeps the keys,' Calzaghe had in fact said, frightened. 'Isn't that so, Vesna?' She'd shrugged in confirmation, watching him closely.

'And Vesna's here every night, not me.' He'd watched Sandro intently, fearfully.

After he'd made his notes their will to go on had petered out, around that table: they all seemed to shut down, out of weariness or anxiety. Giuli had been the first to leave, abruptly, looking only at Luisa. 'I'm on the *motorino*,' she'd said. 'Better get going.' And over her shoulder to Enzo, hurried, evasive: 'See you there, *caro*.'

Stifling a yawn now, Sandro turned into the Via dei Malcontenti, which led down along the bare flank of Santa Croce. The street was dark save for the occasional lit window but there were lamps in the piazza, and their illumination filtered down the narrow, blindsided street. The road of the malcontents: plenty of those. Absently he rubbed his fingertips together, feeling the oil and dirt on them from the plaster wall.

Frazione = Azione, the stencil had said. Someone had crossed out *Gandhi* and put in instead, *Niccolò è nostro re*. Niccolo is our king. From saint to king, raised higher and higher. It would not end well, was all Sandro could think.

On the threshold of the long expanse of the piazza, the statue of Dante at his shoulder, Sandro stopped. Over the three neatly spaced palaces at the far end, the narrow streets fanning out between them off the piazza like a clever experiment in perspective, rose the tower of the Palazzo Vecchio, illuminated against the night sky. Closer, on a bench halfway down the square, sat a girl, legs stretched out in front of her, a boy at her feet, another standing behind her affecting nonchalance, hands in his pockets, and a litre-bottle of wine on the stone beside them.

In Sandro's pocket something jumped and buzzed: his mobile. He hadn't known it was in there. It occurred to him as he pulled it out that he didn't even know if he had his house-key.

It was a message from Giuli.

Need to look over Niccolò's apartment, it said. *Soon as possible. Will he be OK with that?*

So Giuli was awake: she wouldn't have assumed he was, though. This message was intended to reach him in the morning. He looked down, weighing the phone in his hand, itching to reply: *What are you looking for?*

But if she'd wanted to tell him that, she would have. And it was late, he wanted to sleep, and he wanted Giuli to sleep. In the square the boy at the girl's feet was on his knees, upright before her as if he was in church. Slowly the girl leaned down and kissed him, and behind her the standing boy thrust his hands further down in his pockets, shoulders hunched. Turning to leave, Sandro thought, *Just wait. She'll get bored with the kneeling boy and she'll come to you and by then there'll be someone else.*

But for a moment, re-entering the shadows of the Via dei Malcontenti, Sandro found that he could recall exactly the furious power of that raging moment, when the girl won't answer your call or you watch as she kisses someone else and you don't know what to do with yourself. When the hormones rise in you and you could do anything, hurl a stone, break all your knuckles throwing a reckless punch, or jump off a motorway bridge. A pulse of gladness, not to be young any more, was swiftly followed by unease. Giuli wasn't young, was she? And love seemed to be doing for her. Perhaps there was no safe age after all: if he thought he might lose Luisa to another man – or to whatever, he couldn't even name the alternatives – that raging moment would be upon him before he could blink, and he'd be lost.

Doggedly Sandro retraced his steps, working these thoughts out of his system. Thinking with determination of his bed and the need for some sleep at least. By way of distraction listening out for those other feet, the brisk clicking heels: only there was nothing. By the time he got to the corner of the Via dei Macci he'd cleared it. They were rational creatures, he and Giuli and Luisa; their little unit would survive. He stopped.

He could smell the fresh spray paint before he even got there, acrid and chemical in the night air that should have smelled of flowers. Someone had been there, in the shadows, around the corner, no more than a hundred metres behind him.

Frazione = Perversione, it read now. And where five minutes earlier he'd read that Niccolò was their king, a brutish angry scribble had been drawn obliterating the words completely. Above it now, in huge black letters, *Rosselli è pedofilo*.

Frazione = Perversion. Rosselli is a paedophile.

And there he'd been, thinking that he might even get a good night's sleep.

Chapter Twenty-Two

SOMETIMES YOU JUST KNEW.

Luisa knew, before she opened her eyes, in that moment between sleep and waking she'd always been half afraid of because it whispered to you things you didn't want to hear. A dangerous moment, your dreams still hovering, your fears unrationalized. This fear had dug in, it sat under the skin like a tick.

She'd known about her lump in exactly the same way: the morning of the first appointment with the breast doctor. Sandro was beside her just as he was this morning, tangled in sheets after a restless night and snoring. She'd lain in bed, listening to the November rain, and quite calmly she had understood that this was not going to be good news and it would have to be dealt with.

No rain this morning but the air had cooled, she could almost feel the sky thickening with the approach of autumn. Luisa opened her eyes.

This wasn't anything as concrete as a tumour, but the fear was there. There was something wrong, something badly wrong. *This is not good*, were the words in her head. And this time it wasn't Luisa who needed help. *You're in trouble, aren't you?* She felt it from across the city. Somewhere out there, in her pale high-heeled shoes, in her floating pretty dress, Chiara was drowning.

Luisa's appointment at Careggi was at eleven-thirty. No point saying anything: Sandro would only worry unnecessarily. It was just routine anyway, it was the check-up and the reconstruction talk. She'd cancel it, of course. There were more urgent things. There was Chiara.

Uneasily she turned over in bed, unconsciously setting her back against Sandro. She needed to talk to him, just not yet: about Chiara. There would have to be a strategy for the whole Pietro thing. That was madness, it was out of control. But it came to her that it wasn't just Sandro's old stubborn streak, his touchiness, his paranoid reticence where his former partner was concerned. Pietro *had been* behaving strangely. There *was* something he wasn't telling them: in the cool, sharp early light it became quite clear to Luisa. He'd been funny with her yesterday, his eyes constantly darting away from hers.

Beside her Sandro shifted, but didn't wake. What time had he come in? Two, perhaps three: he'd have had no more than five hours' sleep. Luisa sat up: carefully she eased out of the bed. She shivered.

In slippers and dressing gown she padded into the kitchen and began to dismantle the coffee pot.

He came up behind her, his breath sour from sleeplessness but his arms warm: she relaxed back fractionally against him, the coffee pot still in pieces in her hands.

He cleared his throat. 'So when's your appointment again?' he said.

*

A woman stood outside the taped door of the Frazione Verde's offices in the grimy alley and looked at the handwritten sign.

Another came up beside her. They were both middle-aged, with weathered faces: one had wiry grey hair and the other dyed black, with a squared-off fringe. They were wrapped up in layers of clean, warm, unfashionable clothing, and their noses wrinkled against the alley's smell of urine and garbage.

'It's a shame,' said the dark woman, frowning hard. A man, a little older, wandered up behind them, neatly dressed in a waxed jacket and carrying some shopping from the market. He peered at the sign.

'*Thank you for your continued support, friends,*' it read. '*The closure of our offices is temporary, due to police intervention: we will soon be opening a new centre of operations where all will again be welcome. Please refer to our website for details.*'

'It's more than that,' said the grey-haired woman grimly. At the end of the alley some teenagers appeared, thumbs flicking over their mobiles: three girls, two boys, late-teens, closer to twenty. They lifted their heads as they approached and stood for a moment in front of the sign, mobiles now abandoned.

'OK,' said the tallest of the girls, lanky in jeans. Cheerful. 'So. What's the plan?'

*

Perhaps this was how it worked, thought Giuli, standing at the ugly little bar around the corner from the Women's Centre and waiting for her coffee. You pretended nothing was the matter and hoped for the best.

Had he been unable to meet her eye, as he left? Swinging his USB keys nervously. 'I'm going into work,' he'd said. 'I want to monitor the Frazione website, people will want to know what's going on. They'll be posting stuff.'

Or had she been unable to meet his?

'Sounds good,' she'd said. 'I'll call you.'

It was eight o'clock: the Addictions clinic opened at half-past, and she'd arranged to see Barbara in here. Best for both of them to stay away from the Centre for this chat.

The barman yawned as he set her coffee down, showing tobacco-stained teeth. Another reason to give up: just not today, thought Giuli. She smiled her thanks warily.

Say nothing, don't rock the boat. The alternative was impossible: she couldn't *ask* him. Enzo, do you know anything about what the vice squad were looking for? *Was it you?*

She knew it had to be arrived at rationally. Pulling the coffee towards her, Giuli thought without hope of Sandro's diligence, the way he could just shift the irrelevant and the unreasoned out of the way, and focus. Trouble was, she didn't feel rational, she felt like there was nothing in her body that was fixed, no ticking brain, no bone or muscle, only a jelly of hormones and panic – soft, frightened girl stuff.

She'd watched Enzo pack his briefcase with his back to her, transferring the USB keys from his pocket to the case as though they were the keys to Fort Knox. Zipping carefully, something deliberate about the way he wasn't turning round. 'I'm going to be a bit tied up this morning,' he'd said, as he left, turning away too quickly on the stairs. 'I'll call you.'

She spooned some of the froth on her cappuccino into her mouth.

Of course it wasn't him: he knew too much about computers, he'd have been able to hide it if it had been him. Plus, she knew him. This was Enzo, he didn't have a bad bone in his body.

That wasn't logic, that was emotion. That was love. Back to rational, OK? Look at his behaviour. Was he acting guilty? Some people might see guilt: he'd been horrified and panicky, he hadn't been able to meet her eye.

Or had that been her, not meeting his? She took a sip, tasted the creaminess with gratitude, felt the kick of the caffeine.

He wasn't acting nonchalant, that was for sure, and that would be worse; that would be cast-iron evidence of guilt.

The barman's head lifted: Barbara stood in the doorway. From the look of her, Giuli thought the nurse might turn on her heel at the slightest provocation so she turned back to the barman, asked for two more coffees and took them, without a word, to the furthest corner of the small space.

'Best to meet here,' said Giuli warily as she approached. 'Farmiga had a go yesterday. I don't know what her problem is.'

'Her problem is, she's a bitch,' said Barbara, and a flush appeared on her cheeks. She pulled at her collar and lifted the cup. 'She hates the lot of us. Her latest man's supposed to be giving her trouble, but she doesn't need an excuse. I don't know what she's doing working at the Centre at all.' Her smile was pinched. 'Unless she's a plant.'

Now it was Giuli's turn to flush. Did Barbara think she was some sort of conspiracy theorist? It seemed to her that it was like everything evil in the world; if you were lucky, you could go through life not seeing it – the babies with cigarette burns, the abused nine year olds, the family men trawling the internet for sex, the bent policemen, the government working against the people. But once you saw it, you saw it everywhere. What *was* Farmiga doing working at the Centre?

'Who'd have her?' she said almost reflexively, although she knew plenty of them would. A woman like Farmiga was good news for a particular sort of man: he could treat her how he liked, she wouldn't flinch. Did people see Giuli like that? She was tough enough.

'Some good-looking Nazi,' said Barbara. 'Some tall handsome bastard full of testosterone.' And laughed drily. 'Who'd want one of those?'

Not me, thought Giuli, looking up startled because it was

true, and because she hadn't thought that someone like Barbara would want one either. Or Chiara. And for one tiny, warm second Enzo's face appeared before her, frowning, serious, kind. True. Not rationally, but in her gut, she knew it: he was true.

She lifted her coffee to her lips and, suddenly queasy, set it down again untasted. Barbara's face was pale and set.

'It's all right,' Giuli said. 'You don't even have to tell me, not right out.'

'I don't?'

'I think I know. I know why Flavia came to talk to you, I know what her – addiction was. I don't know who – who else was involved, I don't know how it started – but I know what she couldn't give up.'

Barbara stared.

'Same old, same old, wasn't it?' said Giuli. 'It was love.'

*

If anything, Giovanni Bastone's office seemed dustier, dimmer and more cluttered than when Sandro had first seen it. Remembering with surprise how deftly Giuli had taken control then, he wished she were with him this time, too.

The lawyer sat behind his heaped desk under the high coffered ceiling: all those ancestors, all that wealth, reduced to this dishevelled hulk of a man in his grand but decaying apartments. 'Niccolò'll be here – ah, soon,' he said helplessly. 'I don't know where Enzo is. I've called him but his phone's switched off or something.' He looked grey.

'He's been a help, I imagine,' said Sandro, still standing. 'I'm sure he'll be in touch, and we've an arrangement to go and see Niccolò. But it's you I wanted to talk to.'

In fact, he'd said to Luisa, 'I can talk to Bastone later, I'm coming with you.'

He'd known from the way she stiffened as he mentioned the hospital appointment that she hadn't been going to say anything: he wouldn't have put it past her not to turn up at all.

'No way,' she'd said firmly, turning in his arms. 'It's just routine, I don't need you there. I *don't*, *caro*, darling, sweetheart, I don't. I can manage.'

'On your own? On the bus?' He didn't set her free.

There'd been a fractional hesitation. 'Gloria's coming,' she'd said. 'I asked her the other day. She – she'll drive me.'

And that had been that. Had she been lying? It wasn't a question you could ask Luisa: in any marriage it was the question you waited longest to ask.

'They won't let us back into the Frazione's offices,' said Bastone now, and he seemed close to tears. Had this man ever practised as a lawyer? It came to Sandro that the qualification, the beautiful consulting rooms, the books and the panelling and the view of the piazza were all a distraction, a rich man's toys.

And the money was why he'd come to Bastone. It all came down to sex or money: if anyone wanted to pull the Frazione down, it had to be because of money. 'Some business interest or other,' like Colonello Arturo had said. And was that why he couldn't get the soldier's face out of his head?

If it hadn't been for the computer raid, it might not have occurred to Sandro. But who had access to those computers, real access? Rosselli, Enzo, Bastone. Would Rosselli want to bring down his own party? Drive his own wife to suicide? And Enzo? However much he liked the boy, had learned to trust him, Enzo was still an unknown quantity, Sandro had to remind himself of that. Enzo had the expertise.

But Bastone. . . He had known Flavia Matteo as long as she'd known Rosselli. Luisa had told him what Maria Rosselli had said about Bastone, and his family: tightwads, misers – not vulgar, though, heaven forbid. The old school of Florentine landowning semi-nobility: incapable of earning a decent living, selling off bits of land, cranking rents out of failing *contadini*.

So if what Pietro had turned up at the land registry was accurate, it looked like Bastone – or his family – had a financial stake in the Frazione's downfall. *Should it come about*, and Sandro almost muttered the words superstitiously. He found himself hoping fervently that by some miracle this shambolic little unit, this ragtag mob of hippies and do-gooders and eco-recyclers, would survive to fight another day. Not for him, but for Giuli, and Enzo, and Chiara.

Chiara. The girl's face appeared to him, fresh, dark-eyed, eager: when had he last seen her? When she'd thanked him for the iPod, a year ago? Children grow up, we have to get used to that. He thought of Luisa's shoulders set stiff in his embrace this morning as she had told him: *I woke up certain she was in trouble, I mean real trouble.*

The Frazione was in trouble too.

Then Giuli had called, the phone ringing even as he unclasped his arms from around Luisa, to say that she would meet him in the piazza at eleven. She was on the trail of something: he had known better than to interrupt her with questions. The message had been the same as last night's: he had to sort it with Niccolò Rosselli for them to go over the apartment with a fine toothcomb; Giuli still hadn't said what it was they were looking for – and Sandro hadn't asked. So Bastone would have to be dealt with first.

And if the lawyering was a kind of smokescreen for the fact that Bastone was so wealthy he didn't have to work, where had the politics come into it? To assuage his conscience? A young man's indulgence? Only now Giovanni Bastone was no longer young.

Sandro had called Niccolò straight after hanging up on Giuli. He had sensed Luisa listening from the kitchen.

Rosselli had agreed to the request without hesitation.

'We would try not to – cause too much disruption,' Sandro had said, taken aback. Could this man really have so little to hide? Or nothing left to lose.

'Eleven's fine,' Niccolò had said. 'My mother – my mother will take care of the child. Do you want me there, too?'

'I – um – sure,' Sandro had said, improvising. 'I'm sure we'll need your help, at least initially. It's your apartment, after all, she was your wife. But if it becomes distressing—'

Like Sandro, Rosselli hadn't asked what it was they'd be looking for. Which was just as well.

Now Bastone was looking at him with undisguised panic, getting to his feet from behind the desk. He looked as though he hadn't shaved or slept in a week.

'You want to talk to *me*?' he said.

'Sit down,' said Sandro gently, although it was not his place. Obediently, however, Bastone sat.

Sandro remained standing, his hands on the back of a beautiful polished wooden chair. 'Do you practise much?' he asked, almost by way of polite conversation. 'What kind of law is your speciality?

'Land law and tenancy agreements,' said Bastone, looking bewildered. 'But I – no – well. My mother isn't so keen on – I'm taken up a great deal with the Frazione. With helping Niccolò.'

'Yes,' said Sandro. 'And with family matters, I suppose?'

'Family matters?' Bastone was wary, at last.

'Well, I understand your family owns a great deal of land. Your expertise must be useful.'

'I don't understand what you mean,' said the lawyer stubbornly. 'I don't understand what this has to do with – with Flavia.'

Something about the way he spoke her name. 'It's not just Flavia, though, is it? It's more complicated than that now.'

Bastone seemed frozen behind the heaped desk. Did he read these dusty books? The photograph of the lawyer's mother stood behind him on the shelf: it seemed to Sandro to display the kind of sweet smile that disguised selfishness, caprice, greed, jealousy. He noticed that there was another photograph further along, of three figures standing in an awkward group at some social function. Niccolò Rosselli, Flavia and Bastone, the pale woman at the centre all the more radiant somehow, even from where Sandro stood, for her dowdy, ill-fitting dress.

'Are you an only child, Dottore Bastone?'

Bastone just stared as though he had renounced all hope of understanding Sandro's approach. 'I am,' he said, barely audible.

Sandro inclined his head. 'So your mother depends on you?'

'It's in the nature of the relationship.' A fight back. 'I don't understand what you're asking me.'

'Does she mind your involvement with the Frazione?'

Uneasily, Bastone twisted his head on its broad neck. 'She's not interested in politics. She doesn't understand – my relationship with Niccolò.'

So the mother was hostile: obviously, she would be.

'Not interested in politics,' Sandro said. Interested in money, though, I bet, for all Maria Rosselli said they weren't the vulgar sort. 'Did she just think it would be a passing phase? And now – it's time to return to your responsibilities?' Sandro paused. 'I mean, as a landowner. I imagine she has exerted pressure?'

Bastone paled, and Sandro knew he was right. 'It is true, isn't it?' he said gently. 'That your family will become considerably richer if that road is built, the road the Frazione Verde opposes?'

Now Bastone was on his feet. Unperturbed Sandro continued.

'I have information –' and he took a breath, thinking of Pietro, of those dreary offices in the Via dell'Agnolo where taxes were estimated and historic ownership of patches of wasteground proven, 'that the land registry shows the purchase of your *terreno* – your building land – is under way. The permissions have been granted for the commercial centre. I imagine the price goes up as each obstacle is overcome. The Frazione – against all the odds – the Frazione seems to be the only thing left in your way.'

There was a long silence: Bastone stood, pale but steadier somehow than Sandro had seen him before. At last the lawyer spoke.

'In *my* way?' He tilted his head, like a large, predatory bird, and for the first time Sandro could after all picture him in a courtroom. 'My way is the Frazione's way, you forget that. Flavia and Niccolò and the Frazione – *they* are my family.' But there was a stiffness in the way he said it. 'My mother—' And he clicked his teeth, a sound of uneasy frustration. 'My mother doesn't understand.'

You bet she doesn't, thought Sandro. His gut feeling about this man was shifting despite himself, but he resisted. There was something buried deeper than he had yet dug.

'They might have been your family,' he said, 'a kind of family. But blood is thicker than water. It is hard to resist a mother, if you're an only child. And all this—' He looked around: the lovely long windows with their aspect on to the flank of the church, the polished wood, the great dark wall sconces. 'Did she threaten to take all this away?'

From the look on Bastone's face, he knew he was right.

'Wouldn't it have been enough to say, "Withdraw your support, leave them"? Were you funding them?'

Bastone stood very still. 'Niccolò wouldn't take money from me, even if I had it to give,' he said. A question hung unanswered: Why not? Sandro pressed his advantage. It seemed to be time for the direct approach.

'Did she demand that you bring the Frazione down? You had access to those computers. You seem to have allowed the vice squad in without a fight. Did you know what they were looking for? Did you know all along?'

The light shed through the windows was grey today, and standing in it Bastone was greyer still. 'They said it was illegal material,' he said, and his voice shook. 'They said the thieves – the burglary – it was connected. They said they believed that whoever stole the computers made the tip-off. They had the correct warrants, all the documentation was in order, I was obliged—' But Sandro interrupted him.

'You were first on the scene of the break-in,' he said. 'It seems an extraordinary coincidence to me. First Flavia,' and he saw Bastone flinch, 'then the break-in, then the vice squad. The illegal material. What material is this? You know, don't you?'

'Indecent images,' said Bastone, once more barely audible. 'That's what they said.'

Sandro thought of what Luisa had told him about Maria Rosselli's haughty dismissal of Carlo Bastone. Not very intelligent: a boy who'd wanted Niccolò Rosselli's life. And when he couldn't have it? When Niccolò Rosselli refused to take his money?

'You know,' he said. 'You know. What images?'

'I did nothing to harm the Frazione,' said Bastone, and Sandro saw tears, real tears, in the creases of his pouchy eyes. Saw the pudgy schoolboy whom no one would befriend. 'I would never – never! I told Mamma. I told her that I wouldn't leave the Frazione, she could do what she liked.' He waved a hand helplessly, turned his face away from the grey light. 'She only cared about money. Money is nothing.'

Easy for you to say, thought Sandro, but Bastone's voice held the ring of truth. Carlo Bastone didn't know what it would be like without money, so he probably meant what he'd just said. There was something he wasn't saying, though: Sandro burrowed back through the exchange, listening in his head for the words that Bastone had faltered over.

Flavia. He looked into Bastone's eyes and didn't even need to say it.

'I loved her,' said Carlo Bastone. 'I've always loved her.'

And in the thin light of the great room he closed his mouth. He put one hand to it and then another, like a child trying to stop himself saying another word.

Chapter Twenty-Three

I T WAS THE RIGHT time to be going.

There'd been thick low cloud over the sea at dawn and the town was dull and sunless close to midday as Vesna turned towards the station. The season was over and done.

Calzaghe had said that as she wasn't giving notice, she'd have to go without the previous week's wages. Never mind that he'd have let her go at the end of the week without any warning, anyway.

He'd tried to inject triumph at his own cunning into the dismissal, but it had fallen flat. She had caught him looking up at the Stella Maris in sullen confusion, the striped police tape still flickering from the railings, as if only now realizing that the hotel was never going to make him his fortune. Vesna felt only relief as she walked away, her suitcase surprisingly light in her hand. She'd never been one to accumulate things: there'd be time for that. There'd be time and family and home, for that.

Outside the dry cleaner's – his blind down, only open three days a week, now that September was almost over – litter was blowing in the street. As Vesna frowned at it, following a crumpled length of cellophane unfurling in the breeze, there he was. Coming around the corner after it in his luminous jacket, stabbing with a kind of pincer arm to catch the ribbon. He looked up, at her face then down at the suitcase in her hand. Vesna couldn't help but feel rewarded by his transparent dismay.

'You're leaving,' he said. Rubbed his forehead, leaving a smear. He took off a glove and looked at his hand: scrubbed, nails clean, observed Vesna.

'Yes,' she said. And smiled, the smile broadening at the thought of her escape. 'I jumped before I was pushed.'

'When's your train?' he asked abruptly.

'Not sure,' said Vesna. 'I was just going to turn up and wait.' She felt completely at ease. However long she had to sit on station platforms today, it would be worth it, to leave this place behind.

'Had enough of us?' he said, half-reading her mind.

'Not all of you,' she said, beginning a smile, then she felt her face fall.

'Would you have a coffee with me before you go?'

She hesitated.

'There's something I wanted to tell you.'

They stood in the Bar Cristina on the front: he'd suggested they go to the station and wait there but Vesna wanted to be alone for that, that last moment of departure. What was half an hour, anyway? The journey across the breadth of the country – Florence, Bologna, Verona, Trieste – mapped itself in her head, the slow *regionale* trains, the lit-up windows, the deserted stations at midnight. She wouldn't be home till midday tomorrow.

They knew each other's names, after a year's nodding acquaintance, but they didn't use them: it seemed too late to become familiar. He bought her a *caffè latte* with grave politeness: he was probably only her age, Vesna realized. When he took off his cap she saw a band of startlingly pale skin at the hairline. And this morning he didn't have that whiff about him, of dregs and stale grease. Perhaps there just wasn't so much rubbish now the tourists had mostly departed.

She should go.

'Have they decided, then?' he asked quickly, as if to detain her. 'About the woman? Flavia Matteo: it's all in the papers. It was suicide?'

Tweaking her hair in front of a mirror behind the coffee machine, Cristina looked along the bar at them for a second. The dustbin man bobbed his head down and drank his espresso quickly, staying out of Cristina's range. Vesna wondered what it was he wanted to tell her.

'I mean, otherwise they probably would be asking you to stay around.' He gave her a lopsided smile.

'I don't know anything about it,' she said quickly, wishing she didn't, wishing she'd never come to the Stella Maris. These men with their kind, serious, searching looks: Sandro Cellini and now this one – as if she didn't feel sorry enough.

'I just meant—' His face fell. 'Doesn't matter.'

Cristina was closer to them now, refilling the already full sugar dispenser, spilling some on the bar.

'It *was* suicide,' said Vesna. 'There's no doubt.' And she shut up, sipping the coffee. She didn't mention that Flavia Matteo had been dressed in her underwear. That tugged at her too painfully. The modest woman, whose limbs had probably never even been exposed on a beach.

She should have made the detective listen more closely, about what she'd seen written on Flavia Matteo's hand, but what good was it now? She didn't belong here. Sandro Cellini's departure had left her feeling more alone than she had since she left home.

'She wanted to buy a mobile phone,' Vesna said, surprising herself: a good fifteen years since her last confession but the urge somehow seemed to be intact. 'There was a number. . .'

The dustbin man nodded, thinking of something else while Vesna waited for him to absolve her, but before he could say anything Cristina pounced.

'She'd been here before,' she said. 'She was here last year, this time last year. Season ending. I saw her.' And she stood a little straighter, proud of her announcement. 'She didn't stay with you then, did she?'

Dumbly, Vesna shook her head.

'She was at the Miramar,' said the dustbin man quietly, wiping his lips with a scrap of paper napkin, leaning down to dispose of it carefully in the tall copper waste bin under the bar. They both stared at him. 'She was there for one night, the first Saturday in September, the same night as the Festival of the Sea.'

'Did you tell him?' said Cristina. Vesna frowned. 'The detective guy,' said the café owner impatiently. 'Or did you tell the police?'

'I've been working it out,' said the man calmly. 'I wasn't sure. I have a memory system, you see. Plenty of time in my job, to work through things. Take it slowly is always best, work backwards from the details.' Neither woman spoke: they both still gazed at him.

'Well, for a start the Festival of the Sea generates a lot of refuse,' he said, serious-faced. 'I start very early. I saw her coming out of the Miramar that morning.' His frown deepened. 'Early. I didn't realize it was the same woman for a while – she looked – she looked different. That morning. I looked at the picture over and over, the picture in the paper.'

Cristina reached under the bar and without a word set *Il Tirreno* down between them. There she was. Flavia Matteo – pale, beautiful, closed. Unhappy. 'Something about the mouth, the hair. . . it had to be her. And I asked to look in their log, you know, the visitors' book.'

Vesna looked at him, tried to imagine the desk staff at the smooth, modern hotel watching him walk in off the street with his request.

'The Miramar,' said Cristina, contemptuous. 'That's the problem with those chain hotels. All trained up somewhere in America not to notice people. Like it doesn't make the world go round, noticing people.'

'I explained,' said the man mildly. 'I kept saying, "It's the woman in the paper." In the end they gave in. The police hadn't been there, the receptionist didn't know what I was on about. She was foreign.' He darted an apologetic look at Vesna.

'I don't think the police really bothered much,' Vesna said. She felt the sadness lying in wait. 'They knew it was suicide.'

'*You* noticed,' said Cristina. 'I bet.'

Vesna felt weary. 'You should call him,' she said. She wanted to pick up her suitcase and go to the station, because she had nowhere even to sit down in this town any more. But she couldn't. 'The detective guy. Sandro. Tell him: tell him when you saw her before. Tell him where.' Her shoulders dropped. 'Have you got his number?'

The dustbin man shook his head: they were both looking at her with kindness and Vesna thought she might scream if they didn't stop. She pulled her bag across her front on to the bartop and began to dig through it. 'It's all right. I've got it here somewhere.'

Halfway through the search she paused, looked up. 'You said she looked different? Coming out of the Miramar.'

'She looked like an angel,' he said. 'She was shining.'

*

From the way he stared at her in dismay, Giuli knew this was going to be one of those aspects of the modern world Sandro would have trouble with. Around them the piazza was in chaos: half of it being dug up, the market stalls shifted into one corner. A carabiniere sitting in his car at the military police post in the corner.

'She'd been having a what?'

There was the tall journalist, leaning against the wall of the house neighbouring Niccolò Rosselli's, smoking. His eyes met Giuli's and languidly he pushed himself off it and sauntered away, into the Via Mazzetta. It seemed an age ago, passing him in the doorway at the Frazione's meeting. Before all this kicked off.

How to explain it to Sandro? In his time you'd have talked to a girl at a – God knows, a First Communion or something. A dance. Gone for a walk with her parents chaperoning. Times had changed: well, even Sandro had kept up, up to a point. He knew about the internet, he knew things had moved on and you didn't have to communicate by pigeon these days.

The thing was, it had jumped too fast. One minute, even in Giuli's childhood, not everyone had a telephone, and if you did have one, it would be on a table in the hall and everyone could hear what you were saying. Now – you could call someone from a lilo floating in the sea. You could send them a photograph from up a tree. You could send them a video. You could say the most secret things to someone you'd never met, and it had got dangerous.

'It's like any addiction,' Barbara had explained to her in the bar. 'Like cigarettes, like heroin. At least, that's how I tackled it. I said to her, You can't expect to stop wanting it. I mean, Jesus, I gave up alcohol fourteen years ago and I still want a drink.'

'You did?' Giuli had stared at her. 'You do?'

Barbara had shrugged. 'They say ex-addicts make the best counsellors. I don't know about that. But I said, You'll still want it, it's just you get to the point when you know you're not going to have it.'

'But that means you're never safe.' Despite the warm fug of the bar, Giuli had felt cold.

'Life's not safe, is it?' Barbara had said. 'We've all got our private needs. Wants. And it's why we're not still living in caves, isn't it? It's wanting what we can't have that drives us on.' She'd smiled sadly. 'I don't say that to them, though. The addicts. Not to many of them.'

Their coffee cups empty, Giuli had stared through the glass and seen a long-legged woman climb out of a car on the corner of the Piazza Tasso. Good legs, black hair, too much make-up. Farmiga. Giuli had watched her lean down into the window to say something to the driver.

Barbara had sighed then. 'I don't know how patient I was,' she'd said, and rubbed her eyes. 'I'm used to dealing with it all at the other end, when it's all gone to shit, when the – the – what they think was love turns into drug-abuse and booze and they're on the streets, and they're sick. They're physically destroying themselves, that's what you have to manage. Flavia was a woman of privilege, it seemed to me sometimes. She had the intelligence to deal with it, she had Niccolò, a home. I couldn't understand how she got herself in so deep.'

'She wasn't born into that life, though,' Giuli had said. 'You know that? She left home at sixteen, came here to study. Her dad beat her once too often, her mother died.'

Barbara's face had set. 'I didn't know that,' she'd said. 'She didn't tell me that.'

The car that had dropped Farmiga off had slid past the plate glass of the window where they'd sat, and involuntarily Giuli had looked down as the driver looked up. He'd smiled at her: she'd turned away.

'That's her type, is it?' she'd said. 'I suppose that figures. A man in uniform. Good-looking, though.'

'Him?' Barbara had said. 'He's a creep.'

There'd been a brief silence then, and Barbara had slid off her stool. 'I'd better get in,' she'd said. 'Especially if Farmiga's in a temper.'

'Did Flavia show you?' Giuli had asked. 'Did she show any of the messages to you?'

Barbara had shaken her head. 'Told me about them – a bit. The kind of things he would say. I suppose she wanted to show me he wasn't an ordinary guy, not the kind of man who'd pick a woman up on the street and give her a line.' She'd shaken her head once more. 'Don't we always think that? I tried to tell her. I told her, You're turning him into something he isn't. It's the problem when it's only words, when a relationship's just words. Just because he reads Tolstoy, just because he listens to Bach, doesn't make him good, doesn't make him – anything.'

At the door, weighed down by bag and coat and looking too small suddenly for the job she was heading off to do, Barbara had turned back to Giuli, still sitting there.

'She'll have written them down somewhere, though,' she'd said. 'She told me she was deleting them all, but she'll have written them down. It's a human instinct.'

Now, in the piazza a digger had roared into life and Sandro was shouting over it.

'I don't understand,' he said. 'What is all this? How did you work it out? There was nothing on her phone. No messages.'

'It was Wanda.' The digger stopped, and Giuli's voice was abruptly too loud. 'The colleague. The maths teacher.'

Giuli glanced up at the window of Niccolò Rosselli's apartment: the shutters were closed.

'What she said about being out on a walk with her and Flavia's phone bleeped, like she'd got a message. Flavia answered it straight away. Like a pro, Wanda said, but not like the Flavia she knew. Wanda showed me.'

Moving her thumbs, deft and quick, over the little keyboard.

'She said she realized then she'd never heard Flavia's phone make a sound before: had hardly been aware she had one.'

A text-message relationship: it sounded stupid, and tawdry. It sounded like something for teenage girls or losers.

'And then Barbara – the addictions counsellor at the Centre – she confirmed it. Sounds like the guy, whoever he was, really did a job on Flavia. Wouldn't let up. Like a full-on seduction, old-style. Only Barbara did say – she thought it was possible it never went further. It was just an intellectual thing.'

Giuli told Sandro what Barbara had said, trying to remember all the stuff about fantasy and reality, about why people need drugs. About adrenaline, and addictive relationships, and the chemicals produced by what you could call love, or sex.

Sandro was chewing the inside of his cheek, as he did when something was getting to him. 'What kind of man would do it?' he said. 'Someone – inadequate? Someone – what's the story, the guy with the nose? Cyrano? Does it all with words, seduces the woman who'd never look at him twice in the street?'

Giuli didn't know what he was on about.

'There was a movie – never mind,' said Sandro. 'That might explain – if it didn't go any further.'

'Have you got someone in mind?'

'Bastone just told me he loved her,' said Sandro shortly. 'I went in there to grill him about the land deal, and—' He looked defeated suddenly. 'I ended up feeling sorry for the guy. He's been in love with Flavia for years.'

'Him?' Giuli tried to fit Bastone into the frame, the scruffy, unshaven lawyer, with his anxious face, rumpled forehead. 'It sounds like these messages were – well. Not all love poems and platonic stuff.'

'He certainly had their mobile number,' said Sandro slowly. 'He used it to call us, in the middle of the night.'

'You haven't still got the phone, have you?'

Sandro shook his head, slowly. It couldn't be Bastone. 'Niccolò's got it now.' He tipped his head back and they both looked up at the window.

'What are you going to tell him?' said Giuli, feeling abruptly nauseous. 'What are you going to say to Niccolò?'

'I think I'll have to tell him – something. Say there may have been some kind of a relationship he doesn't know about. Connected with Flavia's – state of mind.' Sandro sighed. 'He said all he wanted was the truth. It might even *be* true.'

They stared at each other and Giuli knew Sandro was thinking what she was thinking. They should never have started on this: Barbara had been right, Clelia Schmidt had been right. Who would gain by finding out that Flavia Matteo had been – if not unfaithful, then in love with someone else?

As she watched, Sandro took out his phone and looked at it. 'Text messages,' he said. 'So that's why—'

'That's why she left the mobile behind when she went to the seaside. When she checked into the hotel, to – to—'

'To kill herself,' said Sandro, frowning furiously. 'She didn't want to be tempted.'

'She was – it was like flushing the drugs down the toilet, pouring the booze down the sink. But there's always more booze, if you know where to look.'

'And so Flavia went looking for another mobile.'

'She didn't go through with it, though. She didn't buy the mobile, she didn't send the message. Although I don't know what it would have said, or what reply she'd have got. Would it have saved her? Or did she just want it to send her suicide note?'

Sandro made a curious movement with his shoulders as if trying to shake something off. 'She tried to write something, they said. She sat down to write something. Maybe she just – couldn't.'

'It would be a tough thing to explain,' said Giuli. 'I'm leaving you alone, for this.'

'But a woman like that?' he said, agonized. 'Educated? After the life she'd made for herself? It's so – so – it's like the way kids behave. Hysterical. She killed herself over that? You mean, she didn't even – they didn't even sleep together? It was just words?'

'We don't know what kind of woman she was,' said Giuli. 'I don't know for sure if they slept together or not. The child was Niccolò's, though.'

She sighed, suddenly weary of it, of being female, of men's ideas – even Sandro, even her beloved and loving ersatz dad's ideas – of what women should be, what women were good for or capable of. She tried again.

'We know what she tried to turn herself into alongside Niccolò, her white knight, a man who was only good.'

They both looked up again and the shutters shifted as they did. It was Maria Rosselli who leaned out to push them open and instinctively both Sandro and Giuli stepped back, behind the trunk of one of the square's elms. In the quiet Giuli became aware of an unfamiliar sound, somewhere not too far off to the west, the Piazza del Carmine perhaps. A low murmur that rose to chanting.

'We don't know what that relationship was like. What she didn't get out of it, for example.'

Sandro looked tired suddenly. 'Well,' he said. 'I see. Yes.'

'And we don't know what he said to her, this man she couldn't get away from. We don't know if it was just words, either.'

And as if on cue Sandro's phone, still held out in his hand in front of him like a talisman or a bomb, began to ring.

Chapter Twenty-Four

A T TEN-THIRTY EXACTLY GLORIA'S worried face appeared at the door of the Portakabin where the breast clinic had been 'temporarily' relocated two years ago, squeezed up against diabetes and renal disorders. Luisa lifted a hand: that twinge pulled at her under the arm, and she thought of the family she'd served – was it only thirty-six hours ago? – in the shop.

She'd thought about just lying to Sandro all the way, not going: after all, saying Gloria was going to come with her had been a lie at the time. She could cancel the appointment, she could head into the city, to the university perhaps, looking for Chiara's friends.

What had stopped her was the knowledge that she'd really be cancelling the appointment because she was afraid. So she'd thought, right, I'll call Gloria, she won't be able to come, that's my decision made for me. Only Gloria had said yes, immediately, and Luisa had heard it in her voice, all the anxiety of sitting at home fretting over husband and daughter. Gloria needs something to do, she'd thought.

But judging from the way she sat now, close but not too close, and from the calm and kindness with which she insisted on talking about it to her friend, counselling would come naturally to Gloria, nursing too.

'It's OK,' said Luisa, adjusting to the sight of the others in the cramped space as Gloria talked on, soothing. This was the worst bit. Seeing the young frightened women, with small children. The elderly ladies, complacent and unflustered, a lump in the breast no worse to them than a bit of deafness or rheumatoid arthritis, all part of the deal. Luisa neither one nor the other, not a mother, not a grandmother. Not young, not old enough to be reconciled to the prospect of death. She had thought she was sanguine but it turned out she was not.

'I'm only here to talk about the reconstruction,' she said. 'I'm not worried about the rest.'

Gloria gave her a look but said nothing. In the silence Luisa saw her face change, new thoughts creeping in to replace all that chatter about gold-standard breast reconstruction and annual check-ups and five-year prognosis.

'Have you heard anything?' Luisa said. 'Has she called?'

Gloria shook her head slowly.

'She used to text,' she said. 'Little messages. . . *Hello, Mummy. . . You're the best mother in the world.* Nothing. There's been nothing, since she left.'

Luisa felt something tighten in her chest. 'Chiara used to say that?' she said. 'Your tough cookie?'

Gloria looked at her shyly, a faint flush on her cheeks. 'It was like a secret,' she said. 'Oh, you know. Some people act tough, but they're soft inside, like my little Chiara. She could be like that – in a message. Kind of an alter ego, her soft side. She knew how it used to cheer me up. She was a thoughtful girl.'

The past tense hovered between them. 'She is,' said Luisa. That's why—'

'That's why we can't understand it,' said Gloria, despairing.

The door opened: murmurs of complaint rippled around the packed space as bodies shifted to accommodate the new arrival.

'How long's it been going on, d'you think?' asked Luisa. Something occurred to her then. 'You don't think it's connected with – when she got interested in politics? The Frazione Verde stuff. Because—' She hesitated. 'Well, it seems to have changed Giuli's life. Meeting a new group of people.'

'Not long,' said Gloria. 'I've been going over and over it in my head, and I don't think it's that long. She started going to the Frazione meetings months ago, but she was still my same girl. Then maybe – six weeks back? If anything, she eased off on the political arguments with Pietro, more – clammed up over it. Stopped – being my loving little girl, stopped with the messages, didn't call in at work and say hello. But evenings she seemed always to be off in some corner talking to someone else. Him, I suppose.'

'Talking?'

'On the mobile. Texting, talking. It's a different world, Luisa.'

'Luisa Cellini?'

She knew the middle-aged nurse who called her name, looking around the room over her hornrims. She had a severe manner but her hands were always gentle. Luisa stood up.

'You want me to come in with you?' Gloria was getting to her feet.

'Wait,' said Luisa. 'Just wait here.'

In the end she barely noticed what they said to her because as Luisa got to her feet she saw him across the room. Giancarlo, Chiara's gay friend, reading a dog-eared magazine in the other section of the Portakabin. The sight of him immediately alarmed her. Was he ill? Was he waiting for someone?

Perhaps he was waiting for her. He hadn't looked up when they said her name – but then maybe he wouldn't have remembered it.

Oncologist first, a flying visit, head round the door with her notes in his hand. Didn't even sit down, just smiled and dropped the notes on the desk for the breast surgeon.

'Are you taking this all in, Signora Cellini?' The surgeon turned out to be a woman. 'It's sometimes better to have someone with you for these consultations, you know. Doesn't have to be your husband. To make sure all the information is – ah – on board?'

'I know what's involved,' Luisa heard herself saying. 'I've done a bit of looking into it.'

'So we'll pencil you in for a reconstruction just before Christmas?'

She nodded: it seemed she'd made her decision.

Walking back out into the waiting room she looked for Giancarlo but she couldn't see him.

No sign of any recurrence. The scan is clear. Had the oncologist said that? He must have said that, calculated Luisa, otherwise they wouldn't have scheduled the reconstruction. The brain was a peculiar mechanism: she'd waited for those words all year it seemed, and at the moment at which they were delivered, she'd managed to absent herself.

'Luisa?' Gloria was breathless, on her feet. 'You're so pale. What did they say?'

'Everything's fine,' she managed to say. 'I'm going to be reconstructed.' She tried a smile. 'Let's just sit here for five minutes. Is that OK?'

Gloria bustled about, rearranging them. 'Of course. It's a big decision – oh, that's great, Luisa, that's such a relief!'

Was it? Luisa decided she would think about it later.

'There's someone—'

She stopped. Someone I want you to meet? There were tears in Gloria's eyes: she'd always been an emotional woman. There was nothing wrong with emotion, decided Luisa, wanting to put her arms around her friend, whose tears, she knew, were of gratitude for Luisa's results.

'I saw Pietro yesterday,' she said, trying to make it sound casual. 'Did he tell you?'

Gloria flushed. 'He did.'

'I suppose he said I was trying to pump him for information. Or gossip, or something.'

Gloria frowned furiously. 'No, he – no.' So he had.

'I don't like it either, you know,' said Luisa, abruptly impatient with all this pussyfooting around. 'I knew there were things he wasn't telling me, I'm not stupid.'

Gloria just shook her head tightly. Luisa leaned in towards her.

'Since when did we all stop being proper friends, friends who trust each other, help each other? Is it to do with Sandro's job? Sandro's petrified of overstepping the mark with Pietro, you know that? Their friendship's more to him than anything.'

Gloria seemed to collapse in front of her, pink with agitation.

'It's the job,' she said, rubbing at her eyes. 'It's this job he's on – he isn't even supposed to tell *me* about it. It's to do with the Frazione – he's been seconded to – to another squad. Now he thinks that's why it's all gone wrong with Chiara, why they both stopped being able to talk to each other. Because he got so het up over her becoming involved politically, and especially with the Frazione – because he was worried something might happen to her.'

'He wasn't supposed to tell you about it?' said Luisa slowly. 'This job?' Hush-hush. 'But he did?'

Gloria's wide eyes pleaded with her.

'He's looking into the Frazione Verde's activities?'

'Not exactly,' said Gloria, fidgeting in her seat. 'It's connected. Or it may be connected. There's a group – right-wing people – they're acting unlawfully—' She put one hand to her mouth.

Luisa seized the other hand in hers. 'Do you know what?' she said. 'I think you're right to be worried about Chiara. I think – I wanted to say, relax and it'll all be fine. I wanted to say, It's just growing up. But I think there *is* something not right about it all, and this – this politics. They think it's all fresh and new, it's all about good intentions and justice – but it doesn't stay new for long. It's dangerous: this country, politics here is dirty stuff.'

The colour had gone from Gloria's face. 'You think Pietro's work – has something to do with it?'

Luisa threw up her hands in exasperation. 'If he doesn't say what he's working on, this top-secret project, how can we know? Something's wrong, though, and I just don't know what we do about it. I don't know how we find her.'

'How we find her,' repeated Gloria, trembling. 'You think – do you think something's happened to her?'

The door to the diabetes consulting room opened, and Giancarlo came out.

Luisa stood up, straight as a totem.

'I think we need to find her,' she said.

*

Sandro exploded. 'Oh, for God's sake! You didn't think it was worth mentioning?'

The seaside pathologist's telephone manner had reverted to icy formality. 'In my opinion – my humble opinion – it did not constitute evidence of any useful kind. However, once the images are available I shall certainly email them to you. With police approval and the permission of the next-of-kin, naturally.'

It took all Sandro's reserves for him to thank the man civilly.

'Anyway,' said the pathologist carelessly, 'the body'll be coming back to you for burial within twenty-four hours. Unless he wants that done here. Burial or cremation, or whatever. We're done with it.'

Burial: not there. It'd be in the city, the big, dirty city.

Niccolò Rosselli's wife had been involved with another man: she had been away with him, she had been to Viareggio with him. To a hotel by the seaside, the first weekend of last September.

They didn't have the man yet.

A pneumatic drill set up and instinctively Sandro put his hands to his ears: what in the name of Christ were they doing now? He swung around, looking at the wire fencing, a digger languidly raising its bucket while below it a man in earmuffs was jerked by the drill. The eddying marketgoers being channelled this way and that, this great democratic space cramped and cordoned off. The carabiniere still lounged against his car, indifferent, infuriating, as if satisfied with the chaos.

The drill stopped and for a moment Sandro thought there was a kind of after-echo in the air but it was something else. A loudhailer, someone shouting through a loudhailer a block or two away, and calls in response.

On the phone the pathologist was shouting, 'Hello? Hello?'

'Sorry,' said Sandro, without sincerity. 'It's the city. Noisy here.' He took the man's email address and gave his own, and hung up. Giuli was looking at him expectantly: for all he knew Maria Rosselli probably was, too, from the window above. It was eleven-thirty, and they were late.

Luisa would have seen the doctor by now.

Niccolò Rosselli and his mother would have to wait just five minutes longer.

'Vesna,' Sandro said. He sighed. 'The Bosnian maid who found Flavia's body. What the police would call a good witness, and fortunately for us, she seems to have something like a conscience.'

'Right,' said Giuli.

'She was talking to – a guy. Dustbin man, as it happens.'

Giuli raised her eyebrows.

'The kind of guy you don't notice in the street, I suppose, but he notices everything. A bit sweet on the girl, I thought. I met him, he gave me directions, a decent bloke. Anyway, this guy had seen Flavia in the town before, last year. The first Sunday in September, he seemed precise on that point because it was some festival or other the night before.'

There'd been one in Castiglioncello when he and Luisa had been there this summer, seemed like a lifetime ago. Men in robes carrying banners on long poles along the esplanade, chanting. He'd got impatient with it, a lot of mumbo-jumbo, but there'd been fireworks afterwards.

'He was sure it was her? One hundred per cent?' Giuli's voice was urgent.

Vesna had put the man on to Sandro: he'd been able to hear the hiss of the coffee machine behind their voices and remembered that bar, the blinding white seaside light and the woman's candyfloss hair. Cristina.

He'd repeated it, and Sandro had believed him. 'She looked different, but it was her. She looked so happy.'

Vesna had taken the phone back. 'What he said to me was, she looked like an angel. Trans. . . whatever the word is. Gone up to God and made new.' Her voice had grown gruff then, perhaps embarrassed at the flight of fantasy. Perhaps sad for the joy gone, ended in a cold bathtub.

Ecstasy on Flavia's face as she walked out of a hotel lobby into the September sunshine. Who had she left upstairs in the room?

He'd thanked her, earnestly: had heard her soften. 'You're off, then,' he'd said.

'You've got my number now,' she'd said, hesitating. 'But there's something else before you go.'

Before she had even said it, the image had been waiting in his head, that fragment he'd been too impatient to hear to the end when she'd been trying to tell him, in the Stella Maris's bare kitchen.

The image of something scribbled in haste on the body, like a tattoo.

'There were some numbers written on the palm of her hand. Like – a phone number.'

Because Flavia hadn't taken her phone with her, where the number would have been stored.

'I don't suppose – you don't—' And he hadn't even finished the sentence because unless Vesna was some kind of savant, she wouldn't remember a number glimpsed in the dim bathroom, a dead woman sodden in her arms.

'It was mostly worn away,' she'd said. 'I don't know, I can't remember the numbers, but I think only two or three – the middle numbers in the row – were visible.' She had sounded bothered by the memory.

'It's all right,' Sandro had said. And taking a breath, had added quickly, 'She was lucky she had you. To find her. To care about her – enough.'

Giuli had clamoured to be told, there and then, what was going on, but he'd made her wait. While he had obtained the number of the pathology lab and spoken to them, and then it had been twenty-five minutes of name-checking and obstructiveness before he'd got anywhere.

'A telephone number?' said Giuli now. 'Well. That figures. She made herself leave her mobile behind, the number would have been on it. But she couldn't quite – couldn't quite make the break. Wrote the number on her hand – maybe she tried to scrub it off?'

'Maybe,' said Sandro slowly. 'Maybe she deleted it from the phone she left behind, too.'

'Or maybe she didn't,' said Giuli, glancing up. 'Like Barbara said, it's human not to be able to let go. She said, it's human to want to salvage something, to remember, to record. We hate the idea of obliteration.'

Sandro stared at her, because quite suddenly the statement seemed startlingly, unavoidably true. Obliteration. Suicide was an attempt to obliterate, wasn't it? But something was always left behind: the dead body, the traumatized maid, the baby. And Sandro and Giuli were trying to rescue Flavia from those traces.

'Let's go up,' said Sandro. 'Time to face the music.'

When Niccolò opened the door to them, he was holding the baby on one shoulder. Sandro could see Maria Rosselli behind him at the window with her arms folded across her body and it seemed to him that there'd been some kind of a shift here, between these people, inside these four walls. Something had changed.

Rosselli's hand sat lightly on the child's slumbering back: he moved gingerly to one side to let them pass.

'Niccolò,' said Sandro. 'If I may. . .'

'You need to have a look around,' said Rosselli, his face quite calm behind the thick glasses. 'That's fine.'

At the window his mother let out a small snort of contempt.

'Mother,' he said mildly, but Sandro heard the warning note in his voice.

'There've been journalists, do you know that?' she said. 'Ringing our bell. Why don't the police do something about that?' She glared at Sandro. 'Why don't you?'

'Perhaps we should leave you alone to look around, after all,' Rosselli said quietly. 'Mother and I.'

'Don't worry,' said Maria Rosselli, shifting herself heavily away from her position at the window. 'I'll go out. Give me the child.'

'No,' said Rosselli. The word hung coolly between them. 'You've done enough,' he said, as the silence lengthened, and the ambivalence of the phrase wasn't lost on any of them. 'Thank you, Mother. He's asleep, anyway. I can manage.'

'Oh, yes,' said Maria Rosselli bitterly, 'I suppose you think you can.'

'We'll be fine, Signora Rosselli,' said Giuli. 'I can take him out in his – his pram. If he wakes up.'

With a furious movement Maria Rosselli swept past Giuli without answering or looking at her. At the door she stopped, face to face with her son.

'You had better tell them,' she said, almost spitting. 'Or I will.'

'They may already know,' said Niccolò Rosselli, still quite calm. On his shoulder the child slept on.

'Know what?' said Giuli, before Sandro could say anything.

'That *that woman* was a whore,' said Maria Rosselli. 'I could see it in her when she was twenty, coming from where she came from, from the people she came from. Look at how long she strung him along. . . years! The only surprise is it took her so long.' And she was past her son, out on the landing and the door slammed behind her. Under Rosselli's hand, against his shoulder, the baby gave a start but did not wake.

There was a silence.

'Nothing wrong with his hearing, then,' said Giuli finally. Rosselli looked at her, and for the first time since Sandro had met him, his face appeared to have life in it: ordinary life. A smile appeared, rusty with underuse.

'He's been crying all morning,' he said. 'Since my mother came. He's worn himself out.'

Sandro rubbed his eyes. How could you ask: *What did your mother mean?* Although her meaning had been clear.

'Your mother—' He stopped. Rosselli looked at him a second then, when he didn't continue, extended an arm to usher them into the sitting room.

The windows and shutters had been opened and from outside in the piazza came a harsh grinding noise as the machines continued with their work of excavation. For a moment it seemed to Sandro that the sounds were of a city under siege, that those in power simply didn't know what they were doing and covered the fact up with random, pointless decisions. Dig here, build there, extend, demolish, an endless cycle of diversionary activity. What was it all for?

They all three sat, Giuli and Rosselli on the brown corduroy sofa, Sandro on the matching chair. Very gently Rosselli lowered his son on to the sofa beside them. Carefully he placed a cushion between the child and the edge of the divan.

'You said you wanted to look for something,' he said.

Sandro hesitated, then nodded towards Giuli. Let her find an explanation. He saw a fraction of a second's panic in her eyes, then it was gone.

'A diary,' she said. 'Something like that? I mean, it sounds obvious, but it might help? A notebook or a diary?'

Slowly Rosselli moved his head from side to side, less to say no, it seemed to Sandro, than to ease some internal pressure. 'She didn't keep a diary,' he said. 'We wrote things down on the calendar.' He nodded towards the cluttered desk and its pinboard. 'I don't know about a notebook.' He frowned. 'When Flavia was teaching she had one of those black notebooks, a big one, with an elastic band around. For teaching plans, that kind of thing.' He looked around helplessly. 'I don't know where it would be. The desk was always mine. I haven't seen it in there.'

Giuli opened her mouth, hesitating, Sandro knew, to ask if she could rummage through his life.

'You're welcome to look,' Rosselli said. He frowned. 'But Flavia worked in the – in the room where the baby sleeps now. That's where she would have kept her things.' He frowned, as if something had just occurred to him.

'What?' said Giuli. 'Did you remember something?'

'It's where I found the phone,' he said slowly, and with the words felt in his pocket, pulled it out. 'Our mobile.' He looked down at it. 'It's odd. Since she died, I seem to have started carrying it around with me. Which I suppose is what one is supposed to do.'

Giuli and Sandro both stared at the small silver object in Rosselli's hand. Sandro had slipped the mobile back into the man's jacket when he'd dropped him off at his apartment; he very much doubted Rosselli had even noticed. And now, calmly, as if dealing with a nervous animal, Giuli extended a hand, and Rosselli obediently placed the mobile in her open palm.

Giuli flipped it open, with her expert thumb scrolling through something Sandro couldn't see.

'You didn't expect to find it in there?' she asked.

'It was on the ledge above the cot,' he said. 'Beside the baby monitor.' He raised his head. 'There was something – weeks ago. It makes that noise, you know, when it receives a message? I was trying to think when I'd last seen it. And then I realized I'd heard it. Not long after the baby was born. Flavia was putting him down and the baby monitor made a sound. That sound.' Abruptly Giuli and Sandro were both on their feet.

'In the nursery,' said Giuli quickly. 'In there?' And without asking if she could, she crossed the soft red tiles of the floor and went in through the open door, where the white-painted corner of a cot was visible.

On the threshold behind her Sandro and Rosselli stood shoulder to shoulder as Giuli moved through the room. A white mobile hung over the bed, and a battered clown's head was fixed to the bars of the cot: together with the white plastic baby monitor standing on the shelf, they were the only concessions to the child's presence. Would Rosselli, Sandro found himself wondering, buy this child all the other things it needed? Those small towelling garments? The nappies, toys, and in due course the right books?

Giuli had stopped at eye level with the monitor on the plain white shelf. She put a hand up and brought it back, dusty. She looked along the shelf: between some bookends stood a couple of paperbacks.

'Was that all there was on here?' she asked, turning back to look at Niccolò. 'Just those few books?' She took one down: Sandro saw it was a guide to pregnancy and childbirth, well-thumbed. Rosselli took a step into the room, and frowned. He crossed over to stand beside Giuli and put his hand up to the bookends.

'No, she—' He broke off. 'There were some other books here. I don't know what she—' And he looked around. 'Only school textbooks,' he said, almost on the verge of panic now. 'But if she – that's where her notebook would have been. I don't know where they've gone.'

Giuli opened her mouth, then closed it. Without a word she was past them and back into the sitting room; by the time Sandro was through the door she had her jacket on.

'I'll see you at the office,' she said. 'I'll be there in half an hour.' She turned to Niccolò Rosselli. 'I – I'll let you know what I find,' she said. 'I – I'm sorry.' And she was gone.

The room seemed abruptly much emptier without her whirlwind presence. On the sofa the child slept on: both men looked at him.

'I should put him in his cot,' said Rosselli. 'It's safer.'

'He'll wake up,' said Sandro. 'He's safe while we're here.' Neither of them moved.

'Your mother,' he began, and something seemed to clear in Niccolo Rosselli's face: he looked at Sandro full on, and focused.

'My mother,' he said, then stopped. Started again. 'My mother has just informed me that Flavia and Carlo were having – that they were involved with each other.'

Sandro cleared his throat. 'Do you believe her?'

'I don't know,' Niccolò said, and sat down. Sandro sat beside him. From behind the thick lenses Sandro saw the frowning earnestness of his effort, actually to understand, to approach the question logically. 'She said—' He stopped, looked down at his sleeping son and his hand strayed towards the child, resting on the small, rounded shoulder.

'She said Carlo had been in love with Flavia for many years.'

Sandro nodded involuntarily, because he knew that much already: Niccolò frowned.

'He's your friend,' said Sandro. 'Do you think it's true?'

Rosselli made a small shrugging gesture and under his hand the child gave a shudder before settling back into sleep.

Sandro pushed, gently. 'Do you think – she reciprocated?'

She strung him along, was what Maria Rosselli had said.

'My mother has never liked Flavia, I couldn't escape that,' said Rosselli. It wasn't an answer to the question: it was the first time Sandro had detected evasion in him. There was something he wasn't saying, yet.

Rosselli let out a long sigh.

'My mother thought the child was his. Carlo's. She pushed for the doctor to have the blood tests done. Which involved DNA testing. I didn't really understand – it was nothing serious, a mild allergic reaction they couldn't identify. But of course I didn't object: why should I? And my mother was forceful.' He sighed.

Sandro was almost holding his breath: this was not the thing that was hidden, not yet. 'Did Flavia seem anxious about the tests? The outcome?'

'No,' said Rosselli. 'She was quite resigned to their being done. Submissive.' He shook his head a little. 'She was worried about him: I told her, it was only a rash. The tests showed that he didn't have the gene they were looking for. And that he was my child; naturally that was not presented to me as though it had ever been in doubt.' He turned his head to look down again at the small body under his hand. The child's side rose and fell evenly with each breath. 'And the rash cleared by itself.'

'Do you think Flavia was having an affair?' Sandro asked. There were shouts from outside and abruptly the mechanical noise ceased, replaced by something that was not quite silence.

Rosselli looked at Sandro and before the man spoke, he knew, this was it.

'Flavia strung him along all these years, that's what my mother said. I think it was a source of satisfaction to her, to say it.' I bet it was, thought Sandro, but Rosselli sounded only bewildered. 'She said, "So finally she let him have what he wanted."' A raggedness had crept into his voice, the frayed edges, at last, of grief and despair.

'She had proof.' It wasn't a question.

Rosselli's head tipped back, just a fraction, where another man might have howled, or raged. As he waited for him to speak, Sandro realized that although the drilling and scraping in the piazza outside had ceased, it was not silence that had replaced it but the distant rise and fall of chanting.

The doorbell squealed, a hideous intrusion, and Rosselli raised his head as if trying to recognize the sound. He got to his feet, and Sandro saw him put a hand to his pocket, feeling for something, in a kind of nervous reflex. The mobile, thought Sandro, and in the same moment understood that Giuli had taken it. Rosselli lifted the intercom receiver.

'Come up,' he said, quite calm, and pressed the buzzer once, twice, to be sure.

'Photographs,' he said. 'My mother said Carlo had photographs.'

The tread on the stairs was a heavy one: before Rosselli opened the door Sandro knew who would be there.

It was Carlo Bastone.

Chapter Twenty-Five

CORNERED BETWEEN THE TWO women at a table in the hospital's stuffy bar, Giancarlo looked acutely uncomfortable.

'Diabetes,' said Luisa, in an attempt to defuse the situation. Although sometimes situations had to be like this. 'I thought it was drugs. The little syringe.'

'Insulin,' said the young man with a wan smile. 'I guess it's kind of a drug. Not all drugs are bad: not that simple, is it?'

Beside her Luisa could feel Gloria's tension, and put a restraining hand on her forearm.

'Sorry to kidnap you like this,' she said. 'I've just been for an appointment of my own. It's nice, don't you think, to see a friendly face in one of these places?'

He glanced at her warily, not persuaded.

'Have you been in to the university today?' she said. He laughed weakly. 'Never before eleven,' he said. 'I'm not an early riser. And I had the tests to do, out here.'

'My daughter,' Gloria said, unable to wait any longer. 'You've seen my daughter?'

Panicking, Giancarlo looked at Luisa, then back at Gloria.

'You're Chiara's mum,' he said. 'I wouldn't have seen it. She's so dark.'

'She looks like her father,' said Gloria, in an agony of impatience and fear. 'Have you seen – this man? The one she's moved in with. Do you know him? Is she safe with him?'

Uneasily Giancarlo shifted.

'Safe,' he said, his eyes evasive. 'I don't know about safe. Do you think safe's what we want? What Chiara wants?'

'That's not useful,' said Luisa sharply. 'I don't know what you mean. Are you talking about sex?' Beside her Gloria flinched. 'We want to know if you've seen him, what he looks like. Has she told you anything – anything concrete about him? Such as where he lives? His job, his age?'

'She's told us none of these things,' said Gloria with dignity, and reluctantly Giancarlo met her eye. Without a smile Gloria, a woman who'd always seemed to Luisa like a happy child, looked her age.

Giancarlo took in her misery. 'I haven't met him, no,' he said unhappily. 'But you know what girls are like: the guy's all they want to talk about, how amazing he is, the little things he does, says. . .' He looked away, swallowed. When he went on, he spoke as if giving evidence. 'She finds him exciting. He's a dominant sort of guy, alpha-male type, kind of cold, and kind of clever. That's the impression I get. But no, I haven't met him. Nothing concrete. Reading between the lines?'

'Yes,' said Luisa. Beside her Gloria was mute and pale, hands knotted on her knee. The boy went on.

'He's older than her. A lot older. Don't they say, it's only the old men have the bad habits? He makes her feel small and naïve and inexperienced, and only he can teach her. Alternates between loving and stern, just like he was training a dog.' He sighed. 'I tried to explain that to her but she looked at me like I was cruel, so I let her think the love was real. Well, it might be, mightn't it?'

They both looked at him, appalled, and he hurried on. 'Anyway, I thought perhaps he's got a good job – a responsible job. Perhaps in a position of power?' He wiped his forehead, and with a twinge of pity Luisa wondered about the diabetes. 'Or perhaps he's just a nasty bastard.'

A nasty bastard. What was it Giuli had been talking about, last night at the table? About Flavia Matteo's dream, a man with a sword. Which signified sex that was like violence, she'd said, not able to meet Luisa's eye. Luisa was not a woman of experience, not in that way. She and Sandro – well. It had never been like violence, and she didn't feel like she'd lost out.

Flavia Matteo had dreamed of a violent man, with longing. Maria Rosselli had said of her that she was weak. Luisa frowned: that was Flavia, this was Chiara. They were different.

'Bad habits?' she said.

'All right, I'm talking about sex,' mumbled Giancarlo. 'Rough stuff.'

'He hurts her?'

'Not yet,' said Giancarlo, his unease deepening. 'But she thinks he might. She's frightened – but it's exciting. Until it happens, it often is.' He let out a long breath and stood up. 'I've got to go,' he said. 'I've got to collect my tests.'

'Don't go,' said Gloria, grasping fruitlessly for him, her hand slipping from his arm. He looked down, then took it in his own.

'She's a clever girl,' he said. 'I thought that meant she'd come out of it OK. I don't know. She's just gone off the radar now, and I don't know any more. I should have said something.' He tipped his head back, stared at the ceiling, spoke without looking at them. 'The thing is, it's not always just a game. The strangeness is what she likes, but he might be stranger than she thinks. He could hurt her. He could film her, photograph her, post it on the internet. . . '

Gloria made an awful choked noise in the back of her throat, and Giancarlo abruptly brought his head back down and looked at her.

'She wouldn't tell me where she was living,' he said. 'My impression is, he told her not to say, not to anyone. But there was something she let slip – about the Via Pisana, the road to the seaside, about being near the river too.'

They were all three on their feet now, but it was Gloria who spoke. 'And?'

'I think she's in the Isolotto,' said Giancarlo.

*

By the time she got to the Via del Leone, Giuli was sweating. What in God's name was going on? Traffic stationary up and down the Via dei Serragli, the Via Romana, access blocked. There was noise everywhere, chanting from towards the Cestello, the lazy siren of a police car stuck on the Via Mazzetta, and a van full of soldiers jeering at her as she hurried by.

'A demo,' said a big woman standing outside the ambulance post in the Via Mazzetta. 'In the Piazza del Carmine. They're all lying down in the street, apparently, corner of Santa Monaca, Porta Romana, and nothing's moving.' A smile of deep satisfaction appeared on her face. 'Police can't get there, too idle to get out of their cars and walk.'

In other circumstances, Giuli might have stopped to argue that not all policemen were lazy. Sandro never was. Or Pietro. But she'd been to see Wanda Terni, and in her pocket she held her prize. She let herself in, out of the midday heat of the street and into the cool hall, looking forward to the shuttered peace of the office.

It had all suddenly fallen into place at Niccolò Rosselli's apartment. The mobile phone, the baby monitor, the shelf – the books.

Wanda had mentioned them the first time she and Giuli had met – the books Flavia had returned just last week even though Wanda couldn't remember lending them to her. What if Flavia had wanted to hide the evidence of something, but she couldn't bring herself to destroy it? And what if she had known she wasn't coming home – she'd not have wanted Niccolò to find that something, would she?

Giuli had waited in the corridor, listening to the lesson inside, interpreting the sounds. It had been nearly lunchtime and the kids were restless: you could hear the shuffle of feet, the rising level of backchat. Wanda Terni's tired, hopeful voice. Then a bell had shrilled tinnily in the recesses of the building and there'd been the thunderous scraping of a classful of chairs being pushed back, and they had streamed out of the door.

'I think so,' Wanda had said uncertainly in response to Giuli's question. To her surprise, the teacher had visibly brightened at the sight of her in the doorway.

'Yes.' She had sounded more certain now. 'Where did I put them?' She had begun to pull open drawers: Giuli had seen the disarray on her desk, breathed the stale air heavy with the smell of kids and their unwashed socks and half-eaten breaktime *merende*. Giuli had never been sent to school with a snack; most days her mother had been comatose till late in the afternoon.

And there they had been: Wanda Terni had emerged triumphant and dusty from her bottom drawer with a small stack of books. *Primary Mathematics, Child Psychology for Teachers*. A copy of a Russian novel: *Anna Karenina*. A battered black notebook fastened with an elastic band.

Giuli could tell something was wrong even before she began to climb the stairs to the office, something about the light. As she rounded the stairwell she saw that the door was off its hinges and the sunlight streamed through.

It could have been worse. Nothing had been scrawled on the walls or smeared on the desk. It was almost orderly, only all the drawers in the filing cabinet stood open, and the computer was gone from the desk.

In her chest, though, Giuli's heart thudded as though it might break through: she felt it in her throat as if it might choke her. They'd been here. They'd been here too.

They? Who were they? The same people that had broken into the Frazione's offices, and tipped off the police there was porn on the computer? It was as though the city was contracting, drawing tight like a net around her and Sandro and poor lost Chiara, and she couldn't breathe. *They* – were they everywhere?

Breathe. Think.

Who knew Sandro and Giuli were investigating Flavia's death? Bastone, Wanda Terni, Clelia, Barbara. Farmiga knew, so no doubt her good-looking boyfriend knew too. Did the police know? Did the undercover guys, AISI? The army, the press? That journalist who was everywhere, he'd know, he'd seen Sandro and Giuli going in to Niccolò's apartment.

Breathe.

Paranoia, that's how Sandro would have described it a mere three days ago: conspiracy theories were just that, theories. But things were different now. With a trembling hand Giuli reached to close the shutters; she lowered herself on to Sandro's chair. Don't touch anything. She reached into her bag and took out her phone.

For a moment she stared at it and didn't understand: this was not her mobile. Then she remembered: this was Flavia and Niccolò's phone. Gingerly she laid it down on the desk in front of her: she opened her grubby canvas bag and withdrew the notebook Wanda Terni had allowed her to take away, and laid it next to the phone. Only then did she locate her own mobile.

The names came up in her call history, Sandro, before that Enzo.

Her guys for an emergency: Sandro, she told herself, would be still in with Rosselli. She clicked down on to Enzo's name, *dialling*, it told her and even as she heard it ring she knew he'd make everything all right. Knew she shouldn't have doubted her man, not for one minute.

'*Cara?*' He sounded different. Hyped, excited, afraid. 'Sweetheart. I was just about to ring you. Something's happened.'

'We've been broken into,' said Giuli, and she heard her voice shake. 'I mean, at the office.'

'I'm coming,' he said. He hung up before she could say, There's all sorts going down in the street.

Sitting on the chair, Giuli found that she couldn't move. She could see that the open filing cabinet still contained the same paltry few pieces of paper: the insurance documents for the office and the business, the certification from the trade association. Nothing was kept on paper these days. It was all on computer. She *shouldn't* move, either, should she? There might be evidence.

Then again, the police might not be on their side. They hadn't been on the Frazione's side, had they? After that burglary. She looked down at the notebook. This was about Flavia, wasn't it? And as she stared, she knew this was what they were after. Slowly she peeled off the rubber band.

Lesson plans, notes. She stopped, frowned, thought. Turned to the back pages and there it was.

I just wanted to say hello.

There was a date: August last year, the first entry. *Botanico*, a tiny sidebar in red.

The Botanic Gardens?

She flipped through the pages without looking, at first, working backwards through the notebook, wanting to see how much there was. Page after page after page, covered with tiny dense writing in fine black ink, running on and on and on. Times and dates, his messages, her responses, in tiny neat handwriting, the writing of a teacher.

The writing of someone trying to compress something huge into a small space.

Words sprang out at her from the tight-packed sentences: Love. Beautiful. Philosophers were named, poets.

The parts of the body.

She noticed that there was no entry for the first Saturday in September, but another little sidebar told her she was right. *Sea*, it said. The messages started again, the following day.

She turned back to the first page and began to read.

By the time Enzo came through the door, saying something about the traffic in an incredulous voice, his laptop under his arm, she'd read it all, twice. Her heart felt like lead in her body; it was as though she was Flavia herself, and as though she had cut her own wrists in that bathtub.

She looked up at him, amazed that her eyes were dry as she should have been weeping.

'I'm only surprised she didn't do it sooner,' she said.

The phone rang: it was Sandro.

*

The university might as well have been on the moon, not the other side of the city; Chiara just couldn't see herself ever going there again.

She'd put on jeans but the disobedience frightened her and she'd pulled them off in a sweat and stuffed them at the back of the drawer. She'd put on a skirt, a neat blouse, looked down, trying to see herself through his eyes.

Dressed, then, and ready but somehow unable to open the front door, Chiara thought of the university courtyard, the old cloister off the Piazza San Marco, the road leading up to the Botanic Gardens and the barracks. She didn't really belong there any more, it seemed to her: it was kids' stuff to sit and gaze adoringly at some bearded lecturer or other. To jostle into the crowded bar and talk political theory, to go up to the Biblioteca delle Oblate with the others, to sit writing their assignments together on their laptops with the red dome of the cathedral filling the skyline. Chiara felt a twinge of loss. This was her home now. The suburbs, the green canopy of trees outside the window, her balcony, her man.

She set down her college bag on the ugly console in the hall and gazed through the doorway into the kitchen. It was a shame it was all so shabby, but it couldn't be helped. The thought that he might have found them somewhere more suited to a couple starting their life together was one that had come to her early on, but she'd dismissed it. It was childish, it was superficial, decor didn't matter.

Anyway, she'd only just have had time to get to the lecture and back, if he was going to be home at lunchtime. And wanted her there. She walked into the bedroom, the big, smooth bed, the old-fashioned walnut headboard and the painting over it, a kitschy oil painting of a child with big eyes.

The huge mirrored wardrobe that covered one whole wall. It faced the bed.

Chiara stood facing the wardrobe for a long time. She removed her clothes and looked at herself in the mirror, then she looked up. Something looked back at her.

Chapter Twenty-Six

'**T**HERE'S A RALLY,' SAID Bastone, breathless in the doorway. 'Someone's leaked something on to the internet about the police raid, and they're gathering. In the Piazza del Carmine.'

Sandro's mobile chirruped: a message. And then another. Surreptitiously he reached a hand into his pocket. The message was from Giuli: *Found her messages*, it said. *She was targeted. She was groomed.* He turned it off, the words still glowing behind his eyes. Groomed. He knew what that meant, but he couldn't make it fit, not with this woman. Not with these men, Bastone and Rosselli: they didn't inhabit a world where cold-blooded strategy was employed to lure the vulnerable into a trap, where images were collated and disseminated. Rosselli hadn't even had a mobile phone of his own.

Niccolò Rosselli got to his feet. Sandro could see the effort required for him to stand firm, one hand extended just a little towards the sofa where his son slept, as if monitoring him through the air between them. He looked gaunter than ever, but his gaze was steady as it fixed on Bastone's pouchy, anxious face.

'What do they say on the internet?' he said quietly.

'It's that journalist,' the lawyer said eagerly. 'I'm sure of it. He started a blog, just for the purpose of bringing you down. It calls itself *Vigilante*. He's at every meeting, he wrote the initial report of your collapse, I know his style.' His voice was breathless, hoping against hope, Sandro could see, that Flavia would not be mentioned.

'And the blogger, this *Vigilante*, he says what?'

'Well, it's just inference, he talks about the seizure of illegal material. But it's obvious he's putting the worst possible interpretation on it. We can stop him – legally, if we can get his identity. Prove he's behind it.'

'They're calling me a pornographer.' Rosselli's voice was flat. 'It's too late to stop him. A paedophile. I've seen it. . . I've seen it written on the walls.' His gaze flickered sideways, to the sleeping child, then back to Bastone. 'Free speech,' he said. 'You can't only believe in it if you have nothing to fear.' The apartment door was still open and as Sandro stepped to close it he heard the click of the front door below, and paused.

'It's not free speech if they hide behind anonymity,' said Bastone, pale but determined. Sandro looked at him, startled by signs, at last, of a lawyer's acuteness. 'They say anything they like and aren't accountable.'

Rosselli didn't seem to hear. 'So it's a lynch mob,' he said. 'I'll go and talk to them.'

There were footsteps on the stairs and Sandro saw Niccolò Rosselli's expression deaden as he recognized them.

'No,' said Bastone, earnestly, 'you don't understand. It's the Frazione, they're rallying for you.' He took a breath. 'They're behind you.'

'It has to be faced, Carlo,' said Rosselli, as if he hadn't heard Bastone. 'You can't leave things to fester. That's how we got here, how this country got here. It's been buried alive and it has to be torn up, out of the ground.' Something kindled and caught behind the man's eyes. 'Things buried have to be brought up to the air. We need to breathe.'

Sandro almost stepped back at the tone of his voice, the rage hardly contained, the conviction like the blast of heat from an oven. In that second he saw that such certainty could go either way: a man like Rosselli might murder, might shame a woman into suicide, might turn fanatic and lay waste to his country. Or might be the only one to save it.

'So are you going to tell him, Carlo?'

Maria Rosselli was in the doorway and the voice was hers, level and poisonous. At the sound of it, on the sofa, the sleeping baby started, let out a whimper. Her big bony hand was on Bastone's crumpled sleeve: he looked down at it as if a snake had laid itself over him.

She hissed, 'I think you'd better tell him.'

On the divan the child had not settled back to sleep: he twisted and arched, as if in pain. The three – mother, son, lawyer – seemed locked in a horrible silent struggle, like dogs unable to detach from hostility. Sandro went to the sofa, bent over the child. He glanced back at the trio in the open doorway: too late, he supposed, to worry about what the neighbours might think.

'What does she mean?' Niccolò Rosselli asked, suddenly quieter and looking into his childhood friend's eyes.

'I loved her,' blurted Carlo. 'I did. There's no crime in that.'

'I know you loved her,' said Rosselli, almost impatient. 'Do you think I'm a fool?'

'I could never have taken her from you,' said the lawyer, miserably. The child arched his back on the sofa and Sandro smelled a sweetness off him released by the movement, of talcum powder, of clean sweat. He put out a hand and felt the warmth of the small body under the rough towelling fabric. 'Shh,' he murmured.

Maria Rosselli made a sound of contempt and Carlo Bastone turned to her, briefly dignified. 'I couldn't. I loved her, but she didn't love me. She didn't even need to say it. And you had your child together, it was proof she loved you only. How could I have harmed you?' Looking at Rosselli. 'What harm was in it?' The man was almost crying.

'Did you send her messages?' Sandro asked from beside the child. Bastone looked bewildered, blank. 'Messages?' he said. 'What do you mean? I saw her every day. Letters, you mean? I didn't write to her.'

'I saw you,' said Maria Rosselli. 'I saw you looking at something two, maybe three weeks ago, some photographs. I saw you put them in a drawer quickly when I came in. At the offices of the Frazione, you put them in a drawer, in a folder.' Bastone's face was suddenly grey. She leaned into his face. 'I opened the folder, when you'd gone. I know what you were looking at.'

Niccolò Rosselli said nothing: Bastone turned to him beseechingly.

'I – they – I never—'

'Dirty pictures,' said Maria Rosselli with relish. 'You were looking at dirty pictures of her. Whose bed was she on?'

The child beside him let out a cry, startlingly loud, like a cry of pain. 'Shh,' said Sandro helplessly. What was he supposed to do now? He had no idea. He slid a hand around the child's small warm torso, put another at the back of his neck, he'd seen that done. He picked the baby up and placed him against his chest. Was his shirt clean enough? He stood, joggled: the child snuffled and was quiet. He was warm, heavy as a sandbag, and still.

'Photographs of Flavia,' said Niccolò, and his voice was hollow.

'Someone sent them,' said Bastone. 'They were sent to the Frazione, to me. I opened the envelope. Then they emailed them, too. I burned them. I burned the copies.'

'Not straight away,' said Maria Rosselli. A furious flush spread up Bastone's neck.

'I didn't know what to do with them,' he said, in agony. 'She – she looked – she didn't look as though she was enjoying it. She looked—' He covered his face with his hands and what he said was muffled. 'I thought they might be evidence of some – some wrongdoing. Then I couldn't bear it – if they were still there, you might see them, *she* might see them. I thought I should talk to you – talk to her—'

'Did you talk to her?' The hollowness was gone, there was something else now in Rosselli's voice: an awful, stifled kind of pain. Grief. Bastone shook his head, his face still covered. 'I burned them. Only that was when an email arrived with them attached. I hid it on the computer. I left it there in a folder labelled Expenses, just for a week. I didn't know what the right thing to do was, and then I deleted them from there too. But they seemed less dangerous on the computer.' The hands left his face.

'Only of course it's more dangerous,' said Rosselli. 'Things can be recovered from them. Or they can be planted. Perhaps those photographs are what the police are looking at now. Pictures of my wife.'

'You never married her,' spat Maria Rosselli.

Niccolò Rosselli turned his head very slowly and looked at his mother as if he could have struck her down, there and then, in a single blow. 'She was my wife,' he said. 'I loved her, and she was my wife and my soul.'

Maria Rosselli, at last, was silent: her jaw set heavy, she looked as though she'd been turned to stone.

'They're gone, then,' said Sandro. 'The photographs? The evidence.'

And slowly Bastone nodded. 'They're gone.'

'Someone else knew,' said Sandro. 'The same person who

sent the photos. Who broke into the offices. Who tipped off the police.'

Who pursued Flavia Matteo, who forced love or some version of it into her straitened life. Who opened her and broke her. *Groomed* was a small word for what had been done here.

Suddenly feeling useless, Sandro shook his head and held out the sleeping baby to Niccolò Rosselli. Maria Rosselli didn't move. Once he was in his father's arms the child's eyes opened. They were dark, almost black, and they fixed unwaveringly on the face above them.

Uneasy, Sandro looked away: looked down at his phone, which was switched off. He turned it on.

Two missed calls. One from Luisa. And Pietro Cavallaro, another missed call. An instinct throbbed, not for nothing had this man been his working partner for decades; was it Chiara? Not only. It was Chiara, and it was Rosselli, and it was the Frazione: they were connected, he knew it, and Pietro knew it too.

His oldest friend: it looked like Pietro did need him, after all.

*

'My God,' said Gloria, to herself as much as to Luisa. The Piazza del Carmine was packed to its edges: people stood wedged between the parked cars, against the barred windows of the yellow stucco palaces and on the steps of the great church of Santa Maria del Carmine. Overhead the sky was a hard, brilliant September blue.

After their encounter with Giancarlo, Gloria had been all for driving over to the Isolotto and up and down those quiet streets of apartments until they saw Chiara, coming out of a shop perhaps or on a balcony, hanging out washing. Instead, Luisa had called the office when Sandro's mobile went to answerphone, and had got Giuli.

'I'll keep trying him,' Giuli had said. 'He's in with Rosselli. There's something here he's got to see, though.' There'd been such a dull emptiness to her voice that Luisa had had to ask. 'You've found out what happened? To Flavia?' It wasn't that she'd forgotten Flavia, it was only that the woman was dead, and Chiara was the one who needed their help now.

'I know why she killed herself.'

Gloria had been too distracted to listen to what Luisa was saying, which was just as well. They'd abandoned the Cavallaros' little red car in the Borgo San Frediano, up on a pavement, unable to move any further.

'Who are they?' Gloria asked now, bewildered. 'Who are all these people?'

Dreadlocked youngsters in patchwork coats occupied the terrace of the Dolce Vita: the proprietor had ceased his attempts to shoo them off and stood beside them, watching proceedings. Fierce old women shouted, bearded boys, respectable types. A brigade of schoolchildren, barely more than sixteen, in formation like Roman soldiers and pushing cheerfully to and fro in the middle of the throng.

'This is the Frazione,' said Luisa. 'This is Giuli's lot. Chiara's lot. The young people's party.' Gloria scanned the faces more urgently, but even supposing Chiara had been among them, it would have been like finding a needle in a haystack.

NIC. CO. LO!

On the steps of the church someone had a loudhailer, and a banner that Luisa was not close enough to read. He was calling through his megaphone and the crowd answered him.

Behind him and inside the great church the frescoes stood quiet in their chapel, telling that old story, thought Luisa as she surveyed the scene, of sin and temptation. Adam and Eve, the fallen woman covering her face with her hands as she runs from the Garden of Eden, her mouth gaping in a howl of horror and shame.

Flavia Matteo.

Giuli's voice had been ragged as she told Luisa on the phone, as though she were the woman betrayed and abandoned. 'A man came after her. She fell in love with him, with the way he spoke to her, through his messages. He – he seduced her, and she was helpless. She'd never been in love before, not like that.'

Even a modern woman, it seemed, even a woman who didn't believe in the snake and the apple, could fall: could run out of the garden and die of shame.

Luisa didn't find it surprising, not for a minute. Didn't it lie in wait for all of them, the most virtuous woman and the most sophisticated alike?

She spied an opening, round to the side, that would lead them to the Via del Leone. Did Giuli know all this was going on, five hundred metres from the office?

NIC. CO. LO!

The crowd swayed and roared. Luisa quailed at the thought of what would happen when he came.

*

They sat, side by side, the notebook open on the desk in front of them. Enzo's laptop sat beside it, humming into life.

'Don't look,' said Giuli. 'Don't read it. No one should read it.'

She felt as though in that small book was everything any woman had ever had to be ashamed of. The longings and the weakness and the need – all of it.

'I don't want to,' said Enzo, and he took Giuli's hand. He'd turned his head slightly away from her as he did so, and Giuli understood, with a small pulse of pity and love mixed, that he couldn't look at her in case she should see he was talking about something precious to him; that he was also too fearful it wasn't precious to her to be able to look her in the eye.

She just shook her head, mute.

'How did it start?' On Enzo's face she saw pity fighting with disgust.

'Don't judge her,' she said quietly, and he darted her a quick look. 'She was walking in the Botanic Gardens. She tripped or something, and he helped her. He asked for her mobile number because he was worried about her, he said. And that night he sent her a message, to ask if she was all right.' Giuli found she couldn't actually bear to talk about it. She wished Luisa would come.

His last message to Flavia, two weeks after the child was born. The phone sitting on the shelf beside the baby monitor.

Dai, finiamo. Non mi diverto più.

Come on, let's finish it. I'm not having fun any more.

He'd kept it going more than a year. That showed stamina. Had it been strategic? Had he been waiting for something to happen before he pulled the plug on her? He had: there'd been a number of things he'd been waiting for.

She'd got pregnant with her husband's child, that must have slowed things down for him. Flavia had hoped it would cure her, but it hadn't.

And she'd hung on a month after that last message. She must have looked at that little screen a thousand times a day, waiting. She would have done anything to have that feeling back but it had left her, as a chemical left the body, leaving only its toxic residue. Giuli blinked something back.

'What's going on out there?' she asked. 'Was that what you were going to tell me? About the demo?'

'They want Niccolò,' Enzo said. 'I was all morning on the computer – ' he flushed ' – I was supposed to be servicing the computers at a textile warehouse but I got a tweet. Someone said there was going to be a flash rally, down here, in support of the Frazione. It went viral: the kids are really on to it, you know? The technology.' There was the briefest inflection of pride, before he sobered. 'I had to bring up the Frazione's website on my laptop to monitor activity.' His flush deepened. 'The site was crashing every few seconds under the weight of it, so people were tweeting instead.'

He gazed through the window, marvelling. 'So many people. Some journalist had been stirring it online, gloating over the police raid, and people just flipped.' He shook his head. 'They're sick of being manipulated. By the authorities: the army, the carabinieri, the police, the press – everyone. We're being watched everywhere. Let them watch us now.' He was almost on his feet.

'This was what you were going to tell me?' Giuli asked.

Enzo sat back down, his face suddenly pale. Slowly he shook his head again.

'Flavia was groomed?' he said. 'That's what you think? She was targeted.'

'I think,' Giuli concentrated on keeping her voice steady, on not letting the rage she felt contaminate her argument, 'that he watched her in the gardens. She walked every day in the Strozzi, or the Boboli, or the Orto Botanico.' She frowned. The Orto Botanico was near the university, wasn't it? Where Chiara studied. . . 'He might have seen her in any one of those places: everyone knew who she was, he might have tracked her in all of them. I think he waited for his opportunity. He might have waited a long time before he got his opening.' She looked at Enzo. 'She must have been a sitting duck. All that emotion, kept in check all those years. Just a question of pressing the right buttons. A technique some men have.'

'She slept with him.' Enzo's voice was flat with disillusion.

Slowly, Giuli shook her head. 'We don't know for sure.' She

couldn't repeat those parts to him, the hotel room by the sea. And later, when he'd taken her to an empty apartment.

'He was playing a long game,' she explained. 'He took her to the seaside to make her fall in love with him, once and for all. To show her he wasn't only about sex.' She blinked. What had Sandro said? The man who saw her come out of that hotel said Flavia had looked like she'd died and gone to heaven.

'And he wasn't. He was all about power.'

Enzo opened his mouth, hesitated. On the desk the telephone rang. Giuli stared at it, startled that it should still exist, nearly obsolete technology, untouched by the break-in. She picked up the receiver.

The voice was peremptory, the bad temper of a provincial official begrudgingly giving in to pressure. 'I've received permission from the next-of-kin, and the police have authorized it, God knows why.'

It was the coroner in Viareggio, wanting to double-check the agency's email address before he sent the image of Flavia's wrist.

'Oh, yes,' she said, thinking furiously as she looked at the empty desk, Damn, damn. 'Look. Our computers are – are down. You're going to have to send it to a different address. I'm Sandro's assistant.'

'This is irregular,' he said, and she heard the twitchiness in his voice. 'I don't want these autopsy pictures getting into the wrong hands. For obvious reasons.' He wouldn't want much of an excuse to change his mind, permission or no permission.

'It's a number,' she said. 'Isn't it? I was standing next to Sandro when you talked to him. Look, call him if you want.' Silence. 'It's so important,' she said, because it suddenly seemed that it was, that she couldn't wait one moment longer to nail this thing. And it might have been that the official heard the anguish in her voice but he let out an impatient sigh and said brusquely, 'All right. All right then. Give me the address.'

'Photographs?' Enzo said, after she'd hung up.

'One autopsy photograph,' she said. He was even paler. 'There was something written on Flavia's hand,' she said. 'A number.'

Nervously Enzo clicked on his email, send and receive. Nothing. 'So what were you going to tell me?'

He clicked again, and the message began to load. 'High resolution, I expect,' he said, still fidgeting.

She just looked at him.

'I found some photographs,' he said, shame-faced. 'On – on my memory stick.'

'Ah,' she said.

The message was through: Enzo opened the attachment, and there it was.

A blown-up image of Flavia Matteo's dead hand filled the screen, the fingers curled inwards, the flesh bloodless white, puffed from water immersion. What drew the eye was the wound, on the lower edge of the frame; a razor had done it because the edges were clean, gaping across the wrist, scored to the bone, tendon freed. And the faded remains of a line of numbers, written across the creases of her palm. Enzo leaned down, enlarged the image, zoomed. He tipped his head on one side. He pulled a piece of paper towards him and wrote the numbers down: five numbers visible: it looked as though they were the last five. He looked back at Giuli.

'Give me the phone,' he said. 'You said you'd got her phone?' She handed it to him and he opened it. 'If this is the number she was calling,' he said, 'if she left the number in her address book on the mobile, with five out of ten numbers, we can match it. You want to know the odds?'

'First show me your photographs,' she said.

They were looking at them, shoulder to shoulder, when Luisa walked through the door with Gloria.

Chapter Twenty-Seven

SANDRO DIDN'T HAVE TO ask, why here? He knew his friend was ready to talk.

Out of uniform, Pietro looked smaller somehow, less visible; he was standing in the porch of the church of San Marco, in the big square where all the buses converged. Beside him the austere façade of the monastery hid its treasure, the monks' cells, each with its glowing fresco, and fleetingly Sandro thought, maybe there's something in it. A little white cell, daily observances, brotherhood. Maybe that's what we should have opted for, Pietro and I, no fretting over wives or children. Mortification of the flesh, and communion with God, though: they might have been tricky.

On the adjacent side of the square stretched the deep umber stucco of the university buildings with their long, handsome windows, a gaggle of students in the doorway. Pietro was watching them as Sandro approached.

'This way,' his friend said without turning his head, and heading north out of the square they fell into step. The crowds fell away behind them. They walked in silence as far as the bar opposite the Botanic Gardens, then they were inside, behind the ornate gilded façade.

The place was close to empty, only one khaki-clad soldier propping up the bar today, though it was almost lunchtime. Silent as the grave. Sandro looked around, then he thought of the chaos around Santo Spirito and wondered. Would the army have been called in? Had it got that rough? Then something else came to him, the detail he'd been trying to recover, on and off, since Luisa had told him about the man she'd seen Pietro talking to in the street. . . the detail he'd confused with Flavia Matteo's autopsy and the number written on her hand.

The lad with a tattoo on his wrist: he'd seen a man in this very bar, raising a coffee to his lips and his sleeve falling back to expose a blue-black snake tattoo. Pietro wouldn't have chosen this bar by coincidence, would he?

'I couldn't tell you,' said Pietro, pushing the coffee cup across to Sandro. 'You understand that?' They were seated in the dim recesses of the back of the bar: opposite them the wide window was filled with a view of the green jungle of foliage behind the garden's high railings.

'But you can now?' Sandro asked quietly. 'Has there been an edict from above? Have you asked permission?' He didn't say, *You couldn't tell me what?* Pietro looked at him, his eyes turning hard and angry, and then the look was gone. He exhaled.

'Start from the beginning,' said Sandro.

'An arson attack,' said Pietro. 'That was the start. A routine investigation: an arson attack on the house of a Frazione supporter. A police matter: only then a man from AISI came calling. He was waiting in my office at eight the following day. Sitting at my desk.'

The secret service. Sandro listened, admiring, fearful, almost envious. Almost. If he'd been a younger man, still in the service, might he have refused? An undercover operation, they'd have used all the buzzwords. Inter-disciplinary co-operation, a merging of skill sets, cross-fertilization. Plus, of course, you didn't get a choice.

'There's an agenda,' said Pietro. 'There's always an agenda. You know that, I know that. You think, are they really looking for these people, this right-wing cabal, or am I just a patsy? Have they picked me because I'm the cleverest cop they could find, or the dumbest? Or just because I happened to be the investigating officer on the arson attack, and they want to put me off the track?'

Sandro remembered it, dimly. A petrol bomb had been lobbed into the garage of some teacher from a left-wing *liceo* who'd been vocal in his support of the Frazione.

'And so you just have to make the best of it, because orders are orders. It came at a bad time, too: it wasn't long after they approached me that Chiara started going out with this guy.' As he said it, Pietro's expression tightened, closed, warning against Sandro's questions. 'And I was distracted. Bad-tempered. Just when I should have been talking to her, I cut her off: it didn't help that she'd got involved with the Frazione too. What was I supposed to do? Every time I tried to hint that she should be careful, she thought I was coming on as heavy-handed fascist dad.'

'So the guy Luisa saw you with—'

Pietro rubbed the back of his neck uneasily. In front of them their coffee cups were long empty. 'Matterazzi. Informant turned undercover operative. Used to be a soldier.'

'I saw him in here.'

'You would have done.' Pietro's mouth clamped shut.

Sandro felt suddenly weary. 'Look,' he said. 'I don't want to force anything out of you.' In his pocket he gripped the phone. 'But this is turning nasty for me. This morning the office got broken into and this time *my* computer's gone. It's one thing when politicians steal and spy and all the rest amongst themselves – but I'm just trying to make a living here.'

'They broke into the Via del Leone?' Pietro's face was grim.

Sandro leaned across the Formica towards him. At the bar the soldier was taking his time drinking the coffee. The barman was wiping a glass for the umpteenth time very slowly.

'Why did you bring me here?' he asked. 'And to tell me what?'

'What did you find out about Flavia Matteo's death?' Pietro asked softly in return. Sandro straightened.

'She killed herself,' he said, and he felt the sorrow that had sat inside him since he entered that awful shuttered bathroom harden and fuse with something more like anger. 'That was clear to me. But I think – we think – she was targeted. Almost certainly her suicide was incidental, although it probably will have served someone's purpose well enough. Someone who wanted to bring Niccolò Rosselli down. To dirty that shining armour of his.'

'Targeted?'

'Groomed. Someone thought she'd be ripe for a sex scandal and they went after her.' He swallowed, not wanting to say it, not even to his oldest and most trusted friend, because once it was out, it was out. *Niccolò Rosselli, paedophile. Flavia Matteo, whore.* It'd be graffitied on a hundred walls, whatever Bastone thought.

'Have you told him?' Pietro spoke quietly. 'Rosselli?'

'He knows,' said Sandro wearily. He'd seen it in Rosselli's eyes, in his answer to Bastone, to his mother. 'I told him some of it – enough. He knows his wife. He knows this is two things. That this is someone using his wife to get to him. That this is his wife being human, not wicked.'

Pietro swallowed, nodded.

'There were photographs: of Flavia Matteo. Dirty pictures. That's what they planted on those computers, that was the "illegal material" the vice squad were tipped off about. If Flavia knew about them, that would have been enough to drive her to suicide, don't you think? A woman like that, who'd led a blameless life, a nun's life until then.' He took a deep breath. 'And that's what you need to tell me. Who *they* are.'

Pietro stared at him, mesmerized. At the bar the soldier was taking his time to pay, but when he saw himself observed, he turned sharply on his heel and was through the door. The barman turned away.

Sandro spoke again.

'And what I most want to know is, who *he* is? The man who did this to her. All this *they* – that's how they do it, they do evil and they hide behind *they*. But when it comes down to it, it was one man, talking to one woman.' He looked into his old friend's grim face, and waited.

There was a silence: an ambulance passed, its siren wailing. Pietro nodded once, twice, as if giving himself a signal.

'They,' he said slowly. 'Yes. *They* exist. They don't have a name, though one of them writes a blog called *Vigilante*. An extreme right-wing group, a coalition as loose as the Frazione, but everywhere. Everywhere. In the press, in the civil service, in the police.' He looked at the barman. 'In the law, in the army. Their most pressing objective seems to be to bring the Frazione down.' He blew out. 'I signed the secrecy forms. What do you think they'll do if they know I've told you?'

Sandro didn't answer. 'In the army,' he repeated, thinking of the surly, handsome soldier chatting across his reception desk while Sandro waited patiently for his attention. What had been the name on that badge? He couldn't remember.

'The call came from here.' Pietro spoke so softly Sandro could hardly hear. He nodded towards the ancient payphone booth in the corner. 'Sloppy, that, or perhaps they didn't care about being traced to a bar opposite a barracks?' He spoke with resignation. 'Come to think of it, they almost certainly have someone in the vice squad.'

'The tip-off,' said Sandro. 'It came from here.'

He slid off the barstool, on his feet, a nameless fear rising in him. 'Why do I get the feeling we're in the wrong place? Why's it so bloody quiet?'

And as if on cue from Sandro's pocket his phone shrilled.

*

It was clear to Luisa that Giuli hadn't known what to do when they'd walked through the door. She'd put a hand to the laptop screen as though to shut the lid, but the expression on their faces, as she looked back over her shoulder at Luisa and Gloria standing in the doorway, seemed to freeze her.

Outside, the noise levels were rising steadily: it was like a sea, like the rhythmic crash and suck of waves in a rising sea.

All Luisa could think was, it's not Eve who covers her face, is it? As she runs out of Eden, Eve covers her body: it's the man who covers his face. Adam.

Giuli had spread herself to cover the screen, but it had been too late. In the picture Luisa had seen, Flavia Matteo covered neither body nor face, though her face seemed to plead silently to become invisible. The three women had stared together: Enzo had shoved back his chair, clutching something. A piece of paper, a mobile phone: he had looked like he wanted to run, too.

Luisa spoke first.

'This is why she killed herself.' A flat statement. 'She knew about these.'

'No,' said Giuli, on her feet. 'Isn't it enough,' she said, her face wild, 'that she killed herself because she believed a worthless man had stopped loving her? It's too much that he did this to her as well.'

'Look at her eyes,' said Luisa. Reflected in a bank of mirrors, Flavia lay on a wide bed, her knees up and together, as though waiting for a doctor to instruct her. She was naked: her skin, Luisa registered automatically, was smooth and pale, lightly freckled on the shoulders.

From outside the chanting came, swelling to a roar. There was something frightening about it; or perhaps, thought Luisa, the frightening thing was in this room.

'They're stills,' said Enzo, from his corner. 'They're not photographs. She probably didn't know she was being filmed at the time.' He was pale, he wasn't looking at the screen, but he was determined. 'She's scared, you're right. But there would be other reasons for that, perhaps. She was doing something she'd never done before. She's trying to please someone she doesn't know very well.'

'What's this?' The question came from Gloria: Luisa saw that she had positioned herself behind the laptop, so she couldn't see the pictures. She'd seen enough.

Luisa always thought of Gloria as a child, in that way: Pietro her only man. A shy girl. . . she'd always been a shy girl. They'd all wondered where Chiara got her boldness from. Luisa stepped over next to her and put an arm gently around her shoulders. Gloria had picked up a black notebook, the pages spidery with fine, cramped script, and as she felt Luisa's arm, she raised her head, eyes round. 'Love letters?' she said, faltering.

'Text messages,' said Giuli from behind the laptop, raising her head tentatively to meet Gloria's eyes. 'A year's worth. From the man who made her do this.' Her hands rested still on the keyboard as she watched the other woman's expression.

'Aristotle,' said Gloria wonderingly, her finger pressed to a word. 'Chiara's been reading Aristotle. Tutor to Alexander the Great, did you know that? I didn't know until she told me.'

'Text messages about philosophy? And then he brought her to this – this room and made her do this?' Luisa felt sick.

'The right kind of bait for the right fish,' said Enzo, and the women turned to look at him. He didn't flush any more; he looked stricken. 'I don't think she'd have – I mean, just telling her she was beautiful wouldn't have worked on Flavia.'

'Text messages,' said Gloria, turning the words over with horror.

Giuli was staring at the screen, sallow under her tan. 'He's in this photograph.'

And then the three women were in front of the screen. Luisa felt Enzo step back, as if out of deference or perhaps shame. He was in the corner, clutching the little mobile and the piece of paper, his shoulder half turned to them like a child sent to the corner in school, busying himself. Like one of those children who can't look you in the eye, who distract themselves from their fears with some small mechanical activity.

'This is the number,' he said, but no one was listening. 'It matches this one. It says *Anna K.*'

It's the man who covers his face. But not always out of shame.

In the image on the screen, the white expanse of bed, the lines of the mirror, the pale soft body spread as though a doctor had given instructions, Luisa noticed three things.

A man. Standing, leaning against the mirrored wardrobe: the camera had been angled so that his face could not be seen. He was tall, and he was clothed; a forearm the only flesh visible, in the attitude maybe of the thinker. Watching.

A line ran from Flavia Matteo's navel downward, the dark line that pregnancy left behind on a body.

'She didn't sleep with him,' said Giuli, choked. 'It's in the book. In the messages: she wrote them all down. She didn't sleep with him because she couldn't do it: he said he loved her, then. But later he changed tack: he began to say other things. To imply that she wasn't a real woman, that she was – frigid. So she went to this place, this apartment, after the child was born. No more than a few weeks ago: a last attempt maybe. And then the messages ended.'

She bobbed her head down. 'He said he wasn't enjoying himself any more.'

And something else. Luisa put her face close to the screen. 'Can you blow this up?' she said. She pulled back and Giuli moved in, deftly sliding something to adjust the image.

This was a room where no woman washed the sheets, this was a room meant only for this kind of liaison, where women came and went, under the tacky pastel of a child over the bed, the ugly mirrored wardrobe. Under the eye of the camera.

'A laundry mark,' Luisa said, her face close to the screen. 'Verna, it says. Lavanderia Verna.' She turned back and they were all staring at her now, even Enzo, who seemed to have been interrupted halfway through forming a declaration of his own. 'I must have passed the Lavanderia Verna a hundred times,' she said. 'It's on the Via Pisana. On the road to the seaside.'

'Through the Isolotto,' said Gloria, bewildered. 'I don't understand,' she said. 'This is Flavia Matteo. We're talking about her, not Chiara, in the Isolotto. Aren't we talking about her?'

'Perhaps we're talking about both of them,' said Luisa.

*

Chiara lay on the wide bed and saw herself reflected in the mirror: saw her girl's arms, her narrow calves too slender as they emerged from under the pale pink silk. I'm nineteen, she told herself. I'm only nineteen. All of her strained to listen for him: through the window she could hear the old women's voices on the balcony below. Now she knew what that warning was, that she had always heard in the voices of women older than her. Sometimes you don't know, they were saying. You think it's what you want, but you don't know. You think you're in control, but sometimes they're too strong for you.

A car pulled up outside.

Chapter Twenty-Eight

WAS THAT WHAT SANDRO'S old brain had been trying to find a place for, ever since that morning when he'd sat in the car and watched the traumatized insurance claimant smoking on the balcony? That name. 3 September, 3.20 p.m., the first Friday of September last year. Two cars behind the accident, a good citizen had given his name and a witness statement – although his female passenger had not been named. They had been on their way to the seaside.

Had it frightened Flavia Matteo, on her way to that luxurious hotel with a near-stranger? A car accident: it must have seemed like fate. A narrow escape.

The two men stood outside the barracks, the eye of a surveillance camera on them. They'd spoken their piece into the intercom but the doors were still closed: Pietro stood with his fists clenched as if he would need no persuasion to begin battering on the door.

Giuli had been as cool as a cucumber on the phone: that's my girl, Sandro had thought as she'd delivered her evidence, piece by piece.

'I've seen him,' she'd said. 'He's in the photographs. Enzo'd saved everything on those computers on his USB key, two weeks ago. He does it routinely.' She'd taken a breath. 'I've seen the man, and I've read his messages. I wouldn't recognize him in the street, because he keeps his face hidden, but I know what novels he reads. I know how he thinks. I know what he thinks of us. Of women. I've got his number: and I've got it literally, too. I know his phone number: she called him Anna K.'

And when the name had come to him, and the face attached, it had been as though Sandro had known it all along.

He wasn't sure he should have told Pietro. That was a worry, looking at his old friend's clenched fists now, his face almost unrecognizable, almost deranged.

But how could Sandro not have told him?

'They think it's the same guy,' he'd said. 'Luisa and Gloria – and Giuli too. It was Gloria saw it first, Giuli said. Your Gloria, she said, *And now they're trying to get to Pietro*. Through Chiara.'

They wouldn't have gone for his wife, would they? Not for Gloria. She wasn't damaged like Flavia Matteo, she hadn't spent her life repressing anything, she wasn't at a dangerous age. So they went for little Chiara, the bold, rebellious child everyone knew and loved, that member of the new generation of girls who thought they could handle it all. Maybe each new generation thought that.

'Looks like he's got a place in the Isolotto,' Sandro had said. 'Do you think that might be where Chiara's living now?'

And with a dark look of pulverizing, murderous rage, Pietro had shoved past him without a word and out of the Bar dell'Orto, almost shattering the glass door as he flung it violently open. Sandro had thought he might scream something in the quiet street. But instead it was Pietro's turn to ask the same question Sandro had asked him. 'Never mind *they*. I want to see this bastard's face.'

Was it the sword that had given him the answer? Not the copy of *Anna Karenina* – Anna K? – not the bust of Aristotle, not the description of him leaning against the mirrored wardrobe, tall and lean, an older man. An arrogant bastard, Giuli had said, with contempt.

Yes: the sword. The man Flavia had dreamed of, the man who cut women into pieces, the man who pursued her down the city's dark, luxurious streets.

And that photograph of a man in full dress uniform standing on the shelf in his office alongside the Tolstoy and the philosophy and the chessmen. The soldier's hand resting on the pommel of a sword. Sometimes in a dream a sword is just a sword.

He would be up above them in his room now, with his long legs stretched out as he contemplated his victory over the left-wing rabble.

The barracks door swung inwards.

'I'm sorry,' said the soldier in fatigues whose name Sandro only in that moment remembered as Canova and who stood now blocking their path with his careless good looks and his unassailable indifference.

Even before he finished speaking, the heavy door was beginning to close steadily between them. The soldier stepped back into the shadows as it moved.

'I'm afraid that Colonello Arturo has left for the day.'

Sandro and Pietro could only watch as the door closed, and they were on the outside again.

*

'They'll find her,' said Giuli, looking into Gloria's golden eyes, her pale face contracted with terror. On the other side, Luisa held her friend's hand.

'You have to leave it to her father,' she said. They'd closed the lid of Enzo's laptop but the images hadn't left anyone's head. 'He needs to be the one.'

'They'll find her,' repeated Enzo, from his corner, clutching the mobile. 'Those two – if anyone can do it.'

Were they all thinking the same thing? wondered Giuli as she heard the uncertainty in his voice, and no one spoke. That there comes a time when those we've always looked up to, the all-powerful parents, are suddenly too old, too slow, too late?

'Can you give me that?' she said, and obediently Enzo handed her the phone. She looked down at the name, and the number attached to it.

'It was the novel she was reading,' Giuli explained. 'One of the books Flavia left with Wanda Terni, along with her notebook. *Anna Karenina*. Anna K.'

And then there was a silence. Not just in the room between them but outside, something like a vast collective intake of breath and a sudden hush that was almost suffocating after the rising din, as though a great blanket had been thrown over the crowd.

'Niccolò,' said Enzo. 'I knew he'd go out there.' He looked at Giuli, and she saw he was afraid. 'What will they do to him?'

She held up a hand: she was dialling. She felt the adrenaline rise in her, in her throat, as she waited to hear his voice, at last.

*

Chiara had put the little case in the kitchen so he wouldn't see it, but he knew as he came through the door. Even though she was wearing what he'd told her to wear, lay where he wanted her to lie, on the white bed under the ugly painting. She made sure not to look in the direction that would give her away.

He came through the door, his head tilted to one side, long and lean and handsome in his off-duty clothes. She'd never seen him in his uniform, but he'd told her about it. He'd told her with pride that he even had a sword. 'Of course, it's meaningless,' he'd said in a throwaway manner: she'd believed him, then. She'd thought when he began talking to her in that way of his – all that lulling, deep-voiced insistence brought to bear on her, Chiara thinking herself so sought out in the university cloister – that here was a man at the heart of the old order who had only contempt for it. 'Just pen-pushing,' he'd told her with his lazy, amoral smile. 'I don't fancy a war zone.' Together what might they not overthrow? But at the same time, buried somewhere deep, she'd liked the idea of that sword too, of that uniform. She'd wanted it all.

The way he held his head, the half-smile on his face, the pause in the doorway. He knew.

'Darling,' he said, smoothly amused, and she saw his gaze flick up to the camera she'd found, behind the painting, a tiny eye. She gazed steadily at him, not following his glance: she felt a great surge of misery. Had she still been hoping that this was her own paranoid imagination? That they were still twined souls in rebellion? That he loved her? But it wasn't her imagination. This was a horrible dirty story, an old, disgusting story about a stupid girl and a wolf, a virgin and a Bluebeard, a house full of locked doors. She was a fool.

He stepped towards the bed and his hand was on her thigh under the silk: his face came close to hers and she smelled the onion on his breath.

His mobile rang.

The smile fixing on his face, he pulled back and reached into a pocket for the phone. His face over hers stilled as he looked away from her and down, at the cellphone's screen.

'No,' he said, his expression darkening.

'No,' she said, lifting herself from the pillow, with her eyes fixed over his shoulder on the little eye of the camera and with her hand groping for the only weapon she had, hidden under the pillow, her last resort, no time to call for Dad. Downstairs someone was shouting her name.

*

They had to leave the car at the end of a long private parking lot, and vault the locked gate: with difficulty, in Sandro's case.

They'd driven in near-silence until they got to the Viadotto dell'Indiano, the viaduct that would lead them in a wide overhead curve around the congested centre and to the Isolotto. The sedate rows of apartment blocks flanking the river rose to greet them through their canopy of trees: so calm, so secluded, so private.

'The Oltrarno's gridlocked,' Pietro had said. 'The Frazione Verde are demonstrating. As if that'll make any difference.' His mouth was set in a line.

'The Isolotto's a big place,' Sandro had said, despairing, and Pietro had looked at him.

'D'you think I don't know where to find my own daughter?' And when Sandro had just stared, Pietro had turned his face away and said stonily, 'I ran a trace on her mobile phone through the computers the morning after she left.'

'You knew where she was,' Sandro had said. 'All along, you knew? And you didn't come after her?'

Pietro had stared at the road ahead as he'd answered: a lorry was blocking their exit, moving horribly slowly. 'I didn't make the connection,' he said. 'I was watching the Frazione, my daughter had grown up and left me. They were different things. Do you seriously think that if I'd had the slightest inkling she'd got involved with this guy – *this* guy – I'd have let it lie?' Ahead the lorry began to move.

Sandro looked at his friend's tormented face. 'No,' he said, his chest tight.

'I had to let her go,' Pietro said, still not looking at him. 'What, sit in a car outside in the street, watching her? Fascist dad. Big Brother. What if she saw me? Or *he* did?'

'You didn't even come and get a look at him?'

'I didn't know!' Pietro had said in anguish, and his hands had gripped the steering wheel. 'I thought I had to let her go. But I had to know where to come for her, when the time came.'

And the time had come.

Now, though, ten years younger than him, Pietro was pulling away from Sandro as they ran through the parking lot.

Chiara!

An old woman in black looked over her balcony at the sound, at Pietro bellowing like a maddened bull in the orderly, shrub-lined grounds below her. Looking up, Sandro saw something in her beady, dark eyes, a kind of satisfaction: recognition. She turned her head to look along the block and up, and pointed.

They ran under the elevated building to a liftwell, and pressed all the bells in turn at the locked door. A click came, and they were through. 'Third floor,' said Pietro, and he was on the stairs before Sandro could even think about the lift. Sandro's lungs were burning before they got to the first floor, he was dizzy with the effort and with wondering, which door?

And, could either of us even batter a door down, at our age?

But the door was open and Chiara behind it dressed only in a pink slip, struggling with a tall man. Absolutely recognizable even in his jeans, the lazy-smiling soldier with his big jaw, taller than her and pinning her, like a child, by holding her arms over her head. He turned an expression of amazement on them as they entered.

Arturo. The tall colonel with deepset eyes, climbing out of his cramped army vehicle in the Piazza del Carmine. Stretching his long legs in his office opposite the Botanic Gardens, looking at his watch as Sandro tried not to like him, a bust of Aristotle on the shelf. Flavia Matteo had ended her life in that marble tomb of a bath, in that bathroom where the distant reflection of pale seaside light played on the walls, for this man. Who was worthless, and she had known it.

He looked at Sandro and Sandro saw a flicker of recognition in his eyes, the beginnings even of amusement. We can be men together about this.

'She hit me,' he said, and Sandro saw on his temple a trickle of blood and a reddening abrasion. In one of the hands he held by the wrists, Chiara clutched her mobile phone: her knuckles were grazed and bleeding. 'There's no need for it.' He sounded affronted. 'As if I can't control myself. There's no need for violence.'

Drawing back his fist, Pietro punched him.

*

Someone had found an amp and a microphone and had plugged it in, God knows where. Across the wide piazza the crowd swayed, silent. They waited.

In the corner of the square where they'd arrived and been unable to move further stood Enzo and Giuli, pressed against each other shoulder to shoulder, Luisa and Gloria with their arms tight around each other. No one in all the great hushed mass of people was looking anywhere but at Niccolò Rosselli, who stood on the steps of the great church of Santa Maria del Carmine.

He wasn't alone: from against his father's chest Rosselli's son stared with beady black eyes out over the crowd.

Rosselli spoke.

'Go home,' he said, and there was a murmur, a groundswell of menace.

'I need to mourn my wife,' he said, and the murmur fell away. Giuli felt Enzo's hand close warm around hers.

'I need you all to go back to your homes.' His voice was weary but firm. Giuli held her breath: they were all holding their breath, and then he spoke again.

'Go home. And wait.'

He stepped away, one hand holding the back of his son's head as he turned, and Giuli saw the child look up at him in the absolute silence.

And then, like a wave breaking in the great piazza over all the heads, over the man and his child, then came the roar of approbation.

Chapter Twenty-Nine

GIULI KEPT THE SCHOOL notebook with its elastic retainer. She didn't know what else to do with it, was her excuse: she didn't want to destroy it, nor to hand it over to the police to have men poring over it.

'I'll let Pietro have it,' she said to Enzo as they laid the table for Luisa and Sandro's arrival for the dinner long postponed. 'When he asks. It's evidence, I know that.'

She might have destroyed it. That might have done the trick, the trick of putting it all behind them and moving on. But, as Barbara had said, we don't like obliteration.

She'd told Enzo what was in the book – some of it. 'He was really into it, you can tell,' she said. 'She wouldn't have fallen for it otherwise. He liked the game of it, and Flavia was an intelligent woman, a good match for him. In that way.'

Enzo understood: he was the one who'd said it, after all. The right bait for the right fish.

'It might even be why – he didn't sleep with her. Didn't force her. He had his evidence, he only did the minimum. Perhaps he saw no need to harm her more than was necessary.'

'Maybe,' said Enzo dubiously. 'He harmed her enough.'

Even now, folding napkins, laying them on the neat place settings, slicing the tomatoes as Enzo had shown her, Giuli felt a knot of rage and grief form in her at the thought of it. Arturo had taken Flavia to the seaside and shown her his idea of love: he'd talked to her about Aristotle and stroked her pale freckled arms in a hotel bedroom. He had said he'd wait: she had come out of the hotel in the early morning so radiant with it that even a street sweeper had stopped to watch her face.

She'd waited: she'd struggled and fought against it, she'd turned to her husband and had her child, and it hadn't worked. Arturo had lured her back two weeks after the baby was born, even as he was working on Chiara, to a flat in the Isolotto – his dead mother's flat, it turned out, as he was shacked up, most of the time with Nicoletta Farmiga – and had filmed her removing her clothes. Because this in the end was what it was about: documentary evidence.

Had Arturo enjoyed it? Had it started out as a kick for him, an ego trip? Maybe. Probably. Or a power trip too. Perhaps. Had he and Farmiga cooked it up between them, because everything about Flavia got to Farmiga: her political idealism, her shame, her purity? Farmiga wasn't talking, but Sandro thought it was possible. A bit of nasty fun, maybe, a challenge, see if you can pick her up. And then: that'd show them. What would it look like for Rosselli if his wife were caught in bed with another man? The saintly Flavia.

Then if there was documentary evidence too, pictures that could go out on the internet, it could be turned into a weapon for the cause – their cause that was the negative image of Rosselli's commitment to openness, to justice, to clean hands.

And when, having got what he wanted, the soldier had stopped returning her messages, when he'd already started turning his attention elsewhere, Flavia had tried to hold on to her sanity for a month. Flavia Matteo, who'd trained herself for a lifetime not to feel except on behalf of others, not to need except for others' needs, had been unable to keep going. She'd gone back to the glittering waves and white seaside light, and had put herself out of her misery.

The little book told it all. It was Flavia Matteo's creation, it was her love story. One day, Giuli told herself, she would destroy it.

When Flavia had turned up dead and it had looked like there was a chance of a sympathy vote for Rosselli, they'd had to stage the break-in and tip off the police to go looking for dirty pictures.

'Right,' said Giuli, stepping back and looking at her perfect table, smelling the food on the stove. She went over to Enzo and put her arms around him and felt him relax.

'I love you,' she said.

*

'Tie?' asked Sandro, frowning into the wardrobe. Luisa looked at him in surprise.

'For Giuli?'

He shrugged. 'It feels like a special occasion,' he said, and Luisa nodded.

'Besides,' he said, 'it's turned cool out there. Might even wear a jacket too.'

Luisa was in her slip: he saw her put a hand up to her left side.

'It was so easy for him, in the end,' she said with sorrow. 'An intelligent woman, but he destroyed her.'

'I don't know if it was so easy,' Sandro said. 'But perhaps that was part of the kick. To them it's all part of the same game: politics, sex. Get one better. Triumph.'

Luisa's hand stayed where it was, at her flattened breast. 'And Chiara?'

He shrugged, uncomfortable. 'The agenda might have been a little different, the techniques too. He might – he might have been pleasing himself more. The same game, though. Still the same game.'

'What's going to happen to him?' Luisa asked.

'He's been suspended on full pay while the investigation continues,' said Sandro. He still couldn't think of Arturo without a churn of nausea: the man's charm had taken him in as easily as a girl. The philosophy and the intelligence glittered on the surface, and underneath a darkness moved, alive with greed, venality, self-interest. It was the world.

Sandro took out a tweed jacket: too heavy. He put it back in the wardrobe and took out a light wool one, frowned at it. He could hardly remember where half these things came from. Luisa must have bought them for him: she was still in her slip in front of him.

'Is it even a crime?' she asked. 'Seducing a woman.'

He turned to her, put his hands on her arms, trying to manage the love he felt for her closed, intent expression.

'The concealed filming is a crime,' he said. 'A good thing there's evidence to back that up. . . the photographs Enzo managed to retrieve. If they can prove conspiracy, blackmail – all those things.' He thought of Pietro: he'd been removed from the investigation, for obvious reasons. Was there a winner here? Chiara was safe: that was all Pietro cared about. And the vigilantes had been dealt a blow, and they knew it.

'They'll get on to the internet, won't they, though?' Luisa was still frowning furiously. 'It'll get out.'

'Maybe,' said Sandro. 'Maybe. But then again, maybe people are not as terrible as we think. Maybe no one wants to see pictures of a naked woman on the verge of tears, a woman who went on to kill herself out of shame.'

'I don't think it was shame,' said Luisa. 'I think it was grief.'

Sandro raised his head. 'She left behind a child,' he said. 'Perhaps people will have pity.'

'He's strong enough, isn't he? Niccolò. He seems strong enough, after all.' She spoke hesitantly.

'To keep going with the Frazione?' Sandro rubbed her arms briskly. 'You're getting cold.'

'To bring up the child,' said Luisa, and as he took his hands away she brought her arms up across her chest.

'Yes,' he said, and gently he prised one arm away. 'He'll bring up the child very well. His mother's not going to live for ever, is she? And she'll come into line.'

Luisa looked down at him, waiting to know what he was going to do next.

'I was getting quite fond of this,' he said, touching her scar under the silk. She pulled her head back in surprise.

'Now he tells me,' she said, and he saw pink rise up her throat. He put his mouth to her neck and breathed in.

'Which is not to say,' his voice sounding muffled against her skin, 'I won't be fond of the new one, too.' Sandro pulled his head back and smiled. 'Now get dressed, girl of mine,' he said. 'You'll catch your death.'

*

Five hundred kilometres away, Vesna stepped off the train and breathed in a new but familiar city. She saw a station hotel, an avenue of lime trees, dark and sticky at the end of summer, smelled cooking and exhaust fumes and the cool undercurrent of sea air. An old man – two years older than the last time she'd seen him – stood with his hat between his hands at the taxi rank and waited for her.

'Hey, Dad,' she said.

He bent and took her bag.